Praise for the Gethsemane Brown Mystery Series

MURDER IN G MAJOR (#1)

"Gordon strikes a harmonious chord in this enchanting spellbinder of a mystery."

— Susan M. Boyer,
USA Today Bestselling Author of *Lowcountry Book Club*

"Just when you think you've seen everything, here comes Gethsemane Brown, baton in one hand, bourbon in the other. Stranded in an Irish village where she knows no one (but they all know her), she's got just six weeks to turn a rabblesome orchestra into award-winners and solve a decades-old murder to boot. And only a grumpy ghost to help her. There's charm to spare in this highly original debut."

— Catriona McPherson,
Agatha Award-Winning Author of *The Reek of Red Herrings*

"Gordon's debut is delightful: An Irish village full of characters and secrets, whiskey and music—and a ghost! Gethsemane Brown is a fast-thinking, fast-talking dynamic sleuth (with a great wardrobe) who is more than a match for the unraveling murders and cover-ups, aided by her various—handsome—allies and her irascible ghost. Can't wait to see what she uncovers next!"

— Chloe Green,
Author of the Dallas O'Connor Mysteries

"A fast-paced drama that kept me engaged in all aspects in the telling of this multi-plot tale that was hard to put down...The windup to the conclusion had me quickly turning the pages as I had to know how this will play out and to the author, I say "bravo" because now I need to read the next book in this captivating series."

— *Dru's Book Musings*

The Gethsemane Brown Mystery Series
by Alexia Gordon

MURDER IN G MAJOR (#1)

A Gethsemane Brown Mystery

MURDER IN G MAJOR

ALEXIA GORDON

HENERY PRESS

MURDER IN G MAJOR
A Gethsemane Brown Mystery
Part of the Henery Press Mystery Collection

First Edition | September 2016

Henery Press, LLC
www.henerypress.com

Copyright © 2016 by Alexia Gordon
Author photograph by Peter Larsen

Trade Paperback ISBN-13: 978-1-63511-057-9
Digital epub ISBN-13: 978-1-63511-058-6
Kindle ISBN-13: 978-1-63511-059-3
Hardcover Paperback ISBN-13: 978-1-63511-060-9

Printed in the United States of America

Dedicated to my parents, who let me have an unrestricted library card as soon as I was old enough to check out a book, never said "no" at the bookstore, and let me stay up all night in the summer watching spooky movies on TV.

ACKNOWLEDGMENTS

I am indebted to The Writer's Path program at Southern Methodist University, especially to Suzanne Frank and Daniel J. Hale. Without the program, this book would never have been written. Thanks, Dan for asking, "What's your story about?"

Thanks to Terri, Stephanie, Kim, Kaitlyn, Heather, and all of my other Writer's Path compatriots for sharing your energy and enthusiasm.

Thanks to Alexia Isaak for telling me to say "percussion" instead of "drums."

Thanks to Kendel Lynn, Rachel Jackson, and Erin George at Henery Press for taking a chance on an unpublished writer and for helping me turn my manuscript into a book.

Thanks to Paula Munier of Talcott Notch for representing me and helping me understand the business side of this writing business.

Thanks to Dru and to the other hens in the Henery Press Hen House for your support and encouragement.

Thanks to my instructors at Vassar College, especially Nancy Willard, for teaching me the value of good storytelling.

Thanks to Emilie for making me go to that MWA cocktail party and practice my first pitch.

Thanks to Adrienne and Meg for understanding exactly.

Thanks to Chad and Jay for making Fort Leavenworth in January fun.

Thanks to the Dallas Symphony Orchestra for providing the musical inspiration.

Thanks to The Joule, Dallas and Weekend Coffee for letting me occupy your space for countless hours and keeping me caffeinated and fed.

Thanks to Trinity Hall Irish Pub for furthering my whiskey education.

Thanks to Fort Work Dallas for letting a writer hang out with the tech startups.

Thanks to Serj Books for the crayons and the jokes.

Thanks to the Church of the Incarnation for the spiritual inspiration.

And thanks to my parents for always believing I could write.

One

Gethsemane Brown leaned closer to the windshield. She could just make out a thatched cottage through the gray curtain of rain pounding southwestern Ireland's coast. The whitewashed house perched a few hundred yards from an ominous cliff. Farther up the road a lighthouse stood sentry over the rocky landscape. She rested her head against the window's cool glass, trying to ignore the sound of tires skidding on wet gravel, and reconsidered her any-job-is-better-than-no-job philosophy. Right now unemployment sounded appealing.

Next to her the car's driver, Billy McCarthy, kept his eyes on the tortuous road. "I hope you'll like Carraigfaire Cottage, Dr. Brown." Gethsemane flinched and held her breath as a rock wall loomed into view. Billy swore and spun the steering wheel hard. Car under control again, he continued. "Sorry about yer luggage."

One more disaster in a string of disasters. Stolen luggage, stolen money, stolen career. She'd been *promised* the assistant conductor position with the Cork Philharmonic. A shoo-in. She didn't even have to interview. She gave up everything for it—her apartment in Dallas, her furniture, her fiancé—and booked a one-way ticket to Ireland. To have it snatched by the music director's mistress...She bit back an expletive. Now look at her, stranded halfway between the airport and the back of beyond, reduced to racing up a suicide hill toward—what? A deserted cottage in some village she'd never heard of. Why not go back? All the way back to the beginning, before the international concert circuit, before moving from place to place and job to job while climbing the ranks of the orchestra. Why not admit her ambitious, workaholic, jet-setting lifestyle ended up a bust and go back to Virginia where she'd grown up? Start over. And face Mother's disappointment and her eldest sister's ridicule? Gethsemane clutched her violin case to her chest and shuddered. Could be worse. She could be back in Finland where she'd been the only African American in the orchestra *and* she hadn't spoken the language. At least here they spoke English.

The car swerved. Billy wrestled the vehicle and swore again, not in English.

Gethsemane tightened her grip on her case. "What?"

"Nothin'. 'Twas Irish. *Gaeilge*. Not fit to translate in mixed company."

So much for speaking the language. To drown out the pounding of her heart she asked, "How long's it been since anyone lived at Carraigfaire?"

"About twenty-five years. Since my aunt and uncle died. Maybe you know of my uncle?"

"Of course I know Eamon McCarthy. I performed his "Autumn Nocturne" at my first recital. I was devastated when he—I mean, um…"

Billy spared her a glance. "Murdered his wife and then committed suicide? That's the official story." He skidded to a stop in front of the cottage. "Unofficially?" He shrugged.

They dashed through the barrage to the front porch. Gethsemane tugged her rain-sodden dress, its navy skirt now more fit than flare, while Billy hunted on his key ring. Two days' continuous wear and a Second Coming-caliber downpour. How much more could her only outfit take? Even worsted wool had its limits. She silently cursed whoever stole her luggage. Then she cursed herself for having packed her raincoat and umbrella. Who goes to Ireland without keeping raingear handy? She looked wistfully at the car. At least her violin was dry. Billy fumbled a key into the bright blue cottage door. Gethsemane started to grumble then bit her lip. Her new landlord would think her as sullen as the weather. Instead she said, "When I was in New Orleans years ago with the chamber orchestra I heard voodoo priestesses paint their doors bright blue to keep out spirits."

"We don't try to keep our spirits outside in Dunmullach." Billy swung the door open triumphantly. "Wouldn't be hospitable."

Gethsemane stepped over the threshold. Mackintoshes and a newsboy cap hung from a coat rack. Two pairs of Wellingtons nestled underneath a bench.

"I thought you said nobody lived here." Water puddled around her feet.

"No one does." Billy hung his mackintosh next to the others. "This is a tableau."

"A tableau?"

"I plan to turn Carraigfaire Cottage into a museum. Arrange everything the way it was when Uncle Eamon and Aunt Orla lived here. It'll look like they just stepped out for a moment. Let me get you a towel." He disappeared upstairs.

Gethsemane padded down the hall, trailing wet footprints as she peered into rooms. A Steinway piled with sheet music dominated one to her right. Opposite, a massive roll-top desk shared space with a well-stocked bar cart, a leather sofa, and floor-to-ceiling bookshelves. A lacy afghan draped over the back of the sofa provided the room's only feminine touch. Gethsemane sniffed. A faint odor, woodsy. Billy hadn't worn cologne. Had he? She sniffed again. The smell was gone.

Billy returned with a towel. "I think the time's right to open a museum. Uncle Eamon's garnered a new legion of fans since that woman's book came out."

An American author had recently published an unauthorized biography of Eamon. *Trash.* Gethsemane had tossed it into the recycle bin after the third chapter. The book reached number eight on the bestseller list the day she quit her job as concertmaster with the Dallas String Ensemble.

Billy offered to start a fire. He talked as he worked. "You'll have the run of the place. The lighthouse, too, if you like. Be careful on the stairs if you go up. A bit dicey."

Gethsemane toweled her hair. Let Mother call her nappy-headed. Her natural style held up better in the rain than relaxed tresses. "I appreciate your letting me stay here. You saved me from sleeping in the train station."

The fire roared to life. "I'm happy to find someone to look after the place. I travel on business. Makes it hard to take proper care of things here."

Gethsemane dried her feet then grimaced as she slipped them back into her still wet shoes. She backed up to the fire, enjoying the burn on her calves. "Ever think of turning this place into a B&B?"

Billy waved the suggestion away. "I'm no innkeeper. I'd have to hire someone. Even with increased music sales, Uncle's royalties barely cover restoration and maintenance, never mind a salary."

"Why not sell?"

"I've had a few offers, but none tempting enough to make me give up on the museum."

Gethsemane felt her skirt. Dry. "How about a tour?"

Billy led her through the rest of the house. Two bedrooms upstairs with a bathroom between. A parlor across the hall. The delicate furniture and gilt accents marked it as the lady of the house's answer to the downstairs man cave.

Billy gestured to the front bedroom. "Use this one." Inside, a bureau topped with men's toiletries and a silver-framed photo of a stunning brown-eyed blonde abutted an armoire. Opposite, a vanity laden with women's toiletries and a silver-framed photo of a handsome dark-haired man with a strong resemblance to Billy stood near a chifferobe. Gethsemane recognized the man as Eamon McCarthy. His eyes seemed greener in the photo than in magazines.

Gethsemane thanked Billy and followed him downstairs to the kitchen. She caught another whiff of the woodsy cologne.

"What're you wearing?"

"Wearing?" Billy asked.

"Your cologne."

Billy looked puzzled. "I'm not wearin' cologne. I'm allergic." A worried expression replaced the puzzled one. "And I don't smell anything."

"Leather, cedar, pepper, hay." Gethsemane took a deep breath. "Nice."

"I smell rain and peat, smoke from the fire."

"My imagination." Gethsemane chuckled. "Or a ghost."

Billy swallowed. "You're, er, not afraid of ghosts, are you?"

"I can't be afraid of what doesn't exist." Grandma's stories of the farmhouse door unlocking and swinging open at three a.m. without aid of human or animal notwithstanding.

Billy swallowed again. "It's only fair to tell ya that folks—not everybody mind ya—report hearing strange noises up here and seeing things out on the cliffs."

"Optical illusions, misinterpretations of natural phenomena." Gethsemane pressed her finger against the window and traced the outline of the mist-shrouded lighthouse looming atop the cliff's head. Forget Grandpa's account of a gray man materializing from the fog to portend death in the family. "Products of overactive imaginations stimulated by an eerie landscape."

"That's what I like about you Americans. Always ready with a rational explanation."

A recollection from Sunday school poked her in the back, sending a shiver down her spine: King Saul hiring a medium to conjure Samuel's ghost. She pushed it away.

"The pantry's stocked, so's the bar." Billy wrote on a notepad by the phone. "My number's here as well as the grocer's and the guards'. That's the *gardaí*, the police. I'll also leave Teague Connolly's number. Call him if you need anything while I'm gone."

"Teague Connolly?"

"A good mate of mine. Orla's baby brother. Half-brother." He finished his notes. "Any questions?"

"How long does it take to walk to St. Brennan's from here? I have a meeting with the headmaster at five."

"It's about a twenty-minute walk. I'll send Father Keating, the school chaplain, up to give you a ride."

Billy retrieved Gethsemane's violin from the car and bid goodbye. The crunch of tires faded away. Time for a shower and nap before her appointment with the headmaster. She needed to be on her A-game if she was going to salvage her disaster of a life.

Upstairs, she studied her reflection in the vanity mirror. Mother was right, her thick hair was nappy. She sighed and examined the items on the vanity top. A sleek perfume bottle labeled *Maywinds* in gold script held the fragrance of vetiver, powder, roses. She lifted a squat cologne bottle from the bureau, *Gaeltacht*. A spray released a familiar aroma—leather, cedar, pepper, hay. Odd, Billy hadn't smelled it.

Remembering why she came upstairs, she found a bathroom cupboard with towels and *Mrs. Leary's Buttermilk* soap. Steaming shower water provided solace from disappointment and relief from the niggling unease of mysterious smells and murder-suicide.

Refreshed by her nap and shower, Gethsemane arrived at St. Brennan's School for Boys a few minutes early for her appointment. Father Tim Keating, parish priest as well as school chaplain, escorted her to the school office, a dim wood-paneled cavern. A few uncomfortable-looking students sat on uncomfortable-looking benches along the near wall. The secretary ushered Gethsemane and the priest to a door affixed with an oversized engraved brass plaque which read, *Richard Riordan, Headmaster.*

A cultured voice answered the secretary's knock. "Enter."

Inside, a distinguished-looking, impeccably dressed man rose from an ornately carved wooden desk to greet them. "Good evening, Dr. Brown. Father Tim, always a pleasure."

"Likewise, Richard," Father Tim said. "Now, if you'll both excuse me, I'm presiding over the Garden Committee's monthly meeting." He winked. "You know how the ladies get without a chaperone. Best of luck to you, Dr. Brown."

Gethsemane and the headmaster settled into chairs around his desk. Riordan opened a folder and turned pages. "Bachelor of Arts in music from Vassar College, Doctor of Arts from Yale University, a certificate in orchestral conducting from Yale as well. Multiple awards, including the Strasburg Medal and the Fleisher Prize. What an honor to have a musician of your caliber join our faculty, Dr. Brown."

"I can't tell you how much this opportunity means to me, sir." Not without admitting she'd rather play her violin for change on the nearest street corner than slink home defeated.

Riordan outlined Gethsemane's duties. "Four periods of general music education thrice weekly, individual music instruction twice weekly. You play the violin and—?"

Gethsemane counted on her fingers. "Piano, viola, cello, guitar, percussion."

"Excellent. Your primary concern will be the honors orchestra, upper school boys selected by audition and recommendation. Unfortunately, the orchestra's been," Riordan crossed the room to a display case, "at sub-peak performance."

Gethsemane twisted in her chair. "Just how far 'sub-peak'?"

Riordan didn't answer.

Tchaikovsky's "Pathétique"—her early warning system—sounded in Gethsemane's head. "How much time do I have to get them to peak performance?"

The headmaster rapped his knuckle against the display case. "This year marks the seventy-fifth anniversary of the Annual All-County School Orchestra Competition, returning, after twenty-five years, to Dunmullach's Athaneum Theater."

Tchaikovsky played louder. "When's the last time St. Brennan's won the competition?"

"St. Brennan's won"—Tchaikovsky screamed—"the inaugural competition, also at the Athaneum."

Gethsemane peered into the case. On the center shelf a golden piano-shaped trophy claimed pride of place. "When's this year's competition?"

Riordan's expression reminded Gethsemane of a boy hiding a failing report card from his parents.

"End of Michaelmas term," Riordan said. "Six weeks."

"Six weeks?" Gethsemane's eyes widened. "Six *weeks*? That's..."

"Not a lot of time, to be sure." Riordan's expression brightened. "But you have the talent, expertise, and dare I say, genius required for the task. With your leadership, hard work, and a firm hand, I'm confident St. Brennan's will triumph."

"Firm hand?"

The headmaster hesitated. "The boys are a bit—spirited. You know boys."

"I have two younger brothers."

"Then I'm sure it's nothing you can't handle. You're doubtless up to the challenge."

That word. Gethsemane hadn't backed down from a challenge since she was ten.

Riordan clasped his hands. Eyes downcast, he said, "It's only fair to tell you some of the faculty expressed—concern—over my decision to hire you."

"Concern?"

"They were unfamiliar with your work, your reputation." Riordan met Gethsemane's gaze. "You'll show them."

First a challenge, now a dare. Getting an orchestra in shape to win a competition in only six weeks was impossible, but refuse a dare? Admit she couldn't do it? She could hear her sister snickering. If Holst could do it for St. Paul's..."Don't worry, sir. St. Brennan's will rise like a phoenix." She fought the urge to cross her fingers behind her back.

"Excellent." Riordan returned to his desk and shuffled papers, dismissing her. "I expect you want to get back to Carraigfaire, settle in."

No time to settle in. It's not like she planned to make

Dunmullach a permanent change of address. Six weeks was no time and, if she judged the headmaster's euphemistic assessment of the orchestra correctly, she'd be starting in the abyss.

Six weeks. Gethsemane banged open the cottage door, weary after the twenty-minute uphill trudge through the ever-present rain. She hung the borrowed mac on its hook on her way to the study where she flopped onto the sofa. Who was she kidding? Veronika Dudarova, herself, couldn't turn slacker school boys into a championship orchestra in six weeks. She should call Riordan, tell him she changed her mind. Suck it up and go back. It wouldn't be so bad. The "disappointed look" from Mother, relentless heckling from her eldest sister, smothering pity from the other...

Blech. Even if crawling home didn't sound less fun than a gaping head wound, how would she get there? She'd canceled the stolen credit cards. Which were maxed out anyway. She had her passport and a hundred euros. She might get as far as Dublin or Shannon, but then what?

She studied the bottles on the bar cart and lifted a stout one with a bold black and red label. Waddell and Dobb Double-oaked Twelve-year-old Reserve single barrel bourbon, from Kentucky. McCarthy had good taste. She poured liquid amber into a heavy leaded crystal whiskey glass. Maybe she could borrow money. Not from Mother or her sisters—unless she wanted to hear about it until doomsday. Her brothers? They didn't have any more money than she did.

Her old professor. The *maestro* had helped her before. He'd gotten her into the Strasburg Competition, arranged her audition for the Cleveland Symphony, her first professional gig. He'd be at his villa this time of year, hiding from the modern world. No phone or internet. She'd write him a letter.

The roll-top yielded stationery and a fountain pen in a brass violin-shaped pen stand. One shake sent ink drops jetting from the nib where they spread in Rorschach patterns across the dark cherry wood. Gethsemane cursed and ran to the kitchen for a rag. Returning, she froze a moment in the study's doorway then moved to the desk. The ink spill was gone, the pen back in its stand, the stationery back in its box, the whiskey glass back on the bar. She hadn't imagined pen and paper and bourbon, so how—?

"Is it American custom to take without askin'?"

Gethsemane grabbed a letter opener. A tall, broad-shouldered, unsmiling man leaned against a bookcase near the window, arms crossed.

Gethsemane ran—out of the cottage, down the driveway, and into the path of a slow-moving car. Brakes squealed, gravel sprayed, the car stopped inches from Gethsemane's knees. "Are you all right?" The driver, a stocky brown-eyed blond, about a decade older than her, jumped out.

Gethsemane gasped the story of the intruder.

The driver gestured up the hill. "C'mon, we'll take a look."

There was a fine line between brave and stupid and she wasn't crossing it. She watched horror movies in college. She knew better. "If Jack Torrance's up there—" She aimed a thumb at the cottage. "I'm staying down here."

"I shouldn't worry. No deranged caretakers 'round here in at least a hundred years."

Gethsemane didn't return the man's smile.

"Would you feel better if I went up myself and looked around?" he asked.

"Who are you?" Gethsemane asked.

"Teague Connolly."

Teague Connolly. Billy's friend and Eamon's brother-in-law. Gethsemane took a closer look at the blond hair and brown eyes, so like the woman in the photograph. "You're the man Billy McCarthy told me to call if I needed something. I'm Gethsemane Brown."

"I know. Whole village knows. News travels fast 'round Dunmullach. Wait here." Teague got back into his car and continued up the road.

Gethsemane listened to the wind howling down over the cliffs, conscious of the gathering darkness. Psycho killers grabbed people on isolated roads too. She hiked back up to the cottage in time to meet Teague at the front door.

"No one's there," he said.

"He was in the room with the desk, over by the window."

"I looked in all the rooms. Not a livin' soul inside. You know, the light up here plays tricks this time of evening, casts weird shadows."

"He spoke to me. Does the light form complete sentences?"

"What'd he look like?"

"I dunno. Big. White."

Teague scratched his head. "You might have seen Kieran Ross."

"Who?"

"Kieran Ross. Roams the cliffs, does errands. Harmless, an Irish Boo Radley."

Boo Radley wasn't harmless.

"What's he doing in the cottage?"

"Kieran keeps an eye on the place." Teague frowned. "Never known him to talk, though, 'cept maybe to the Nolan girl. I'll tell him to keep clear."

"Thank you, Mr. Connolly."

"Teague." He opened the trunk of his car. "I brought these for you." He lifted out two shopping bags filled with clothes.

Gethsemane stepped back. "You keep women's clothing in your trunk?"

Teague laughed. "Not as a matter of course, no. These belonged to Orla. Billy told me you were about her size."

"You won't mind me wearing your sister's things?" She looked through a bag.

"You're doing me a favor. My wife's been after me about getting rid of them. Sentimental, she calls me. I'd rather see 'em put to good use than end up in the rubbish."

Rubbish? Gethsemane pulled out a dress. Halston. Another. DVF. What philistine would toss designer dresses in the rubbish, even if they were twenty-five years old? She held up a suit. Chanel. Eamon wasn't the only McCarthy with good taste.

Back inside after Teague's departure, Gethsemane locked the door. She was sure—almost—she'd bolted it when she'd gotten home. How had Kieran Ross gotten in? She shrugged it off and went back to the study. The letter to the maestro needed to go out in the morning mail.

The scent hit her near the desk. Leather, cedar, pepper mingled with soap. *Gaeltacht* and *Mrs. Leary's.*

Then the voice. "Wouldn't Connolly give ya a ride back to town?"

No letter opener. Gethsemane swore. She must have dropped it outside. She grabbed a paperweight and faced the large man, drawing back her arm. "I'm warning you. I was starting pitcher in the Girls' State Fastpitch Softball Championships."

The man laughed, rich and throaty.

"Go ahead. Throw it."

Gethsemane hurled the weight. It sailed through the man's chest, disappearing into him like a sugar cube into hot coffee, and thudded behind him. She gasped. She'd thrown a low fastball dead center. A direct hit. He should be on the floor.

Had it really gone right through him? Gethsemane grabbed the pen stand and let loose an overhand pitch with heat like Jonathan Broxton. The stand stopped mid-air, hovered motionless, then fell to the ground.

Not. Humanly. Possible.

"Stop before ya break something." The weight and pen stand floated back to the desk.

Gethsemane ducked behind the wing chair. When had the laws of motion been repealed?

"Don't grip the chair so tight. You'll mark the leather."

"You're not Kieran Ross." He looked like—no, he couldn't be. She wished the chair was larger.

"Brilliant. My first conversation in a quarter century and I land a dullard."

Gethsemane scowled. Her brain must be playing tricks. How could Eam—? "Who are you?" she asked, afraid she knew the answer.

"Eamon McCarthy, owner of this cottage."

She forced her lips to speak the words. "Eamon McCarthy's dead."

"Be that as it may, I'm he."

"Him. And that's not possible," she said. *Not possible. Notpossiblenotpossible...*As if repeating it would make it true.

"Yet here I am." He cocked his head. "What's the matter? Don't believe in ghosts?"

She felt dizzy. "There's no such thing." What did generations of Mother's people—uneducated country-folk—know?

The man stepped closer. "Damned silly remark, since you're looking right at me. And stop cowering. It's unbecoming. What have you got to be afraid of if I'm not real?"

Gethsemane squeezed her eyes shut. Reality check. She recited her name, birthdate, current location. She opened her eyes. The man looked solid, real. He existed. But a ghost? Her physician mother left country superstition behind when she went away to college, married a mathematician and raised children—a chemist and a nuclear physicist, for God's sake—in a world filled with science. Not ghosts. But this wasn't her world.

"Decided yet?"

Eamon McCarthy. Gethsemane leaned around the chair.

Grandfather, the paternal one, had taken her to see McCarthy perform Debussy at the Peabody in Washington, D.C. when she was seven. Her first "grown-up" concert. She formed a crush on the Irish pianist with the wild dark curls, clipped his picture from a magazine and had kept it in a pink heart-shaped frame next to her bed until she went off to Vassar. This was the man in the heart-shaped frame, the same man in the silver frame on the vanity upstairs—Eamon McCarthy, dead twenty-five years.

"Well, which is it?" Eamon frowned down at her. "Ghost? Trick of the light? Or maybe a psychotic break? Or drunk on my bourbon?"

Her father's professorial words came to mind: if evidence forces you to reject your null hypothesis—ghosts don't exist—you must accept your alternative hypothesis. Mother would choose option C: psychotic break. She preferred Father's reasoning. "Ghost." She dropped into the wing chair. "Excuse me if I take a moment to become accustomed to you."

"Gene Tierney, *The Ghost and Mrs. Muir.* One of my wife's favorite movies."

Gethsemane reached for Eamon's leg. Her fingers buzzed as they passed through to the desktop. "You look so—here."

"I *am* here. And sticking your hand through people's rude."

"Sorry." She yanked back. "I meant solid. Flesh and blood."

"How'm I supposed to look?"

"I don't know. You're my first ghost."

Eamon dematerialized until only a vestige remained. "You prefer this?"

Gethsemane counted stars through his chest out the window beyond. "Not at all, Mr. McCarthy."

Eamon re-solidified. "You knew me before I told you my name." An accusation, not a question.

"Yes," she admitted. "I knew who you were. Are. Were, whatever. Gifted pianist, brilliant composer, notorious hothead. I saw you at the Peabody. You played Debussy."

"One of my better performances." He looked Gethsemane over. "You're not old enough."

"I was seven."

"School field trip?"

"Birthday present from my paternal grandfather. A cellist."

"You're musical?"

"Yes."

Eamon looked her over again. "Smart, talented, easy to look at. Has some bone in her back." He stroked his chin. "She'll do."

"Hey, Irish." Definitely a ghost. Hallucinations would've had better manners. "I'm right here. What'll I do?"

"Help me."

"Help you? Go to the light?"

Eamon waggled his fingers and made cartoon ghost noises. "Where'd ya get that?"

"I heard it on an episode of *Ghost Hunting Adventures.*"

Eamon snorted. "A skeptic watching such rubbish?"

"I wasn't actually *watching* the show." Gethsemane felt her cheeks redden. "The TV happened to be on and it happened to be playing."

"And you *happened* to catch a glimpse over your shoulder as you passed by on your way to return Jane Austen to the library."

The press hadn't exaggerated when they described Eamon as brusque and arrogant. They'd understated. "I know why you don't want to go to the light. Because, in your case, it's the glow from the fires of hell."

"Do you want to try scared speechless again? I liked that better than snarky."

"*Me* snarky?" Gethsemane got up. "Go haunt someone else."

"This is *my* house. Go live somewhere else."

"Fine." She started for the door.

Eamon blocked her path. "Wait."

"I'll walk through you."

The study door slammed shut.

Or not. "Well, if that's the way you're going to be about it." Gethsemane returned to the wing chair. "What do you want?"

"Your help. Pay attention."

"Are you going to get to the point or are we going to play twenty questions?"

Eamon crossed his arms and glared down at her. "Are all Americans as contrary as you?"

Gethsemane crossed her arms and glared up at Eamon. "Are all ghosts as contrary as you?"

"Stop." Eamon threw up his hands. "You'd think after ten

years of marriage I'd have learned better than to argue with a female." He looked her over a third time.

"Quit ogling. I'm not a bug on a pin."

"Not much bigger than one. But you give as good as you get. Though she be but little she is fierce."

"Though she be but little she is leaving." Gethsemane stood. "I'll find lodging at the school."

"Hear me out." The lock on the study door turned. "Please."

"Unlock the door."

Nothing happened.

"Unlock the door or I'll go through the window."

The lock turned again. Gethsemane hesitated. What if she left? Would he follow? Rematerialize at some inopportune moment? Push her off a cliff? No harm in listening. She didn't have to agree to anything. "All right, out with it. What is it you *need* me to do?"

"I need you to prove I didn't murder my wife."

"Oh, is that all?" Thirty-six years old now, she'd been too young to analyze reports of the McCarthy murder-suicide with any depth at the time they happened. She remembered feeling disbelief her idol could commit such atrocities. She also remembered news coverage sounding certain, to her eleven-year-old mind, of Eamon's guilt. "No problem. And while I'm at it maybe I can prove the Easter Bunny exists and find the lost city of El Dorado."

"I'm serious."

"So am I. If such evidence existed, wouldn't the police have found it twenty-five years ago?"

Eamon snarled. "The guards?" Gethsemane gagged on the sudden cologne-soap blast. A ropy blue vein popped out on Eamon's temple, coursed upward to disappear into his tangled curls, and exploded into a pulsating blue halo. Fists clenched, he paced. "Declan Hurley and the rest of the feckin' gardaí wouldn't have found evidence wrapped in a gold cloth and hand-delivered by Saint Nicholas himself. Bunch of feckin' gowls, the lot of 'em."

Every muscle in her body screamed, "Run!" but Gethsemane held her ground. "The legendary McCarthy temper in action."

The glow and the scent faded. A calmer Eamon offered apologies. "I was no fan of the Dunmullach An Garda Síochána and they were no fans of mine."

"Considering your high opinion of the local constabulary, if I managed to find some evidence clearing you of your wife's murder to whom would I deliver it?"

"To the guards."

Gethsemane pressed the heels of her palms against her eyes. If McCarthy was this maddening when he was alive, it's a wonder his wife hadn't killed him. "You just said—"

"Declan Hurley's long since retired, the drunken bastard. So have his cronies. The guards have a new man now, Inspector O'Reilly. About your age. He heads up the cold case unit. He's got a bit of a stick up his arse and he owns a cat—I'm a dog man, meself—but he seems like a sharp fella."

"And you know this how?"

"I get out and about. Can't stay in the cottage all the time, I'd go insane."

"If you can leave the cottage, why don't you just go to Inspector O'Reilly yourself?"

Eamon sighed, sorrow and frustration palpable, and sat opposite Gethsemane. "I tried. O'Reilly can't see or hear me. Not everyone can, you know."

"How'd I get so lucky?"

"Maybe you have a gift."

"For music, not for seeing dead people."

"I don't know why we can communicate. Maybe us both being musical's got something to do with it. Ghost rules are complicated. I haven't sussed 'em all out yet."

"No *Handbook for the Recently Deceased*?"

"No, and no signpost up ahead either. I'm glad you're finding this amusing."

She stared out the window into the darkness, stars and moon now obscured by clouds promising more rain. "I find nothing about this situation amusing, including you." She turned back to face

Eamon. "I find you presumptuous. How do you know I believe you? Maybe you really did kill your wife. You wouldn't be the first murderer to swear he didn't do it."

Eamon vanished, replaced by a buzzing blue orb. The glowing ball rose and shot toward Gethsemane's head. She ducked. Heat burned her cheek as the orb whizzed past an ear and slammed into a picture frame on the opposite side of the room, shattering the glass. In her other ear, a voice with Eamon's accent but the low, cold tone of her father during one of his spells, said, "Don't you *ever* say that again. Orla was the air to me."

"Okay, okay, I believe you. You didn't murder your wife."

Eamon re-materialized, solid, surrounded by a faint blue glow. "Damn. I liked that picture."

Safe from orbs, she stood. "You didn't murder your wife and *all* you want me to do is find evidence proving you didn't kill her and take the evidence to the police."

"That and one other—" Eamon held his thumb and forefinger a fraction of an inch apart "—wee thing."

"What? Find Jimmy Hoffa's body?"

"Find out who *did* murder Orla and me."

"You mean find out who murdered Orla. You committed suicide. You murdered you."

"I did no such thing. Do I seem like the sort of man who'd off himself?"

Gethsemane studied Eamon from the top of his tousled mop to the tips of his oxfords. Six feet, three inches, one hundred seventy pounds of talent, temper, and ego. "No, you definitely seem more like the type of guy someone else would murder. Shoot, stab, bludgeon, garrote—"

"You can stop now. And, for the record, I was poisoned."

"How do you know?" Reports of Eamon's suicide stated he'd taken poison which, of course, you'd know if you'd done yourself in. But if someone slipped it to you?

Eamon nodded toward the bar. "Are you a bourbon drinker or will any libation do so long's the proof's high enough?"

"I'm a Bushmill's drinker, but I don't turn my nose up at Ardbeg, Laphroaig, or Waddell and Dobb."

"So you know your whiskey well enough to know when something's been added to it." Gethsemane nodded. Eamon continued. "I know the taste of my Waddell and Dobb as well as I know the sound of my music or the smell of my wife's hair."

Gethsemane paled. "You were poisoned with the Waddell and Dobb Double-oaked?"

"Not the bottle you so liberally familiarized yourself with. Don't worry, you won't wake up dead."

"I wasn't worried about that. I was thinking what a waste of a good bottle of bourbon." She ignored the blue sparks around Eamon's head. "You being a connoisseur, one sip should've told you the bourbon was off. Why'd you drink more? Assuming the poison wasn't so powerful it killed you with one sip."

"One gulp. My wife had just been murdered, smashed to bits at the foot of a cliff. Everyone believed I'd done it based on the say-so of a crooked inebriate of a cop and a sociopathic thug named Jimmy Lynch who lied about seeing my car. 'Eamon's a hothead.' 'Eamon lost his temper again.' 'Flew into a rage and sure he done it.' Never mind I'd cut off both hands before raising one of them against Orla. I spent the week between her death and mine planning her funeral and trying to convince that gobshite Hurley to get off his arse and check out my alibi. I gulped bourbon, I didn't sip it. By the time I noticed the fatal glass didn't taste right it was too late."

"What were you poisoned with?" She couldn't remember hearing the specifics twenty-five years ago and didn't recall the poison being named in anything she'd come across recently, not even that ridiculous book.

Eamon shrugged. "Dunno. Something bitter, slightly spicy."

"That narrows it down. Not. Didn't you ever check the toxicology report?" Could ghosts check toxicology reports?

"Dunmullach's a village in the middle of nowhere. We weren't on the bus line back then and the train stopped here even less often than it does now. If you think we had some fancy toxicology lab and an expert forensics unit, you've been watching too much TV. We had the embalming room at the funeral parlor and a GP who was one of Hurley's drinking mates and senile to boot. The doc put less thought into examining Orla's and my bodies than you put into choosing your outfit in the morning. He didn't perform an autopsy on my wife. She's lying on the rocks with a broken neck and a smashed skull and no bullet holes or stab wounds. Cause of death was obvious on external exam. Why bother cutting her open? He saw me dead with an empty glass nearby, dipped his tongue in the bourbon, declared death by self-administered poison, signed off on the death certificate and that was that. Everybody down to the pub for a round. No one asked questions, they were too afraid of Hurley."

Gethsemane doubted Eamon's complaint was much of an exaggeration. She knew her mother, a psychiatrist, had been pressured more than once by a busy funeral home director to sign off on a death certificate as the "physician of record" and her mother's friends who volunteered as death examiners were family physicians and internists, not pathologists. Not that a toxicology report would have cleared Eamon of suspicion. A solid alibi, on the other hand..."Everyone said your alibi was bogus."

"Who's everyone? The press? Bunch of feckin' vultures. They didn't even wait 'til the bodies were cold before they started feeding. My alibi wasn't bogus, just unverifiable. I gave a house concert for some friends relocating to central Africa to do missionary work, my farewell present to them. They were on the airplane by the time I found Orla. Ever try to track someone down in rural Africa?"

She had. Her baby brother was a missionary. He'd worked in Chad, Sudan, Rwanda. Communication was sketchy at best, even in the era of internet and cell phones. Twenty-five years ago? No wonder no one had confirmed Eamon's alibi. But what about his car? "You said someone saw you in the area."

"I said someone lied. Jimmy Lynch is a cancer. A malicious

bastard who'd cut his own mother's throat for a Euro. The world would be a better place if he'd been drowned at birth."

"Cancerous sociopath or not, why would he go out of his way to frame you for murder?"

"Jimmy's had it in for me ever since we were teens. I caught him peddling dope to some boys from the lower school. Another lad had died of a drug overdose a few days prior. I mangled Jimmy, broke his nose. He never missed an opportunity after that to get revenge on me. Orla's death was his chance to do me in once and for all. Orla died sometime around midnight, according to the wee bit of exam the GP performed. Jimmy told the guards he'd seen my car turning onto Carrick Point Road at eleven thirty p.m. on All Hallows' Eve. I actually got home from Dublin at four o'clock in the morning on All Saints' Day. I slept at the lighthouse to avoid waking Orla. I found her on the cliffs after sun-up as I was walking back to the cottage. As for Hurley going along with Jimmy's lie, rumor had it Hurley took bribes from Jimmy in exchange for turning a blind eye to his dope dealing. He'd have backed up anything Jimmy said."

The blue aura deepened. "Dunmullach's a peaceful village, neat, orderly, at least on the surface. Murder's messy. Attracts attention. Not the good kind. The kind that shines light into corners best left dark. It was easier to put it all on me. A dead scapegoat. Case closed. No guards poking into your private business, uncovering your secrets. No wondering if the person chatting across the hedge or sitting in the pew opposite was a double murderer. Write the whole sordid situation off as a bad memory. Get on with life the way it was."

Gethsemane thought of her sorority sister, an attorney with the National Justice Project. Dozens of cases of people railroaded into prison by corrupt small town law enforcement stuffed her file cabinets.

"I'm asking you again, will you help me? Prove I didn't murder my wife and find out who did."

"I can't."

"The first part, then. Clear me of murdering my reason for living. I can rest easy if the world knows I never did such a thing."

"No."

"Do you want to take a moment to think about it?"

"I don't need a moment. I don't need a second. I'm a musician. I'm a *maestra*. I'm not some Miss Marple-wannabe. I don't know anything about investigating murders."

Eamon dropped to a knee. "I'm doing something I never did while I lived. I'm begging. You're my best, my only, hope of being able to rest in peace. I can't cross over to anywhere, be it heaven or hell, with this hanging over me."

Memories of King Saul poked her again. "Don't psychics find justice for restless spirits? Contact one of them."

Eamon spat. "Charlatans, con artists. You're all I have."

"Then you have nothing. I can't help you." Forget about idolizing him growing up. "I have six weeks to turn three dozen slackers into a championship orchestra, I've got to come up with lesson plans for boys as interested in music as I am in video games, and I have to find a permanent job, preferably back in the States." Forget about his heartbreakingly beautiful music. "I don't have time to investigate crimes solved a quarter of a century ago." She massaged her temples. "Even if I had time, I wouldn't have a clue where to start. I'm sorry."

"I need you."

"I'm really sorry."

Forget the bond his music created between her and her beloved grandfather, a connection not shared with anyone else in the family.

Eamon faded feet first, bit by bit. His eyes vanished last. Were they glistening before they winked out? Maybe it was the light. Gethsemane sniffed. No cologne. No soap. She smoothed her dress and squared her shoulders. She couldn't help Eamon McCarthy. Really.

*   *   *

Upstairs again, she stood in the middle of the master bedroom. Orla and Eamon stared at her from their photos, imploring. No way could she sleep in here. She relocated to the back bedroom and undressed. She caught sight of herself in the mirror. Dark circles ringed her eyes, a frown creased her forehead, her hair stood out at odd angles. A right mess, Grandma would say.

"How can I help you?" she asked aloud. "I can't even help myself."

Gethsemane tossed and turned most of the night. War raged in her brain. *You imagined the whole thing* battled *you saw it with your own eyes. Overactive imagination triggered by a strange place* fell victim to *you've spent your life traveling to strange places. Someone cleaned up the desk* slew *delirium-induced hallucination.* Around three a.m. the tide of battle shifted. Voices, infrequent at first, soon became steady like the drip-drip-drip of a slow leak. Selfish. Uncaring. Not how you were brought up. The voices sounded like Grandfather and her baby brother. Her brother, the missionary physician who'd passed up a partnership in an exclusive Washington, D.C. practice to build a women's clinic in Zambia. Elegant, dignified Grandfather, always working extra shifts at month's end to make up the rent money he'd spent on food for the widow next door or medicine for the pensioner downstairs. They'd have helped.

"Leave me alone." Gethsemane threw a pillow and knocked over a lamp. "I can't help. I'm not a detective or a ghost whisperer. I don't want to be anybody's hero. I just want my sensible, orderly life back." She pulled the covers over her head and squeezed her eyes shut. Sleep came, eventually, trailing with it the faint aroma of leather and soap.

Two

Gethsemane abandoned her fitful sleep early and arrived at St. Brennan's before morning bell. The smart, red-orange suit she'd chosen from the clothes Teague brought her complemented both her brown skin and the season. She felt authoritative in a suit. She pulled her mac close against the crisp October air and inhaled deeply. The aroma of bacon, toast, and coffee revived her and lured her toward what she hoped was the dining hall.

As she stepped onto the emerald quad, someone called from a nearby colonnade, "So you're her."

She spun. A tall redhead in wire-rimmed glasses, wrinkled khakis, and a tweed jacket, which looked as if it had been handed down from a brawnier older brother, leaned against a column. Gethsemane introduced herself.

"I know who you are," the man said. "Always thought St. Brennan's savior would be taller."

Putting up with this type first thing in the morning required more sleep. "I have a rule. You're not allowed to insult me before I've had coffee unless I know your name. So, Mr. Whoever-you-are, if you'll please excuse me, I'm on my way to breakfast."

"Grennan. Francis Grennan." He didn't offer his hand. "I teach maths."

Did mathematics create oddballs or only attract them?

Gethsemane imagined her father sitting in a pub having an esoteric conversation with this man about Fibonacci numbers.

"My friends call me Frankie."

"And what should I call you?" Gethsemane asked.

"Grennan will do."

Why did she notice his eyes were the same luscious shade of green as the quad's soft grass and his short hair shone like a new copper penny? Hunger? Certainly his attitude did nothing to make him attractive. Gethsemane gave in to the rumbling in her stomach and the entreating aromas wafting from the far side of the quad. "Excuse me, *Grennan*. Somewhere sits a plate of bacon with my name on it."

She made it halfway across the grass before he called after her. "It's impossible, you know."

"What's impossible?"

"Winning the All-County."

"Why?" She turned and went back to where he still leaned. "Why impossible?" Odd ducks often had brilliant insight. Her father had been downright spooky sometimes.

Francis didn't hesitate. "No passion. No commitment to the community."

He couldn't mean her. He hadn't known her five minutes. Or was a guilty conscience so obvious?

"We've had a string of conductors using St. Brennan's as a stepping stone present uninspired music with mechanical instruction. Lackluster leadership yields lackluster performances. Then the maestro moves on and leaves Dunmullach to deal with the disappointment."

"Is the All-County such a big deal?"

"Perhaps not to a musical prodigy stuck in an Irish backwater."

"I'm serious, Grennan. Where does the All-County rank on the competition circuit? I don't know the Irish honors orchestra scene."

"About forty-five percent of winning musicians are offered scholarships to conservatories or music programs. About twenty percent of musicians in winning orchestras go on to professional music careers. And the event pumps about half a million euros into the host village's economy."

"A big deal," Gethsemane said as much to herself as to Francis.

Francis scuffed his shoe. "Of all the years to invite Peter Nolan to judge."

Gethsemane forgot the bacon. "Peter Nolan?"

"Peter Nolan, the executive director—"

"Of the Boston Philharmonia, the preeminent orchestra in the eastern United States. What's Peter Nolan doing judging a high school orchestra competition?"

"Slumming."

"Oh, stop it. I don't care how important the All-County is to Dunmullach or to all of western Ireland, for that matter. Peter Nolan judging a high school battle of the honors bands is like Julia Child judging a barbeque battle. Which, before you say anything, people in my part of the world take seriously."

"Or sort of like the winner of the Fleischer Prize teaching music to school lads."

Gethsemane bit back her un-ladylike response.

"Peter Nolan must get a gazillion requests to judge competitions. Why this one?"

"Dunmullach's Nolan's hometown. His nephew, Colm, is in the orchestra. Plays strings."

Rumors flew in the classical music world about Peter Nolan looking for a new music director for the Philharmonia. Why not her? She liked Boston: history, culture, clam chowder. She'd worked hard her whole life to succeed where people told her she didn't belong because she was the wrong race or the wrong gender. She'd climbed to the heights of her profession. She deserved Boston.

"Dr. Brown?"

"What? Sorry, I was someplace else."

"If you're dreaming about catching the next train out of town, it leaves Thursday at half-nine in the morning."

"Actually, I was wondering whether the All-County judges would prefer a concerto or a symphony."

Francis shoved his hands in his pockets. "Maybe you'll get lucky and find a long-lost Eamon McCarthy composition hidden in a book. Or maybe you can summon his ghost and have him whip up a brand new piece for you."

Francis tromped off along the colonnade. Maybe he was on to something.

Gethsemane got lost twice between the dining hall and the music room, arriving just as the bell rang to signal the start of the period. Fifteen pairs of eyes stared at her and fifteen voices fell silent as soon as she opened the door.

Gethsemane took a deep breath. She had this. She'd performed before *New York Times'* music critics at the Lincoln Center. She could handle teenagers. Look confident. Step into the room.

"Hi. My name is Dr. Gethsemane Brown. I'm your new music teacher."

A pencil dropped, a chair scraped, but no one spoke. More seconds passed. Gethsemane opened her mouth to ask for the roll book when a boy on the front row stood up.

"Welcome to Introduction to Music, Dr. Brown."

She examined the boy: Titian red hair, about sixteen years old, taller than her, stocky, somewhere between boyish and manly with hints of muscle starting to replace what had likely been fat before testosterone kicked in. She asked his name.

"Aengus Toibin."

"Well, Mr. Toibin, if you're supposed to be in Introduction to Music you'd better leave and come back third period." She walked to the chalkboard. "This," she said as she wrote, "is Intermediate Music Theory."

Another boy, about the same age and height as the first, rose. He stood blond and lithe and beautiful, with eyes greener than

Grennan's, the sort of boy from whom parents tried—and failed—to keep their daughters. "Stop acting the maggot."

The redhead sat down and flashed a smile any crocodile would have envied.

The blond boy addressed Gethsemane. "He knows what class this is. And his name's not Aengus, it's Feargus. *That's* Aengus." He nodded at a third boy, the redhead's identical twin.

"And you are?" Gethsemane asked the blond. He reminded Gethsemane of someone.

"I'm Colm Nolan, Head Boy." He pointed to a shiny enameled pin on the lapel of his uniform jacket.

Peter Nolan's nephew. Dangerous good looks ran in the family.

Colm continued talking. "Feargus is Deputy Head Boy and he thinks he's funny."

Gethsemane noticed a similar pin on Feargus's jacket. She remembered a book she'd read about a Head Boy and his deputy. Vicious bullies put on trial for driving a younger boy to suicide. She clenched her jaw. Teaching teenaged schoolboys was going to be almost as much fun as defending her dissertation to a hungover committee head who'd lost his tenure and his wife in the same week. Almost.

Gethsemane read the lunch menu posted near the cafeteria: Battered cod portions, carrot batons, vegetable curry, rice, and fruit salad. No wonder the boys behaved badly. Dyspepsia.

"The cod's not bad." She recognized Francis Grennan's voice. He stood behind her, hands shoved deep into the pockets of his wrinkled khakis. "Avoid the vegetable curry like the plague."

His earlier remark about trains leaving town came to mind. "Transportation options, dietary advice. You're a one-man information bureau."

"I deserved that," the math teacher said. "But I've been in Dunmullach my whole life and at St. Brennan's through half a dozen music directors. History tends to repeat itself in this village."

"I'd be lying," she conceded, "if I claimed the chance to impress Peter Nolan enough to offer me a job back in the States didn't excite me or if I pretended I didn't take this job because it paid better than open mic contests at the pub. But," she forced certainty into her voice, "now I'm here, I don't intend to lose."

"The legendary American self-confidence. Lunch line's this way." Francis disappeared into the crowd before Gethsemane could figure out if he'd insulted her or complimented her.

She followed him through the serving area to the faculty dining table. She sat across from him and introduced herself to the other teachers.

"Bit of a boys' club," Francis said. "You're one-fourth of the female faculty."

Gethsemane hid her carrots under the clumped rice. If the vegetable curry was worse...

Francis continued. "The women formed a 'ladies only' book club. A show of solidarity. I think they're reading that true-crime about the McCarthy case this month. You might be interested, given your current lodgings."

"Or not. The book's garbage." She stabbed the sole cherry amongst her fruit chunks. "Sensationalized distortions of fact propped up by rumor and innuendo."

"Such passion. One would think you knew the McCarthys personally."

One of them, anyway. Or, at least, his ghost. A snarky, demanding, irritatingly charming ghost who, in one meeting, had convinced her of his innocence. She wished, she admitted with a guilty twinge, she could help prove it. "Not personally. I was eleven when they died. But I know Eamon, through his music, as well as I know my name. He's—he *was*—no murderer."

"While you're up at Carraigfaire maybe you'll uncover a clue to the real killer hidden in some dusty tome and convince Iollan O'Reilly to open one of his cold cases."

Iollan O'Reilly. The cop Eamon told her to go to. Was Francis joking? She searched the math teacher's emerald eyes for signs of mirth. Inscrutable. She couldn't figure him. Cynical and curmudgeonly one minute, solicitous the next. She took O'Reilly's name coming up as an omen and decided to play it straight. "You know Inspector O'Reilly? What's he like?"

"Sound fella. Straight-laced, serious about his work. Good to have at your back in a fight. Why? You're not really going to ask him to re-open the McCarthy case?"

Spooky. Like her father. Or was she so obvious? "Just— curious. His name came up somewhere."

"If you hurry you might be able to satisfy your 'curiosity' and catch him on campus. He dates the English teacher and usually has—lunch—with her in the Shakespeare garden."

Gethsemane cocked her head. This guy puzzled her more than the quadratic equation.

"What?" he asked.

"Nothing. Never mind. Thanks for the tip, Grennan."

She tossed the remains of her lunch and hurried from the dining hall. She crossed playing fields dotted with students enjoying afternoon break on her way down to the brick-walled Eden halfway between the main campus and the boathouse.

Espaliered fruit trees lined the perimeter. Manicured boxwoods taller than Gethsemane and gravel paths divided the space into quadrants around a central fountain. No visible sign of anyone. Voices, a man's and a woman's, rose from the other side of a hedge. The woman sounded angry. "You always say the same thing, Iollan."

Iollan. Inspector O'Reilly. Gethsemane hesitated, then leaned her ear toward the hedge. It wasn't really eavesdropping. The garden was a public place. You couldn't argue in public and expect privacy.

The woman's volume rose. "Why does work always come before me? Four months we're together and you've canceled as many dates as you've kept. When do I get to be a priority?"

"You have to understand," O'Reilly pled. "Work's diabolical. Hundreds of open cases in the archives."

"By now you should have solved every cold murder in the county back to eighteen sixty-two," the woman said.

Gethsemane clamped a hand over her mouth to keep from laughing. She tried to peer through the boxwood. Only tangled brown branches and leathery green leaves.

The argument continued. "I work hard too, Iollan. Do you think teaching's easy? I spend all day in class then I come home and grade papers and prepare lessons. Yet, I still make time to cook a fancy meal for your birthday and what happens?"

"I explained," O'Reilly said.

"You explained folks a decade dead were more important than me."

"That's not exactly what I said."

"You might as well have. One night, Iollan, one night. Your cold cases wouldn't have been any colder if you'd let them wait one night. Why couldn't you do that for me?"

"The cold case unit is my responsibility. I'm all alone right now. As soon as the funding comes through and the department adds some more men—"

"When will that be? A month? Two? A year?"

Silence. Gethsemane counted ten.

The woman spoke. "However long it takes, don't expect me to be waiting. Goodbye, Iollan."

Light footsteps retreated along the gravel in the direction of the garden's lower gate. A string of expletives and a rant on the general uselessness of females accompanied heavier footsteps approaching Gethsemane. She looked around. No escape. Her sister's voice popped into her head—if you can't get out of a situation, take control of it. She was waiting for O'Reilly as he rounded the hedge. Startled, the inspector swore.

"Hello." Gethsemane extended a hand. "You must be Inspector O'Reilly."

O'Reilly, unsmiling, adjusted a tweed stingy-brimmed fedora.

"How long have you been there?" His gray eyes, the color of a gathering storm, fixed hers.

Gethsemane held her hand two inches from O'Reilly's nose. "I'm Gethsemane—"

"I know who you are." His handshake, though perfunctory, was firm. The strength of his grip and the smooth skin on the back of his hand belied the salt-and-pepper gracing his temples. "Giving music lessons in the garden today?"

"Just on a break." Gethsemane glanced at her watch, taking in O'Reilly's lean, five-ten frame, nondescript suit, and ordinary tie. "Which ends in five minutes." She noticed his shoes—black leather monkstraps, expensive-looking, designer, probably Italian, out of place with the rest of his attire.

"I won't keep you." O'Reilly stepped to one side.

Gethsemane blocked his path. "I did want to ask you about one thing. The McCarthy case."

"Murder-suicide." He stepped the other way, colliding with Gethsemane as she blocked him again.

Sandalwood and clove greeted her nose pressed against the inspector's neck. His cologne was spicier, more exotic than Eamon's. She lost her train of thought. The crunch of gravel beneath O'Reilly's foot as he moved away brought her back to the garden. "Is the McCarthy case one of the cold cases you're investigating?"

"The case isn't cold, it's closed."

"Eamon McCarthy was never convicted of killing his wife. He never even went to trial."

O'Reilly readjusted his hat. "Maybe the legal system operates differently in America, but here in Ireland we don't put dead men on trial."

"In America we presume you're innocent until you're proven guilty in a court of law. No trial, no conviction, no closed case."

"Welcome to Dunmullach." He made a show of pushing back his sleeve to expose his watch. "Your break."

"What about it?"

The gray eyes fixed hers again. "It's over."

Gethsemane stepped aside as O'Reilly strode to the upper gate. She waited until he disappeared beyond the playing fields before heading the same way. She paused at the gate long enough to tell a murder of crows come to roost atop the boxwood what she thought of ill-tempered policemen, even if they did smell good and remind her of a movie star.

Gethsemane sprinted from the Shakespeare Garden to reach the music room as the afternoon bell announced Honors Orchestra. She opened the door on three dozen boys from third through sixth year. Some, like the Toibin twins, she recognized from the morning.

"Good afternoon. For those of you I haven't met, I'm Dr. Gethsemane Brown, your maestra."

"What's a maestra?" one boy asked.

"The feminine of maestro, the conductor." She surveyed the room. "Who can tell me what the conductor does?"

Laughter followed an anonymous, "Stands down front and waves that little stick."

Aengus Toibin raised a hand. "The conductor keeps the time and tempo. He—or she," he flashed an obsequious smile, "ensures the different sections of the orchestra work together as a cohesive unit. He expresses the emotions of the music through the musicians."

Feargus mumbled, "Then quits the day after the All-County."

"What piece did you perform in last year's All-County?" Gethsemane asked.

No one spoke.

"Someone must remember."

"Beethoven," a boy near the window offered.

"Beethoven's 'Symphony Number Six in F.'" Colm Nolan grinned around the room from the doorway. "And we did that for Parents' Day. We performed one of the maestro's own compositions for the All-County."

"You're late, Mr. Nolan."

Colm sauntered over to the other boys. "Sorry."

Not. But no point starting a war when you're outnumbered. Time to speak to Colm about his tardiness later. Gethsemane addressed the group. "Arrange yourself by instrument, as you would for a performance."

A few moments of jostling and chair scraping and the boys had positioned themselves into smaller groups: percussion, winds, reeds, brass, strings, first and second violins. The first violin chair nearest the conductor's podium sat empty.

"Who's concertmaster?" Gethsemane asked. The leader of the first violin section, a "first among equals," had a job almost as important as hers. The concertmaster tuned the orchestra, coordinated the bowing and phrasing of the strings, and communicated the maestro's musical vision to the rest of the orchestra. He had to blend in with the rest of the strings when the entire orchestra was playing while arising to the challenge of a solo when the music required it. As servant of both orchestra and conductor, the concertmaster needed to be at the top of his craft.

"He went up to university."

"Which of you have been a featured soloist?" The star of the show, the main attraction.

No hands raised.

"Looks like we'll have some decisions to make soon."

Colm slouched and crossed a foot on his knee. "Important decisions."

Gethsemane tossed her mac, missing the coat rack by a foot.

The coat levitated and hung itself on a peg. "You missed." The cologne-soap smell accompanied Eamon's voice. "You look fetching in that suit, by the way. It was one of Orla's favorites."

"Thank you," Gethsemane poured a double bourbon. "Why can't we lock boys up between the ages of twelve and thirty-two? Or send them to a remote island, *Lord of the Flies*-style?"

"Where's the fun in that?" Eamon materialized beside her. "Alcohol poisoning's not going to make them any more tolerable."

"That's funny, coming from you. And stop appearing out of nowhere. Getting used to a ghost is hard enough without him popping up everywhere."

"I see the rigors of a day spent shepherding schoolboys has done nothing to dull your tongue."

"I guess they're no worse than my brothers at that age. I'll have to ask Mother if she was this exhausted by the end of the day." Gethsemane flopped onto the sofa. "You used to be a teenaged boy. Give me some insight. What made you tick?"

"Short skirts and long legs."

Gethsemane rolled her eyes.

Eamon leaned back, his torso melting into the seat cushions. "Seriously, all I can tell you is, when I got up to mischief, I got up to it because I knew it was wrong. That was the whole point."

"How'd you not end up in the hospital or jail or worse?"

"I had Orla and Pegeen Sullivan to keep me from going too far astray. I think Ma paid them."

"Who's Pegeen Sullivan? Your governess?"

"Governess? Ya think we were minted? She's an old friend. Grew up together, Peg, Orla, and me."

Gethsemane sipped her drink, savoring the bourbon's warm spicy finish.

"Feeling better?"

"Microscopically." She emptied her glass. "I need to win the All-County."

"Wouldn't have anything to do with a certain judge from Boston?"

"How do you know about Peter Nolan?"

"In Dunmullach, even the ghosts are in on the gossip. Allow me." Eamon waved a finger at the bar cart. The bottle of Waddell and Dobb Double-oaked floated to Gethsemane and poured a refill. Eamon waved his finger again, returning the bottle to its previous position.

"Neat trick," Gethsemane said. "You must be a hoot at cocktail parties."

"That's nothing. You should see me pull a rabbit out of—"

Gethsemane shot him a warning look.

"A hat."

"So what *can* you do? Besides cleaning up spills, pouring drinks, and vanishing into thin air. Read minds?"

"If I could, I'd know who killed Orla and me."

"Point taken."

"I can go pretty much anywhere I went while I was alive." He sat up straight. "Except Our Lady."

"Our Lady?"

"Our Lady of Perpetual Sorrows. Father Keating's church."

"Why not?"

"Because I'm labeled a suicide. Erroneously, but labeled nonetheless. I'm buried in unhallowed ground, so I'm eternally banned from the church and church yard. Can only go as far as the front gate."

"Where's your wife buried?"

A blue aura framed Eamon's head. "At Our Lady."

"Where you can't visit her."

The blue deepened.

Even after all these years, her mother visited her father's grave once a week.

"Can't you contact her on the other side?"

"The 'other side' is devoid of mobile phone technology and social media."

Blue sparks popped.

"Snippiness is not attractive in grown man nor ghost. You can materialize all over town, listen to gossip, levitate objects, and smash pictures with glowing blue orbs. Why can't you go find your wife?" Eamon's expression prompted an apology. "I don't mean to sound flip. I want to know."

Gethsemane strained to hear Eamon's whispered reply. "I *have* tried to find Orla. Over and over I've tried. Sometimes I hear her or glimpse her hair or catch a hint of her perfume. I call her, she raises a hand or starts to speak but then a gray fog appears and I've lost her."

"What's blocking you?"

"I wish I knew."

"My over-the-top rational, psychiatrist mother swears she still feels my father's presence in the house they shared."

"It's worse here than anywhere. I can't sense her at Carraigfaire at all." The blue aura faded to yellow. "I'd have thought if I could reach Orla any place it would be here. Carraigfaire meant the world to us, ever since we discovered it together as kids. It'd sat abandoned for a century, a ruin unfit for habitation, but as soon as we found it Orla and I both knew we'd live here someday." Eamon laughed sadly. He leaned close to Gethsemane and laid his hand through hers. She shivered as a buzz zipped up her spine. The cologne fragrance enveloped her. "I think injustice keeps Orla and me apart as sure as Pyramus and Thisbe's brick wall. I have to believe finding our killer will set things right, cosmically speaking. Then maybe I can find my wife. But I can't do it without your help."

"Why me? I know music, math, baseball, and old movies. I don't know anything about murder investigations."

"You arrive on my doorstep a few weeks before the twenty-fifth anniversary of my wife's murder *and* you can see and hear me. It's a sign. I'm not asking you to solve the crimes yourself. Just find enough evidence to convince the guards to reopen the case and do the job right this time."

"I still say contact a psychic. They help police solve cold cases all the time."

"You don't believe in psychics any more than you believe in vampires or alien abductions."

"Or ghosts, until yesterday."

"Touché. *I* don't believe in psychics. Teague hired one soon after I died. Took Teague's money and gave him nothing but mumbo jumbo that could have applied to half the village. I stood right next to the whacker, even poked my finger in his eye, and he never knew it. Could have gone after him with a cricket bat and he wouldn't have noticed. A rank con man."

Gethsemane went to the hall for a coat. "I still think you've got the wrong girl. I don't see how I can help you."

"Where're you going at this hour?" Eamon appeared beside her.

"For a walk."

"Are you bolloxed? It's getting dark out and fixin' to lash." On cue, raindrops hit the porch.

"Do you control the weather or merely predict it?"

"Neither. You don't have to be a ghost or a psychic to know it's fixin' to rain in Dunmullach. You just have to live here for more than ten minutes."

Gethsemane buttoned her mac and grabbed the newsboy cap.

"You're not really going out there? If you don't fall off the cliff, you'll catch your death from pneumonia."

"I'll stay away from the cliff's edge. And bacteria and viruses cause pneumonia, not rain. Trust me, my mother's a doctor."

"Have it your way, but don't expect me to come running if you go tumbling down the mountainside." Eamon vanished.

"I don't need your help." Gethsemane slammed the front door and started up the road to the lighthouse. "You need mine."

She ruminated as she walked, ignoring the rain's sting. Her orderly, safe life had devolved into a mess. Her star had tarnished; she'd disappointed her mother. She wasn't used to failure. A job in Boston—not ghosts and murders—was her ticket back to normalcy, to golden-girl status. How to get there? She tried to ignore the tiny voice in her head echoing Francis Grennan's sarcastic suggestion: enlist the help of the greatest composer of the late twentieth century.

Three

Gethsemane arrived at St. Brennan's with the morning bell, mood lifted by a night's sleep. Ireland had wrapped its spell around her in her dreams.

Her good mood lasted the time it took Headmaster Riordan to cross the quad. "Dr. Brown." He gestured to the lanky, gray-haired, expensively suited man accompanying him. "Meet Hieronymus Dunleavy, a good friend to St. Brennan's for many years."

Good friend. Code for major donor. Gethsemane greeted the duo.

"An honor to meet you, Dr. Brown," Dunleavy said. "I'm a fan. I had the pleasure of hearing you perform in New Orleans."

"Mr. Dunleavy is a true music lover and patron of the arts."

Gethsemane didn't need Tchaikovsky to warn her what came next. She'd heard it enough throughout her career.

"Richard told me you were marshaling the troops, so to speak, gearing up the orchestra for the All-County."

Riordan placed hands on both their shoulders. "With Dr. Brown at the helm, I've no doubt about the outcome of this year's competition. Her leadership virtually guarantees a trophy for St. Brennan's."

Wait for it.

Riordan stage-whispered to Gethsemane. "Mr. Dunleavy is considering a generous donation to St. Brennan's music program."

Bam.

Dunleavy stood taller and puffed out his chest. "A complete overhaul of the music room, sound-proofed practice rooms, new instruments, and an acoustically-engineered auditorium. St. Brennan's deserves a music space that reflects the potential of its music program."

Riordan grasped his lapels and rocked back and forth on his heels, the kid who won the Golden Ticket to Willy Wonka's factory. "Mr. Dunleavy showed me the plans for the new auditorium. They include a lovely trophy display case."

Translation: win the All-County, St. Brennan's "good friend" donates enough money to the school to feed a non-industrialized nation for a month. Gethsemane flashed her best professional musician smile. "Thank you both for your confidence in me. I'll do my best to give St. Brennan's an orchestra it can be proud of." Thus ensuring Mr. Dunleavy's continued friendship and generosity.

After handshakes all around, the men went their way. Gethsemane closed her eyes in silent prayer. Winning the All-County to convince Peter Nolan to offer her a job was big. Winning to convince Hieronymus Dunleavy to donate a fortune to the school was huge. Her reputation would never recover from the hit of losing a major donor. She'd be poison, lucky to land a gig conducting a prison orchestra in Outer Mongolia. And she'd be labeled as the one who cost St. Brennan's its auditorium, disappointed the village, a stigma she'd carry in her heart long after she left Dunmullach behind. She'd disappoint them.

The spell was broken.

The day's lunch menu—chicken supreme, creamed potatoes, beetroot, sweet corn—sounded even less appetizing than the previous day's. Hunger quelled by thoughts of chicken chunks swimming in bland sauce, Gethsemane opted for a walk in the Shakespeare Garden. She half hoped to run into Inspector O'Reilly again—only to ask him to reconsider opening the McCarthy case, not because his eyes reminded her of gathering thunderclouds on a sultry day—then dismissed the thought. Of course he wouldn't be there. Having been dumped, he'd have no reason to be on school grounds. Regardless, a stroll in the brisk autumn air surrounded by a Bard-inspired landscape would cheer her up.

She retrieved her mac from the faculty cloak room and headed out. A display case in the hallway near the exit, filled with newspaper clippings, photos, letters, and small artifacts, caught her eye. A card identified the case as being dedicated to the notable achievements of St. Brennan's alumni. One newspaper headline stood out: *Three Generations of Morrises Choose Life of Missionary Service.* The photo accompanying the article showed two couples, one elderly, one middle aged, and twin boys who looked to be in their early twenties. One twin posed with a video camera. All of the males shared a family resemblance.

Gethsemane scanned the article. The senior Morris headed the Road to Emmaus Missionary Society, dedicated to building schools and spreading the Gospel in central and eastern African nations. His entire family—wife, son, daughter-in-law, and grandsons—had joined him in his work. The Society held a fundraiser—Gethsemane caught her breath—to send the Morris family to a permanent mission in Sudan where they planned to start a school and a church. The yellowed clipping was dated a few months before Eamon gave his departing missionary friends the gift of a house concert.

The garden walk would have to wait.

Gethsemane surveyed the school library. Deserted except for her. A sign on the desk admonished students to stay away until after lunch. She hesitated. Even if the Morrises were the friends Eamon performed for, the chances of contacting them to give a statement about the time Eamon left their home were slim after all these years. They could be anywhere in the world. And what if she did contact them? Would they remember the details of a night so long ago? And wasn't searching for them getting deeper involved in Eamon's problem, which she'd vowed not to do?

She shook her head. Just checking wouldn't hurt. It would only take a little while and she could hand anything she found over to O'Reilly. Let the police do the leg work. It's not like she had to track them to Africa or wherever herself.

Bypassing the newspaper stacks in favor of more modern technology, Gethsemane sat at a computer terminal. An internet search on "Morris," "Road to Emmaus mission," and "Africa" soon yielded the information she wanted.

Or didn't want. There'd be no statement from the Morrises. They'd all died in Sudan, victims of that country's civil war.

Skipping tea in the faculty lounge after school in favor of whiskey at the Mad Rabbit, Gethsemane found the crowd of regulars already gathered. They ignored her as she claimed an empty seat at the bar.

"What'll ya have, miss?" Murphy, the stocky barman, asked. He set a whiskey glass in front of Gethsemane. "We do have wine if you prefer."

An urge struck her. "How about bourbon? Waddell and Dobb Double-oaked Twelve year-old Reserve."

"Sorry, haven't got it. Eamon McCarthy's only one who ever drank it. The Off License used to special order it for him. Billy McCarthy still gets a case from time to time. 'For verisimilitude,' he says. Wants the cottage kept the way his uncle kept it. Between you and me and the lamppost, if it's just for decoration, why's he need replenishments? Who's drinkin' it? Eamon's ghost?"

Gethsemane stifled a laugh and chose again, her usual. "How about Bushmill's Twenty-one? Neat."

"I admire a woman who appreciates a fine whiskey," Murphy said as he poured. "And, might I add, Orla McCarthy's dress looks good on ya."

Gethsemane recognized a few faces from St. Brennan's in the crowd. Still no one noticed her. A woman drinking hard liquor alone in a pub in the late afternoon didn't seem to be occasion for excitement in Dunmullach.

A newspaper lay abandoned on the bar. Gethsemane slid it over then slid it back. The words had been gibberish, not the fault of the whiskey.

Murphy handed her another. "That one's Irish," he explained. "Try this one, the *Dunmullach Dispatch*. It's English."

Gethsemane flipped through the pages, skimming articles about the upcoming Michaelmas Festival and the rugby team's chances for next year. An ad on page three jumped out at her:

Village Psychic

Sister Siobhan

Helps in All Areas of Life

Contacts the Departed, Answers All Questions

Reunites Lovers, 10 Euro Special

065 555 4070

Gethsemane traced the ad with her finger. A sign? Twenty-four hours after telling Eamon to contact a psychic an ad for one practically falls in her lap. She asked Murphy for a pen.

"Thinking of hiring her?" he asked.

"Just writing the number down for future reference. In case the cottage turns out to be haunted or something."

"Wouldn't be a proper Irish cottage if it didn't. No need to waste ink, though." Murphy gestured to the rear of the pub. "Sister Siobhan's sitting over there."

Gethsemane swiveled. A pudgy female face sandwiched between a multicolored turban and matching scarf hunched in a corner booth. The tips of her chandelier earrings grazed the rims of empty pint glasses as her head bent over a smartphone. A red caftan hid everything below the scarf. "That's Sister Siobhan?"

Murphy nodded. "The one and only." Under his breath he added, "Thank God." He refilled Gethsemane's Bushmills. "Take it. You'll need it."

Thus armed, Gethsemane made her way across the pub. As she neared the corner booth she took in the rest of Siobhan: Aladdin slippers protruded beneath the caftan's hem, ring-encrusted fingers grasped the smartphone, red rouge and lipstick tinted cheeks and lips. Gethsemane waited for Siobhan to look up. Fifteen seconds, twenty. Gethsemane cleared her throat.

"What?" Siobhan kept texting.

Gethsemane slid onto the bench opposite. "My name is—"

"I know who you are. Whole village knows."

"Your ad says—"

"I know what my own ad says, don't I? If ya want me to find your stolen luggage, I don't do that sort of thing."

Gethsemane took a deep breath and a gulp of Bushmills. "What about ghosts. Do you do that sort of thing?"

Siobhan's thumbs slowed, but she kept her eyes on her phone's screen. "Mebbe."

"You know I'm staying at Carraigfaire."

"What of it?"

"You know it's rumored haunted."

Siobhan snorted. "This is Ireland, dearie. Every place is rumored haunted." Her thumbs sped up.

Gethsemane drained her glass and congratulated herself on not bouncing it off the turban. "What if something—What if I...had a dream, an incredibly realistic dream? And in this dream Eamon McCarthy tried to tell me something important?"

"Like what? Where to find his secret fortune? Or more of his wife's clothes?"

Gethsemane made a mental note: Never shop resale in Dunmullach. "Like he and his wife were murdered and he wants to know who did it."

Siobhan put down her phone and grinned, revealing a silver tooth and a mercenary gleam. "Pathétique" fired off in Gethsemane's brain. She should have listened to Eamon.

Siobhan pushed aside the pint glasses. "How may Sister Siobhan assist you?" She reached for Gethsemane's hand. Gethsemane evaded her by raising her whiskey glass to signal for a refill. Siobhan's grin disappeared. Her gleam did not. "Sometimes a dream is just a dream, not a communication from the other side."

Gethsemane leaned forward. "But this was different. Eamon's presence was almost physical. Like I could have reached out and touched him." Or put a hand right through him.

"Here's your drink, miss." A barmaid replaced Gethsemane's empty glass. "And another for you." She set a pint in front of Siobhan.

"Well? Off with ya, then." Siobhan waved her hand. The barmaid frowned and spun on her heel. "Nosy girl," Siobhan said when the barmaid was not quite out of hearing.

"Eamon told me how he died. Poisoned with his own bourbon. Twenty-five years wasn't so long ago. Maybe the poisoner is still alive. Maybe it's not too late for justice."

Siobhan twitched. An odd expression crossed her features for an instant. Then the grin reappeared. The practiced saleswoman returned.

So did Tchaikovsky. "I thought maybe you could reach out to Eamon and talk to him, or whatever you call it. Pick up a clue to take to the police."

"Let's not be hasty." Siobhan scratched her chin with a finger adorned with a grape-sized ruby.

Hasty? How was a quarter of a century 'hasty?' And how well did psychic services pay?

"You can hardly walk up to the garda station, knock on the door, and say, 'Guess what a ghost whispered in my ear?'"

"No," Gethsemane said. "Of course not."

"You need hard evidence to back up your psychic communications."

"Yes, of course."

"Evidence can be hard to find."

Gethsemane wondered how others couldn't hear Tchaikovsky blaring in her head. She forced herself to concentrate on Siobhan. "And probably costly to find."

Siobhan leaned back and shrugged. Her grin widened. "How can one put a price on justice?"

How indeed. "What would this—process—involve?"

"Oh..." Siobhan circled her hand in the air. "I would come to the cottage and conduct several sessions—"

"Several?"

"One can't hurry these things. The spirit realm is unpredictable."

Con artists, psychic or otherwise, were not. "Ballpark estimate. How many?" Did she only imagine a voice whisper, *Just enough to bleed you dry*?

"Murder is a delicate business. I'd say six or seven. Possibly eight."

Yep, just enough. "Not to sound crass about such a 'delicate business,' but what does a spirit communication session retail for?"

"One-fifty."

"Dollars?"

"One hundred fifty Euros. Cash."

Murder was an expensive business. No wonder Siobhan wore rubies. Time to backpedal. "The more I think about it, you're probably right. This was just an ordinary dream. Nothing worth wasting your talents on."

Siobhan's expression darkened and her fist tightened around her glass. Her voice lowered. "You're a perceptive woman, I can tell. You wouldn't have come to me if you thought this—dream—was anything other than remarkable."

Gooseflesh popped out on Gethsemane's arms. The wrong side of Sister Siobhan would be a bad place. "Perhaps a preliminary session, a psychic scouting trip, for say, thirty-five Euros?"

"I don't offer discounts. Or payment plans."

Gethsemane sipped Bushmills and prayed to the whiskey gods for inspiration. "Never mind. I'll just poke around on my own and see what I come up with. Who knows? I may find a masterpiece, even if I don't find evidence."

Siobhan snorted again, setting Gethsemane's teeth on edge. "What masterpiece?"

"Surely you don't think "Jewel of Carraigfaire" was Eamon's

last piece? He died suddenly. No doubt he left unfinished works behind. Probably even finished compositions he never had time to give to his publisher."

"So?" Siobhan went back to her phone. "Just some old music."

"Just some old music?" Gethsemane laughed. "Everything Eamon is hot right now, thanks to that book. Sony Classical just released a digitally remastered twelve-CD set of his early works. Sold out within an hour of hitting the shelves. Think of the bidding frenzy an undiscovered work would kick off."

"Billy would've found—"

"Billy travels. He hasn't checked under every floorboard and every eave. He's no idea what's hiding. Jimmy Hoffa could be stuffed up the chimney and he wouldn't know it." Gethsemane hid her crossed fingers in her lap.

Siobhan pursed her lips. Gethsemane held her breath. The phone disappeared beneath the caftan. "If some new piece turned up, I don't suppose anyone could say for certain where it'd come from."

Gethsemane shrugged. "Could've fallen out of an old library book."

"I don't usually do this, you understand." Siobhan flashed the tooth. "Seeing as you're a newcomer to the realm of psychic phenomena, I could do a—What did you call it?—preliminary session to find out if this dream holds any significance..."

Greed trumped justice once again. "I appreciate your making an exception."

"For eighty-five euros. But—" Siobhan held up another finger, dressed in an emerald. "I must have unrestricted access to the cottage."

"Treat Eamon's house as your own." Gethsemane jumped as a sharp pain hit her between the shoulder blades. She detected the faint aroma of leather.

Siobhan frowned. "What's wrong with you?"

"Nothing," Gethsemane said. "Just a hunger pain." Which she'd better get used to. Eighty-five Euros was most of her money.

Siobhan signaled the barmaid. "I knew them, the McCarthys."

"Close friends?"

Siobhan glared at the barmaid as she downed half her pint. "Another. And be quick about it. Don't stop to flirt on the way." She emptied the glass and plunked it next to the others. "Eamon and Orla McCarthy weren't never friends with the likes o' Siobhan Moloney. Moved in different social circles." She snatched her new drink from the barmaid's tray and sent its contents in the direction of its predecessors. "Though I'd've been a better friend than some." She dabbed her mouth with her scarf and produced a compact to reapply her lipstick.

"When—"

"Tomorrow night." She jabbed a hand at Gethsemane. "I'll have the cash in advance."

Gethsemane patted her skirt and her bodice.

"My wallet..."

Siobhan adjusted her turban with a harrumph and slid from the booth. Much taller than she'd seemed when sitting, she stared down at Gethsemane. "Tomorrow then, without fail." She left without waiting for an answer.

Five minutes passed before Gethsemane realized she'd been stuck with the tab.

School's hectic pace—music lessons, orchestra rehearsal, a playground scuffle, a lower-school boy sick in the hallway from overindulgence in double-chocolate cookies—kept Gethsemane too busy to think about ghosts, psychics, or unsolved murders. The bizarreness of her situation hit her as she walked home after school. She, an avowed skeptic about the paranormal, had moved into a haunted house and hired a psychic to communicate with the ghost in an effort to find his killer and help him cross over to the other side. What would her sisters, both professional scientists, say? Nothing. They'd say nothing because she'd never, ever, under threat of having her fingers cut off, tell them. She silently apologized to her maternal grandparents for dismissing their supernatural tales.

She rounded a corner onto an unfamiliar street. She'd been so preoccupied she walked the wrong way. She turned to retrace her steps but spied something that changed her mind—a bookstore. Unable to resist a bookstore's pull—one of few traits in common with her mother—she detoured inside.

Books filled almost every available space in the small shop. Patrons browsed narrow aisles, periodically flattening themselves against overstuffed shelves to let others scoot past. Gethsemane headed toward the history section when a man, his line of sight obscured by a stack of books, jostled her. She bumped against a table, knocking over some books—the detested American true-crime tome and a collection of poems by Orla McCarthy. Gethsemane caught a whiff of roses and vetiver as she picked Orla's book from the floor.

"Poetry fan?" Gethsemane recognized the speaker as St. Brennan's faculty.

"Oh, no, I just bumped..." Gethsemane replaced the book on the table. "Limited knowledge of poetry. Of Orla McCarthy too. I know plenty about her husband. Eamon McCarthy inspired me. I think I was always a little jealous of Orla for taking my fantasy dream man off the market. Silly, since I never met either of them."

"I felt the same way about that prince fella who married Grace Kelly. You'd have liked Orla if you'd met her. Everyone did." He lifted the true-crime book. "Don't believe any of this claptrap. A load of aspersions and insinuations. Should be shelved under fiction."

At last, a kindred spirit who shared her low opinion of the work. "Tell me about Orla. It's strange living in her house. The McCarthys' presence is palpable. You feel you could turn around and find them standing behind you." One of them, anyway.

"Orla personified beauty. Not only because she was beautiful to look at, though she was that. Long blond hair, intense brown eyes, elegant. About your size. Inner beauty poured forth from Orla like a wellspring. Everything she touched took on some of her glow. If you spent five minutes in her presence you came away determined to be a better person."

"What about her poetry?" Gethsemane opened a book titled *Preface to a Soul's Destruction* and scanned a page. "Is it any good? I can't judge."

"Some call it haunting, some brilliant, some fundamental to the understanding of Irish poetry. She won countless awards and accolades. Hobnobbed with the leading lights of the poetry world—Diane di Prima, Gregory Corso, Thomas Kinsella. Amiri Baraka and Seamus Heaney came to her wedding."

"Given you think this," Gethsemane tapped the cover of the true-crime book, "is trash—I agree with you, by the way—what do you think actually happened to Eamon and Orla McCarthy? The book claims murder in a jealous fit followed by suicide due to overwhelming remorse."

"Well," the man thought for a moment, "No one denies Eamon McCarthy was a hothead, even growing up. Threw legendary temper tantrums. Got expelled from a school or two. Plenty of news reports about trashed hotel rooms and overturned restaurant tables. But he never, not once, directed anger at Orla. Quite the opposite. He could be in the midst of a raging hooley, she'd lay a hand on his arm, and he'd calm down quick like she'd flipped a switch. Meek as a sleeping babe. Eamon adored the very air she breathed. Mention her name in passing and his face lit up like the noonday sun." He paused. "No, I don't think Eamon McCarthy murdered his wife. Committed suicide in his despair, perhaps. Killed Orla, no."

"Who do you think killed her?"

"I don't know. Can't imagine anyone wishing Orla a bad day, let alone dead. Maybe someone passing through the village on the way to somewhere else. Tourists occasionally stop to view the cliffs, hike up to the lighthouse."

Or to report their stolen luggage at the first police station they come to. "A random act of violence by a stranger?"

"Makes more sense than someone who knew her killing her."

"Thank you for the insight." Gethsemane picked up a second volume of Orla's poems to go along with *Soul's Destruction*. "I'll read these and see if they'll convert me into a poetry lover." Except her credit cards and most of her money were in the stolen bags. She set the books back on the table. "I can probably find copies at the cottage."

"I hope you find some long-forgotten clue proving Eamon's innocence tucked behind a bookshelf. Some of us would like to see his reputation restored."

Gethsemane's anxiety grew as Siobhan's visit drew near. How much did Eamon distrust psychics? Enough to smash half the cottage if one crossed the threshold? Trifling with the infamous McCarthy temper courted peril. Her father's rage fits involved apoplexy, not property destruction.

By quarter to seven, her head throbbed. She paced. "Chino Smith. Right field. Nineteen-twenty-six to nineteen-thirty. Four-sixty-five. Jud Wilson. First base. Nineteen-twenty-two to nineteen-thirty-six. Four-forty-six. Cristobal Torriente. Center field. Nineteen-thirteen to nineteen-twenty-eight. Four-thirty-four."

"What are you on about?"

She stopped pacing. Eamon reclined on the entryway bench. She hadn't noticed the leather-soap smell until now. "Baseball stats. Negro League on-base percentages."

"Apropos of?"

"I recite baseball stats when I'm nervous. Heavy Johnson, right field, nineteen-twenty to nineteen-twenty-eight. Four-thirty-two. Oscar Charleston. Center field. Nineteen-fifteen to nineteen-thirty-six. Four-twenty-four."

"What have you got to be nervous about?"

"You know. Being haunted by the ghost of a murdered composer, having six weeks to get an orchestra ready for a major competition, having my future job prospects riding on the outcome of said competition. The usual stuff."

"You're not telling me something."

"Paranoid's not a good look for you, Irish." She paced again. "Josh Gibson. Catcher. Nineteen-thirty to nineteen-thirty-six. Four-two-two. Merito Acosta. Left field. Nineteen-thirteen to nineteen-twenty-three. Four-twenty-one."

"What is it with Americans and baseball?"

"As opposed to Europeans and cricket? Or soccer?"

"Football, you Philistine."

Someone knocked. Seven o'clock sharp.

"Expecting company?" Eamon asked. "Haven't been here long enough to have a gentleman caller."

Gethsemane opened the door to an outstretched hand and a mountain of gold fabric capped by a bejeweled Cleopatra wig. Her eighty-five Euros disappeared into the fabric's folds before she could bid Siobhan hello.

Siobhan pushed past her and stopped mid-hall. She threw her arms up and arced her head left and right. "Listen."

Gethsemane listened. "I don't hear anything."

"Ssssssh." Siobhan licked a finger and held it up. The lights glinted off the ruby.

"We're indoors," Gethsemane whispered. "There's no wind."

Siobhan drifted toward the study, swinging her head and sniffing the air. Head right-pause-sniff. Head left-pause-sniff. A fat golden hound on the trail of something.

"I don't smell anything," Gethsemane said. Had she left something on the stove?

Siobhan stopped short in front of the study. Gethsemane plowed into her back, surprised to find solid mass under the gold tent. Siobhan spread her arms, craned her neck, and closed her eyes. She started up a hum which rose in pitch to a level between a blender and a power saw. Gethsemane plugged her ears. Siobhan stopped humming. Arms kept raised, she looked left-right-left-right again.

"What?" Gethsemane's eyelid twitched. "I don't hear, see, or smell anything. What is it?"

"A vibration," Siobhan said, still scanning the room.

"A vibration?" Gethsemane's eye throbbed. She pressed her thumb against her eyelid.

"In the ether." Siobhan lowered her arms.

"What does that mean?"

Siobhan ran to Eamon's desk and rifled papers. "It means a portal to the spirit world has been opened." Hands outstretched, she squeezed her eyes shut and screwed up her face.

"Are you all right? Are you in pain?" Was she serious? "Do you need the bathroom?"

"Ssssssh!" Siobhan, eyes still closed, extended her arms and spun, the Tasmanian Devil in a dress. The hem of her caftan flared, exposing pasty, muscular trunks above the Aladdin slippers.

Gethsemane dove to save a vase and a lamp. "Now what?"

Siobhan stopped spinning. She lowered her arms and opened her eyes. "I've lost it."

No kidding. "Lost the vibrations?"

"The fluctuations."

"Fluctuations. In the ether?"

"In the protoplasmic miasma." Siobhan clucked as though Gethsemane was a particularly slow child.

"The protoplasmic miasma." Walking into a movie theater during the third reel made more sense. Gethsemane's eye throb bloomed into a full-on headache. "Meep."

"Are you not the full shilling?" a man's voice asked, close to Gethsemane's ear.

Leather-cedar-soap hit Gethsemane's nostrils. Siobhan, oblivious, hummed again. Gethsemane whispered, "Eamon? Is that you?"

"It bloody well isn't a fluctuation in the ether or a vibration in the protoplasmic steak and kidney pie or whatever the hell she's on about." Eamon materialized, solid as a stone wall. Siobhan kept humming. "Why's she doing that?"

"Trying to raise the dead, I guess. How'd I know?"

"If anything could raise the dead, that noise would."

"Silence." Siobhan pointed a finger at Gethsemane. "How can I be expected to contact the spirit realm with you standing there jabbering to yourself?"

"To myself? But—" She jerked a thumb at Eamon.

"Silence!" Siobhan turned her back.

"She can't see you, can she?" Gethsemane asked Eamon.

"Watch." Eamon walked over to Siobhan and held his face an inch from hers. "Siobhan Moloney, what the bloody hell are ya playin' at?"

Siobhan flung her arms toward the ceiling, sending her hand through Eamon's crotch.

Eamon jumped back. "Watch it, ya eejit! I don't know ya that well."

Gethsemane clamped her hands over her mouth, smothering her laughter. Siobhan twirled, slowly at first, increasing her speed until her caftan puffed out like a circus tent.

"I'm dizzy watching her," Eamon said.

Siobhan froze. Gethsemane held her breath. Siobhan flung an arm out and pointed to a corner nowhere near Eamon. "There."

"Where?" Gethsemane asked.

"Where?" Eamon repeated. Behind her back, Gethsemane gave him the finger.

"In the corner," Siobhan said. "Can't you see it?"

"See what?"

"A mist, an ectoplasmic emission."

Eamon turned blue. "Make her stop."

"Enough." Gethsemane grabbed Siobhan. "I just thought of something. What if the ectoplasmic emission isn't coming from Eamon?" She ignored Eamon's guffaw. "What if it's coming from—" Gethsemane peered over her shoulder and leaned close to Siobhan, dropping her voice to the merest whisper. "What if it's coming from a *dark* entity?"

"What do you know about—"

Gethsemane shushed her.

Siobhan dropped her voice to match Gethsemane's. "What do you know about dark entities?"

Finally, all those episodes of *Ghost Hunting Adventures* paid off. "I know when a portal opens sometimes spirits of the departed aren't the only ones to come through. Sometimes inhuman spirits slip past the veil." She glanced over her shoulder again. "Before you go any farther, I should call Father Keating and arrange a house blessing as a precaution." She crossed herself.

Siobhan flashed her silver grin. "No need to disturb Father. The poor dear's so busy, what with catechism class and the garden committee and the roofing committee...I have plenty of experience dealing with inhuman spirits. I can come back tomorrow with some smudge sticks and St. Michael medals—"

Eamon growled. Blue sparks flew from his head.

"No, no. This is a matter for the church." Gethsemane tugged gold polyester satin until she finagled Siobhan into the hall. If her legs were trunks, her arms were sturdy branches. "Besides, tomorrow's not good for me. Orchestra rehearsal." She elbowed Siobhan toward the door.

Neither Siobhan nor her one-hundred-twenty-five-pound advantage noticed.

"Monday next, then. That will give me time to order some candles."

"Monday next's no good either." Gethsemane pushed with both hands. "Tutorials." She might as well have pushed a Buick.

"Put your back in it," Eamon said.

Gethsemane made a face. *Come help me*, she mouthed. Eamon sighed. The neck of Siobhan's caftan bunched up, grabbed by an invisible hand, and her slippers rose a tenth of an inch from the floor. She twisted her head toward Gethsemane. "You're stronger than you look."

"Comes from bowing the violin. Builds upper body strength."

Siobhan moved forward, pushed-carried to the door, Gethsemane right behind her. The door swung open and Siobhan went through it, stumbling on the steps on the way down. The door slammed shut, just missing Gethsemane's nose, and locked.

"What the hell was that?" A cobalt aura surrounded Eamon. "Your idea of a joke?"

Gethsemane rested her forehead against the nearest wall. "That was my idea of a ghost whisperer."

"Ghost whisperer?" The cobalt dimmed to robin's egg. "Are you serious?"

"Kind of. Pretty much. Yeah."

"What happened to not hiring a psychic, who neither of us believe in anyway?"

"A ghost, which I used to not believe in, begged me to help solve a double murder, which I've never done before. Desperate times make for bizarre behavior."

"Fine, I deserved that. But Siobhan Moloney, for the love of God? The whole village knows she's as phony as the Fiji mermaid."

"Well, the whole village forgot to tell the new girl."

"Come on, you're no eejit. You've got eyes in your head. You didn't cop on to that ridiculous act of hers?"

Tchaikovsky *had* warned her. "Just because she's a con artist doesn't mean she doesn't have any psychic abilities."

"Please know I'm laughing *at* you, not with you. How much did it set you back?"

Gethsemane stared at the floor. Oh, if only it would open up right now.

Eamon's face materialized under Gethsemane's nose. "How much?"

"Eighty-five Euros. Down from one-fifty." Gethsemane raised her head. "Don't look at me like that."

Eamon stared for half a minute, then a rich, full-throated laugh welled up from his feet and spilled from his mouth in waves. Surrounded by an aura the color of spring grass, he doubled over, arms wrapped around his midsection.

"Stop!" Gethsemane balled her fists. "I hope you make yourself vomit."

Eamon choked out, between peals, "Ghosts don't vomit."

Gethsemane bit her lip. A snicker escaped, followed by a giggle. Then she laughed as hard as Eamon. She fell back onto the entryway bench and banged her head against the wall which made her laugh harder. Soon coughs and gasps mingled with the laughter.

"Are you all right?" Eamon asked, hands on knees. His chest heaved.

Gethsemane nodded as she struggled to regain control. She wiped tears. "I'm sorry."

Eamon sat next to her. "Me too."

"Truce?" they asked simultaneously.

Gethsemane held out a hand.

"I'd shake it, but..."

"Sorry, forgot."

Neither spoke for a while. Eamon broke the silence. "It's good having someone to communicate with after all these years."

"Even a willful, opinionated female?"

"Willful, opinionated females are the only sort worth talking to."

"Am I really the only person in Dunmullach you can talk with?"

Eamon nodded.

"Only person anywhere. I tried my publisher in Dublin, the managers of theaters where I performed my concerts, friends. One or two could see me, a few others could tell I was hanging about but none could hear me, at least not well enough to carry on a conversation."

"You didn't try your floating object trick?"

"That only scared them. Literally shite-less, a couple of 'em."

"It scared me."

"You didn't show it. You've a good arm, by the way."

"I meant it about being starting pitcher for Girls' State. My whole family plays baseball or softball. It's one thing we have in common. The thinking family's game."

"How'd you manage to play ball and music? Weren't you afraid you'd break a finger?"

"I gave up music."

"You're coddin'."

"For a year. My rebellious phase. Swore I hated music and wanted nothing to do with it. Threw myself into ball with the same determination I'd devoted to the violin. Ate, drank, and slept softball."

"How'd you end up back this side of the fence?"

"Team went to championships and won. I showed everyone I could do whatever I set my mind to. Had the chance to be part of something bigger than me and make some non-musical friends. Realized I didn't just love music, I existed for it." Gethsemane shrugged. "So I came back."

"Good thing. The world needs music. Baseball it can manage without."

"That remark borders on sacrilege. What's your sport?"

"I'm a rugby fan. Orla loved cricket."

"If I had to sit through a cricket match, I'd be a rugby fan too."

"I said almost the same thing to Orla once." Eamon smiled. "She hit me in the shin with a cricket bat."

"You miss her."

Eamon's shoulders slumped. "Horribly, terribly, every day."

"My father died years ago. He was a—difficult—man, odd, hard to get close to. But I loved him and still miss him. So does Mother. She still brings him flowers every week and sits and talks to him for an hour."

Eamon patted Gethsemane's hand. Small shocks traveled up her arm as his hand passed through hers.

"Do you really think clearing your name will let you cross over and find Orla?" she asked.

"I have to believe that. Spending eternity without Orla would be worse than any hell God could sentence me to."

Hell. Being condemned to haunt the home you shared with the love of your life because everyone believed you murdered her must be pretty close to hell. Gethsemane studied Eamon—semi-transparent, the outlines of the macs hanging from their hooks visible through him, yellow aura, sad—before speaking. "Tell me again about this house concert. Were the Morrises the only ones who attended?"

Eamon looked surprised. "How'd you know their name? I never told you."

"I found some information at school and made an educated guess. Were they the only ones there?"

The yellow aura shimmered red along its edges. "Does this mean you're helping me? For real?"

"Not if you don't answer my questions."

Eamon solidified, his aura full-on red. "Gethsemane Anna Brown, I'd kiss you right on the mouth if I could. You've made a dead man happy."

She blushed. "Yeah, well make a newbie amateur detective happy. Tell me the Morisses had guests that night."

"Afraid not. Family only."

"No servants, caterers, anyone like that?"

"No. Their cook and housekeeper had already received notice since the Morrises weren't planning on returning to Dublin. Why? What did you find?"

"Not good news. The Morisses were murdered in Sudan during the war."

"Damn." The red glow turned yellow again. "I'm sorry to hear that. The Morrises were fine people."

"I'm sorry too. That leaves us with only the hope Lynch will recant his statement about seeing your car or Hurley will admit to running a crap investigation or the GP—"

"Long dead."

"Lynch or Hurley then. I could talk to them—"

"You can stay away from them. They're both nasty pieces of work, especially Jimmy. Convince Inspector O'Reilly to speak to them. I want your help, but I don't want you getting hurt. Besides," he added under his breath, "I've a better chance of being reincarnated as a tutu-wearing pachyderm in an Uzbek three-ring circus than of either of those two confessing."

Gethsemane couldn't help grinning. "You care if I get hurt?"

"Yeah," Eamon said. "You're starting to grow on me."

She slid over on the bench until she felt a buzz as her shoulder passed through Eamon's. "Likewise."

Four

Gethsemane opened the door the next morning to a near collision with Father Keating. He stood on the porch, hand raised to knock.

"Morning, Father." Gethsemane pulled her mac close against the crisp morning air.

Father Keating removed his cap. "Top o' the morning to ya, Dr. Brown."

"What are you doing here so early? Nothing's wrong, is there?"

"No, no, nothing wrong. I forget the only thing worse than seeing a priest unannounced on your doorstep is seeing a priest with the gardaí. I just stopped by to offer you a ride to school."

"You shouldn't have troubled yourself, Father. I don't mind the walk."

"'Twas no trouble. I'm headed that way myself. Chapel services today. Trying to make good Catholics out of the lot."

"In that case, I accept. Thank you."

"The ride comes with one condition."

"Which is?"

"You're not allowed to call me 'Father.' I'm Tim."

"I'm Gethsemane."

"A nice Biblical name."

"Grandmother's idea. Father wanted to name us all after Nobel laureates. Mother just wanted the names to be pronounceable with no unnecessary apostrophes."

Father Keating laughed and held the car door. "How're you fixed for provisions?" he asked as he slid into the driver's seat.

"Plenty of bourbon. A bit light on food."

"I'll be happy to run you by the grocer."

"Really, that's too much trouble for you. And don't tell me you were on your way there anyway to convert heathens in the frozen food aisle."

"I aim to do the Lord's work wherever I can." He pulled out of the drive.

They pulled up in front of St. Brennan's a short while later. Father Keating helped Gethsemane out of the car.

"Thanks again for the ride, Fath—Tim," she said.

"I meant it about the groceries."

"And I meant it about not troubling yourself."

"How about a compromise? Borrow my bicycle. Keep it for the length of your stay, and I won't worry about you walking at all hours. She's a lovely machine, a Pashley Parabike, hunter green with a wicker handlebar basket. A gift from my mother when I got my first parish."

"Won't you need it?" Gethsemane asked.

"Alas, no." Father Keating patted his knees. "Messrs. Arthur Itis and Rumy Tism have cured me of the habit. Poor old Bess sits hidden away in the garden shed dreaming of being ridden through hill and dale. Do her good to get out. I'd be happy to see you ride her."

"All right." A cool breeze rushed past Gethsemane's cheek. She pulled her coat collar tighter. "Autumn's good bike riding weather. I'll come by church later and pick her up."

Father Keating tipped his cap. "Now off to turn some sinners away from the road to perdition. Wish me luck." He headed off toward the chapel.

Gethsemane called after him. "Say a prayer for me while you're at it." She looked up at the four-story brick classroom building and found the music room's windows. A breeze brushed her cheek again. "Lord knows I'm going to need it."

A twig snapped in the distance. Gethsemane turned to see a dark-haired boy and a blonde girl beneath a tree, close enough for her to identify the bespectacled boy as one of the orchestra students—something O'Brien—but too far away to hear their words. The boy held a leaf, brilliant red, as though it was the actual jewel with whom it shared its color. The girl accepted it with the same reverence and slipped it into her coat pocket. They smiled then dropped their gazes. Did Eamon and Orla behave that way once upon a time, when they first realized their childhood friendship had blossomed into something more?

The boy and girl looked up at Gethsemane simultaneously, as though she'd spoken her thoughts aloud. The girl's startling green eyes—where had Gethsemane seen them before?—locked onto Gethsemane's for a second then the girl darted off across the quad. Before Gethsemane could call to him, the boy ran off in the opposite direction, toward the dorms. Young love. When had she last felt that way? She shook her head. No matter. No time for romance. Time to concentrate on practical matters, like breakfast and rag-tag orchestras and reputation repair.

Gethsemane stood in front of the century-old red brick Dunmullach post office during her lunch hour, clutching the letter she'd written asking for a loan. A backup plan never hurt.

She paused inside the post office entrance and scanned the lobby for a mail slot. Something hit her in the back, nearly knocking her over. A fat, balding, red-faced man swore as he struggled to squat to pick up several envelopes scattered on the floor.

"Watch where yer goin'," the man said.

Who'd bumped into whom? She shoved her letter in her coat pocket. "Let me help." She read the name on the return address, "Declan Hurley."

"Yeah. What of it?"

He snatched the envelopes from Gethsemane's hand.

"You're the police officer who investigated Eamon and Orla McCarthys' deaths."

"So?"

Gethsemane took in Hurley's close-set eyes and over-round cheeks. A childhood image popped into her head: the cartoon pig advertising the local BBQ joint on billboards in her hometown. "May I talk to you about your investigation?"

"No you may not talk to me, about anything." Hurley shouldered her. "Out of my way."

Gethsemane fell back, banging her head against a row of mailboxes. Other postal patrons turned to stare. Gethsemane winced and called after Hurley, "Why didn't you check Eamon McCarthy's alibi for the time of his wife's murder?"

Hurley spun. "What are you gettin' at?"

He radiated meanness the way Eamon radiated colors. "I'm not getting at anything, Mr. Hurley," Gethsemane said, "Pathétique" playing in her ear. "I just asked a question. Eamon McCarthy had an alibi for the time of his wife's murder. Why didn't you check it?"

"I heard ya. It's a damned stupid question and it's none of yer damned business." Hurley could have intimidated the Pope into confessing to the McCarthy murders, plus Kennedy and the Lindbergh baby.

Gethsemane remembered her eldest sister's advice. Anytime you're facing down a big dog act like you're bigger.

"I would think Eamon's alibi was a matter of public record. Maybe murder investigations are conducted differently back in the States."

"Yeah, mebbe they are. 'Round here people leave the question-asking to the guards."

"Because the guards 'round here ask the right questions of the right people?"

Hurley moved fast, stopping with his face inches from Gethsemane's. "I did my job." He shook a beefy finger under her nose. A millimeter closer and she could've bitten him. "Who are you to say I didn't?"

Gethsemane wiped onion-scented spittle from her cheek. "I'm sure you did your job to the best of your ability, Mr. Hurley. But you haven't answered my question. Why didn't you verify Eamon's alibi?"

"Alibi," Hurley spat. "I had a witness put McCarthy in the area in plenty of time to throw his wife off a cliff."

"A reliable witness, I'm sure."

"Reliable enough for me. Eamon McCarthy killed his wife and then offed himself." The beefy finger folded into a beefier fist which hovered near Gethsemane's chin. "Case closed."

Bluff, bluff, bluff. Most dogs were all bark. "I hear the police department's opened a new cold case unit. Maybe you should let the cold case detectives look at your notes from the McCarthy investigation. A second set of eyes never hurts." Gethsemane leaned closer. She forced herself not to gag on the stench of sweat and stale cigarette smoke. "Even the best of us miss things."

"I didn't miss anything," Hurley said. Paper crinkled as his other fist closed around the envelopes Gethsemane had helped him pick up. "Case. Closed."

Gethsemane wiped spittle from her other cheek. Some dogs bit. She heeded Tchaikovsky and shrugged again. "Case closed."

Hurley stomped to the counter to conduct his business. Gethsemane waved to the other postal patrons, still staring, then left the building. She forgot to mail her letter.

Shouts hit Gethsemane's ears before she reached the music room. Fight in progress. She opened the door on a semi-circle of boys cheering something in their midst. She pushed through the perimeter. Aengus—or Feargus—Toibin sat on a boy half his size, raining punches. The smaller boy tucked his hands into his armpits, protecting them from the blows. Gethsemane grabbed the Toibin twin by the wrist as he drew back his arm to deliver another punch.

"Ow! Let go!" The twin started to swing. Gethsemane tightened her grip. "That hurts!" the twin said.

"No more than you hurt him." Gethsemane pulled the stocky redhead to his feet. "Which one is he?" she asked one of the spectators.

Aengus, his identity confirmed, tried to pull his wrist free. Gethsemane had learned a few things about breaking up fights from her brothers. She sat Aengus in a chair and kept a hand on his shoulder.

"Help him up." She nodded at the boy on the floor.

A couple of the others helped Aengus's victim—the boy from that morning, with the leaf and the girl—stand. The disheveled, bruised brunet wiped his bloody nose on his jacket sleeve. Someone handed him a tissue.

"Ruairi started it," Aengus said. He tried to shake Gethsemane's hand off his shoulder. He couldn't.

"Ruairi O'Brien started a fight with *you*?" She looked from Aengus to the younger boy. Someone handed Ruairi his glasses.

"He talked shite to Feargus." Aengus jerked his head toward his brother.

"Watch your language," Gethsemane said.

A voice came from the rear of the crowd. "Feargus does all the talking but leaves the fighting to Aengus."

The boys all giggled. Feargus and Aengus glared at them. The giggling stopped.

Gethsemane looked at Ruairi again. He was the smallest boy in the orchestra, smaller even than some of the boys in the lower grades. He hadn't spoken in class other than to tell her his name and which instrument he played. Gethsemane could hardly imagine him saying hello to a boy as big as Feargus Toibin, let alone smarting off to him. She turned back to Aengus. "I don't care what he said or to whom he said it. You're older, bigger, and stronger than he is. You might have seriously injured him."

Aengus stared at the floor and mumbled an apology.

The door banged opened. Colm Nolan strolled in.

"You're late," Gethsemane said.

"Sorry, Dr. Brown." He didn't look it. "Did I miss a hooley or something?"

"Or something," one of the boys said. "You missed a fight."

Colm strolled over to the group. "Hate to miss a good reefin'. What's the carry-on about?"

"Aengus tried to mangle Ruairi."

"'Cause Ruairi smarted off to Feargus."

"'Cause Feargus blathered about your sister."

Colm was on Feargus before Gethsemane could move. He grabbed a handful of Feargus's shirt and twisted the collar tight. "What'd you say about Saoirse?" He twisted the shirt tighter.

Feargus clawed at his neck.

Aengus jumped up.

"You're chokin' him!"

Gethsemane threw out an arm and short-stopped Aengus mid-leap. He fell back into the chair. She pushed past several gaping boys and grabbed Colm's ear. She twisted it as hard as he twisted Feargus's collar. Colm let go of the shirt.

"Ow! You'll rip my ear off!"

Gethsemane let him go. Colm clapped a hand to his ear, as red as the twins' hair.

"Sit down," Gethsemane said.

Colm stood still.

Gethsemane repeated the command. "Sit. Down."

Every boy in the room complied.

"You should be ashamed of yourselves," Gethsemane said. "This is a classroom, not a cage match."

"He shouldn't have talked about my sister." Colm kept his hand over his ear.

"No, he shouldn't have. And you shouldn't have tried to strangle him. You're Head Boy. Act like you warrant the responsibility." She looked at Aengus. He stared at his shoes. "And you shouldn't have beaten up a smaller boy for defending her." Gethsemane looked around the class. "*All* of you should be ashamed. I can see why the school hasn't won the All-County in seventy-five years."

"We're a right bunch of savages," a boy said.

"I don't know what you've gotten away with before I got here but it stops now. We've got less than two months to get ready, and I'm not going to stand in front of Cork County and be made a fool of by a bunch of unruly brats."

"What do you care?" Colm asked. "It's not like you'll be staying on."

"I'll be staying on long enough to send you to detention—or whatever the Irish call it—for the rest of the week, Colm Nolan. You too, Toibins."

"You can't do that," Feargus said.

"Want to bet?"

None of the boys moved.

"Don't make me drag the three of you to the headmaster's office," Gethsemane said.

"You'd better go," the boy closest to Aengus said. "I think she can take you."

The twins stood first, followed by Colm. They waited for him to lead the procession out.

When they'd gone, Gethsemane said to the boy next to Ruairi, "Escort him to the nurse's office, please. The rest of you get your instruments. We've got a lot of work to do."

"Don't see any bloodstains." Francis Grennan, looking less taciturn but just as wrinkled, stood in the doorway polishing his wire-rimmed glasses with his shirt tail.

Startled, Gethsemane dropped a stack of sheet music, sending papers fanning across the floor. "What do you want?" she asked him as she scooped them up.

"Heard the boys were acting the maggots," the math teacher said, "had a bit of a kerfuffle."

"Nothing I couldn't handle."

"You are woman, hear you roar." He adjusted the glasses on his face and nodded at the papers. "What's all that?"

"I'm trying to find something for the competition, something 'wow' but not so complicated the boys won't manage it."

"'Chopsticks'?"

"*Did* you actually want something?"

"Just stopped by to see how you were getting on."

"Fine. Sorry to disappoint you. Now if you don't mind..."

"I don't mind." Francis sat on the edge of Gethsemane's desk. She caught a whiff of his fresh, citrus-y cologne. He thumbed through a pile of music. "Beethoven, Mahler, Schubert, Schoenberg."

"Who's your favorite?"

"Davis."

"Sharon or Anthony?"

"Miles."

"Jazz fan?" Gethsemane grinned. "I'd have guessed death metal."

Francis crossed his legs. "Bet you wish you really could find an undiscovered work by McCarthy. With that and a miracle, St. Brennan's might take second."

"Why are you so down on the orchestra? Or is it just me you don't like?"

The blush on Francis' cheeks made his eyes seem greener. "I don't dislike you. I told you, I dislike folks swooping in all pomp and circumstance, filling the boys full of false hope, watching 'em crash and burn, then slinking off to something better first chance, leaving a mess behind for someone else."

"How do I convince you I'm not that person?"

"Tell Peter Nolan you've no interest in a job with the Philharmonia."

"How else?"

The math teacher stood. Gethsemane put a hand on his arm. He stiffened and she withdrew it.

"Come on, Grennan. Who'd I fool if I pretended I wouldn't

knock down old ladies in the street for a dream job leading the Boston Philharmonia? But my career plans don't include a scorched earth policy. I want to leave on a high, not sneak away in shame like the Colts out of Baltimore. I'm going to turn this orchestra into a winner and bring the trophy home to St. Brennan's before I go."

"Now you sound like Riordan about that damned trophy. Are you trying to soothe your wounded ego, too?"

Why was he so damned perceptive? "What do you mean 'too'?"

"I'm talking about Riordan's disastrous stint with the orchestra. He played clarinet when he was a student here. Got into honors orchestra based more on family connections than talent. He performed in the All-County three years running and St. Brennan's placed last in each. The year after he left school, St. Brennan's placed in the top six. Folks called Riordan a jinx. He never recovered from the humiliation. He's been chasing that trophy ever since he took over as headmaster, trying to redeem himself."

Everyone had an agenda. "Why are you so concerned about the fallout from the All-County? You teach math, not music. You like jazz, not classical. Are you related to one of the boys? Or are you that Shakespearean character who hangs around the edge of the action making pithy comments passing judgement on the foibles of others?"

"Just say I know how it feels to have someone pin all their hopes on you then be left to deal with the burden of their disappointment when you don't measure up."

Gethsemane's throat tightened. He'd pinpointed the heart of her fear of going home in defeat. She warmed to him a bit, despite his moodiness. "You don't know me so you have no reason to cut me slack but I'm asking you to give me a chance. If I don't win, I promise I won't leave the boys to deal with the loss by themselves. But I *am* going to win." This time, the certainty wasn't forced.

"From your lips to," Francis raised his eyes toward the ceiling, "His ears. May I borrow some of your bravado should the need arise?" He walked to the door then paused on the threshold. "Speaking of caring about things that shouldn't concern you, why are you investigating the McCarthy case? Word's out you're doing some serious digging."

"I believe a man I admired suffered a horrific injustice. Didn't you ever go to bat for someone you thought was wronged?"

"Once." Francis grinned. "And here I thought you were just being nosy."

"You say nosy like it's a bad thing. And I prefer curious."

"Call it as you will, it's dangerous for an outsider. Secrets are all right in the family but we mustn't let them outdoors."

"What secrets are you keeping, Grennan?"

"Me? I'm an open book. A book with a worn cover and dog-eared pages," he adjusted his over-sized jacket, "but open nonetheless. But I have poked my nose into others' codices on occasion."

"You? A snoop? Details, please."

"Ah," he raised a finger and winked, "that would be telling." He disappeared into the hall.

Gethsemane sputtered. "That would—telling—but you—" She sank into her chair. A second later she jumped up with a scream. "Do you mind?"

"Do *I* mind?" Eamon asked. "Who sat on whom?"

"Keep your voice down." Gethsemane shushed him and glanced toward the door.

"You're the only one who can hear me, darlin'."

"You're not the only one who can hear *me*."

"Then you'd better keep your voice down." Eamon stretched out in her chair.

"Is this National Aggravating Males Day? I wish I'd known, I'd have bought you a card. Please, make yourself comfortable."

"You're in a foul mood."

"Francis Grennan stopped by to cast aspersions on my motive for taking this job. And to mess with my head."

"Which motive? Wanting to win to impress Nolan so he'll take you back to the States or wanting to impress Dunleavy so he'll buy the school a new auditorium? Which they'll name after him."

Gethsemane twisted and turned, trying to see over her shoulder.

"What are you doing?"

"Looking for the sign on my back that says, 'Mercenary.'"

"Stop." Eamon waved a hand. "No one blames you for trying to get out of Dunmullach. Why should you want to stay? You didn't plan to come here. This was just the first train stop after you noticed your luggage was gone."

"I *will* win this competition." Gethsemane swept her arm across her desk, knocking over the pile of sheet music. The pages froze mid-air, then floated upwards and reassembled themselves into a neat stack.

"Leave the temper tantrums to me," Eamon said.

"Sorry." Gethsemane leaned against her desk. "I'm not used to things not going my way."

"Are you referring to the theft or the situation in Cork?"

Gethsemane flushed. "How do you—"

Eamon held up his hands. "Ghosts get in on gossip, remember. We're excellent eavesdroppers. I overheard some old music friends in Dublin. You're quite the hot topic. Brilliant young conductor done out of a job by the boss's bit of fluff. Never met a musician who didn't love a scandal."

Gethsemane pressed the heels of her hands against her temples. She was a water cooler topic. Or, worse, a happy hour topic. "I was referring to the All-County, but thank you for reminding me my life sucks."

"Calm down. You haven't lost the All-County yet."

Yet. Unless...Twice, Francis mentioned an undiscovered Eamon McCarthy composition. And here was Eamon McCarthy, one of the world's most gifted composers, sitting in her chair, so close she could lean over and touch him—

"Hey, watch where you're putting your hand."

Gethsemane jerked her fingers from Eamon's nose.

"What?" he asked.

"What 'what'?"

"I can see the wheels turning, darlin'. You've got a plan. Out with it."

"Write something for St. Brennan's to perform in the competition."

Eamon stared at her for a full minute then laughed the same deep laugh Siobhan's spectacle had triggered.

"I'm serious."

More laughter.

Spell exhausted, Eamon spoke. "No."

"Why not?"

"It won't work, that's why not. How would you explain the appearance of this previously unknown masterpiece?"

"I'll say I found it in the lighthouse."

"The competition's little more than a month away. When would the orchestra have time to learn a piece that's not even composed yet?"

"Write fast. You wrote 'Requiem for a Fallen Angel' in four weeks. You finished 'Adagio for Two Violins' in less time. 'Twelve Etudes' and 'Arabesque Number Seven' only took three days apiece."

"But you need a symphony or a concerto."

"'Symphony Number Thirteen in B-flat Minor.' Sixteen days."

Eamon opened his mouth. Then closed it. "You're damned hard to argue with."

"Thanks, Irish, I'll take that as a compliment. Does that mean you'll do it?"

"No."

"Why not?"

"Because I don't think you have a chance of winning, and I don't want my name associated with defeat."

"Of all the arrogant—" She looked for something to throw. "So you think I can solve a twenty-five-year-old double murder but can't win a high school orchestra competition?"

"One's got nothing to do with the other. Besides, I'm not asking you to solve the murders—"

"You're only asking me to find probably nonexistent evidence to take to the police so the police can solve the murders."

"You're not going to cry, are you?"

Gethsemane had never resorted to crying to get her way. Flattery, however...She stood over Eamon, her arms braced on either side of him. "If I have to enter this competition with a work by any other composer—Beethoven, Paganini, Bernstein, Copeland—St. Brennan's has zero hope. But with an Eamon McCarthy composition, especially a world-premiere Eamon McCarthy composition, I know we can win. The sheer brilliance of your music, the genius of it, would be enough to snag the trophy, even if trained monkeys performed it. Which they won't. The boys will pour their hearts and souls into doing justice to your composition. Their blood, too, if need be."

"You're full o' shite, darlin'. You know that?"

"Will you do it?"

"Yes."

"Eamon Padraig McCarthy, I'd kiss you if I could."

Eamon glowed pink.

"Are you blushing?"

"'Course not. Ghosts don't blush." Eamon cleared his throat. "Symphony or concerto? Or funeral dirge?"

"Concerto."

"Violin or piano?"

"Violin."

"You'll need a soloist."

"One of the boys."

"I have doubts."

Gethsemane sat on her desk.

"Why? You have no doubts about my ability to clear your name, yet I've never investigated a murder. I've won lots of orchestra competitions."

"I've got a feeling about you and the murders. Intuition. A hunch." He dimmed. "Why *did* you agree to help me? Not so I'd owe you a favor."

"I'm not sure, Irish. I'm just—*supposed* to." She tried a brogue. "Intuition. A hunch."

"You really need to work on the accent."

"Why'd you agree to help *me*? Not just because I stroked your ego."

Eamon put on an American accent. "Dunno. I'm just—supposed to." He vanished.

A loudspeaker crackled to life. Gethsemane stared up at the brown box in the corner. Tinny Debussy floated down—the same piece Eamon had played to open his concert at the Peabody.

Gethsemane headed to the Athaneum after school, eager to see what space she had to work with. Cheered by Eamon's promise to compose a violin concerto, she whistled as she approached the one-hundred-fifty-year-old building. Once a venue for a steady stream of operas, plays, lectures, and variety shows, the Athaneum now sat dark except for quarterly productions by the Dunmullach Amateur Dramatical Society and, when Dunmullach took its turn hosting, the Annual All-County School Orchestra Competition.

Inside, her whistling took on a nervous tone as she waited for the theater manager to turn on the lights. She'd never liked darkened auditoriums. Empty seats lurked like gremlins in the gloom. She relaxed as the familiar ch-chunk of overhead lights transformed the hulking shapes into velvet-covered chairs. Gethsemane walked down the center aisle trailing her fingers along the faded blue fabric as she passed. Fuzzy. The theater's Victorian beauty reminded her of Miss Havisham, past her prime but still proud. She closed her eyes and imagined the sounds of an orchestra filling the auditorium. String, woodwinds, brass, percussion. A soft thud from the orchestra pit jolted her back to the present. Something white flashed by. She craned farther over the rail and spied an arm partially hidden in shadow. She called, "Hello."

No answer.

"I can see you there. Come on out."

Movement in the pit. Gethsemane looked down at a delicate blonde girl dressed in a white top and a skirt the same shade of blue as the velvet. She recognized the green eyes from that morning. "What's your name?"

The girl dropped her gaze and remained silent.

She tried again. "My name's Gethsemane. What's yours?"

"Saoirse," the girl whispered.

Colm's sister. "A lovely name. What are you doing down there, Saoirse?"

Saoirse scuffed her shoe at a spot on the floor.

"Well, whatever you're doing," Gethsemane said, "I think you'd better come up."

Saoirse disappeared from view. Footsteps approached then the girl stepped from behind the curtains. She descended the steps from the stage and stood next to Gethsemane. "They used to have magic shows." She dashed back up the steps and ducked into the wings.

Gethsemane followed. She found Saoirse staring at an old advertising poster proclaiming the appearance at the Athaneum, for three nights only, the astonishing Sullivan the Magnificent performing feats of prestidigitation to delight and amaze both young and old.

"Sullivan the Magnificent," Gethsemane said. "Can't say I'm familiar with his work."

"He only did tricks, illusions. He didn't do real magic."

"Real magic?" Gethsemane studied Saoirse's face. The girl wore a serious expression, no sign of joking. "What are you talking about?"

A door latch clicked. Gethsemane turned toward the sound. When she turned back, Saoirse had gone. The theater manager stepped backstage.

"All finished, Dr. Brown? I was hopin' to head out. The missus'll have dinner ready soon. Don't like to keep her waitin'."

"Did you see where she went?" Gethsemane asked.

"The missus?" The manager looked puzzled.

"No," Gethsemane said, "the girl. Saoirse. She was here beside me a minute ago. I looked away for a second and she was gone."

"Oh, the Nolan girl. She's an odd duck, that one. Always popping in and out. Doesn't go to school. Doesn't play well with others, I hear." The manager shrugged. "Her parents have money so they hire tutors. Father Keating and Peg Sullivan most recent. Other than that they pretty much let her be."

"Let her be to just roam the village unsupervised?"

"Sure, she's never done no harm. And she's not exactly unsupervised. We all keep an eye on her, make sure she wanders home eventually. She spends time at her lessons every day. Real smart, she is, a certifiable genius. Father Keating and Miss Sullivan watch her then. Kieran Ross in particular looks after her. The two of 'em 'talk' to each other. The girl's a bit strange but harmless. Although, truth be told," he lowered his voice to a whisper and leaned close to Gethsemane, "she does give ya the creeps sometimes. You'll turn 'round and find her standing there, staring at ya like she's trying to see inside ya. And she knows things."

Gethsemane lowered her voice to match his. "What things?"

"Things that haven't happened yet. She sees things too, things other people don't see."

Gethsemane bit her lip to keep from smiling. She and Saoirse had something in common. "How do you know, if you can't see them?"

"Sometimes you'll catch her looking at empty space, but not like she's daydreaming or sleepwalking. Like she's looking at something or someone she sees as clearly as I see you."

"Why are we whispering?" Gethsemane asked.

"You never know," the manager looked around, "who might be listening."

Gethsemane straightened up and thanked the manager in her normal tone of voice. With a last look at Sullivan the Magnificent's poster she headed for the exit, peering into the orchestra pit as she passed, unable to resist the urge to see if two green eyes would meet hers.

*   *   *

The pink-orange glow of sunset shone through a gap in the ever present clouds as Gethsemane walked up the stone steps leading to Our Lady of Perpetual Sorrows. The hinges of the iron gate in the fence standing sentry around the Gothic church squealed as she pushed it inward. Gethsemane started for the main entrance but changed course toward voices coming from the path near the graveyard. Around a corner, Father Keating knelt in a flower bed. Colm Nolan stood over him.

"Evening," Gethsemane said as she approached the duo. "Not interrupting prayers, am I?"

"Not prayers," Father Keating said. "Weeding." He held up a handful of freshly yanked plants, dirt dripping from their roots.

"I've come to fetch my sis," Colm said to the priest.

"You'll find her in her usual spot," Father Keating said. "You know how she loses track when she's in the garden."

"Do you really think it's a good idea, Father, teaching Saoirse about poisons?"

"Not just poisons, Colm. All aspects of botany."

"But the poison plants are the one she goes on about. Why's she need to know about mandrake root and wolfsbane?"

"Curiosity, Colm. Saoirse's got a curious mind. Besides, knowledge never hurt anyone. It's what you do with the knowledge that matters. And I don't think Saoirse's planning to bake any poisoned biscuits." Father Keating extended a hand to the boy. "Help me up, would you? There's a good lad."

Colm pulled Father Keating to his feet. Father Keating brushed dirt from his pants. "I seem to remember you asking for some botanical advice not so long ago. Wasn't it a love potion for a certain young lady on the choir?"

Colm blushed and glanced at Gethsemane.

"N-no, it was just, um, flowers for, for Ma's birthday. Asked what kind to get. You, um, must have me mixed up with one of the other lads, Ruairi maybe. He's the lovesick one." He jerked a thumb over his shoulder. "I'll be off after Saoirse now." He nodded at Gethsemane. "Miss."

Gethsemane returned the nod. "Colm. See you in class tomorrow. On time." Colm didn't answer. He turned and headed toward a wrought iron enclosure beyond the graveyard.

Gethsemane moved closer to Father Keating. "What was all that about poison?"

"Our poison garden." Father Keating pointed in Colm's direction. "Down there."

"The church has a poison garden? As in *Arsenic and Old Lace* poison?"

"More like Socrates. Arsenic's a metal." The cleric removed his cap and scratched his head. "We've got foxglove, hemlock, belladonna, aconite, Jimson weed, oleander, some others."

"I'll rephrase. *Why* does the church have a poison garden? Incentive to tithe?"

"The Church hasn't been that severe since the Inquisition. Our garden's of historical interest. The nuns of the Sacred Society of Apothecaries had their abbey here in the fifteenth century. They planted the garden for medicinal purposes."

"The garden's six hundred years old?"

Father Keating shook his head. "This garden is an exact replica of the original. Well, maybe not *exact*. We added some additional safety measures—an industrial grade lock, cages around some of the deadlier plants."

Gethsemane looked up at the church building. "A Gothic church with a poison garden on the far side of the graveyard. It's very—"

"Irish?"

"I was going to say operatic. Maybe I'll write one. Has an opera ever won the All-County?"

"First time for everything." Father Keating looked at the darkening sky. "If you plan to do some composing you'd best get home. You won't make it before nightfall as it is. This way to the bike."

Gethsemane followed Father Keating to a small stone outbuilding at the rear of the church. He put a key in the lock. It wouldn't turn. He tried the handle and laughed as he swung the door open. "Always forgetting to lock this thing." He reached inside and flipped on a light. "Not that there's anything to steal except the bike, I guess, and you're about to take care of that."

Gethsemane followed the priest down a short flight of stone steps. Garden tools and flower pots hung from hooks and filled shelves along two walls. A wheelbarrow rested in a corner. The shelves on the third wall held books crammed into every inch of shelf space, stacked next to and on top of each other. Gethsemane moved closer to read the titles: *Malleus Maleficarum*, *Psychology and the Occult*, *A Practical Treatise on the Banishment of Daemons*, *The Book of Enoch*. Gethsemane turned to Father Keating for an explanation.

"My inheritance from my late brother, also Father Keating. An exorcist."

"An exorcist? Like William Peter Blatty, three-sixty head spins, Georgetown steps exorcist?"

"Not quite that dramatic. No head spins."

"A legitimate exorcist?"

"Church sanctioned. In fact," Father Keating said, "the Church is recruiting. Trying to replenish the dwindling supply. So if you run across any boys thinking of taking Holy Orders..."

Gethsemane jumped at a noise outside. The hair on her arms stood up. "The bike?"

"Yes, of course. What you came for. You have to rein me in sometimes. I *do* get to talking." Father Keating pulled aside a canvas tarp and revealed a vintage Pashley, hunter green with wicker basket.

"She's gorgeous," Gethsemane said.

"She's meant to be ridden, not to prop up a canvas sheet."

Father Keating and Gethsemane maneuvered the bicycle up the stairs.

Gethsemane climbed on. "Don't forget to lock up."

Father Keating thanked her and locked the door.

"Thank *you*," Gethsemane said. "I promise to take good care of her."

"I know you will. See you in church on Sunday?"

"I'm Episcopalian."

"Come anyway. Maybe I'll make a true believer out of you."

"Stranger things have happened," Gethsemane said as she pedaled off toward Carraigfaire. "Stranger things, indeed."

As she rode she spied two women sitting on a bench on the green in front of the post office. Both slender and gray-haired, the taller wore her hair in loose waves that tumbled to her waist. The shorter wore her hair pinned up in a style borrowed from another era. They both wore dresses, the former billowy and floral, the latter tasteful and buttoned-down. Only the shorter woman wore shoes. A pile of books sat between them on the bench. The women stared at Gethsemane so intently as she passed she almost stopped to ask if something was wrong.

Eamon materialized on the Pashley's handlebars. Gethsemane swerved and nearly fell. She swore as she struggled to regain control of the bike.

"Careful, darlin'. You don't want to wreck Father Tim's lovely machine. And such language. What would your mother think?"

"Who do you think taught me to curse? Get off my bike."

"I'm not too heavy for you, am I?"

"You're not see-through."

Eamon dematerialized enough for Gethsemane to see the road through him.

"That better, darlin'?"

"What are you doing here? And quit calling me darling."

"It's dark so I'm here to escort you home. And I didn't call you darl*ing*. I called you darlin'. I call most women darlin'. The ones I like, anyway."

"It's annoying."

"No more than you Southerners calling everyone 'dear' or 'hon.' Or you calling me 'Irish.'"

"Touché, Irish." She jerked her head back toward the post office. "Who were those two women?"

"Nuala Sullivan and Deirdre Lynch."

"Why were they staring at me?"

"Why were they staring at the most remarkable thing to hit this village since the Famine? One guess. Kieran Ross stared at you, too."

"I didn't see anyone but the women."

"You don't see Kieran unless he wants you to. But he's always there, watching, listening."

Gethsemane shivered but not from the night air. "This is how you make a girl feel safe on the ride home?"

"Sorry. How's this?" Eamon's aura lit up a bright green-red, illuminating the bike and the road for several yards in front of them.

Gethsemane glanced around.

"Don't worry, no more gawkers. Even if there were, they wouldn't be able to see my light."

"Thanks."

"How about some music to go with the light show?" He whistled.

"'Put on a Happy Face'? Seriously?"

"One of Orla's favorites. Never failed to cheer her up."

"Probably because the idea 'gray skies are gonna clear up' in Western Ireland struck her as hysterical."

"Whatever works. Join in if you know the tune."

Eamon whistled and Gethsemane hummed the rest of the way back to the cottage.

Five

Her home-to-school commute time shortened thanks to Father Keating's Pashley, Gethsemane arrived at the cottage the next day with energy and time to spare before supper. The bright sun and crisp autumn breeze beckoned her up to Carrick Point. She'd walked the lighthouse grounds before now but hadn't gone in, Billy's warning about the stairs fresh in mind. Today, emboldened by clear skies over wildflower-studded cliffs and calm waters stretching out from the beach at their base, she grabbed the ancient wooden door's handle—

And swung it open with ease, to her surprise. No squeaking, no shower of rust as the hinges moved. Someone maintained at least this much of the place.

Light penetrated from windows in the wall high above her to the ground level, casting shadows over large boxes crowding the floor between the entrance and the spiral staircase coiling up the tower's center. Gethsemane stepped inside and immediately banged her shin on the edge of a box she failed to notice protruding into the doorway. She let a string of swear words fly and hobbled to the wrought iron stairs. She sat on the lowest tread only to jump up as plaster rained down from anchor screws loosened in their sockets under her weight. A "bit" dicey, Billy said.

"Kieran will see to that."

Gethsemane, startled, banged into another box. "Damn it." she said to Eamon's apparition materialized behind her. "Would you stop doing that?" She rubbed her other shin.

"Doing what, darlin'?"

"Sneaking up on me."

"I'm not sneaking. This is my normal method of going from place to place. See?" He vanished and reappeared at the top of the stairs. He vanished again and popped up next to her.

"Yeah, well, you oughta warn people. Send a blast of your soap and cologne before you just—" She made a "pouf" motion with her fingers.

"Did you hurt yourself?" He nodded at her legs.

"Yes. No, not really." She kicked a box. "What's in all these?"

"Books, papers mostly. A few bits and bobs Billy collected."

Gethsemane pulled up the corner of a box top. "Anything that might help your case?"

"No. I checked." He sat on a box; the backs of his thighs disappeared into the cardboard. "Orla used to write her poems up here. No boxes then. She set up an office in the clockworks."

"You and Orla worked together up here?"

"Not in immediate proximity. 'Worked well with others' is not engraved on my headstone. I was terrible company when composing, so deep into each new piece you could've set fireworks off in the front yard and I wouldn't have noticed. I had a desk and a cot on the floor below Orla. I'd spend days up here with little more than a guitar and a pen. Orla'd bring food and remind me to eat. She'd work up here when I was at the piano. My banging on the Steinway, or maybe my cursing while I played, kept her from concentrating on her poems. We often climbed up to the lantern together and stared at the landscape for hours, not saying a word."

"I bet the view's amazing."

"'Tis. When it's clear you can see halfway to forever. When the fog's in you feel like you're floating on clouds." Eamon passed a hand through the stair's iron railing. "I used to come up here all the time as a lad. I'd drag Orla and Peg with me and we'd play pirates or explorers or some such game. Sometimes we'd picnic on the cliffs. Lighthouse was pretty rundown then. Ma'd blow a fuse at me for coming up here, especially with the girls, convinced one of us would fall to our death." His aura turned yellow. "Ironic."

Orla died near the lighthouse. "Do you want to talk about it?"

"Talk about what it was like finding my wife dead? How I felt when I saw her lying broken on the rocks?" Eamon closed his eyes. The yellow aura took on a blue tinge. "No, I don't."

Subject change. "Sounds like you, Orla, and Pegeen were close as kids."

"Thick as thieves as they say. Orla was the glue who held me and Peg together. An antidote to my temper and a balm to Peg's pain. She no doubt saved us from bad ends: me from jail for reefin' some git who'd set me off, Peg from an institution for—well, thanks to Orla, it didn't happen."

"Peg's pain?"

"Father abandoned her, mother and sister had mental and legal problems, Peg served as primary caretaker for both. Neither of them appreciated Peg's efforts. Villagers snickered behind her back. Peg dealt with a lot from a young age. She built a shell around herself, studded it with bristles."

"If you don't let anyone near you, no one can hurt you. What about you? What stoked the fires of your temper?"

Eamon chuckled as red edged out the yellow and blue. "My musical genius. Aren't all musical geniuses hot-blooded and mercurial? It's part of our charm."

"Charm's not the word I'd have chosen." The light from the window dimmed. "Time to head back down. I need to get supper and I have some lesson plans to write."

"Race you."

"Funny." Gethsemane's foot landed on something small and hard. "An earring." She turned the turquoise bauble over in her hand. "Orla's? How'd it get up here?"

"Not Orla's. How do you think it got up here? The door's never locked. Pirates and explorers aren't the only games people play at Carrick Point."

*   *   *

Colm showed up late for orchestra rehearsal.

"Again," Gethsemane said as he took his time joining the other violins. She waited for the class to settle then resumed auditions. Her head hurt. She massaged her temples as the next boy executed a technically competent but uninspired selection from the first movement of Beethoven's Symphony No. 3. Talent alone wouldn't win the All-County. She needed a soloist with passion to pull off a McCarthy concerto. Eamon's compositions were notorious for arousing emotion. Some women even claimed listening to a McCarthy piece brought them to—

"Dr. Brown?"

"Sorry, Ruairi, go ahead."

Boys snickered as Ruairi fumbled his sheet music. He pushed up his glasses, positioned his violin...

And played the violin solo from fifth movement of Bernstein's "Serenade, after Plato: Symposium" so beautifully Gethsemane dug her nails into her palms to keep from crying. Every trace of awkwardness vanished as Ruairi became one with his music.

Silence followed Ruairi as he resumed his seat. He wiped his glasses on his sweater and stared at the floor.

Colm Nolan took his place at the music stand. No fumbling. No snickering. He shouldered his violin and raised his bow in a fluid motion and played a cadenza from Rimsky-Korsakov's "Scheherazade."

Gethsemane reminded herself to breathe. Transcendent. Genius. Colm brought forth the voice of God from his strings. The headache dissipated. She had her featured soloist. Ruairi'd make a fine concertmaster. St. Brennan's actually had a chance of bringing home a trophy.

Gethsemane stood at the foot of the staircase leading to the Dunmullach public library's second level, where they housed their music collection. She closed her eyes and inhaled the almond-vanilla smell of old books, one of her favorite scents. She trailed her hand along the rail as she climbed the stairs, wood and marble both worn smooth by generations of visitors. Had they come to check out a recording of Eamon's music? Or a volume of Orla's poetry? Had one of them murdered the McCarthys?

She approached a smartly-dressed woman seated behind a semi-circular desk through an arched entryway. The brass sign at the woman's elbow read *Mrs. Toibin, Head Music Librarian.*

The woman looked up from her computer monitor. "Ah, you're Dr. Brown, new music director up at St. Brennan's. Hope the twins aren't acting too much the maggot. Have the guards found your luggage yet?"

Eamon hadn't exaggerated Dunmullach's gossip mill. "No, ma'am, not yet."

The librarian eyed Gethsemane's pink suit. "That's a lovely outfit. One of Orla's?"

"Yes." Small villages in Ireland were as bad as small towns in Virginia. "Teague brought some of her things over."

"It's quite fetching on you."

"Thank you. Lucky Orla and I were about the same size."

Mrs. Toibin shifted in her chair. "Now then, how may I help you? I'm sure you didn't come by on your half day to talk fashion."

"Eamon McCarthy."

"What about him?"

Gethsemane caught herself in time to keep from saying, "I need evidence to prove an incompetent cop and a malignant thug set him up for murder." She drummed her fingers on the desk while she fashioned a plausible lie. "I'm studying his later works, particularly his last piece, his sonata, 'Jewel of Carraigfaire'."

"His masterpiece in my opinion. Did you know he composed it for Orla? For her birthday. Her last as it turned out. Eamon's last composition too." She jumped up, nearly heading Gethsemane in the nose. "We have a complete collection of recordings of Eamon's work. Emanuel Ax performing 'Etude for Piano in C Major', Hilary

Hahn performing 'String Quartet in A Minor', Vladimir Horowitz performing 'Nocturnes', Leonard Bernstein conducting 'Symphony Number 7 in B-flat Minor'. And, of course, recordings made by Eamon himself."

Gethsemane followed her toward shelves packed with CDs. "How well did you know Eamon?"

"Quite well. We were at school together. I was two years ahead of him. My sister was in his class. All of us girls had fierce crushes on Eamon. But even then we knew he'd end up with Orla." She blinked several times and wiped her eye with the back of her hand before continuing. "None of us could quite believe what happened."

Gethsemane whispered, "Do you really think he killed his wife then committed suicide?"

"He must have, mustn't he? Lost that famous temper of his, pushed Orla to her death, then poisoned himself, overcome with remorse by what he'd done."

"But he loved Orla. Deeply."

"Maybe he loved her too much. Some men do, you know."

Gethsemane put her face near the librarian's. "But what if Eamon *didn't* murder Orla? What if someone else killed her?"

"And what, framed Eamon?"

Gethsemane nodded.

"Who'd do such a thing? The McCarthys hadn't any enemies." She cocked her head and thought a moment. "Well, Orla hadn't, anyway. A true angel. Everyone adored her. Prettiest girl in the village. Smartest, too. And such a sense of adventure. She'd lead Eamon and Pegeen on what she called 'Grand Expeditions.' They'd roam the cliffs collecting specimens—flowers and rocks and things. Orla would display their finds in class next day and tell fantastic stories about their exploits. When they weren't exploring, the three of them would climb up to the top of the lighthouse—none of the rest of us were brave enough to go up there—and scout the bay for pirates and sea monsters. They spent all their time together, the three of them." Mrs. Toibin waved a hand. "But you're not interested in ancient history. You're here about music."

Music. What secrets hid in the melody, the harmony, the notes themselves? Maybe the coded name of the killer? Ridiculous. Eamon couldn't have named his killer *before* he was murdered. Gethsemane hurried to catch up.

"Eamon's entire *oeuvre*." The librarian swept her arms at shelves on either side of them. "All of the definitive performances by the world's leading musicians—Fyodorov, Kaminski, Ivanova, Bergich—as well as Eamon's own recordings. But," she punctuated her words with a finger, "perhaps you'd rather *see* Eamon perform."

"See?"

"I'll bet you're too young to have had the privilege of seeing Eamon perform live."

Gethsemane laughed.

"I may not be as young as you think. I did see Eamon McCarthy perform live once, a few years before he died. Debussy at the Peabody in Washington, D.C. I was seven. My first concert. My grandfather took me."

"Ah, so you know." She nodded as if Gethsemane belonged to the same secret society. "Unfortunately, I can't summon Eamon's ghost to give another concert performance—"

Gethsemane coughed.

"But I can offer you the next best thing to a live performance. The library owns more than three dozen concert videotapes, a recent gift from one of the Morris heirs, God rest their souls." Mrs. Toibin bowed her head for a moment. "There was a nasty, drawn out legal battle over the estate. Long lost relations popped up on three or four continents. When the courts finally settled their affairs a fourth cousin in Canada ended up with several boxes of photos and videos. I guess he was a bit chuffed about his legacy because he left the boxes in storage for donkey's years. His daughter finally got 'round to sorting through them. Turns out one of the Morris twins was a fan of Eamon's as well as a keen videographer."

Gethsemane recalled a boy in the newspaper photo holding a video camera.

Mrs. Toibin continued. "He recorded many of Eamon's

performances. The fourth cousin's daughter, an archivist, thought we might appreciate having the tapes and shipped them to us."

Videotapes. Gethsemane snapped her fingers. She remembered watching a movie from some years ago, when she'd had nothing else to do while snowed in at a Denver hotel, something with Kellie Martin on The Women's Network. A detective identified a singer's killer by studying the audience in concert footage. The killer—a stalker—showed up in every film. An obsessed fan might kill your wife...

"Dr. Brown?"

Gethsemane hoped her smile didn't appear over-eager. "Mrs. Toibin, I can't think of anything I'd rather do right now other than look at those tapes."

Ten minutes later, the librarian set a stack of videos next to Gethsemane in front of a video monitor. She showed Gethsemane how to operate the attached VCR. "I wish we had the funds to transfer these to DVD. Or at least the staff to properly catalog them."

"I'm just glad you have them," Gethsemane said. "St. Brennan's has gotten rid of everything Eamon McCarthy-related."

"What purpose does that serve? Getting rid of Eamon's works won't bring Orla or him back. Eamon was a brilliant composer and gifted musician, regardless of—whatever. Discarding his work only compounds the tragedy. Let me know if you find anything exciting. Haven't had time to look through the tapes myself."

Mrs. Toibin made her excuses and left to go assist a woman whose infant was using a Bob Dylan CD as a teething ring. Gethsemane lifted a tape from the stack—Eamon performing Debussy at the Orenburg Opera House—and loaded it into the machine. She put on headphones and pressed play. Eamon sprang to life on the monitor's screen. His long, sinewy fingers flew over the Steinway keyboard as Debussy's *"Les sons et les parfums tournent dans l'air du soir"* filled Gethsemane's headphones. She was seven years old again, clutching her grandfather's hand with her right and the concert program with her left, sitting motionless on the edge of a mauve velvet seat, her patent-leather-clad feet dangling inches above the theater floor.

After Debussy came Haydn with the New York Philharmonic, then Tchaikovsky, Sousa, and Berlin at a Fourth of July concert with the Boston Pops. The Anchorage Symphony Orchestra world premiere of one of Eamon's own compositions, "*An Fhuaim Agus An Fury,*" followed. All thoughts of scanning the footage for shots of potential stalkers in the audience evaporated as Gethsemane lost herself in the music.

She removed the headphones just as the library's clock chimed. The four thirty warning. One half hour until closing. Gethsemane shuffled through the remaining tapes, hoping to find some Beethoven to wrap up the day. She held up the next to last tape in the stack and stared. On the label:

"Jewel of Carraigfaire"

Morris Farewell Concert

Dublin, Ireland

The date? Thirty-one October, twenty-five years ago. Eamon's last performance. The Morris boy. The "keen videographer" who recorded Eamon's concerts. Of course he would have recorded Eamon's farewell gift to his family. Her pulse quickened and she cursed as she fumbled the tape into the player. She took a deep breath to slow her heart rate, replaced the headphones, and pressed play. Eamon reappeared on screen. She caught the faint scent of leather and soap. She glanced around. No one there except other library patrons gathering their belongings. Gethsemane watched and listened to Eamon play his sonata, the music he'd composed for the one he loved best, as a gift for the friends seated only a few feet away from him, their faces enraptured. The piece ended and Eamon began to play Beethoven. Gethsemane fast-forwarded to the end of the tape. The time stamp lit up in a corner of the frame. Ten thirty p.m. Orla died around midnight November first. If Eamon McCarthy was playing the piano in Dublin at ten thirty p.m. on

Halloween, could he make it back to Dunmullach in time to murder his wife at midnight on All Saints' Day?

Someone tapped Gethsemane on the shoulder. Gethsemane jumped, knocking several tapes to the floor. She turned to see Mrs. Toibin stooping to pick up the fallen videos. Gethsemane bent to help.

Once the videos had been restored to order on the table, Gethsemane asked, "How far is it from Dublin to Dunmullach? Driving? Time wise?"

The other woman thought for a few seconds.

"Oh, I'd say about four hours. Maybe more if you hit traffic in Dublin."

"Even if you were speeding?"

The librarian laughed. "My son, bless his soul, who's notorious for his driving, has made the trip in three and a half hours. No one's beaten his record."

Gethsemane curled her toes. She felt like doing a happy dance. "So if you were in Dublin at half past ten there's no way you could be on the road up to Carrick Point before midnight."

"Half ten in the morning?"

"No, ten thirty at night."

"Not unless you'd managed to get hold of one of those transporter things they use on *Star Trek*. Or Dr. Who loaned you his Tardis."

"No matter who said they saw your car," Gethsemane said under her breath.

"What's that?"

"Nothing. Just thinking out loud." She offered her hand. "Thank you, ma'am. Thank you very much. You've been more helpful than I can say."

"You found what you needed, then?"

"Yes, ma'am," Gethsemane said. She didn't add, "Proof that Eamon McCarthy's no murderer."

*   *   *

A short bike ride later, Gethsemane caught Inspector O'Reilly in the parking lot of the garda station. He wore his fedora but carried his suit jacket over his arm.

"I was just on my way home, Dr. Brown." He tried to side-step past her.

She blocked his path. "This will only take a minute."

O'Reilly side-stepped in the other direction. "If you'll come by the station in the morning—"

Gethsemane blocked him again. "Half a minute."

O'Reilly sighed and readjusted his jacket. "Go on."

"Eamon McCarthy couldn't have killed his wife."

"Did I mention it was late?" O'Reilly stepped forward. His Oxfords—brown leather this time, but just as expensive-looking as the monkstraps—missed her toe by an inch.

Gethsemane caught sandalwood and clove again. She held up both hands. "Hear me out. Please."

Another sigh. "Talk fast."

"I have proof Eamon couldn't have killed his wife."

"Show me."

"I can't show you—"

"Dr. Brown—" O'Reilly hooked his jacket over a shoulder with one hand and fished in his pants pocket with the other. "The only reason I'm not arresting you for obstructing an officer of An Garda Síochána is because I'm too tired to do the paper work." He pulled out a key fob. "Now if you'll please excuse me—"

"The proof is at the library. On videotape."

O'Reilly paused with his thumb on the key fob. "Videotape?"

"I just watched a videotape of Eamon McCarthy's last performance. The one he gave in Dublin the night Orla McCarthy died." Gethsemane waited. O'Reilly said nothing. "It was a live performance, for friends moving to Africa. One of them recorded it."

"And?"

"And the time stamp on the videotape says ten thirty. Ten thirty p.m. On October thirty-first. In Dublin. Four hours away from Dunmullach."

"Three hours and fifty-two minutes." O'Reilly put the key fob back in his pocket.

"Too far away to make it up to Carrick Point in time to throw your wife off a cliff at midnight, November one," Gethsemane said. "Even if Eamon left his friends' house right after the concert, he wouldn't have made it home before two thirty. Orla was dead by then."

O'Reilly pushed his hat back on his head, closed his eyes, and massaged the bridge of his nose.

Gethsemane counted to five. "I know it's late, Inspector. You've worked hard. Your feet hurt. Pizza delivery's on the way, beer waits in the fridge, the game's on TV, and I'm a pain in the ass." O'Reilly kept his eyes closed. "But I'm a pain in the ass who's just seen a video that exonerates a man of murder. Murder, Inspector. Doesn't that rate a look?"

"Tomorrow." O'Reilly opened his eyes. "Tomorrow I will go to the library and watch the videotape. It better be there."

Gethsemane assured him it would be. Mrs. Toibin had promised to safeguard it.

"Fine," O'Reilly said. "But right now—" He pulled out his key fob again. "I'm going home. You should do the same." A pointed look made Gethsemane move out of his way. "Playing detective on top of your teaching duties must be exhausting." O'Reilly settled into the driver's seat. "By the way, my feet don't hurt because I wear good shoes, a tip I picked up from Da. And it's osso buco and ruffino I'll be havin', not pizza and beer." He slammed the door and sped away.

On her way home from the garda station, Gethsemane stopped her bicycle at the turn-off to Carrick Point Road, little more than a rocky, serpentine path leading uphill to nowhere except

Carraigfaire cottage and the lighthouse. She listened. Only her own breathing and a desolate wind howling off the cliffs. Light from the Mad Rabbit and Our Lady of Perpetual Sorrows shone in the far distance. No cars or pedestrians passed by. Little chance Jimmy Lynch or anyone would just "happen" along and see—

Something blindsided Gethsemane. The object hit her full force in the ribs and knocked her to the ground before she had time to register pain. She lay still on her back for several seconds watching the reflection of moonbeams on clouds. One cloud reminded her of her college roommate's cat. She pinched herself. Focus. After a manual survey verified her neck bones remained in a straight line and her scalp remained in one piece she turned her head.

The Pashley lay on the ground, front wheel still spinning. The lower half of the thing that hit her lay beneath the bike's rear wheel. Its upper half clawed at the bike, trying to disengage yards of fabric from the wheel's spokes. The thing muttered to itself. It pushed a disheveled mass of hair to one side, uncovering a woman's face.

Gethsemane scrambled to her feet and went to assist. She freed the fabric—the folds of a voluminous skirt—from the wheel and lifted the bike off the woman's legs.

"Are you all right?" she asked as the woman got to her feet.

The woman's eyes darted from side to side as she spun in a slow circle, arms outstretched as if to keep something away from her.

"Where is she? Did you see where she went? Where is she?"

"Where is who?" Gethsemane looked around. "We're the only ones here."

"It was her. I saw her. I know it was her." The woman grabbed the bicycle with both hands and held her face an inch from Gethsemane's. "Why won't she leave me alone?"

Gethsemane stepped back and pulled the Pashley toward her chest. The woman held on. Her strength surprised Gethsemane.

"Why won't *who* leave you alone?" Gethsemane tugged at the bike a few times then braced herself and yanked it out of the woman's grasp. "I'm the only other person here. You ran into me. We fell. Do you remember?"

"It was her. She made me do it."

Gethsemane leaned forward to get a better look at the woman. She appeared to be in her sixties. Her tangled gray hair hung in unwashed strings to her waist. Her bony hands ended in long spider fingers, the kind that reminded Gethsemane of fairy tale witches. A pale dress with a high collar, long skirt, and long sleeves concealed everything between her gaunt face and dirty bare feet peeping beneath the hem. The seamstress must have used the entire bolt of fabric.

"I'm Gethsem—"

The woman interrupted. "I know who you are."

"Right, the whole town knows," Gethsemane said. "You have me at a disadvantage, Miss—"

"Sullivan." The woman drew herself up to her full height, several inches taller than Gethsemane. "Miss Nuala Sullivan of the Skibbereen Sullivans, daughter of the famed Joseph Sullivan."

The name rang a bell. One of the women from the bench in front of the post office. Gethsemane imagined her with clean, combed hair. Then she recalled the poster in the theater. "Sullivan the Magnificent? The illusionist?"

"The magician!" Nuala pounced.

Gethsemane blocked her with the bicycle.

"Joseph Sullivan had a gift." Nuala drew herself up to her full height again and looked down her nose at Gethsemane. "I have it too. I'm touched."

"So I see." Gethsemane kept the bike between them. "Do you need help, Miss Sullivan?"

Nuala tensed. "Help?"

"Medical attention. The accident. Are you injured?"

Nuala patted her arms and legs. She relaxed. "No." As if someone had flipped a switch she bowed her head and meekly looked up at Gethsemane through snarls of hair. "I'm sorry. I didn't mean to run into you."

Gethsemane forced a smile. "No harm done. Bike's still in one piece. So am I."

"She made me do it."

"I didn't see anyone else. Who do you mean?"

Nuala looked over her shoulder and whispered, "Orla."

"Orla? Orla McCarthy?"

"Shhh."

Nuala held a finger to her lips.

Gethsemane lowered her voice. "Orla...McCarthy...*made* you run into me?"

Nuala nodded.

"But Orla McCarthy's dead."

"Shhh." Nuala held the finger to her lips again. "She'll hear you."

"I think she knows she's dead."

Nuala rolled her eyes. "I know that. I'm not stupid."

No, just nuts. "Why would a dead woman make you run into me, or anyone, on an isolated road at night?"

"She's punishing me."

"Why?"

"Can't talk about it." Nuala's hand disappeared into her skirt and brought a palm-sized leather book from beneath its folds. She opened the book and read aloud.

The light of God surrounds me.

The love of God enfolds me.

The power of God protects me.

The presence of God watches o'er me.

Wherever I am, God is.

All is well.

The book disappeared back into her skirt. She spun in a slow circle again. "It's all right. She's gone now."

"Oh. Good." Gethsemane climbed on the bicycle. "If you're okay, I think I'll be going too."

"It's been lovely meeting you." Nuala grabbed Gethsemane's hand.

"Um, likewise?" Gethsemane tried to pull free from Nuala's ice cold grasp.

Nuala squeezed her hand tighter. "Tell him it wasn't my fault. She kept them apart."

Gethsemane struggled.

Nuala held on. "She was wrong to do it. They should be together. Tell him!"

"I'll tell him. It wasn't your fault."

Nuala released Gethsemane's hand. "So lovely. We must have tea sometime."

Gethsemane sped up Carrick Point Road. Halfway up the hill, Nuala called her name. She didn't look back.

"Eamon! Eamon! Where are you?"

Eamon materialized in the hallway in front of Gethsemane. "Stop shouting. I—" His eyes widened. "What happened to you?"

"What do you mean?" Gethsemane looked down. Her skirt hem hung loose. Black smudges marked her shins and knees. An abrasion on her palm oozed blood.

"Your face too."

Gethsemane wiped her cheek. "I had an accident. It's nothing."

"Doesn't look like nothing. Are you all right? Do you need to go to A and E?"

"No, I'm fine." Gethsemane waved her hands. "Listen, listen."

"What?"

"I did it. I proved you didn't kill your wife."

"Did the accident involve a head injury?"

"I'm serious." Gethsemane marched through Eamon, ignoring the buzz in her bones and his roar of expletives, into the study and poured bourbon. She raised the glass. "Here's to me. I did it. I rock." She slammed her drink.

Eamon appeared behind her. "D'ya want to slow down and tell me what you're talking about?"

"I," Gethsemane pointed to her chest, "confirmed your," she

pointed at Eamon, "alibi for the time of your wife's death.
Confirmation of the iron clad variety, thank you very much. I found
proof you were performing for the Morris family in Dublin at ten
thirty p.m., too late to have gotten back to Dunmullach in time to
kill your wife."

"What proof?"

"Videotape. One of the Morris boys recorded the entire
concert."

"Video? You're telling me there's a videotape of the
performance?"

"Yep. Color, audio, time stamp. The whole bit. And *I* found it.
I'm surprised you didn't notice the camera."

A whiskey glass exploded against a wall. Eamon radiated
cerulean. "I notice nothing except the music when I perform."

"What's with the flying glassware? This is *good* news.
Shouldn't you be glowing pink?"

"I don't glow bloody pink."

Gethsemane caught the next glass midair and set it on the bar.

"If *you* found the bloody video there's no excuse for Hurley not
finding it." Eamon shone navy. "The whacker didn't fecking look."

"Gee, thanks, Irish. If *I* found it? You mean right after I
learned to chew gum?"

"I didn't mean it that way. Hurley was a bloody guard. At least
he claimed to be. It was his job to investigate. He should have found
that tape years ago. He was too drunk and lazy to do his effing job."

"Well, O'Reilly will find it tomorrow."

"Tomorrow? Why not tonight?"

Gethsemane flopped on the sofa with a fresh drink. "O'Reilly
was tired and hungry. He'd had a long day. Besides, the library was
closed."

"Tired? *He* was tired? Doesn't he think I've been tired of
waiting? Twenty-five years! Why didn't you—"

"Hold on. First of all, O'Reilly doesn't know you're waiting. I
had enough trouble getting him to listen to me without bringing up
ghosts. Secondly, I can't force O'Reilly to do anything. I practically

shanghaied him in the parking lot to get him to hear me out about the tape. He promised to watch it tomorrow. Once he does—" She raised her glass. "Bingo. You're in the clear and O'Reilly can get to work finding Orla's real murderer."

Eamon sat next to Gethsemane. "You're right. I'm sorry. Hurley's not here for me to blast, so I'm taking it out on you. This is the best news I've had since Orla agreed to marry me. Drink one for me."

Gethsemane obliged. "Something else."

"You found proof I didn't off myself."

"No, not that. It's about my accident. Guess who I ran into?"

"You mean literally?"

"Yes. Well, no. Literally, she ran into me. Nuala Sullivan."

"Whoo hoo. There goes all kinds of crazy for ya. She didn't try to set you on fire, did she?"

Gethsemane frowned. "Set me on—No."

"So how'd you meet the infamous Miss Sullivan?"

"Infamous?"

"Whenever anything catches fire mysteriously, the guards check to see if Nuala's been playing with matches again."

"She crashed into me at the foot of Carrick Point Road. I didn't notice any incendiary devices. Get this. Apparently, Orla chased her."

"What?"

"Or maybe she chased Orla. Kind of hard to tell. The point is, she claims she's in contact with Orla."

Eamon stood. "She's not the full shilling, that one. Never has been. Her sister's spent half her life trying to keep her under control. I'm sure she was having hallucinations."

"Just because she's mentally ill doesn't mean she doesn't see ghosts."

"That header no more sees Orla than I see green men on Mars." The blue aura returned. Eamon's hair sparked.

Gethsemane smelled leather. "So what if Nuala Sullivan sees your wife's ghost?"

Eamon bent nose-to-nose with Gethsemane. The leather and soap aroma intensified. "Don't you think I've tried to find Orla? In twenty-five years with nothing to do but wait don't you think I looked for her? If Orla—*my* Orla—was going to come back to someone, she'd come back to *me*, not some—some—fecking—" Eamon vanished mid-expletive.

Gethsemane muttered all the way to the bar. "Fecking temperamental Irish...no appreciation...jealous of a head case." She took the Waddell and Dobb back to the sofa where she stretched out and closed her eyes.

She was asleep before the bourbon returned to the bar, the afghan tucked itself around her, and the pages of a newly-composed violin concerto arranged themselves on the coffee table.

Six

Gethsemane woke from a nightmare as the jangle of the telephone competed with Haydn's "Symphony No. 94" to see which could give her the worst headache. She tumbled from the sofa and blundered to the kitchen, disentangling herself from the afghan as she went. She yelled at Eamon—why was he playing the piano at this hour anyway?—to be quiet, intensifying her headache, and lifted the receiver. She managed a "Hello?" before the throbbing got the better of her and forced her to sit on the floor.

"Good morning, Dr. Brown." Billy McCarthy's voice sounded far away on the other end of the line. Faint chatter went on in the background.

Only inky blackness shone through the kitchen window. "Where are you?"

"New York. It's about eleven o'clock at night here."

Which meant about four o'clock in the morning in Dunmullach. Someone must be dying. "What's wrong?"

"Nothing's wrong. Sorry to bother you at such an unholy hour, but I need something."

Gethsemane's head bobbed as she mumbled.

"Dr. Brown?"

"Yes." Her head snapped up. "I'm here."

"I need you to fax some papers. You'll find them in the study, in a safe behind a watercolor of the Cliffs of Moher."

"Now?"

"No, by nine a.m. New York time. That's two p.m. there."

Fax papers from a safe in the study to New York. Gethsemane struggled to make sense of Billy's words. She pinched herself. She was awake. Was Billy drunk? His speech didn't sound slurred. "I'm sorry, I don't understand."

"I need some papers. The deed to the cottage and lighthouse, Uncle Eamon's will, and tax receipts."

Deed, will, tax receipts. "Pathétique" sounded high alert and pushed aside fatigue and headaches. The hour excused her bluntness. "What for?"

Silence. Gethsemane imagined Billy debating telling her to mind her own business. Finally, he laughed, a forced rather than reassuring sound. "I met a fella out here who wants to look at them. No big deal."

Gethsemane glanced out the window again. A star twinkled. "No big deal" occurred during normal business hours, not four o'clock in the morning. Tchaikovsky in her head drowned out renewed Haydn from the music room.

"Is that music?" Billy asked.

"What? No. Yes. Radio. My alarm just went off."

"I won't keep you. I expect you'll be wanting a cup of coffee and a hearty breakfast before school, yeah?"

"Yeah." That and time to figure out what was up.

"You'll fax the papers?"

"I don't know the combination to the safe."

Billy gave it to her as well as his hotel fax number. He added, "Mark the fax attention: Hank Wayne."

Gethsemane dropped the phone. "Did you say Hank Wayne?"

"Yes. He's the fella wants to see the documents." Gethsemane said nothing. Billy expounded. "I'd have you send them to my attention, but I have to fly up to Boston for a meeting first thing in the morning. Wayne's going to look everything over while I'm up there and we'll talk over dinner when I get back." Gethsemane remained silent. Billy reassured her, "It's all right. Wayne knows to be on the lookout for the fax. You don't have to worry about it falling into the wrong hands."

Something else worried Gethsemane as she agreed to Billy's request and hung up. She'd spent half her life traveling on tours and to competitions. She'd stayed in a lot of hotels. Hank Wayne's logo branded many of them—the tackiest. A vision of Carraigfaire's hardwood floors replaced with hideous pink carpet and its walls covered in matching pink faux wood paneling popped into her head. She shuddered.

Eamon appeared beside her. "Didn't you hear me, darlin'? I asked who was on the phone."

"The prophet of doom."

"Are you still drunk?"

Gethsemane walked through Eamon, hardly noticing the sizzle along her skin as she headed for the safe. Disregarding his comments about people who barged through other's chests, she retrieved the legal documents and took them to the couch. Eamon materialized next to her. "Why were you playing the piano so early?" she asked as she read the terms of Eamon's will.

"Couldn't sleep. Something's worrying me. I always play the piano when I can't sleep. Drove Orla mad."

"Ghosts sleep?"

"Not like when we were alive. We—it's complicated. Easier to just say 'sleep.'" He nodded at the papers she held. "How'd you get the combination to the safe?"

"That was Billy on the phone." Gethsemane hesitated, recalling Eamon's outburst when she'd told him about Nuala seeing Orla's ghost. "Promise you'll remain calm."

"I realize what's worrying me. Why'd Billy call?"

"Ever hear of Hank Wayne?"

Eamon shook his head.

"Do you ever think about what will happen to this place after you're gone? Let's say you're cleared of murder-suicide and you move on to another plane of existence to do whatever one does for eternity. What becomes of Carraigfaire?"

"Have you had too much or too little bourbon? Or do you just not think straight before your first cup of coffee? You know damn well Billy's planning a museum."

"Why do I try to help you?" Gethsemane, papers in hand, marched to the stairs.

Eamon appeared in front of her. "Why *did* Billy call?"

Gethsemane stood on tiptoe to look him in the eye. "Your nephew wants me to fax your will, the deed to this cottage, and tax receipts to Mr. Hank Wayne, a 'fella' he met in New York."

"Wayne's name means something to you."

"Wayne's name means horrid cookie-cutter hotels which make strip malls and industrial parks seem charming in comparison."

Eamon, surrounded by a yellow aura, dimmed.

"But hey," Gethsemane continued, "don't worry. Billy didn't actually *say* he was going to sell your beautiful centuries-old home with the billion-dollar view and priceless memories to a soulless developer with the aesthetic sensibility of a nineteen eighties televangelist's wife. He's only going to let him look at your private papers while he's in another state then chat with him over dinner. So go back to your piano playing, dream up some more insults, or turn into a blue ball and break everything within a ten-mile radius. What do I care? I'm leaving." She stomped up the stairs. Halfway up, she paused. "And don't worry about your precious Waddell and Dobb Double-oaked. I'll stop at the liquor store and replace what I drank." She took the remaining stairs two at a time and slammed the bedroom door.

"I'm sorry."

Gethsemane jumped at Eamon's sudden appearance, splashing coffee down the front of her dress. She muttered curses as she went upstairs to change.

"Orla's green satin gabardine would look nice on you." Eamon materialized at the foot of the bed, a hand covering his eyes.

"Out."

Gethsemane clutched the coffee-stained garment to her chest.

"I'm not looking." He peeked between his fingers. "Besides, I'm dead."

Gethsemane threw a hairbrush which sailed through Eamon and clattered against a wall. "You're the liveliest dead man I've ever met. I can't change with you standing there."

"I'll see you downstairs, then." Eamon vanished, only to reappear a second later. "Don't change. I like you the way you are." He disappeared before the shoe reached him.

Back in the kitchen, Gethsemane's resolve to stay mad melted when faced with the aroma of fresh coffee and hot buttered toast.

"I told you the green would look nice," Eamon said as she sat across from him. "I really am sorry about last night. I shouldn't have snapped at you."

"I'm sorry too," Gethsemane said around a mouthful. "I didn't mean to set you off."

"'T wasn't you. The thought of Nuala Sullivan communicating with my wife when I can't..." Eamon shrugged. "I felt jealous, guilty."

"Guilty?"

"I failed Orla. I had convinced myself the reason I couldn't find her was because she'd passed on or crossed over or whatever. She was sitting on God's right hand reading poetry to angels. She was happy. All I've ever wanted is Orla's happiness."

Gethsemane set her cup down. "If Nuala sees Orla, Orla hasn't crossed over."

"She's trapped here, like me. Without me. And I can't help her. Just like I couldn't help her the night..." Eamon's voice trailed off.

Gethsemane reached for his hand. Her fingers tingled as they clasped air. "Don't torture yourself. Granted, I'm no expert on the spirit realm, but it can't be easy to find someone lost in it."

"You mean the *Ghost Hunting Adventures* boys haven't invented a spectral GPS yet?"

"And there are no social media feeds in the afterlife."

"Thank God."

"Well, maybe in Hell."

Eamon laughed.

"There's the Irish I know and love."

"Flattery will get you everywhere, darlin'."

"Except to school on time."

Gethsemane tapped her watch.

"Before you go," Eamon stood with her, "what *did* Billy want? He's not really planning to sell, is he?"

"He didn't use the word 'sell' but I'm worried. I know Hank Wayne's reputation. He's on the International Heritage Preservation Society's watch list for ruining the historical and cultural value of several properties. I can't think of any innocent reasons why Billy would show him those documents."

Gethsemane followed Eamon's gaze out the window. Sunrise bathed the cliffs in an orange-yellow glow. "Billy can't sell. He knows Carraigfaire's not just a house, it's our Shangri-La, our Eden-before-the-fall." Eamon nodded up the hill. "I composed some of my best work at the lighthouse, and Orla wrote some of her best poetry up there. Billy was dead set on a museum, investing all his time and energy into recovering our things and restoring the house. What changed?"

"Wayne and his billions can be persuasive. I'll see what I can find out. And I'll see if Father Keating can tell me anything about spirit realm hookups. He owns an impressive occult library. *And* I'll replace your bourbon."

"Thank you."

"You're welcome." Gethsemane started for the door. She almost crashed through Eamon as he materialized in front of her.

"One more thing," he said. "I'm glad you're here."

"Me too."

Her cheek buzzed where he kissed her.

*   *   *

Gethsemane's stomach rumbled. As sweet as it was for Eamon to fix buttered toast—her ex-fiancé never made breakfast—it wouldn't hold her until lunch. She glanced at her watch. Enough time to swing by the faculty lounge for a muffin before class.

She sensed something amiss as soon as she opened the door. The lights, usually left burning all day despite the protests of the eco-committee, were switched off. Gethsemane waited. No Tchaikovsky warning. She moved to turn on the lights but a hunch drew her farther into the room. Around a corner the glow from a smartphone flashlight illuminated a cluster of boys huddled near the coffee and tea station. Intent on something, they didn't notice her until she switched on a lamp. Gasps and sheepish grins spread as the smartphone disappeared into a pocket. Gethsemane recognized the Toibin twins and one or two others from the orchestra.

Aengus spoke first. "Morning, Miss."

Gethsemane crossed her arms and waited for an explanation. She eyed a box in Feargus's hands.

"Biscuits, Miss," the boy said.

She spotted a tray next to the teapot half-filled with over-sized homemade cookies. She picked one up and sniffed it. Oatmeal. "Is this faculty appreciation day? School tradition to surprise your teachers with cookies?"

No one answered. Several boys looked at the floor. Aengus and Feargus bit their lips, Gethsemane suspected to hide smiles.

"What's in the cookies?" She waved one back and forth between the twins. She was a college professor's daughter. She knew a prank when she saw one.

Feargus spoke up. "Flour, sugar, oats—"

Brown bits of fruit studded the oats. "Raisins?" Gethsemane asked.

"Prunes, Miss," one of the younger boys confessed. Aengus elbowed him.

Prunes. Nature's Ex-Lax. She grabbed the box from Feargus and dropped the cookie in it. She held the box out. "The rest of them."

Aengus and Feargus stepped aside as one of the other boys dumped the tray's contents into the container.

Gethsemane admired a well-executed prank. Her father's office had been in the engineering building at Bayview University. The math and engineering students often colluded to pull off feats like constructing a replica of the Eiffel Tower on the Dean's lawn and rigging the basketball scoreboard to play Tetris. A few of their better pranks had involved cows. Prune cookies in the faculty lounge, however...

"Boys, this stunt was old when I was your age. It's unworthy of a St. Brennan's lad." She tucked the box under her arm. "Since no harm was done I'll dispose of these and we'll forget this happened."

"Thank you, Miss," the boys said in unison.

"But if I ever catch you again, I'll show no mercy. Understand?"

"Yes, Miss."

"After all," she said in mock seriousness, "the first rule of successful pranking is don't get caught."

The overhead lights snapped on without warning. Gethsemane and the boys jumped. Headmaster Riordan appeared around the corner.

Hands on hips, he demanded to know what the boys were doing in the faculty lounge, strictly off-limits to students. When none of the boys answered he directed his question to Gethsemane.

What to do? Rat on the boys like a responsible teacher? Or remember what life was like at their age and cover for them this once?

"I asked them in, Headmaster." Sympathy and secret admiration drove her decision in part. Selfishness also provided an impetus. Trouble with the headmaster might result in suspension or expulsion. She needed Aengus, Feargus, and the other musicians for the orchestra.

"Allowing students into the lounge is highly improper, Dr. Brown."

"I know, sir, but I, um," her glance fell on the box of cookies, "saw a mouse."

"A mouse?" Riordan looked around his feet. "Where?"

Gethsemane held up the box. "Running across the cookies while they were laid out on the tray. Almost put my hand on him. I ran out into the hall and saw the boys passing by and asked them to find him."

"No luck, sir, I'm afraid," Feargus said.

Riordan pranced as if he feared the rodent in question might skitter across his shoe at any moment. "I'll have the custodians in as soon as possible."

"And I'll dispose of these." Gethsemane patted the cookie box. "I'm sure no one wants cookies touched by mouse paws."

"Quite right," Riordan said. "You boys go to class now."

The boys filed out of the lounge. Gethsemane started after them.

"One moment." Riordan stopped her. "Hieronymus Dunleavy will be on campus today. I'm sure he'll want to pay you a visit, see how rehearsals are coming."

Several curse words flew through Gethsemane's head. Didn't Dunleavey have a job to go to or a trophy wife to amuse? "I look forward to seeing him," she said. Her second lie before morning bell.

Hieronymus Dunleavy's timing sucked. He burst into the music room ahead of Riordan just as the timpani missed his cue, throwing off the clarinets, confusing the flutes, and sending the entire orchestra into cacophony.

"Sounds a bit rough," he said.

"I'm sure this isn't typical," the headmaster reassured him. "Tell him, Dr. Brown."

Before Gethsemane could answer, Dunleavy stepped over to

Colm. "Colm Nolan. You're a head taller every time I see you. You've got your mother's looks."

"Thank you, sir. I take that as a compliment. My mother's beautiful."

Gethsemane slid between them. Did anyone else notice how tightly Colm clenched his hand? She pried his bow loose and steered him back to his seat. "Today's the boys' first run-through of the piece I've selected for the competition."

"And what have you chosen?" Dunleavy asked. "Beethoven? Mahler? Perhaps my favorite, Paganini?"

"It's meant to be a surprise."

Riordan's jaw tensed.

"But I'll let you in on the secret."

"I'm an excellent secret-keeper," Dunleavy said.

"'St. Brennan's Ascendant.'"

"I'm not familiar with the piece," Riordan said. "One of your own compositions?"

"No, sir, it's a previously unknown concerto by Eamon McCarthy."

"My God!" Riordan exclaimed.

"Good Lord!" Dunleavy shouted.

"Who's Eamon McCarthy?" one of the younger boys whispered. Aengus elbowed him.

"Eejit," said Feargus, also whispering. "You've just been playing his music."

"Wasn't payin' attention when she told us his name. Who was he?"

"Eamon McCarthy's the composer who lived up by the lighthouse. Threw his wife off a cliff."

"What'd he do that for?"

Aengus elbowed the boy again.

Gethsemane shushed them.

"How can this be, Dr. Brown?" Riordan asked. "A new McCarthy concerto? He composed his last piece shortly before—" Riordan glanced at the boys.

"He offed himself," one said. Gethsemane's glare silenced the ensuing giggles.

Riordan finished his sentence. "Before his death."

Obfuscate, insinuate. "McCarthy gave a *performance* of his last known work shortly before he died. But he was renowned for his speed of composition. He wrote symphonies in days. And Carrick Point lighthouse is packed with boxes waiting to be explored."

"You discovered the concerto in a box in the lighthouse? Remarkable," Dunleavy said.

Gethsemane spread her hands and shrugged.

"And he called this piece 'St. Brennan's Ascendant'?" Riordan asked.

"Well, no," Gethsemane said. "The title's mine. It seemed fitting."

"What about his nephew, Billy? He inherited the rights to McCarthy's work. He'd have to authorize any performance. I'll need to speak to counsel about the legality—"

"I spoke to Billy by phone." Gethsemane hid her crossed fingers in a skirt pocket. "The premiere of a new piece at a prestigious competition would help future sales. And Billy's all for anything that will benefit the community and honor his uncle's memory."

Riordan clapped his hands. "A world premiere of a lost McCarthy concerto. And on the twenty-fifth anniversary of his death, the seventy-fifth anniversary of the All-County."

"It'll make news if not history," Gethsemane said.

"McCarthy concertos are noted for the complexity of their solos." Dunleavy looked at Colm. "You're sure you've got the right soloist?"

"I'm sure all of my musicians are up to the challenges of the piece." Something in Dunleavy's manner stirred a deep-seated protectiveness toward the boys, even Colm. Where had *that* come from?

"I hope you're right, Dr. Brown. St. Brennan's is overdue for a win. I'd hate a weak link to ruin it." He glanced at Colm again. Colm, flushed, stared at the floor.

"They'll be ready." Gethsemane blocked Dunleavy's view of Colm. "We'll all be."

Dunleavy cornered Gethsemane after rehearsal. "A word about the Nolan boy."

"Amazing. Such impassioned playing. Not many musicians twice his age can arouse such emotion in an audience."

"He's hardly Chuanyun Li."

Dunleavy knew Chinese violin prodigies?

"Colm Nolan's as close to musical genius as most people are likely to come in a lifetime. With him as soloist and Ruairi O'Brien as concertmaster—"

"Had you considered the O'Brien boy as soloist?"

Was Dunleavy anti-Colm or pro-Ruairi? "Until I heard Colm play. He's the better violinist."

"Marginally. Perhaps O'Brien is a bit too reticent to handle the glare of soloist spotlight. What about one of the other boys? This *is* honors orchestra. They wouldn't be members if they weren't skilled instrumentalists."

Anti-Colm. "Technically skilled, yes. But only Colm and Ruairi transcended technical skill to form an emotional connection with the music and translated that bond into a shared experience with listeners. Of the two, Colm did it best." Colm's reaction to Dunleavy in the music room flashed to mind. "Do I sense some animosity toward Colm?"

Dunleavy bristled. "Animosity is a strong word, Dr. Brown. I'm only thinking of St. Brennan's. You must admit, the Nolan boy is undisciplined, unreliable."

"I admit he's horologically challenged."

"I find his playing a bit too fervent."

"Eamon McCarthy's playing was downright fevered. His music demands fervent."

"You've made your decision." Dunleavy straightened his shirt cuffs. "I hope we won't be disappointed."

She heard him before she saw him. Soft humming, Beethoven's "Symphony No. 4," floated from behind a set of bookshelves in the otherwise deserted school library. Gethsemane followed the music to its origin—Colm. He didn't notice her as he methodically flipped each book on the shelf so its pages faced out.

"Looking for a bestseller, Colm? I doubt you'll find it back here in," Gethsemane read the label on the shelf, "transportation."

Colm froze, his hand on a book. "Hello, Miss. Didn't see you."

"Obviously."

"I can explain. I was just, uh, reshelving some books left lying about."

"By turning their spines around so no one can read their titles? Where's the librarian?"

"She, uh, stepped out. There was some mix-up with some books about, uh, female stuff being delivered here instead of the, uh, girls' school."

"Convenient." First prune cookies, now this. "What is going on, Mr. Nolan?"

"It's Pranks Week, Miss. We have a sort of unofficial competition."

"How widespread is this competition? Are all the boys in on it?"

"Practically, at least in the upper school. Some of the faculty, too."

"What faculty?"

"Mr. Grennan."

"The math teacher?"

"He's held the title of Master Prankster since he was a student at St. Brennan's. No one's beaten him. Ruairi's come close."

"Ruairi who doesn't say two words and then only when spoken to?"

"It's the quiet ones you have to watch out for, Miss."

Gethsemane shook her head. "I'm going to watch you turn all those books back the right way. I suggest you hurry before the librarian sorts out the 'delivery error.' I doubt she'll be understanding."

Colm started turning books.

"Out of curiosity, what did Ruairi do that put him in contention for the title?"

"Painted maths equations on three goats and set 'em loose in the halls. The equations worked out to one, two, and four. Took Headmaster an hour to realize there were only three goats."

A variation on a classic. "And Grennan?"

"Invented the Interscholastic Underwater Badminton League. Scores posted in the sports section of the *Dispatch* every week for three years before the league folded. Even had an award, the Leo G. Croyden Prize. Never was any such league. The scores were all fake, no one ever played a game. Most folks still haven't copped on it was a sham."

Francis Grennan in the same class of trickster as Steve Noll and Morris Newburger. Her respect grew.

"You won't tell?"

"What, and disappoint legions of die-hard underwater badminton fans?"

Gethsemane crossed items off her mental to-do list: fax financial documents to man about to sell out his dead uncle, drop bombshell about Eamon's new concerto, alienate major donor by selecting arrogant Head Boy as soloist. Done. Done. And done. What remained? Ask priest how two souls can find each other in heaven and buy liquor. Always save the easiest tasks for last.

As she entered the churchyard a woman called, "Why is a raven like a writing desk?"

Gethsemane recognized the riddle from *Alice's Adventures in Wonderland*, her niece's favorite book. She recognized the speaker's voice from the night of her bicycle accident on Carrick Point Road. Nuala Sullivan, who may or may not be haunted by Orla McCarthy. She followed the voice to the cloister garden, expecting to greet the wild-haired, barefooted creature who'd run into her. Surprise, surprise.

Nuala, thick gray hair twisted into a neat chignon, high-collared dress replaced by a pretty blue tea-length floral, stood in black patent high heels next to a table laid with a tea service and a tiered stand full of finger sandwiches, scones, and sweets. "Have you guessed the riddle yet?"

"No, I give it up," Gethsemane quoted. She'd read *Alice* to her niece at least a dozen times. "What's the answer?"

"I haven't the slightest idea." Nuala held up the teapot. "Join me?"

Cue "Pathétique."

Why did a neat, attractive, calm Nuala in a church garden in the daytime seem creepier than a disheveled, frantic Nuala on an isolated road at night? Gethsemane took a deep breath. Tchaikovsky's warning or no, this was her chance to ask Nuala about Orla. Maybe she'd learn something to help Eamon find her on the other side. "Delighted. Thank you." She sat at the table. Would Nuala remember their run-in? "What a lovely dress you're wearing."

Nuala busied herself with the tea. "Nicer than the one I had on when you crashed into me. But not half as lovely as that dress of Orla's you're wearing."

She remembered. Except for who ran into whom. "About that night. You mentioned Orla."

"Did I?" She held up a sugar bowl. "One or two?"

"Three. Sweet tooth. You said Orla made you run out into the road."

Nuala stirred sugar into a cup of steaming amber liquid. "Can't imagine why I'd say such a thing." She handed the teacup to Gethsemane. "Drink up before it gets cold."

Gethsemane raised the cup to her lips. She hesitated.

Gooseflesh popped out on her arms and "Pathétique" played louder. She set the cup in her saucer.

"Don't you like China black?" Nuala asked.

"Um, do you have milk?"

"Of course." Nuala handed Gethsemane a creamer without taking her eyes off her. No chance to dump the tea.

"You seemed upset the night you—the night of the accident. Distraught. You said Orla made you do it. You said she was punishing you."

"I hadn't been feeling well. I think I had a fever." She sat across from Gethsemane. "I might have said any number of things. You can't put stock in fever speech. You don't like the tea."

"Won't you have some? I hate to drink alone."

Nuala poured tea for herself and stirred in milk and a half dozen sugar cubes. "*Sláinte.*" She drained the cup in two gulps.

Nuala wasn't crazy enough to poison herself. So why did "Pathétique" still play? Gethsemane sipped. Chocolaty, mellow. "It's quite good."

Nuala refilled Gethsemane's cup. "There's an art to brewing proper tea. Most can't. My father taught me."

"Sullivan the Magnificent?"

Nuala's smile made her seem twenty years younger. "You're a fan?"

"I've heard of him. Didn't he perform at the Athaneum?"

"He headlined at the theater. Folks would come from all over the county and queue for hours for a ticket to one of his shows. Peg and I used to help him get ready."

"You said your father had a gift."

"Da was brilliant."

"A gift you share." Gethsemane locked eyes with Nuala. Nuala's grin made her shiver. Fever-schmever. Nuala was crazy like a fox was crazy. She remembered talking about Orla. Why the amnesia routine?

"You must be hungry after a long day at school." Nuala piled finger sandwiches on a plate. "Have some."

Gethsemane took the plate. A variety of salads and spreads nestled between the neat, crustless bread rectangles: tuna, egg salad with dill, chicken, cream cheese.

"Do you like mysteries, Dr. Brown? Novels, I mean."

"I'm more of a science fiction fan." She picked up an egg salad sandwich.

"I love mysteries. Agatha Christie's my favorite. Did you know she worked as an apothecary's assistant during the First World War? That's how she learned so much about poisons. On-the-job training. Dame Christie poisoned a lot of people."

"In her novels."

"In her novels." Nuala smiled. "But wouldn't apothecary's assistant be a lovely job if you wanted to poison someone for real?"

Unsure how to answer, Gethsemane nibbled her sandwich. "What a—unique—tasting egg salad. It's—" *Bitter and slightly spicy.* She looked more closely at the filling. Those green specks weren't dill.

"It's a family recipe."

"Gethsemane!" A hand snatched the mostly uneaten sandwich away. "You'll spoil your appetite. Or did you forget you promised to take tea with me?" Father Keating moved the plate out of Gethsemane's reach.

"Dr. Brown is my guest, Father." Nuala flashed the priest an unholy glare. Gethsemane shivered. A blast of "Pathétique" filled her ear as if Tchaikovsky was saying *I told you so.*

"Some other time, Nuala. Dr. Brown and I have things to discuss. Besides, Peg'll be looking for you. You'd better go on home. Leave these things. I'll have the sextons clean up."

Nuala started to speak, apparently thought better of it, stood and smoothed her dress. She shook Gethsemane's hand. "Lovely chatting with you."

"Thank you for the tea."

"Perhaps some wine next time."

"I don't see any wine."

"There isn't any."

Nuala brushed past Father Keating and disappeared from view.

"I took a bite of that sandwich." Gethsemane gagged. "What'd she put in it?"

"Foxglove. I found it and an empty bread wrapper in the rubbish bin."

"Foxglove?" Gethsemane laid her fingertips against her neck and checked her pulse. She still had one. And she was breathing. "Is that deadly? Do I need to go to the hospital?" Did they still pump people's stomachs?

Father Keating held up the remains of her sandwich. "You only took a wee bite. And Nuala didn't put much foxglove in the food, judging by the amount of the plant I found in the bin."

"Not enough to kill me, just enough to make me ill?" She checked her pulse again. "How fast does foxglove kick in?"

"Why don't we go inside?" The cleric placed a hand on Gethsemane's arm.

She shook it off. "Why don't we call the police?" Was the nausea from anger or the egg salad? "That maniac shouldn't be running around loose."

"I'll call her sister. Nuala's probably off her meds again. Peg'll take her to hospital."

"Take *her* to the hospital? I vote doctor for me, jail for her."

"Finesse in handling folks with Nuala's needs is not the Garda's strong point. They'll only...agitate her. I don't want to push her into setting anything on fire. We'll let Peg handle Nuala. I'll drive you to A and E."

Gethsemane calmed herself. She *had* only nibbled a corner of the sandwich. And the priest didn't seem to think she was in real danger.

"Has Nuala ever pulled a stunt like this before?"

"She used to spike the punch at the spring fete with aloe vera juice. Until we started serving beverages in individual bottles. Never seriously injured anyone."

"I probably didn't eat enough egg salad to harm an adult."

"A onceover by a doctor would reassure you, though."

"Yeah," Gethsemane admitted, "It would."

A couple of hours later, given the all clear by the emergency room physician, Gethsemane accepted tea back at the rectory.

"Bewley's, unadulterated." Father Keating poured. "Tell me how things are going."

"Except for near-poisoning, things are going well. The orchestra's made remarkable progress. They're getting excited about the challenge of an honors orchestra competition. And Ruairi's starting to come out of his shell."

"Colm's not giving you too much trouble?"

"He's yet to show up on time and he's still arrogant and disrespectful when he doesn't have a violin in his hands. But he's already memorized the entire piece and plays the cadenza like he wrote it. I'll give him a while longer to adjust his attitude."

"I'll pray for you both. And I'll go call Peg, make sure she corralled Nuala."

Gethsemane looked around the rectory's parlor while Father Keating telephoned. Books on subjects from aerospace mechanics to zoogeography, in several languages, filled every available space. Framed photos of Father Keating, hair varying from red to gray, posing with people in civilian and religious garb dotted shelves and tabletops. One photo, the largest, featured a redheaded Father Keating in academic cap and gown next to another, almost identical, redhead wearing a priest's collar.

Gethsemane gestured to the photo when Father Keating returned.

"I didn't know you were a twin."

"Not quite. Michael and I were nineteen months apart." He settled into an armchair.

"I have a theological question, Fath—Tim."

"My specialty."

"If one soul preceded another, say a wife's before her

husband's, into the afterlife, how could the two find each other on the other side?"

"Ask me something easy, like explain quantum physics or how many angels can dance on the head of a pin?" He thought for a moment. "I don't know that they can find each other, or want to. The Good Book says 'they which shall be accounted worthy to obtain that world, and the resurrection of the dead, neither marry nor are given in marriage. Neither can they die anymore for they are equal unto the angels.' They're children of God, free from worldly cares or preoccupations."

"What if they didn't make it to heaven or only one of them did? What if they're in different places and one soul's actively searching for the other?"

"Mythology abounds with tales of someone traveling to the underworld to rescue a lost love: Demeter and Persephone, Orpheus and Eurydice, Pare and Hutu, Hiku and Kawelu. But you're asking me something else."

"I'm not sure what I'm asking."

"What's brought this on?"

Tell him about the ghost? The ghosts? "Just brainstorming potential plots for a future work. An opera." What was the penalty for lying to a priest?

"Ah, I love opera." Father Keating waved a hand at his books. "I have several volumes of mythology in my library: Greco-Roman, West African, Japanese. At one point I planned to become a folklorist. You're welcome to borrow any of them."

"Thanks. I'll give you the clergy discount on show tickets." Gethsemane finished her tea. "One more question. Is there anything you know of that would prevent, actually block, souls from finding each other?"

"All of the myths share the theme that if one party breaks the explicit rules of escape from death—eating, looking back too soon, opening a basket—the soul is lost to the underworld forever."

"Could a third party throw up a roadblock? Sorry, that's two questions."

"My brother's Grimoires list banishing and binding spells designed to keep a spirit from wandering."

"Thanks for the information. And the rescue." Gethsemane stood. She motioned to Father Keating to keep his seat. "Don't trouble yourself. I'll show myself out." She hesitated in the doorway. "Did Pegeen Sullivan get control of her sister?"

"Yet again. Sadly, Peg gets lots of practice. You won't have to worry about running into her. You'll be fine."

"As long as I don't accept any more food from strangers."

Gethsemane gave in to the urge to look over her shoulder as she pedaled to the liquor store. No picnic basket-wielding maniacs in sight. If you could poison a woman's sandwich, could you poison a man's whiskey?

Gethsemane flung open the cottage door. "Eamon! Irish! Where are you?"

"I'm right here." He materialized a few inches in front of her. "Why the shouting?"

"Sorry. I get excited when someone poisons me." She shrugged out of her mac. "Or tries to."

"Poison? What are you on about?"

"Today at Our Lady of Perpetual Sorrows Nuala Sullivan fed me egg salad laced with foxglove."

Eamon's aura flashed a mixture of orange-yellow and blue.

"Are you all right? Do you need an ambulance? You should sit down."

He motioned toward the hall bench.

"I'm fine." Gethsemane waved him off and headed to the study. "Father Tim took me to the emergency room. I didn't eat enough to make me ill."

"Where was the good father while the poisoning was going on?"

"He saved me. He ripped the sandwich out of my hand before I could take a second bite."

"Did you call the gardaí?"

"No. I wanted to but Father Tim convinced me to let Pegeen handle Nuala."

Eamon's aura faded to yellow. "Story of Peg's life. Nuala puts on a holy show, Peg gets the call to clean up after her."

"Father Tim said the cops don't handle Nuala well."

"They don't. They deal with her by slapping on handcuffs and dragging her to A and E to be pumped full of sedatives before they cart her off to jail. Nuala's not one to go gentle, either. More than one guard has ended up with a black eye or bruised ribs after tangling with Nuala Sullivan."

"Pegeen must love her sister dearly to put up with so much drama."

"The Sullivan sisters' relationship is complicated. You know what sibling rivalry is like."

Did she ever. Been there, done that, had the t-shirt to prove it. "My eldest sister is mean as hell but she's not dangerously psychotic."

Eamon poured Gethsemane a drink. "I suspect some of Nuala's crazy is sham crazy. She keeps her wits about her enough to throw suspicion for her antics on Peg when it suits her. Like the time she spiked the church garden committee's tea with laxatives. They found an empty pill bottle from Fitzgerald's. Nuala claimed Peg had stolen the pills from work. Lucky for Peg, she went shopping in Cork with Orla the day of the committee meeting, giving her an alibi. Turns out Nuala stole the pills herself when she'd visited Peg for lunch."

"My sisters and I have gotten into it more than a few times but we've never framed each other for crimes. Why would Nuala set up the only person in her life willing to help her? And why does Pegeen put up with it? Why not have Nuala committed? Permanently. With her track record it shouldn't be too difficult."

"Peg promised their father she'd always look after Nuala.

Nuala was the favorite, both sisters knew it. Peg would've done anything their father asked of her, including protect Nuala, to try and win his favor. She resents Nuala—something she'd not admit to anyone in the world except me and Orla. Nuala embarrasses her. She's also afraid people will think she's off her nut, too. Guilt by relation. Nuala resents Peg just as much. Hates Peg being seen as the responsible, respectable sister."

"Responsible, respectable sisters don't set fires or adulterate food."

"Nuala doesn't see things the way others do."

"So two sisters who resent each other are bound together by a promise one made to the father who wasn't there for either of them. Straight out of a daytime TV talk show. At least Pegeen had you and Orla. Did Nuala have any friends?"

"Only Deirdre Lynch, an unholy alliance if ever there was one. Put her in near-constant contact with Deirdre's brother, Jimmy. If you ever wanted to learn creative techniques for breaking the law, Jimmy would be your perfect tutor."

"Do you think Jimmy might include murder in the curriculum?"

"You're suggesting Nuala—" The orange-yellow glow returned. "I don't want to think so, for Peg's sake."

"But it's possible."

"Spiking my bourbon, maybe. Lord knows she's had enough practice spiking drinks. But, honestly, I can't see her pushing Orla off a cliff. I guess she coulda done but," Eamon shook his head, "damn, I'd much rather the killer be some random header passing through. To think of Nuala shoving Orla..."

"Most killers know their victims."

"Offering words of comfort is not in your skill set, is it?"

"I soothe with music, not words." She set her drink on the coffee table and went back to the coat rack. "I'm going to use words to convince O'Reilly to re-open your case. I'll be at the garda station if you need me."

*   *   *

She found Inspector O'Reilly coming from the garda station's gym. His hair was wet, shirt collar unbuttoned, and he smelled fresh from the shower. Gethsemane reminded herself why she came to the station and forced herself to focus.

"You've recovered from your tea party, Dr. Brown?" O'Reilly juggled his necktie and suit jacket.

"May I help you?" She reached for his tie. "How did you know about the egg salad? I didn't report it."

O'Reilly handed her his jacket. "The hospital did after Pegeen Sullivan brought her sister in for stabilization. Are you sure you don't want to bring charges?"

"I doubt she'd be deemed competent to stand trial, even if I did press charges. Nuala needs to be in a secure psychiatric facility."

"I'm guessing you're not here to debate the merits of the legal versus mental health systems with me." He knotted his tie and reclaimed his jacket. "I'm going to live dangerously and guess you tracked me down to talk about the McCarthys, probably to ask about the video you discovered at the library."

"Well, since you mentioned it."

"I have an appointment with Mrs. Toibin in twenty minutes."

"This won't take that long. I think Nuala killed Eamon. Either one of her food-tampering pranks got out of hand or she got tired of just making people sick. And I think Jimmy Lynch killed Orla. That's why he lied about seeing Eamon's car the night of her murder. He needed to shift blame. Or maybe Nuala and Jimmy were in it together."

"You've gone from a single killer to a conspiracy."

"Okay, so my theory's a little messy. Who says murder has to be tied up in a neat package?"

"We gardaí like things neat. If you'll excuse me, I've got to go pick up a video before it's lost for another twenty-five years."

*   *   *

A sign outside Bunratty's Off License, in the heart of Dunmullach and second in size only to Our Lady of Perpetual Sorrows, boasted the largest selection of alcoholic beverages west of Dublin. Gethsemane believed the boast.

A dozen people wandered aisles lined with liquor bottles in every size, shape, and color. Siobhan Moloney, arrayed in a shimmering apple green caftan, chatted with another woman near the wine section at the rear of the store. Compared to the woman's paleness—gray bobbed hair, gray wool blazer, gray tweed skirt, gray low-heeled pumps—Siobhan glowed even brighter than the night of her ghost whispering performance. Gethsemane imagined Siobhan siphoning the color out of the other woman like some sort of polychromatic parasite.

Gethsemane, hoping to escape Siobhan's notice, approached the register. She asked the mustachioed clerk if he carried Waddell and Dobb Double-oaked Twelve-year-old Reserve.

"I'm sorry," he said. "We haven't any in stock. Billy's order hasn't come in yet. I expect it in a few days." Gethsemane remembered the barman at the Mad Rabbit telling her the bourbon had to be special ordered. The clerk went on. "I'll have Kieran bring it up as soon as it arrives."

"How do you know where to have Kieran bring anything?" Gethsemane asked.

"You're Dr. Brown, the new school teacher. Everyone knows you're watching the old McCarthy place for Billy. Dunmullach's a small village."

"Hey! You!" A gaunt man with gray stubble dotting his pockmarked cheeks stood in the doorway. He shoved gloves into a pocket of his worn motorcycle jacket and pointed a bony finger at Gethsemane. "You're the one. What's the idea of stickin' yer damned nose in my business?"

"How could I? I have no idea who you are," Gethsemane said, not keeping the annoyance from her voice.

So tiresome, being known by everybody in town without knowing anyone.

"I'm Jimmy Lynch." He strode to Gethsemane and breathed down in her face. He smelled of onions and cigarettes.

Jimmy Lynch. The one who lied to the cops about seeing Eamon's car in town the night Orla was murdered. Maybe the one who killed her.

He held a finger under Gethsemane's nose, so close it tickled. "Quit stirring up trouble, asking bloody stupid questions about things what don't concern you."

She refused to flinch. She stood as tall as five foot-three allowed and met Jimmy's glare. "What things? Lies about people's whereabouts? Frame ups? Hidden agendas?"

Jimmy lowered his voice to a menacing rumble. "It's been twenty-five years. Leave it be."

"Twenty-five years or twenty-five days, like Kipling said, nothing's ever settled until it's settled right."

Jimmy stepped closer. "Why I—"

"That's enough now." The clerk slammed the counter. "Back off."

Jimmy hesitated, then took two steps back.

Gethsemane realized she'd been holding her breath and exhaled slowly. "Why do you care if I inquire about the McCarthy case? Do you know anything about it?"

"Why should I?"

"You were the one who put Eamon's car on Carrick Point Road in time to kill his wife."

"I saw what I saw."

"Are you positive? Maybe you got the time wrong. Maybe you saw Eamon's car later. Or maybe you saw the real killer's car and mistook if for Eamon's. I'm sure you wouldn't lie outright just to get even with Eamon."

Jimmy balled his fist. Gethsemane tensed.

Someone new spoke up. "Maybe you should leave well enough alone."

Siobhan and the gray woman stood near the register. The gray woman said, "Best to let the dead stay buried. Don't you agree, Siobhan?"

Siobhan shrugged. "Sometimes the dead have things to say."

"Nothing that would interest Dr. Brown. I doubt she has time to be poking into closets, being busy with preparations for the All-County."

"The orchestra will be ready in time," Gethsemane said. "Miss?"

The woman shook Gethsemane's hand. "Sullivan. Pegeen Sullivan." Eamon's friend and Nuala's keeper.

Pegeen said to Jimmy, "You better go. Deirdre will be home soon. You know how she gets when no one's there."

"The feck do I care about Deirdre's moods?"

"Fine way to talk about your own sister."

The clerk cut off Jimmy's retort. "Was there something you came in for, Jimmy? Besides getting in folks' faces, I mean."

He jerked his head towards the coolers that lined one of the store's walls. "The Franciscan Wells Rebel Red," he said. "A case."

"Fine," the clerk said. "You run on home now, before your sister gets there. I'll charge your account and have Kieran bring the Rebel Red by the house in time for supper."

Jimmy started to protest. He looked from the clerk to Pegeen to Siobhan to the cricket bat that had appeared from behind the counter to rest in the clerk's grip. Ten seconds passed. Jimmy shoved his hands into his gloves, adjusted his jacket, then stomped out to a motorcycle parked in a loading zone. Gethsemane relaxed as he sped down the street.

Pegeen whispered near her ear, "He's not one to be on the wrong side of."

"Know him well?" Gethsemane asked.

"Cousin." Her breath brushed Gethsemane's cheek.

"Charming guy."

Pegeen moved away.

"He's not likely to bother you if you don't get in his way.

Selling pills to young fellas and stealing pensioners' checks from post boxes is about all he's good for."

"He hasn't beaten anyone up for a good six, eight months," Siobhan said. She handed her basket to the clerk. The look in her eyes contradicted the smile she flashed Gethsemane. Real meanness lurked beneath Siobhan's peacock finery and ghost hunting mumbo jumbo. Jimmy Lynch wasn't the only one in Dunmullach with a "wrong side."

The clerk rang up Siobhan's purchase—four bottles of Chianti and a pint of vodka—then took Pegeen's basket. Bottles clinked as Siobhan cradled the brown paper bag that held them.

"Having a party, Siobhan?" Pegeen asked.

"I like a glass of wine with dinner. Anything wrong with that?"

"No, nothing." Pegeen pulled her wallet from her purse and counted money.

"Anything else I can help you with?" the clerk asked Gethsemane as he bagged Pegeen's bottle of merlot. "I'm sorry about the bourbon."

Gethsemane waved a hand. "No problem. A lack of bourbon is hardly an emergency, even if it is Waddell and Dobb Double-oaked."

"Kieran'll leave it on the porch if you're not in when he brings it up."

"Maybe you can spare a bottle for Pegeen," Siobhan said to Gethsemane. "No doubt Billy ordered more than you'll be able to drink during your time here." She turned to Pegeen. "Since Waddell and Dobb Double-oaked's so hard to come by you should take advantage and nab a bottle or two."

"What are you on about, Siobhan?" Pegeen held up her wine. "I don't drink bourbon."

"No?" Siobhan shrugged. "My mistake. I thought I saw you with a couple bottles."

Pegeen blinked a few times, then frowned. "When did you see me?"

"Dunno. A while back."

"Maybe thirty-odd years ago, as a wedding present for Eamon. Not since."

"Maybe not."

"You have a good memory," Gethsemane said to Siobhan.

"Never forget a thing. I haven't forgotten about our sessions," she said to Gethsemane.

"Sessions?" Pegeen asked.

"Dr. Brown thinks Eamon McCarthy's spirit is—"

Gethsemane interrupted. "I think I let my imagination get the better of me."

Siobhan clucked her tongue. "Don't be embarrassed to admit you're open to visitations from the other side of the veil. This is Ireland. No one will think you're crazy for saying you see ghosts. Why don't we go ahead and schedule our next appointment?"

"About that. I still don't think the time is quite right. Let me—um—talk to Father Keating and check the—um—*Farmers' Almanac* and I'll get back to you."

"The *Farmers' Almanac?*"

"Yeah." Gethsemane started for the door. "You know, the book that tells you the best times to harvest crops and slaughter pigs and—uh—hunt ghosts." She pushed the door open and stepped out onto the sidewalk. "I'll call you," she said.

The door swung shut behind her, cutting off the sound of laughter.

Seven

Outside, a few elderly women chatted in front of the grocery and boys kicked a soccer ball in an empty lot. No sign of Jimmy Lynch. Gethsemane started for Carraigfaire then thought of Jimmy ambushing her on Carrick Point Road. Best give him time to decide jumping her wasn't worth missing supper. Meanwhile, might as well have a drink at the Mad Rabbit.

Singing—a sonorous baritone—greeted her as soon she opened the door. She recognized "Whiskey, You're the Devil" from the inordinate amount of her senior year at Vassar spent hanging out in an Irish pub in town trying to attract a session musician's attention away from the owner's daughter. She didn't win the handsome bodhran player but she did gain a repertoire of Irish songs.

The crowd of patrons and wait staff gathered near the pub's piano hid the singer. His voice rose above their heads and filled the room with *a capella* lyrics:

> *...Do not wrong me*
> *Don't take my daughter from me*
> *For if you do I will torment you*
> *And after death a ghost will haunt you...*

Gethsemane reflexively fingered the song's notes and hummed under her breath. She moved closer, squeezing between shoulders and dodging elbows as she maneuvered through the throng. At a table, hat at his elbow, tie loosened, black leather monkstraps tapping the rhythm, sat the last person she expected to see singing pub songs like Tommy Maken. "...*O whiskey, you're my darlin', drunk or sober.*"

She gawked. Inspector O'Reilly had a voice.

Applause erupted. O'Reilly stood and bowed then took a long swallow from his pint glass.

"I'm amazed," Gethsemane said.

O'Reilly paused with his pint halfway to his lips. He blinked and frowned. His smile, which didn't reach his gray eyes, suggested good manners more than gladness to see her. "Evenin', Dr. Brown. Takin' a break from the library?"

"No library today." Gethsemane met the inspector's gaze. "Case load lighten up?"

O'Reilly tensed, hesitated, then relaxed into a genuine smile. He raised his glass to Gethsemane. "Da always told me no matter how busy the bastards keep you, make time to slip out for a pint and bit o' craic now and again. Keeps you sane."

Before Gethsemane could respond, a man clapped O'Reilly on the shoulder. "Sing us another."

The other pub-goers shouted agreement. One voice, angry, words slurred by alcohol, shouted above the rest. "Lez hear the 'murican play somethin'. Ain't she some sorta big deal 'muzishun?"

All eyes turned to the bar. Declan Hurley hunched over the glass wrapped in his fist.

Murphy the barman refilled the ex-cop's glass. "Leave be, Declan. Just drink your drink."

Gethsemane shrugged and laughed. "Too bad I don't have my violin with me."

A man in a tweed cap stepped forward and extended a violin case.

"You can use mine if ya like."

"You just happen to have a violin with you?"

The man puffed out his chest and grinned. "Never go out

without her." He held the case out farther. "Go on, you can play her. She won't mind."

"Yes, Dr. Brown." Pegeen appeared near the door. "Please honor us."

Gethsemane accepted the violin with thanks and set it on a nearby table. She opened the case and lifted the violin, cradling it more gently than her newborn niece as she examined the sculptural pegbox, the inscription along the ribs, the marquetry inlaid scene on the back. "This is a Derazey. Mid-to-late eighteen-hundreds?"

The violin's owner nodded. "Me great-great-granddad was a sailor. He saved some French chap from a reefin' by a gang of thugs. Frenchie gave him the fiddle by way of thanks."

"Being a hero has rewards." Gethsemane ran her fingers along the bow. "This is priceless. You're sure you don't mind?"

Hurley interrupted. "He tolja he didn'. Ya gonna play or jes yap?"

Murphy frowned. "Declan, I'm warnin' ya..." Both he and O'Reilly stepped closer to Hurley.

Hurley buried his face in his glass.

Gethsemane positioned the violin and drew the bow across the strings. She adjusted the tuning pegs. Then she played. She opened with "The Spirit of the House." The melody's lonesome tones expressed her sadness and betrayal and anger over being cheated of a promised job, her embarrassment over the mess that passed for her life, her shame over returning home as a failure. Which she wouldn't do. Couldn't do.

She had to win the All-County. A win meant salvaging her career and returning home in triumphal redemption. Her tempo increased into the lighter, brighter "Stranger in Cork and Friendly Visit." A strange sensation filled her chest. Dunmullach's charm pulled her in despite her efforts to remain detached. Western Ireland wove its mysterious spell around her like the morning fog around the Cliffs of Moher. She ended her medley with a jig in their name.

Gethsemane lowered the violin. Everyone stared, not moving

or speaking. Had she committed a cultural faux pas? Broken some unwritten village rule? As the silence reached the point of nerve-wracking, O'Reilly rose from his seat. He clapped once, twice, three times. He clapped faster. The violin's owner joined him. Then Murphy, then one waitress, then another. Soon everyone except Hurley clapped and whistled and stomped their feet. Gethsemane flourished the bow and bowed.

The pub's door banged open and Francis stepped in. "Havin' a hooley are we?"

"Careful with the door, Frankie," Murphy said. "Them walls ain't made o' steel."

"Don't be an old woman, Murph." Francis found a seat at the bar. "What'd I miss?"

"Dr. Brown's virtuosa performance," O'Reilly said. "Looks like St. Brennan's might be a contender in the All-County this year."

"If the All-County was held in a pub," Hurley scowled, "and the judges were all on the piss."

Francis raised his glass to Gethsemane. "Sorry I missed the show. Any chance of an encore?"

Gethsemane waved away the suggestion.

"Come now." Grennan climbed from his barstool and addressed the other patrons. "Who's up for another?"

Cheers and shouts of "Encore!" answered him.

Gethsemane demurred. "Maybe Inspector—"

"Oh, no you don't. I've sense enough not to follow a better act. Besides, it's you they're wantin'."

"Make you a deal. I will if you will," Gethsemane said.

"You first."

Hurley slammed his fist on the bar. "Gwon play," he said, the alcohol's effects rendering his speech almost unintelligible. "Don' pretend yer modest. Play anotherdamsong. Thas' all yer here ferain'tit? To make the music that'll clean the black mark from Dunmullach's sullied reputashun?"

O'Reilly spoke in a low voice. "Watch it, Hurley."

Gethsemane caught Hurley's eye. He glared at her, his gaze

pure meanness. Gethsemane returned the glare, picked up the violin and, without taking her eyes from Hurley's, let fly "The Hanged Man's Lament." The mournful air recounted the tale of an honest man framed for murder by a corrupt officer and hanged.

Francis, now standing behind Gethsemane, chortled. Redness crept up Hurley's face like the tide rolling in. One hand tightened on his glass, the other clenched into a fist. Gethsemane played with more passion, putting particular emphasis on the passages musically depicting the man's torment as his village turns against him, whipped into a frenzy by the corrupt officer's lies. Hurley downed his drink in a gulp and slammed his empty glass on the bar.

"Careful with that, Hurley," Murphy chided. "Glassware's not free."

Gethsemane kept playing. When she reached the last measures, Hurley jumped from his barstool and stepped toward her. He looked at Murphy and O'Reilly, hesitated, then stormed from the pub.

Gethsemane finished the tune as the door swung shut behind him. She lowered the violin and took a deep breath.

Francis whispered in Gethsemane's ear. "Well played, Dr. Brown, very well played indeed."

Gethsemane bit back a smile.

As the applause died down someone reminded O'Reilly he'd promised an encore as well.

O'Reilly tipped his hat to Gethsemane. "Ladies' choice."

"Hmm." Gethsemane tapped her chin. "How about 'Dicey Reilly'?"

"Cute. Hinting at your true feelings about me? You think I'm dicey?"

Gethsemane's grin broke loose. "No hidden meaning, Inspector. I just like the song."

"Dicey Reilly, it is." O'Reilly called to the crowd. "Feel free to join in."

Several men came forward. One sat at the piano, one picked

up a bodhran propped against a wall. One pulled a harmonica from his pocket, another pulled out a tin whistle. A fifth produced a guitar. The tweed-capped man reclaimed his violin. O'Reilly led off with, "*Oh poor old Dicey Reilly has taken to the sup. And poor old Dicey Reilly will never give it up.*" The ad hoc band joined in and soon the entire pub sang the saga of "poor old Dicey Reilly."

At that moment, Gethsemane stopped thinking "poor old Gethsemane Brown."

"The Hanged Man's Lament" replayed in Gethsemane's head. Hurley's reaction convinced her he'd deliberately botched the investigation instead of merely screwing up through incompetence. But why? A grudge against Eamon? Orla? Maybe as a favor or debt to Jimmy Lynch. Maybe Lynch wanted revenge on Eamon enough to blackmail a cop into framing him. How to prove any of this?

Inspector O'Reilly. He'd seemed warm to her at the pub. He hadn't threatened to arrest her, anyway, like he had in the parking lot. Maybe, if she could force herself to check her inner snark demon, she could sweet talk him into letting her examine the evidence from the case. If the garda kept evidence for such a long time. She crossed her fingers.

She rode her bike to the garda station after school, trying not to get too excited. She was probably going on a goose chase. She pedaled faster. She wanted to get to O'Reilly before he got off duty. Even if the evidence had already been destroyed, seeing the inspector wouldn't be a total waste. She could ask him about the Morris video.

She leaned her bike against a wall of the Gothic building and climbed the steps. She opened the door just in time to crash into Inspector O'Reilly coming outside.

The slight scratch of the wool tickled her nose as her faced pressed hard against his jacket. She heard the soft thud of his hat hitting the ground. Two seconds passed. Neither moved. She breathed in the sandalwood and clove of his cologne. She liked sandalwood.

The inspector stepped back. "Sorry." He stooped to pick up his hat. "We seem to keep bumping into each other. Literally."

"Fate. You're the person I was coming to see."

"I'm on my way out."

Gethsemane opened her mouth then caught herself. No snark. She tried again. "When will you be back?"

O'Reilly adjusted his hat and looked at his watch. He looked at Gethsemane then his watch again and sighed. "Will this take long?"

"Only a minute. Or ten." She clasped her hands as if praying. She smiled.

O'Reilly hesitated, seeming to weigh his options. "If I say no, you'll keep at me until I change my mind, won't you?"

She nodded it.

His broad shoulders slumped. "All right. Ten minutes. What do you want?"

"To get into the evidence room or locker or wherever you keep files on old cases."

"No."

"But—"

"Absolutely not. We can't have civilians mucking about in evidence. It's a secure area. Official visitors only and we have to sign in and out."

"You can't make an exception even to let me look at evidence from a twenty-five-year-old case everyone except me considers solved?"

"The McCarthy business. I should have known."

"Please?" She smiled again, her best smile. Her butter-up-potential-donors smile. "Pretty please? I'll buy you a drink. Bushmills. I'll play all of your favorite pub songs on the violin."

O'Reilly stifled the grin playing on his lips. "You're persistent."

"Am I persuasive?"

"That too. I can't let you into the evidence room, but I can go in myself and get the McCarthy box for you. I'll let you examine it in my office for ten minutes."

"Thank you, Inspector." She'd have to keep reminding herself sarcasm wasn't always the best weapon.

She followed him into the station to a bank of elevators. He hummed and twirled his hat as they waited for an elevator car. He seemed to be in a good mood. Why not push luck? The elevator doors opened. "By the way." They stepped inside. "Have you watched the video?"

"What video?"

Gethsemane stared up at O'Reilly, open-mouthed. He pressed the button for the subbasement, his expression deadpan. She sputtered.

O'Reilly watched the numbers over the door illuminate as the elevator descended. "I'm coddin'. I saw it. And I took it into evidence." His expression didn't change.

"Do you play poker? You'd make a killing with your stone face." Forget nice. He owed her for that trick. The doors swished open.

The inspector chuckled. His smile revealed his dimple. "You don't think I pay for these shoes on an Inspector's salary, do you?"

She glanced at his feet. Black leather wingtips. They did look expensive.

She followed him to an office at the rear of the building. A nondescript metal door concealed its interior. He punched a code into the keypad mounted nearby. "Wait here," he said and went inside.

Gethsemane leaned against the wall, wondering what she might find in the evidence box. *If* the evidence still existed. Her confidence in her plan wavered the longer she waited. Would she find much of anything, considering the shoddy investigation? She recalled a case from a town up the road from where she grew up. A man spent eleven and a half years in prison wrongly convicted of murder. The Justice Project decided to help him when the lead detective confessed on his deathbed to coercing a confession instead of actually investigating. The total evidence collected consisted of three photos, a one-page report, and a shoe. There'd been no autopsies on Eamon or Orla thanks to a quack doctor willing to sign death certificates without asking questions. Had anyone taken crime scene photos? Saved the poisoned bottle of Waddell and Dobb? She hoped Hurley had at least taken notes, if only to pretend to do his job.

A moment later the evidence room door opened and O'Reilly stepped into the hall. Empty-handed.

"Inspector?"

"Bloody box is missing."

"Missing? Are you sure?"

"I'm sure. We've evidence from cases a hundred years old. Never had the staff to dispose of it properly. When we started the cold case unit it became my job to organize the damned stuff. I know where I put the box. It's missing. There's an empty space on the shelf where it used to sit."

"Maybe it's just misplaced. Someone moved it."

"I checked. It's not anywhere."

Gethsemane swore. "Sorry."

"Nothing worse than what I said to the clerk. We spent a fortune upgrading our security system six months ago and this happens."

"How do you know it wasn't taken before the upgrade?"

"Do they use the term 'dust catcher' where you're from?"

"Of course."

"That's what those boxes are, dust catchers. So are the shelves they sit on. Covered in dust. We can't keep ahead of it so we stopped trying."

"So?"

"So, the shelf space underneath where the missing box sat is dust-free. Someone took it recently."

"Which suggests I'm not the only one who thinks the McCarthy murders aren't solved."

"Don't get ahead of yourself. That video proves McCarthy

didn't push his wife off a cliff. It doesn't prove anyone else did. Mrs. McCarthy could have thrown herself over the edge. Or fallen. Cliff winds can beat one hundred kilometers an hour."

"How fast is that in English?"

"Faster than sixty miles an hour."

Like being hit by a car on the interstate. Still. "She was murdered, Inspector."

"I know you want to believe that, Dr. Brown, but without more specific evidence—"

"Which has been stolen. Any idea what might have been in the box?"

O'Reilly shrugged. "Not exactly. If I looked in every box I arranged I'd still be at it. Most likely photos, small items of physical evidence preserved from the crime scene, the investigating officer's notes, things like that."

"The officer's notes. Any chance Hurley'd have kept copies of his?"

"I doubt it. No reason to." He paused. "Well, maybe. Da used to file transcriptions of his notes at the station and keep his notebooks at home. In case the station caught fire, he said. Drove Ma crazy." O'Reilly put his hands on his hips and stared down at Gethsemane. "You're not considering going to Hurley and asking him for his notes, are you?"

"Nope, not thinking of asking him."

"Well, don't. Hurley's suspected of some nasty dealings with Lynch and others. No one can prove anything. He covered his tracks too well and witnesses have a habit of developing amnesia and broken bones. Just trust me when I say Declan Hurley is not a nice fella. Best not to cross him." O'Reilly put his hat on, seemed to remember he was indoors, and took it off again. "Can you find your way out?"

"I can. Why, what're you going to do?"

"Paperwork. A theft from a secure area equals security breach. Which equals yours truly spending the rest of the evening writing reports."

* * *

For Sale.

The sign posted in the yard of a house near the garda station reminded Gethsemane to check out Hank Wayne. She detoured to the *Dunmullach Dispatch*'s office. A search of their digital archives revealed two things: Wayne celebrated discovering his Irish heritage by buying properties in Tullamore, Waterford, and Mitchelstown and he'd once again run afoul of preservation societies, in France and England this time, for razing historic buildings, one of them three hundred years old.

"Pathétique" flared in her head. She regretted sending Billy the documents he'd asked for. But what else could she have done? Lied and pretended she'd lost them? And been evicted faster than Billy could've hopped on a plane and come for the deed and tax documents himself. She hoped she hadn't cost Eamon Carraigfaire.

As she logged off the computer a headline caught her eye. "The Wayne Terror: Haunting or Hoax?" Fifty years ago, a Michigan family abandoned their home after enduring months of supernatural horror: objects thrown by unseen hands, visions of a stabbed woman and decapitated man, accidents and unexplained illnesses, the violent death of a pet raccoon. The family's youngest son? Hank Wayne.

Gethsemane filed the information away. If the Wayne terror wasn't a hoax, it might prove useful. If Wayne did come gunning for Carraigfaire—Gethsemane shuddered—a round or two with an irate Eamon would revisit enough childhood trauma to send Wayne and his money far from Dunmullach.

She ran into Teague on the way to the cottage. He pulled alongside her. "Can I give you a lift?"

"I've got my bike."

"I've got rope. We can tie it in back."

Pashley secured, they started for Carraigfaire.

"I've been meaning to check on you," Teague said. "Things going all right?"

"Fine." Considering she was investigating the murders of a ghost and his wife and alienating half the village in the process.

"Any more strange apparitions?"

"No." Eamon wasn't strange. Maddening but not strange. "I'm sure you were right about what I saw that night. Just Kieran."

"Getting used to a new place can be nerve-wracking, especially a place as isolated as Carraigfaire Cottage. If you like, I can drive up nights and check the grounds, make sure everything's secure."

"Please, don't trouble yourself. I'm okay, honest. Just first night jitters, gone now. I've slept in so many strange places I've learned to adapt quickly. Wait, that didn't sound right."

Teague chuckled. "I bet you have, touring the world for concerts and whatnot. Eamon and Orla seldom seemed to sleep in the same city twice. I loved the post cards Orla sent me from the exotic locales they traveled to. Still have them."

"You and your sister were close?"

"As can be. Despite our age difference. She was my half-sister, you know. I'm her brother from another mother."

"Her death must've hit you hard."

"Cried like a baby for weeks. Resorted to some pretty stupid things to try to hold on to her." Gethsemane guessed he meant the psychic Eamon mentioned. "Didn't take it as hard as poor Eamon. Not surprised he committed suicide. People pointing fingers at him, whispering about him, telling outright lies. The gardaí refused to investigate properly. Easier to take the word of a senile inebriate GP and a vengeful dope peddler than do actual work. The blue bottles are interested in closing cases, not solving crimes. Not that Declan Hurley was much of a guard. The only difference between him and the criminals was his badge."

"You believe Eamon is—was—innocent."

"Sure I do. He'd never hurt Orla. He would've killed anyone who did with his own hands. I don't think anyone murdered my sister. She either slipped on the rocks or got blown over by high winds." They pulled into the cottage driveway. "You be careful walking up there."

"I'll stay far from the edge." She thanked Teague for the ride as he unloaded her bike.

"Anytime. And please call me if you need anything, no matter how small."

She found Eamon near the lighthouse, semi-transparent and bathed in yellow. She counted the steps to the lighthouse door through his torso. He stared, grim-faced, at the waves crashing against the shore. Not a good time to tell him the evidence in his case disappeared from the police evidence room or that Hank Wayne was as much of a parasite as she feared.

"Bet I can cheer you up."

Eamon didn't answer.

"Teague believes you're innocent."

"Has O'Reilly agreed to reopen my case?"

"No, not yet. But he's moving in that direction."

"Liar."

"I can't stand seeing you this way, Eamon. Practically my whole life, whenever I felt like the world dumped a giant load of eff-you on my head I'd reach for your music and you'd pull me through the gloom. I'm going to return the favor whether you like it or not."

A smile played on Eamon's lips and red flickered at the edge of his aura. "You're persistent. He jerked his head toward the cottage. "Come on. I'll challenge you to a Beethoven sonata-thon."

At the cottage a few nights later, Gethsemane opened the piano and ran a finger over the keyboard, enjoying the cool sensation of the ivory keys. The Steinway reverberated as she coaxed the opening chords of Eamon's concerto. Teaching had turned out better than she'd feared. If Ruairi stopped being so timid and Colm stopped being "Head Boy," they might provide the inspiration needed to light the emotional spark in the other students.

She played the cadenza and imagined the hum of violins.

Dunmullach held charms: calendar-worthy scenery, fine whiskey, and fine—what had O'Reilly called it?—craic. Handsome men. Not that she wanted any entanglements. She'd had two, with fellow musicians. Neither worked out. The first cheated with a flute player. The second gave her a ring—with the unspoken expectation her career took a backseat to his. When she'd been offered the assistant conductor's position with the Cork City Philharmonic he'd given her an ultimatum: him or the job. She didn't regret not choosing him, even if the job hadn't worked out. She'd never be satisfied putting her own aspirations on the shelf to protect some insecure guy's fragile ego. She learned her lesson. Romance would only distract her. Of course, merely *admiring* copper-red hair or storm-gray eyes wasn't exactly getting *entangled*—

"I'd have played the trill a bit more vibrato."

Gethsemane jerked and bumped the Steinway, sending sheet music to the floor. "Jesus, Irish." She rubbed her elbow and glared at Eamon, suddenly seated beside her. "Stop doing that."

"You should be used to it by now, darlin'." Eamon motioned the scattered papers back to the piano's music rack.

"I *am* getting used to you. A few days ago I'd have thrown something through you."

Eamon nodded at the sheet music, fluttering pages. "So what d'ya think?"

Gethsemane played several measures from the opening of the third movement. "Not bad." She bit back a smile.

"Not bad?" A blue halo flared around Eamon's head. "Not bad? The Giant's Causeway's 'not bad.' The *Book of Kells* is 'not bad.' Beethoven's bloody Fifth's 'not bad.' That concerto—" he jabbed a finger through the paper "—is feckin' brilliant."

Gethsemane laughed. "Okay, the concerto's—it's called 'St. Brennan's Ascendant,' by the way—" she mimicked Eamon's Irish accent "—is feckin' brilliant."

"Unlike your brogue." The aura dissipated. "And it's 'Opus Twenty-seven, Number One, Violin Concerto in G Major,' not 'St. Brennan's Ascendant'."

"It's 'St. Brennan's Ascendant' since Riordan and Dunleavy asked me this afternoon. Besides, 'St. Brennan's Ascendant' fits on the program better than," another brogue attempt, "'Opus Twenty-seven, Number One, Violin Concerto in G Major'."

Eamon grimaced. "Work on that."

The phone rang. Gethsemane rose to answer it. "I'll work on my accent if you work on the violin cadenza."

"Work on the—There's nothing wrong with the violin cadenza."

"Not for an eternally thirty-seven-year-old compositional genius. A merely gifted sixteen-year-old student musician might find the fingering tricky," she called from the kitchen.

"Find a soloist better than 'merely gifted.'"

Gethsemane shushed him and lifted the receiver. "Hello?" The male caller slurred unintelligible words. "Who is this?"

"Yaknowdamnwellwhoshis! Shhurley! Declanhurley!"

"Mr. Hurley. How are you?"

"HowshahellyathinkIyam? DamnReillyrassinme..."

"Mr. Hurley, I'm having trouble understanding you. Maybe—"

"Unnershan this! I know ya sent O'Reilly after me—"

Eamon appeared next to Gethsemane. "What's the story?"

She held out the phone.

"Gowl's hammered," Eamon said.

"No kidding. What should I do?"

Eamon shrugged. "Hang up on him."

Gethsemane put the phone back to her ear. "He sounds pretty bad. Like borderline-alcohol-poisoning bad. Maybe I should call someone to go check on him."

"He wouldn't do the same for you."

"Mr. Hurley," Gethsemane said into the phone. "I'm going to hang up now. I'm going to dial 999—"

"Donshahanguponme! You—" Hurley broke off. When he spoke again his voice sounded distant. "Howdja get in? Whatchawant?"

A loud crack. Gethsemane remembered a baseball game, a

home run with bases loaded in the last inning of the league championships. Nausea rose as realization dawned. Wood against flesh and bone sounded the same as wood against leather.

"Mr. Hurley?"

Glass rattled then crashed. A thud. Silence.

"Mr. Hurley?"

Breathing.

"Hello? Is someone there? Hello?"

A beep then a dial tone.

Homicide detectives questioned Gethsemane about the murder until three a.m. *Why did Hurley call you? Did Hurley recognize his killer? Did the killer say anything?* Afterward, an officer led her to a spartan wooden chair to wait for a ride back to Carraigfaire Cottage. He promised someone would be with her shortly.

Forty-five minutes later, Gethsemane went to find "someone." The direction she thought led to the squad room led instead to an unfamiliar gray-green maze of Formica tile and peeling walls. Offices lined the hallway, dark behind frosted glass door panes except for one at the far end. The placard posted next to it read *Iollan O'Reilly, Detective Inspector, Cold Case Unit.* Gethsemane knocked.

"Come," O'Reilly called.

"Good evening, Inspector," Gethsemane said to the back of O'Reilly's head. "I mean, good morning. Did you stay late or come in early?"

"Both." O'Reilly faced her. "What are you—oh, the Hurley murder. Are you all right? Do you need to talk to someone? We've a victim's assistance officer."

Gethsemane shook her head. Rehashing the details of what she'd heard while some earnest social worker encouraged her to "process her feelings" was the last thing she wanted. "I just need sleep. I'm exhausted."

"Tomorrow maybe, after the shock hits."

"I'll be okay. I won't lie, I didn't like Hurley. Not that I wanted him dead but—" Gethsemane shrugged. "I don't shock easily since I spent a year helping my brother set up mission hospitals in Africa."

O'Reilly grinned. "I suspect you wouldn't let on if you did shock easily. If you change your mind, I've a number you can call."

"Thanks. Can you tell me how to get back to homicide? I tried to find an officer to drive me home and I zigged at fingerprinting when I should have zagged."

"Have a seat." O'Reilly picked up his phone.

More sitting. Gethsemane massaged her back as she examined the inspector's office. His suit jacket and fedora hung on a coat tree. Shelves packed with technical manuals and reference books lined the walls. A mug proclaimed "I'm the Big Brother" from atop English and Irish newspapers stacked on his desk.

"Dr. Brown has waited long enough," O'Reilly said into the phone. "I'd drive her home myself, but I have a meeting with the Superintendent—Yes, yes, she's in my office."

Gethsemane stifled a yawn. O'Reilly's voice devolved into a distant buzz as her eyes glazed. She dug her nails into her palms and blinked at a collection of photos clustered on one of the shelves. A smiling man with a fedora and gray eyes identical to O'Reilly's leaned against a police car in the first photo. In the next, the same man posed with his arms around a beautiful woman who shared the inspector's salt-and-pepper hair. Three young girls and a teen boy sat in front of the couple. The man was absent from the third photo. The boy, grown up into Inspector O'Reilly, stood with an arm around the shoulders of the still beautiful, now gray-haired, woman. The three girls, matured into adults, surrounded them. The youngest, wearing collegiate robes, stood closest to O'Reilly, her arm linked through his. The final photo featured a black cat tangled in silver tinsel.

"Taken care of," O'Reilly said as he hung up the phone. "An officer will be here—"

"Shortly?" Gethsemane asked.

"—in ten or fifteen minutes."

"Thanks." Gethsemane pointed at the photos. "Your family?"

"Da, Ma, and sisters. The youngest, Brigid, is gettin' married next June." O'Reilly beamed.

"The cat?"

"Nero."

"Like the emperor?"

"Like the detective. I adopted him after I closed my first case." He lifted a manila folder from a stack on his desk and opened it. "You mind if I get on with this?"

Gethsemane waved O'Reilly back to his paperwork. Peering over his shoulder, she inhaled sandalwood and clove. "Any leads on the McCarthy case?"

"No," O'Reilly said without looking up. "And before you ask, it's still closed."

She sat on his desk, on top of the file he'd been reading. "How is it still a closed case? You saw the videotape. You know Eamon McCarthy couldn't possibly have murdered his wife. And now the evidence has been stolen and the investigating officer bludgeoned to death."

"As far as my superiors are concerned, the evidence box is misplaced and Hurley's murder is unrelated." Gethsemane strained to hear his muttered, "And none of my business."

He continued in his normal tone. "I need more than amateur videos and hunches to convince my superiors to let me open a case everyone considers solved. Not when there's all this," he gestured toward piles of papers, "to clear up."

"Frierson and McKenzie didn't have anything more than some newspaper clippings and the belief that justice had been denied when they asked a judge to reopen the George Stinney case seventy years later and look what happened."

"We're not talking about a kid being railroaded in mid-twentieth century South Carolina."

"No, we're talking about a man being wrongly blamed for two deaths in late twentieth century Dunmullach. At least Stinney got a trial. A joke of a trial, true, but more than Eamon McCarthy got."

O'Reilly closed his eyes and massaged the bridge of his nose.

"Why don't your bosses think Hurley's murder is connected to the McCarthys'? That his being killed a day after you start asking questions about Eamon McCarthy is a bit too coincidental to be coincidence?"

"Because Hurley's murder was inevitable. More than inevitable, long overdue. Declan Hurley was a crooked garda and a marginal human being. He shook down prostitutes and drug dealers. He took bribes to make evidence appear in convenient places or to disappear altogether. At least a dozen people may have wanted him dead for at least a dozen reasons, none of 'em related to a twenty-five-year-old murder."

"So that's it?"

"Yes, Dr. Brown, that's it. Hurley's murder is an active case being investigated by the homicide unit. I, meanwhile, toil away trying to clean up the messes Hurley and those of his ilk left behind."

"Those messes include the McCarthys," Gethsemane said.

O'Reilly picked up his pen.

Gethsemane yanked the door open. "I'll wait in the hall for my ride."

A hush fell on the audience as she raised her baton. She waited. One second. Two. The down stroke. Cue violins. Wait. Something's wrong. The musician in first chair—Orla. Second chair—Hurley. Bassoon—Jimmy Lynch—

A sudden chord, *fortissimo*, exploded on the piano. Gethsemane shot upright in bed, her bizarre dream already fading into memory. Haydn's "Symphony No. 94" continued playing on the Steinway downstairs. The alarm clock revealed only three hours had passed since the gardaí dropped her off at Carraigfaire. She threw the clock across the room and buried her head beneath her pillows. The leather-soap aroma hit her just before the pillows sailed off the bed.

"Do you have any idea how much I hate you right now, Eamon Padraig McCarthy?" She replaced the pillows with the bed covers.

The covers joined the pillows near the door. Eamon materialized at the foot of the bed. "Sleep later. Talk now. What happened at the station?"

"Some wanker of a cop badgered me with a bunch of stupid questions and O'Reilly told me to mind my own business." She held out her hand. "Blankets."

"Are you always this chatty in the morning?"

"Only when I'm well-rested."

"You've got thirty minutes."

"An hour. And make coffee."

The blankets landed in a heap on her head.

Semi-human after a hot shower and hot coffee, Gethsemane briefed Eamon on her night at the garda station.

"Evidence?" Eamon paced. "What evidence does O'Reilly want? A signed confession?" Blue sparks snapped.

"Something like that. Or at least a good reason why someone would want to kill Orla."

"Don't you mean a good reason why someone would want to kill Orla *and* me?"

"I can think of several of those." Her coffee cup slid out of reach. "Sorry." The cup slid back.

Eamon sat across from her. "O'Reilly's got a point. Thing is, I can't think of one damned reason why anyone would kill Orla. I can't think of a reason why anyone would look at her cross-eyed."

"Maybe Orla's death wasn't premeditated. Maybe an argument got out of hand. High winds, slippery rocks...You can't think of a single person who might have been at least moderately annoyed with Orla? Someone from childhood? I still carry a grudge against Sukie Collins from the sixth grade."

"Orla was a peacemaker. Her father remarried a girl not much older than her. Everyone knew disaster loomed. But a month into the marriage Orla and her stepmother were best friends. When Teague was born Orla became a second mother."

"Surely she pissed off at least one person in all her years on the planet."

"Pissed-off, no. That was my specialty. At worst, Orla may have inspired over-zealous admiration. Never anger."

"You mean a stalker?"

"I wouldn't go that far. Jimmy Lynch's sister, Deirdre, billed herself as Orla's number one fan. Attended all of her poetry readings, wrote her hundreds of letters, even dressed like Orla for a while. Fancied they were 'soul friends'."

"Did she ever get violent?"

"Not towards Orla. Deirdre inherited the Lynch temper. She had a few knock-down reefins as a girl. One was with Siobhan. Don't remember what about but Deirdre got the better of Siobhan despite Siobhan being twice her size. Deirdre always showed Orla the utmost respect, though."

"Nothing weirder than the mini-me dress-alike routine?"

Eamon pointed a finger at the coffee pot which levitated and refilled Gethsemane's cup. "Now you mention it, she did show up here at the cottage at odd hours once or twice. Twice. One time she wanted to discuss a chapbook Orla'd just published. Said she'd deciphered the poems and the message changed her life. The last time, she desperately wanted to see an award Orla won, the Hershberger Poetry Prize. Said it proved her prayers to St. Columba had been answered."

"What happened?"

"The first visit, Orla talked to her for about ten minutes and she went away. The second visit, I called the guards and they talked to her and she went away. Never came back to the cottage. Stopped dressing like Orla, too. Wouldn't speak to me when I ran into her in the village after that, except once to lash into me for coming between two *anam cara*. Shredded a bunch of my sheet music and left a bin bag full of the scraps in the back seat of my car."

"Did you have her arrested?"

"For what? Littering? Poor taste in music? She didn't do anything else aside from write some more letters to Orla."

"What'd the letters say?"

"Don't know. Orla and I had an agreement. I didn't read her fan mail and she didn't read mine." Eamon's aura glowed pink with embarrassment. "Some of mine contained, er, inappropriate requests from female fans. *Never* acted upon but not something I wanted my wife to read."

"Where are the letters now?"

"Teague claimed them. I think he donated them to the library."

"And Orla's award? The Hershberger Prize?"

"A little statuette about yay tall." Eamon held his hands about six inches apart. "Teague must have that, too. It's not at the cottage or lighthouse."

"Looks like I'm going to visit Teague." Gethsemane drained her coffee cup. "Even if he doesn't remember what the letters said he might recall someone from back in the day, someone Orla slighted, even unintentionally. Or someone who imagined Orla slighted them. Little resentments, nursed conscientiously, grow up into big hatreds."

Eight

According to the neighbor, the Connollys had gone to Kilarney for the weekend. A return trip to the library proved just as fruitless. Mrs. Toibin was out and the music department was closed for inventory. A surly librarian guarded the poetry department. Gethsemane could have conducted the whole of Brian's "The Gothic" by the time the woman set a dusty file box in front of her. The papers within consisted of Orla's correspondence with publishers and agents. No personal correspondence or diaries. Nothing hinting at a stalker. Gethsemane returned the box to the librarian who snatched it, sending box and contents tumbling. Papers spread like lava.

The librarian scowled. "Take care."

Gethsemane apologized as the women stooped. Heads collided.

"Leave it." The librarian elbowed Gethsemane out of the way and muttered as she gathered papers. "Bad enough people steal, now folks treat important documents like circulars in the Sunday paper."

Gethsemane clasped a hand against her throbbing head. "Who's stealing?"

"If we knew, they wouldn't be stealing, would they? They'd be in jail."

"What's been stolen?"

The librarian snapped the box shut. "Orla's letters, the ones admirers wrote to her. Her journal, some of her chapbooks." She wrapped her arms around the box, shielding it from Gethsemane. "What's your interest in Orla? Mrs. Toibin said you were a fan of her husband's."

"Scholarly interest. Orla was Eamon's muse."

"She was a genius in her own right."

Gethsemane's throbbing head couldn't take anymore. She beat it back to the sidewalk where she'd left Father Keating's bicycle.

Head still throbbing, she detoured to Fitzgerald's Apothecary. No acetaminophen. Three strikes. Time to go home and curl into a ball on the sofa.

Halfway down the aisle, a voice called, "May I help you?"

Gethsemane explained her dilemma to the woman, some years older than her, who had appeared through a door marked "Private."

"Acetaminophen's called paracetamol over here." The nametag pinned to the woman's white coat proclaimed her *Aoife Fitzgerald, Pharmacist*. Her one blue eye and one green eye matched the colors in the turquoise pendant around her neck. She took a bottle from a shelf and handed it to Gethsemane.

"Thank you."

"My pleasure. It can be a bit confusing with brand names *and* generic names changing from country to country."

Gethsemane agreed and followed Aoife to the counter to pay for the medicine. She looked around as Aoife rang up the sale. A large collection of framed photographs hung on a wall near the counter.

"The history of Fitzgerald's Apothecary captured on film," Aoife said.

Every photo featured the same scene—a group of people posed in front of the pharmacy's display window. Changes in styles of dress and vehicles parked nearby marked the passage of years. Gethsemane guessed the earliest photographs dated to the early 1900s. The most recent could have been taken yesterday. Gethsemane recognized Aoife in several pictures, ranging in age from pre-teen to adult. Aoife often posed standing between two males, her arms linked through theirs. On her right, the older of the two men wore a white coat and shared Aoife's one blue-one green eye color combination. Gray-haired and stoop-shouldered in later photos, he stood next to Aoife long into her adult years. The younger male, a teenager when first seen, disappeared from the photographs by the time Aoife reached her late teens.

"Your father and brother?" Gethsemane asked.

"My father, yes," Aoife said. "The boy's Oisin Ardmore. He started working here as a delivery boy when I was a girl. Dad taught him everything about the business, even helped send him to university. Planned to take him on as a partner, eventually. Probably would've left the business to him. The son he never had." Aoife laughed. "Not that I minded. I had a terrible crush on Oisin. Fancied myself Mrs. Ardmore someday."

"What happened?"

Aoife looked away. "Oisin died." She handed Gethsemane her change and wished her a good day, obviously not wanting to speak more of it.

Gethsemane turned at the door. "One more question. Kind of random. What poisons taste bitter and slightly spicy?"

"Bitter and spicy?" The pharmacist thought for a moment. "I'm afraid I couldn't say. Most poisons are bitter. It's genetic, kept our ancestors from accidentally eating poisonous plants. Bittering agents are added to medicines for the same reason. Why on earth do you want to know that?"

"Oh, one of my students asked about it for a research paper. No big deal. Thanks for the aceta—I mean, paracetamol."

Outside, Gethsemane cursed as she fought to open the medicine bottle, her headache worsening. Half a dozen attempts later, she pried off the cap and shook two tablets into her hand. She jumped at the sound of a voice behind her. Siobhan Moloney. The tablets slid from her hand and rolled into a nearby storm drain.

"They really should sell children with those child-proof caps since children seem to be the only ones who can open them."

Gethsemane closed her eyes and counted three. She arranged her lips into a smile. "Being a psychic must be convenient. People can't sneak up behind you."

"Didn't mean to startle ya," Siobhan didn't look apologetic. "I saw ya standin' here and I thought I might speak with ya for a moment."

"If this is about contacting spirits—"

"It's about your investigation. You *are* investigating the McCarthy deaths?"

Gethsemane shrugged. "More like bringing some inconsistencies to police attention."

"You've found many of these—inconsistencies?"

"A few." Gethsemane shifted her weight. Why did Siobhan care? Looking for an angle for a new con?

"Why don't you tell me what you found? I know this town as well as the Guards."

Gethsemane rattled her medicine bottle. All the paracetamol in the world wouldn't cure this headache. "Maybe some other time, thanks. I ought to be headed home now." She moved toward her bicycle. "Excuse me."

Siobhan grabbed Gethsemane's arm with a force that surprised Gethsemane.

"I'm just trying to help. I've noticed a few—inconsistencies—myself. Big ones."

"Why don't you go to the police?" Gethsemane pulled her arm free.

Siobhan snorted. "Blue bottles. What good are they? They write a report, stick it in some cabinet, and forget about it. They don't take you seriously."

Gethsemane looked Siobhan over. Today's caftan was fluorescent orange with purple trim. She doubted anyone took Siobhan seriously. She rubbed her arm where Siobhan had grabbed her. Not taking Siobhan seriously was probably a mistake.

Siobhan continued. "You're bright. I'll wager you'd appreciate the significance of what I know."

"Tell me now," Gethsemane said.

"Ah," Siobhan said. "I'm afraid it's not as simple as that. These inconsistencies are the sort the individuals concerned wouldn't want brought to light."

"Hmmm," Gethsemane said.

"The nature of these inconsistencies is such that the individuals concerned might be willing to make an investment to ensure that no one ever pointed them out."

"Hmmm," Gethsemane repeated.

"On the other hand, someone else might be willing to make an investment to ensure these inconsistencies didn't stay buried forever."

"An investment in the furtherance of justice."

Siobhan displayed the silver tooth. The hair on Gethsemane's arms stood up.

"I knew you'd understand," Siobhan said. "You *are* a bright one."

"You've certainly given me something to think about." Gethsemane stepped around Siobhan. "And that's just what I'll do," she said as she mounted her bicycle. "Think about it."

"I'll be in touch, then."

"You do that." Gethsemane maneuvered the bicycle around Siobhan. "You know where to find me," she said as she pedaled away.

Gethsemane arrived back at Carraigfaire Cottage to find a large man with sunken eyes, expressionless face, and thatch of straw-colored hair sitting on the porch next to a crate. An Irish Boo Radley. He stood as she approached, his movements surprisingly graceful.

"Hello," she said. "You must be Kieran Ross."

The man nodded.

Gethsemane pointed to the crate. "Is that Billy's order from the Off License?"

Kieran nodded again. Gethsemane waited for him to say something. He remained silent.

"All righty then." Gethsemane led the way inside.

Kieran followed her to the kitchen. He set the case of bourbon in a corner, pulled out a pocket knife, and pried off the lid. Gethsemane hummed the opening measures of "Requiem for a Fallen Angel" while he worked.

A voice behind her called, "'Lo, Kieran."

Kieran smiled at a spot past Gethsemane.

Gethsemane turned. Eamon perched on the kitchen table. Kieran stared just above Eamon's head.

"Good seein' ya again," Eamon said.

Kieran smiled wider.

Gethsemane looked back and forth between the two men. "Kieran, what are you looking at?"

Kieran blushed and ducked his head.

"'S all right, Kieran," Eamon said. "Dr. Brown can hear me too."

Gethsemane raised an eyebrow.

"Kieran can hear me," Eamon said. "Don't think he can see me, though." He shrugged. "Hard to tell since he doesn't speak."

Gethsemane walked over to Kieran and tapped him on the shoulder. "Did you hear a man's voice?"

Kieran shrank away from her.

Gethsemane persisted. "Did you hear Eamon McCarthy say hello to you?"

Kieran kept his head down but glanced up at Gethsemane from beneath lowered lids.

"I heard him too. And I can see him." She pointed at Eamon. "He's sitting on the table with his legs crossed. He's wearing a green cardigan, dark brown tweed blazer, and light brown tweed pants. He needs to comb his hair."

"Don't point," Eamon said. "It's rude."

Kieran giggled. He blushed deeper and rushed from the kitchen. After a moment, the front door latch clicked.

Gethsemane crossed her arms. "You said I was the first person you'd talked to since you died."

"That's not exactly what I said. You're the first person I've come across who could help me. Even if Kieran spoke, no one would listen to him."

"Why can't he talk?"

"Don't know that he *can't*. He doesn't. Good listener. He used to sit with Orla for hours and listen to her read her poetry." Eamon squatted and pointed at the crate. A bottle of Waddell and Dobb Double-oaked rose from its slot and levitated over to Gethsemane. "Have a glass?"

Gethsemane grabbed the bottle and set it on the table. "It's a bit early."

Eamon shrugged and stood up. "It's after noon."

"I'm not thirsty." Gethsemane pulled a chair out from the table and plopped into it. "I'm frustrated." She pressed the heels of her hands against her eyes. "This morning was a bust."

"I do appreciate what you're doing but don't stir yourself into a frenzy. Let O'Reilly handle the heavy digging. That's what the garda pays him for."

"But O'Reilly *won't* go to work on your case unless I convince him he's dealing with a double homicide." Gethsemane sighed. "I think I'll cycle back to town. Maybe Father Keating can put me on to something."

"Maybe you should try the Rabbit. You'll find as much truth in a bar as in church."

"Eamon McCarthy, if you ever do cross over it will be straight to Hell."

"I hear that's where they've got the best tunes."

Headache eradicated by a dose of paracetamol, Gethsemane returned to the village and stopped at Our Lady of Perpetual

Sorrows. She waved to Saoirse, who sat with a stack of books on a bench near the poison garden. She met Father Keating coming out of the garden shed. He couldn't tell her who might have wanted Orla and Eamon dead. She asked about Saoirse.

"She's reading Ovid. She's translating the Latin."

"At twelve?"

Father Keating nodded. "She translated Homer when she was only ten. Saoirse takes to literature and languages as readily as she does to science. Next year her parents hope to find her chemistry and calculus tutors."

The phone rang in the rectory. Father Keating excused himself. Gethsemane walked over to Saoirse. "May I sit?"

Saoirse moved books to make room on the bench.

Gethsemane shuffled a few. "Ovid, huh? Nothing like a little Ovid in the original Latin to make the day go by."

Saoirse stared.

"Well," Gethsemane said, standing. "I'll let you get back to it."

"Don't let Colm bully you."

"What?" Gethsemane sat again.

"Colm. He's a bully. He thinks just because he's Head Boy he can do whatever he wants. Don't let him. He's only Head Boy because our parents donated a soccer field to St. Brennan's."

"Thanks for the warning." Gethsemane spied something in the pile of books. She pushed aside a copy of *Metamorphoses*. "What's this?" Her hand rested on a worn, brown, leather-bound volume she'd seen before—in the garden shed when she borrowed Father Keating's bicycle. "Since when are occult books on the recommended school reading list?"

Saoirse dropped her head and slipped the spell book under her sweater. "You'll tell Father."

"I won't if you promise to use your powers for the forces of good and not evil."

Saoirse remained solemn. "I promise."

"I'm kidding." Gethsemane raised a hand to stroke Saoirse's hair. She caught herself and dropped her hand to her lap. "It's none of my business if you read occult books and learn about poisonous plants."

"Murder's your business. Murder and music."

"What do you know about murder?"

Saoirse bent her head.

"Saoirse, answer me. What do you know about murder?"

"He won't find her. She fixed it that way."

"Who fixed what? Who won't find whom? Give me a straight answer, Saoirse. Crypticism is not attractive in a twelve-year-old."

"Love is an idiot drug." Saoirse pulled out the spell book and read silently.

Gethsemane sighed and stood. "Are you at least reading Latin spells?"

"Yes, Miss," Saoirse said. She looked past Gethsemane and waved. "Hello, Kieran."

Gethsemane jumped. The big man had come up behind her without a sound. He reached past her to hand Saoirse a book. Gethsemane read the title. "That's one of Orla's."

"From the lighthouse. This one's got the poem about the boy who gives the girl a leaf as a promise to wait for her until she's old enough."

"The lighthouse?" Gethsemane looked back and forth between Kieran and Saoirse. "You take things from the lighthouse?"

"Just books. Kieran said Mr. McCarthy said it was okay. And we put them back. Not like her."

"Not like who, Saoirse? Who takes things from the lighthouse and doesn't put them back?"

"Miss Sullivan's acting up again."

Gethsemane followed Saoirse's gaze to a commotion in the cemetery. Pegeen held Nuala by the arm and tried to snatch a bouquet from her. Nuala, several inches taller than her sister, held the flowers out of reach.

"Those are not appropriate for Ma's grave." Pegeen shouted. "They're toxic. What if an animal or a child got hold of them?"

"They're *your* favorites, anyway," Nuala said.

Pegeen glanced toward the poison garden. She let go of her sister. Nuala laid the flowers by a headstone. Pegeen snatched them up. "You always do this to me, Nu. If it wasn't for Da..." She buried her face in her hand. Nuala smiled at Gethsemane then ran toward the front of the church.

Gethsemane turned away from Pegeen. Kieran had disappeared and Saoirse sat absorbed in a book. Gethsemane decided to take Eamon's advice. Maybe she would find more answers at the pub.

Or not. Two Bushmills and forty-five minutes of eavesdropping on gossip yielded no leads. Gethsemane flung the door open as she left the pub. A thud, accompanied by a loud "Ow!" from the other side, stopped it halfway through its arc.

Gethsemane stepped out into the early evening light to find the thin, pale woman from the post office bench rubbing her elbow. Deidre Lynch. Orla's number one fan and possibly her killer. Books lay scattered at her feet.

"I am so, so sorry." Gethsemane scrambled to pick up the volumes. *Moon Shadow, Silver Dust. Nightsong of the Garden. Fire in the Moon.* All by Orla McCarthy. She handed them back to the woman. "I see you're an Orla McCarthy devotee."

The woman beamed as she cradled the books. "Her most devoted. I own everything she's ever written. I can recite all of her poems by heart. Try me. Go ahead. Any poem." Deirdre made her selection before Gethsemane could answer. "'Fire in the Moon.' That's an easy one." She closed her eyes and recited a sonnet. "How about something harder? 'The Wife of Silence.' Deirdre closed her eyes again and recited a lengthy ode in free verse.

"An impressive performance. We haven't been introduced. I'm—"

Deirdre shifted her books and shook Gethsemane's hand. "I know who you are. You're Dr. Gethsemane Brown from America and you've come to help St. Brennan's win the All-County and you're living in Orla's cottage. I'm Deirdre Lynch. What's it like? Living in Orla's house?"

"It's—" Gethsemane hunted for a word "—haunting."

"You must sense her presence everywhere. She must permeate the cottage."

"She's never far from my mind," Gethsemane said.

"You love her, too?" Deirdre grabbed Gethsemane's hand. "Oh, we *will* be friends. Come over for tea. We can talk about Orla."

Gethsemane winced. What did Dunmullach mothers feed their babies to grow such deceptively delicate women? She had no desire to spend the evening chatting about poetry with a murder suspect. She did, however, want to ask Deidre where she and Nuala were at the times of Eamon and Orla's deaths. She agreed to accompany Deirdre home.

Gethsemane stepped through the door of Deirdre and Jimmy Lynch's house into an Orla McCarthy shrine. Posters advertising Orla's appearances at bookstores and lecture halls hung on every wall. Framed publicity stills crowded the fireplace mantle. Gethsemane sniffed. "What's that smell?"

Deirdre frowned. "Don't you know? Anyone who loved Orla would recognize—"

"I *do* know," Gethsemane said. "Powder, roses, vetiver. *May Winds*. Her perfume."

Deirdre laughed. "I scent the cushions and the curtains with it. I feel as if Orla is all around me." Deirdre laughed again. "Jimmy hates it."

Gethsemane walked around the parlor. Books packed every shelf of a glass-front bookcase. She moved closer for a better look.

"First editions," Deirdre said.

"Quite an investment," Gethsemane said. How did she afford them? Or was Deirdre the "she" Saoirse said took books without returning them?

Deirdre frowned. "A labor of love."

"Much nicer than the library's collection." She wandered over to the mantle. "I was at the library. They own Orla's correspondence. A donation from her brother."

"Only her business papers. They don't have her personal correspondence."

They used to.

"Do you have any of Orla's personal papers?"

Deirdre grinned to shame the Cheshire Cat. "I have letters she wrote to me."

"May I see them?"

"I don't know." Deirdre frowned again. "They're meant just for me."

"I understand," Gethsemane said. No point pushing it. "Maybe another time. After we've gotten to know each other better."

"We'll be good friends, won't we?"

Gethsemane bobbed her head. Time to ask what she really wanted to know. "The night Orla died. That must have been traumatic for you."

Deirdre's eyes narrowed. "I don't want to talk about that."

"I wondered if you remembered where you were that night. You must. People always remember where they were when traumatic events happened. Kennedy's assassination, the Challenger explosion, the—"

"I said. I don't. Want. To. Talk. About it." Deirdre's voice rose a few decibels.

"I meant no offense." Gethsemane toyed with the photos on the mantle. "I just—" She lifted a frame. A statuette about yay big sat tucked in a corner.

On cue, the rear door slammed open. Jimmy's, "Deirdre, who's here?" reverberated through the house.

Gethsemane suspected Jimmy Lynch would be almost as thrilled to find her in his parlor as he was about the parlor smelling like *May Winds*.

Deirdre yelled, "I'm entertaining company, Jimmy. Stop shouting. It's impolite."

Gethsemane escaped out the front door before Jimmy could show her how impolite he could be.

Deirdre followed. "Wait, you haven't had your tea."

"Maybe another time." Jimmy stood in the doorway behind his sister. "I just had an inspiration for the competition. I want to get it down on paper before I forget." She mounted her bicycle, glad she'd brought it with her from the pub.

"Do come back," Deirdre said.

Gethsemane answered Jimmy's glare with a nod and pedaled away.

Deirdre's "You will come back, won't you?" followed her down the street.

A late day drizzle punctuated Gethsemane's thoughts about Deirdre's fixation. She'd never be able to question her with Jimmy around. She needed to get her alone.

The drizzle kicked up into a steady rain. No chance of reaching Carraigfaire before getting soaked. An excellent excuse to pop into Roasted, Dunmullach's new coffee house. As she pedaled into the parking lot she spotted a familiar tweed stingy-brimmed fedora going inside. A bonus. She'd ask the inspector his thoughts on creepy poetry fanatics.

She walked up to the counter in time to hear O'Reilly ask the barista, "What's the difference, again, between a ristretto and a macchiato?"

Gethsemane jumped in before the twenty-something brunette with long dark hair and Warby Parker glasses could answer. "A ristretto is a concentrated espresso shot whereas a macchiato is one or two shots of espresso with a dollop of foamed milk." Dating a coffee snob in grad school sometimes proved useful.

"You need a PhD to understand this," O'Reilly said.

"We have regular coffee, if you prefer, sir." The barista pointed to the menu chalked on an oversized blackboard suspended behind the counter. "Ethiopian yirgacheffe, Ugandan gumutindo peaberry, and Honduran opalaca. We can do pour over, French press, aeropress, or cold brew."

"I feel old all of a sudden."

The barista beamed. "You're not old, sir. Bet you've got no more 'n a few years on me Da."

Gethsemane bit back a laugh as O'Reilly reddened. That almost made up for his treatment at the garda station. "The yirgacheffe in a large French press with two cups." She led O'Reilly to a table near a window.

"I'm surprised you're speaking to me," he said. "You slammed the door."

"You were patronizing and dismissive."

"I'm sorry, I didn't mean to be."

"Apology accepted." Gethsemane studied the inspector. His eyes suggested calm, gray seas, a smile revealed a dimple in his right cheek. Bringing up Deirdre would spoil the good mood.

"What is it?" O'Reilly asked as the barista delivered their coffee.

"What's what?"

"Something to do with the McCarthys?"

Gethsemane depressed the coffeemaker's plunger. Best stick to coffee talk. "I was just wondering why a guy who sports Italian leather shoes and rushes home after a long day at work to a dinner of osso buco and ruffino isn't expert on gourmet coffee."

"Seldom drink the stuff. I prefer tea. Bewley's Original Blend."

"Why? Is that what they served Sunday breakfast at the police academy?"

"It's what Ma served every evening when Da came home from work. Didn't matter how late. A pot of Bewley's Original and a plate of chocolate Hob Nobs and we'd sit 'round the kitchen table and tell Da about our day."

"Sounds nice. Childhood traditions have a habit of following us into adulthood."

The jingle of bracelets interrupted them. Siobhan, clad in a silver caftan and matching turban, pulled up a chair. "Forgive the interruption." She flashed a smile as bright as her dress. "I was hoping to borrow the inspector for a moment."

O'Reilly's dimple vanished and his eyes darkened. "How may I be of service, Miss Moloney?"

"About poor, murdered Declan. Azul, my spirit guide, shared information with me germane to the investigation. I felt duty-bound as a law-abiding citizen to pass the information along to the proper authorities."

Gethsemane gulped coffee to drown a snicker.

O'Reilly nudged her under the table. "What sort of information?" he asked.

Siobhan glanced at Gethsemane. "Perhaps the garda station—"

"I'm sure Dr. Brown can be trusted not to go spreading the details of Azul's communication all over the village."

Gethsemane gulped more coffee. O'Reilly stepped on her foot.

Siobhan hesitated, then leaned in. "Azul said—Aren't you going to write this down?"

"I've an excellent memory," O'Reilly said.

Siobhan frowned but went on. "Azul says a vital clue is hidden in the dearly departed inspector's home."

"What clue?"

"Well." Siobhan leaned back and laced her fingers. "Kind of hard to say exactly, right now."

"Message kind of hazy, was it?"

"Hazy, yes. Course, I'd be willing to reach out to Azul again, try to get some clarity. If the garda think I might be of some use to their investigation, that is."

"For the usual and customary consultant's fee."

"One has to make a livin', Inspector."

"You'll want to speak to someone in homicide, Miss Moloney. I'm sure they'll be happy to take statements from you and, uh, Azul as well as discuss remuneration for performing your civic duty." O'Reilly looked at his watch. "If you hurry you can make it to the station before shift change."

Siobhan stood. "Excuse me, Inspector. I forgot you only

concern yourself with old cases." She glared down at Gethsemane. "Speaking of which, have you given any further thought to my offer?"

"Still thinking," Gethsemane said. "One mustn't rush into these things."

"Nor wait too long."

Siobhan swirled, the hem of her caftan brushing Gethsemane's face, and stormed out.

"What offer?" O'Reilly asked.

"Nothing. She hinted she had some information to sell about the McCarthy case. She didn't say whether it came from Azul. By the way, no one in homicide is seriously going to pay her for clues from beyond the veil, are they?"

"No, the boys in homicide are more skeptical than I am. Miss Moloney'll be lucky if they don't lock her up for wasting gardaí time." The dimple returned. His phone rang. He excused himself to take the call. "I'm afraid I have to run," he said when he returned and laid money on the table. "I can drop you by the cottage."

"Thanks, but I'll manage. Rain's stopped."

"So it has. Be wide all the same. The roads can be treacherous."

Through the window, O'Reilly steered his car out of the parking lot. Gethsemane spied Deirdre approaching on the sidewalk opposite. Had she followed her? She couldn't have wanted company for tea that badly. Gethsemane ducked low in her chair as Siobhan sprang out of an alley and waylaid Deirdre. She wished she could overhear their conversation. It appeared intense with heads close together and gesticulations by both women. Gethsemane crept outside and crouched behind a dumpster in time to catch "papers," "missing," and "guards." Deirdre hurried away frowning and Siobhan strolled up the sidewalk wearing a broad, smarmy grin. Gethsemane waited until the two figures receded from view then grabbed her bike.

* * *

Gethsemane had pedaled halfway to St. Brennan's before she admitted what she was about to do. She'd need help. Who? Not Eamon. He'd never been in Hurley's house. And he'd try to talk her out of it. Not the boys. This was no business for children. One of the other teachers? She'd only spoken about anything of substance to Francis. Would he help? He seemed to like her. Sometimes. He didn't hate her. Probably. Anyway, she had no one else. Maybe her plan would appeal to his prankster ethic. She reached campus and, after questioning a few students, located Francis at the boathouse. The math teacher sat with his back against an upside-down boat, red head bent over a paperback book. Which Francis would she get?

"Evening, Grennan."

"Evening, Brown." He marked his place with a finger between the pages.

Taciturn. "I need you to help me do something."

"I'm busy." Francis held up his book.

"This is more important."

He opened the book to the page he'd marked.

"This is almost as good as the Interscholastic Underwater Badminton League."

Francis slipped the book into the pocket of his tweed jacket. "I'm listening."

"I need help breaking into Hurley's house so I can search for his old case notebooks."

"You're not serious?"

"Serious as a tax audit. His notebooks weren't in the evidence room at the garda station. *None* of the evidence in the McCarthy case was at the garda station."

"Because the case is so old, they destroyed it."

Gethsemane shook her head. "Because someone stole the evidence box. Recently, according to O'Reilly. He said there was no dust in the space on the shelf where the box was supposed to be."

"And you think Hurley relocated it."

"Yes."

"Why come to me?"

"The only other adults in this village I know well enough to ask for help are a cop and a priest." She almost added, *and a ghost.* "You don't ask cops and priests to help you break in to murder victims' houses."

Francis stood and pushed his glasses up on the bridge of his nose. "You're right. This is almost as good as the Underwater Badminton League."

Declan Hurley's house sat at the end of a forlorn street, several yards distant from its few neighbors. A weather-beaten privacy fence surrounded Hurley's backyard, the only feature that distinguished the murdered man's rundown lodging from the other equally worn houses dotting the dingy thoroughfare.

Gethsemane and Francis waited in Francis's car until dark then crept onto Hurley's property. The beam from Francis's flashlight reflected off yellow crime scene tape crisscrossing the front door. The duo tiptoed into the backyard through an unlocked gate. Yellow crime scene tape also barred the rear entrance. The windows were all locked.

"Any ideas?" Francis said, his voice a whisper.

"A tire iron," Gethsemane replied.

"In the boot of my car at the other end of the street."

"Hurley's car's parked next to the house." Gethsemane took the flashlight and led the way to Hurley's dented sedan parked in a narrow driveway formed by the fence and a side wall of the building.

"Check the trunk."

Francis looked around. "What trunk?"

"Of the car."

"Oh, the boot." Francis opened a car door and released the trunk latch. Gethsemane lifted the lid and rooted under blankets, old clothes, and empty liquor bottles until she laid her hand on a long, thin metal object.

"Got it," she cried, holding up the crowbar.

Francis shushed her.

"Got it," she whispered.

Francis lowered the trunk lid and they crept back around to the rear of the house. Gethsemane held the flashlight while Francis jimmied open a window.

"Give me a boost."

Francis hoisted her through the window then climbed in himself. She shown the flashlight around. They were in the kitchen.

"If you'd stolen evidence from a police station, where would you put it?"

"Careful." Francis pushed the flashlight beam toward the floor. "Number one rule of creeping around places you've no business being: Don't shine torches through windows. You'll alert the neighbors."

"Do you think any of them will care? Doesn't look like the type of place with an active Neighborhood Watch program."

"Do you want to find out?"

"Point taken. Shall we try upstairs first?"

"No. Hurley was old, fat, and out of shape. He wouldn't have lugged a box upstairs."

"Right. Let's look for a living room or study."

Gethsemane and Francis made their way into the hall. The foyer and front door stood at the opposite end. Three doorways opened off the hall: a bathroom, a closet, and—

"The study," Gethsemane said, shining the light into a cramped room stuffed with a sofa, big screen television, pool table, and stacks of magazines.

"More like a den. I doubt Hurley ever studied anything in here."

Gethsemane moved farther into the room then stopped suddenly. Francis plowed into her back.

"What is it?" he asked.

Gethsemane didn't answer. In a corner, the flashlight illuminated an overturned bar cart. Broken glass littered the floor around it. The light moved to a dark stain on the floor. "This is where it happened."

Francis squeezed her shoulder.

Gethsemane closed her eyes and took a deep breath, held it for a count of five. "I'm okay," she said when she exhaled. "I'm okay. Let's look for the box."

"Why are you so sure Hurley took it?" Francis asked as they searched the room, careful to avoid the stain.

"Because if anyone had examined the evidence they'd have known Hurley, at best, botched the original investigation or, at worst, colluded with a criminal to frame an innocent man. He's also the most likely to have had access to the evidence room. The police won't let civilians in, but they might let a former colleague."

"I don't see anything."

"I do." Gethsemane shone the light on the lid of a cardboard storage box protruding from beneath the sofa.

"The box could be in another room."

"But you know it isn't. Hurley stole the box from the station and his murderer stole the box from him. Something in the box must have pointed to the real killer and it's most likely at the bottom of the Atlantic or reduced to ashes by now."

"I'm sorry for your disappointment." Francis took the flashlight. "But don't you think we'd better get out of here?"

They started for the hall. Gethsemane paused. "One last look."

Francis trained the light in the corner where Hurley died. "Seems our boy died doing what he loved." The light passed over several liquor bottles on a shelf above where the broken glass lay.

"He was pretty drunk when he called me. Stop." Gethsemane put her hand on Francis's arm, holding the light still. "That bottle in the back of the shelf."

Francis retrieved the bottle and held it out to Gethsemane. She recognized the distinctive black and red label. "Waddell and Dobb Double-oaked Twelve-year-old Reserve single barrel bourbon.

Special ordered all the way from Kentucky, just for Eamon McCarthy."

Francis used the flashlight to examine the bottle more closely. "It's been opened." He raked the light over the rest of Hurley's liquor collection. "The rest of these are strictly bottom shelf. Can't have cost more than ten Euros a bottle. This," he hefted the Waddell and Dobb, "isn't Hurley's style. But why's it here?"

"He must have removed it from the evidence box. Twenty bucks—Euros—says this is *the* bottle. The one that killed Eamon. Maybe Hurley knew someone would come looking for it. The best place to hide something is in plain sight. How long do you think poison can be detected in whiskey?"

"One way to find out. I know a private toxicology lab in Cork. The chemistry teacher's sister heads it and he owes me a favor."

"Good points. I knew you were the right man for this job." Without warning, sirens blared in the distance. Gethsemane swore. "I think we woke up the neighbors."

She and Francis ran back to the kitchen and scrambled out the window, careful not to drop their prize. The sirens' wail grew louder as they exited the fenced yard. Flashing lights blinked in the distance.

"What do we do?" Gethsemane asked.

"Run for it."

Francis turned off the flashlight and they dashed through the darkness toward his car. Gethsemane stumbled. Francis grabbed her arm to keep her from falling, nearly dropping the bottle.

"Thanks," Gethsemane said once she'd steadied herself. "But if you have to choose between me and the bourbon, save the bourbon."

They ran again and reached Francis's car as lights and sirens turned onto Hurley's street. They ducked down onto the floorboards.

"Now what?" Gethsemane asked. "If we start the car they'll notice us."

"We'll just wait here until they leave."

No such luck. Sirens drew near. A car pulled to a stop and a car door slammed. Flashing lights reflected off the windshield above them. Gethsemane climbed up into the seat and pulled Francis up by the lapels.

"Kiss me," she said.

"Wha—"

Gethsemane put her arms around Francis and pulled him into an embrace. His glasses clattered to the console. Someone tapped on the car window. Gethsemane held the kiss for a few more seconds then pushed Francis away. She put on her best "Who me, Officer?" face.

Francis rolled down the car window. He seemed to have trouble finding words.

"Is there a problem, officer?" Gethsemane asked.

The garda shone his light around inside the car. Gethsemane slid the bourbon bottle beneath the seat with her foot.

"We got a report of a possible break-in in progress in the area."

"We didn't notice anything."

The guard gave the car's interior a onceover with the flashlight again. Apparently satisfied they weren't cat burglars, he told them to move along. He winked at Francis before walking back to his own car.

Francis put his glasses back on and straightened his lapels.

"Are you okay?" Gethsemane asked.

"Fine," he answered without looking at her. "You?"

"Fine. We'd better beat it before that cop changes his mind."

Francis put the car in gear. Gethsemane fished the bottle of Waddell and Dobb from beneath the seat.

"My friend visits his sister on Sundays," Francis said. "I'll run that by his place tonight after I drop you off."

"Thanks, Grennan." They drove in silence for a while. Gethsemane kept her eyes on the road as she spoke. "That kiss."

Francis kept his eyes forward too. "Yeah?"

"It was nothing personal. It was just, you know, to fake out the cop. Right?"

"Right. Nothing personal."

Gethsemane burst into the cottage. "Irish! I found it! I found it!"

Eamon materialized near the coat rack. "Found what? Where've you been? Have you any idea how late it is?"

"Stop being such a nursemaid and listen. I found it."

"What the hell is *it*?"

"The poisoned Waddell and Dobb. At least, I'm pretty sure it's the poisoned bottle. Why else would Hurley have it?"

"Darlin', are you having a breakdown? Is the shock of Hurley's murder getting to you?"

"No, I am not having a breakdown. Would you listen?"

"Would you make sense?"

Gethsemane took a deep breath and counted to ten. She spoke slowly. "I found the bottle of bourbon I think was used to poison you."

"Found it where?"

"In Hurley's house."

"What the hell were you doing in Hurley's house?"

"Searching for evidence."

Eamon hung his head.

Gethsemane started from the beginning. "I talked O'Reilly into letting me examine the evidence from your case. When he went to get it from the evidence room at the station he discovered it was missing. I had a hunch Hurley might've taken it, so I broke into his place—"

"Darlin', when I asked you to help me I didn't intend for you to resort to felony."

"How else was I going to find out if Hurley swiped the box? Which was a felony on his part. His felony negated mine."

"Not even under American law. You broke in on your own?"

"I, uh, may have had some help."

"Not O'Reilly."

"Course not. He's a cop."

"Frankie Grennan."

"No comment. Anyway, the bottle's going to a lab. I don't know if anything will come of it, but if it does let's pray it points to your killer."

The combination of sun and blue sky Sunday morning convinced Gethsemane to accept Father Keating's invitation to church. After services, she munched cake in the churchyard, courtesy of the Hospitality Guild. She stared past the graveyard to the Poison Garden. She couldn't take her eyes off it. A murderer's fresh market in the middle of town. Something nagged her...

"Beautiful." Francis Grennan stood behind her. Steam from the paper cup he held fogged his glasses. "An effective camouflage for lethality."

"I didn't notice you in church."

"Sat in the rear balcony. You're interested in the poison garden?"

"Curious."

"Ever seen it up close?"

"Up close, no. I glanced through the fence but it was too dark to see much."

"C'mon then." Francis tossed his cup into a trash bin disguised as a statue of Saint Fiacre and started walking. They strode past trees and shrubs arrayed in autumn's red-gold, wound through labyrinthine tombstones, and stopped at the poison garden's wrought iron fence. Francis reached inside a small stone font tucked underneath a nearby holly. He pulled out a key and unlocked the gate.

"How did you know that was there?" Gethsemane asked.

"Everybody knows it's here."

"What's the point of locking the gate if everyone knows the key's hidden under a bush?"

Francis shrugged. He swung the gate open. "Coming?"

Gethsemane followed him inside.

Gravel crunched beneath their feet as they moved along narrow paths. Up close, in the daylight, the garden's plants looked more ominous than they had in the twilight with iron bars keeping them at a safe distance.

Francis pointed out plant names on brass markers. "Castor bean. Progenitor of ricin, a poison favored by Eastern European secret police. Hemlock. Popular with Greek philosophers. Wolfsbane, a personal favorite. Wards off werewolves. And James Joyce used it to kill off Rudolph Bloom."

"James Joyce killed someone?"

"On paper."

"Why do you know this stuff?"

"It's a hobby. Plants, not poison. Come look at these." Francis led Gethsemane to another section of the garden. "Crocus. That's where colchicine comes from. Deadly nightshade. That's atropine. What?"

Gethsemane had stopped reading plant labels. "Thanks again for last night."

"Did something happen last night?"

"Did someth—" She reached up and put the back of her hand against Francis's forehead. "You're not feverish."

"I don't know about you, but last night I was tucked up at home with a book and a glass of whiskey. I was not out committing the serious crimes of breaking and entering and theft. I hope you weren't either."

"Let me rephrase. Not that either of us went out last night, but if one of us had gone out and the other had gone with her and helped her do something that almost got them thrown in jail, one of us would want to say thank you."

"The other of us would say you're welcome. And he'd wonder again why the other of us asked him since he's not exactly been nice to one of us."

Gethsemane searched for words. "You know that one guy you can always count on to go along with whatever scheme you cook up no matter how outrageous or how wrong the plan is? You're that guy. Underneath that curmudgeonly exterior beats the heart of a trickster."

Francis gave a sweeping mock bow, sending his glasses tumbling. Gethsemane stooped to retrieve them. She read the label on the plant where the glasses fell. "Foxglove. That's what Nuala fed me at her tea party."

"Nuala Sullivan? You actually ate food from Nuala Sullivan?"

"I nibbled. I didn't eat."

"Aren't you the brave soul? Nuala sometimes adds special ingredients to her recipes. Did anyone tell you about the punch at the fete?"

"Father Keating."

"Or the cayenne pepper in the cinnamon cookies at the Garden Club bake sale?"

"What's with her? She gets her jollies making people ill?"

"Nuala's psychotic."

"Not all people suffering from psychoses are dangerous."

"Not all dangerous people suffer psychoses. Nuala Sullivan is that rare combination of both."

"Why is this woman roaming the village? She needs to be institutionalized before one of her 'pranks' kills someone."

"She has been. She..."

Francis's words faded as something in the distance behind him caught her attention. Something lying on the ground, peeking out from behind a tombstone. A human foot shod in an Aladdin slipper.

"What is it?" Francis turned to see where she looked.

Gethsemane exited the poison garden into the graveyard. She stopped short next to a statue of St. Bibiane. At the statue's base, purple caftan spread out like a deflated hot air balloon, lay Siobhan Moloney, eyes and mouth open wide. The sun glinted off her silver tooth. An arrow protruded from her chest.

Nine

Gethsemane spent the most of what remained of Sunday in an exhausting repeat of Friday—answering a homicide detective's questions at the garda station. *How well did you know Miss Moloney? What was the nature of your relationship? Do you find it strange discovering two murder victims, being in the village only a fortnight?* His tone and expression told her she was lucky she had alibis for both murders. Or was he angry her arrival in the village coincided with a doubling of his workload?

Warned by the garda not to talk about the case, Monday flew by in a blur of dodging questions from faculty and students. By the end of the day, the only things she wanted to discuss were whether to have Bushmills or Waddell and Dobb and whether to prop her feet on the coffee table or the sofa as she drank it. She gathered her belongings.

"Knock, knock." A wan Francis leaned in the doorway. "How goes it?"

"Haven't dissolved into a quivering heap yet. Tempted, though. How're you? You look rough."

"Didn't get much sleep. Guards kept at me until two a.m. Did you know there are more than a dozen ways to ask someone if they did it?"

Gethsemane tried not to look surprised. "Why would they ask that?" Was "Did you do it?" a routine police question?

"Because I could have come and gone from the rear balcony without being seen, I had a variety of reasons for not mourning the passing of Siobhan Moloney, and I'm a mad decent archer."

Or not so routine. "I thought plants were your hobby."

"I'm a Renaissance Man."

"But archery?"

"Half the village can handle bow and arrow. The archery competition's the most popular event at the Field Day games."

"Seems so medieval."

"So does murder."

Gethsemane collapsed into a chair. "Two murders in one week. Yours and Orla's make four total."

Eamon materialized on the sofa opposite. "Only four murders in a quarter century."

"My hometown boasts six murders in three hundred years. Murder may be common in the big city, but in small towns people are supposed to die in their beds when they're ninety-two."

"It's Nemesis, goddess of divine retribution, evening up the score. Hurley and Siobhan got what was coming to them. The local bookies gave even odds whether Hurley would die by another's hand or at the bottom of a bottle. Dirty cops earn enemies. Can't pretend I'm sorry."

"What about Siobhan? I didn't like her but the death penalty for hosting a few bogus séances seems a bit harsh."

"More than a few. But you're right, 'twas nothing worth killing her for. I'll let you in on a not-so-secret village secret. Siobhan put on the Madame Blavatsky routine to cover up her true stock-in-trade."

"Her true stock-in-trade being?"

"Blackmail. Siobhan's spirit guides whispered sweet nothings from beyond the grave, almost always of an embarrassing or incriminating nature. For a 'small consideration' Siobhan promised to keep the secrets buried."

"Ghosts provided her with blackmail material?"

"Cop on."

"Well, I don't know, do I? In my limited experience ghosts in this village seem to be a prime source of gossip."

"I am not a gossip. But even if an entire heavenly host of specters took over the Information Bureau, it would've been no use to Siobhan. She was as psychic as yesterday morning's toast. She obtained her information the mundane way, from jealous exes, greedy neighbors, and fluthered pub rats. And she wasn't above listening at keyholes and peeping in windows."

"If the whole village knew this, why didn't anyone turn her in? All of the police can't be as incompetent as Hurley."

"No, but some are just as dirty. According to rumor, Siobhan had stuff on several high ranking gardaí. Who'd dare investigate her, even if someone worked up enough nerve to turn her in?"

"Easier to shoot her with an arrow? And cheaper?"

"Not many will miss her."

Gethsemane moved to the window and leaned her cheek against the cool glass as she studied the clouds darkening in the distance.

Oh, to be in Boston. Or Dallas. Or even back in Bayview. Anywhere but in an obscure Irish village with a rising body count.

"Things could be worse," Eamon said.

Gethsemane wrapped her arms around her shoulders. "I guess St. Brennan's could burst into flame shortly after all the boys succumbed to an outbreak of food poisoning brought on by tainted carrot batons. That would be worse."

"Aren't you Suzy Cheerful this evening? Try to look on the bright side. At least the concerto's finished."

Gethsemane held her hands over her ears. "Don't talk to me about the concerto. The All-County is less than three weeks away and the boys are still struggling to perform as a whole greater than the sum of its individual musicians, my brilliant-but-irritating soloist has yet to be on time for rehearsal, and Hieronymus Dunleavy is pushing me to ditch him for reasons I suspect have nothing to do with tardiness. I need more than your concerto to pull this off, I need divine intervention."

"Maybe Father Keating could put in a word."

"You ceased being amusing three minutes ago."

"So forget all this and go home." The leather-soap aroma filled the room.

Home. Where? Dallas? Bayview? One of the countless other places she'd called "home" when she'd performed with this symphony or that ensemble? Places where the only people she'd gotten to know were other musicians who, like herself, had long since moved on? "I promised you I'd help."

"You have. You proved I didn't murder Orla."

"I haven't convinced O'Reilly to reopen your case."

"I release you from that part of the deal. You put a bug in his ear, that's enough."

"But the concerto—"

"Take it. My gift, with thanks. Contact my old manager. He'll help you sell it. It should pay for your plane ticket."

"And then some. But what about Billy? He owns the rights to your music."

"Tell him you found it off-property, at the library or school."

"Can't do it. Even if I thought I could pull it off without being sued by half of County Cork, I'd be going home a failure. A disappointment. My overachieving family holds failure in low regard."

"They'll recover."

"You've never met my family. My eldest sister turned sibling rivalry into a blood sport."

"I'll write some more for you, a symphony, a few sonatas to go along with the concerto. Tell people you found them in a box under the floorboards. Even if someone else lays claim to the rights you'd be famous for discovering them. You could go to the music director of any orchestra in the world and choose any job you want."

"You'd do that?"

"Yes." Eamon's aura shimmered a mix of yellow, purple, blue.

"I'm either going to kick myself or get drunk for saying this, but no thanks. I'm staying. I'll prove you and Orla were murdered and get O'Reilly to investigate."

"Why?"

"Because," Gethsemane returned to the sofa, "friends don't run out on friends."

"Are we friends, then?"

"We tease each other mercilessly, aggravate each other endlessly, and agree to impossible requests by the other. Seeing you miserable and lonely because you can't get to your wife breaks my heart." Gethsemane peered down her blouse. "I do have one buried somewhere beneath this cynical, steely exterior. Of course, I don't expect you to be broken up about me being too ashamed to face my family. My hang up's trivial in comparison to your loss."

"There's nothin' trivial about shame, darlin'. One of the deadliest weapons in the human armamentarium. Shame's been used to control entire cultures for centuries. Ever hear of honor suicide?"

"My family's not *that* bad. You're not expected to commit seppuku or throw yourself in front of a train if you screw up or, worse, quit. You only have to put up with constant reminders about how you disappointed everyone by failing to live up to the family's standards."

"Which may be worse than ritual disembowelment."

Gethsemane laughed.

Eamon's aura morphed into a red halo. "That's the spirit."

"Pun intended."

"I'll pour the bourbon, friend." Eamon levitated bottle and glass. "Meanwhile, why don't you open that?" He inclined his chin toward a plain envelope propped on the desk.

Gethsemane examined it. The front bore only her name and the cottage's address, both typewritten, and a Cork postmark. "Who'd send me mail here?"

"Open it and see."

Her drink and a letter opener set themselves in front of her.

She sliced the envelope's flap and held up a yellowed newspaper clipping. "No note."

Eamon materialized next to her.

"Why can't you just walk?"

"Why be a ghost if you don't take advantage of the perks." He leaned over her shoulder. "Read."

The article, from the English-language *Cork Guardian*, detailed the sudden death of university student, Oisin Ardmore, found dead in his dorm room. No signs of trauma were evident. Several pill bottles lay scattered around the room. Cause of death was ruled cardiac arrest due to accidental drug overdose. It was dated more than forty years ago.

"I know that name," she said. "From the pharmacist, Aoife Fitzgerald. He was in some photographs I asked about. The pharmacist told me he died. She didn't seem to want to talk about it."

"Don't suppose she did. Aoife had a terrible crush on Oisin. Her father treated him like a son. His death devastated the old man."

"You knew him?"

"Well enough to buy him a pint. He dated Pegeen Sullivan for a short while in college. Orla and I double-dated with them once or twice. We didn't care for him. Peg seemed besotted."

"Who'd send this to me? Why send this to me?"

"You asked about him. Maybe one of the librarians thought you'd be interested."

"I didn't ask about him at the library. I didn't hear of Oisin Ardmore until after I'd already been there. Anyway, a librarian wouldn't mail me the original article. She'd make a photocopy and leave it for me to pick up." Gethsemane refolded the clipping. "Another mystery." She couldn't deal with this one right now. Her head hurt. "The line forms on the right." She started towards the hallway.

"Where're you going?" Eamon asked.

"For a walk."

"It's fixing to rain."

Gethsemane called over her shoulder as she opened the door. "It's always fixing to rain around here."

The rain held off for an hour as Gethsemane roamed along the Carrick Point Cliffs. She whistled as she battled the wind, the notes lost in the lonesome howl. Her father had whistled the same tune whenever he worked on a complicated math problem. He'd always solved the problem by the end of the song. Twice through and she hadn't solved anything. She didn't know who killed the McCarthys, she had no idea how she'd convince O'Reilly to take her seriously, and now she had a mystery pen pal.

Every so often Gethsemane stopped and peered over the edge of the cliffs at the waves breaking over the rocks below. She imagined Orla standing in the same spot. She imagined someone—male? Female?—coming up behind her and—hitting her over the head? Pushing her? Struggling with her?

Gethsemane gasped as a gust pushed her back from the cliff's edge, almost knocking her over. Maybe O'Reilly was right, it was an accident. Orla had been blown to her death. Too bad you couldn't arrest the wind. Gethsemane shivered and looked over the edge again. What possessed Orla to come out here at midnight on Halloween?

A raindrop hit Gethsemane in the ear. She looked skyward. Another drop hit her in the eye. She looked at her bootless feet, then toward the cottage, a dot in the distance. How'd she walked so far without realizing it? The path back would be mud before she got halfway home. The thought of slogging through ankle-deep muck in a bone-chilling tempest turned her toward the lighthouse standing watch at the summit of Carrick Point. Closer than the cottage and over a rockier path. If she dashed she might make it before the storm hit full force. She took off at a run.

*   *   *

She arrived at the lighthouse at the same time as the deluge. She ran to the tower and, with a sigh of relief, pushed the heavy door inward. She navigated around the ground floor's boxes—some of them seemed out of place since she'd last been to Carrick Point—with care to avoid bruised shins. She shook the staircase's handrail. No falling plaster. Kieran must have tightened the screws. She circled up toward the lantern, hoping to find the warmth that escaped her downstairs. She reached the first landing and pushed the door open—and found Teague Connolly and Aoife Fitzgerald braced against the clockworks in the center of the room, entwined in each other's arms.

Aoife saw Gethsemane first. She screamed. Teague made a noise and flushed crimson. They untangled themselves and jumped apart, staring at the floor as they smoothed clothes and hair.

"Sorry," Gethsemane said. "Just looking to get out of the rain."

"Us too," Teague said.

"I, um, twisted my ankle coming up the stairs," Aoife said. "I couldn't put weight on it. Teague was just helping me."

"Oh, sure." Gethsemane nodded. "That's what I figured." She crept into the room and inched her way along the wall. "I'm just going to go sit over there in that corner—no, not a corner, the tower's cylindrical, no corners. I'm just going to go sit on that side of the room." She pointed to the wall farthest from the door. "I'm babbling. Don't pay any attention to me. I'm just going to go sit. Over there. Where it's dry. Sort of. Just until the rain stops, then I'll be on my way. Don't mean to disturb you. Just ignore me. I'm still babbling."

Teague and Aoife moved to opposite sides of the room. Teague smacked a gear shaft as he walked by it.

When Gethsemane, huddled beneath a window, tired of pretending to study the derelict clockworks, she stood on tiptoe and looked out. After a moment, she said, "Teague?"

Teague grunted.

"Are you expecting company?"

"You mean besides yourself?"

"Yeah. I mean someone driving your car."

Teague and Aoife rushed to the window, jostling Gethsemane out of the way.

"Oh, God, it's her," Aoife said. "How'd she find us here?"

"She's a damned witch," Teague said.

"Mrs. Connolly, I take it?" Gethsemane asked.

Gethsemane, Aoife, and Teague retreated to their positions and waited. The lower door slammed hard enough to carry over the wind. Heels, stilettos by their sound, clanged on the iron staircase, closer and closer. The smell hit—a blend of berries, coconut, and vanilla. The door flew open, shaking as it banged against the stone wall.

The woman framed in the doorway seemed to block out all light. Her pose—arms and legs outstretched, palms pressed against the doorjambs as if to keep them from collapsing in on her—made her appear larger than she was, like some jungle creature puffing its fur or its feathers to frighten an enemy. Scarlet fingernails stood in for bloody claws.

Gethsemane tuned out the torrent of invective the woman shouted at Teague and Aoife and studied her. She was shorter than Aoife but taller than Gethsemane. Her red hair complemented her green eyes and her flaming temper. She appeared a few years younger than Aoife, thanks to the assistance of a surgeon. Her short skirt and cropped top showed off toned muscles. She wore twice as much makeup and jewelry as Aoife, almost as much as Siobhan. But where Siobhan had seemed garish, this woman looked as if she'd just come from the salon.

Eventually, she noticed Gethsemane. "Who the bloody feck are you?"

Teague answered. "Dr. Gethsemane Brown, you've not met my wife, Eileen Connolly."

"The new school marm?" Eileen sneered. She looked as though she smelled something dead.

"How do you do, Mrs. Connolly?" Gethsemane asked. She didn't add, "It's a pleasure to meet you." Lies shouldn't be obvious.

"What the bloody hell are you doing here?" Eileen's gaze shifted to her husband. "Havin' a threesome?"

"Don't be disgusting, Eileen," Teague said.

"*Me* disgusting?" Eileen launched into another profanity-filled tirade.

After a minute or so, Aoife clamped her hands over her ears and yelled, "Stop it! Stop it! I can't do this anymore."

Eileen rushed Aoife. Teague grabbed his wife.

"Actually, Mrs. Connolly," Gethsemane positioned herself between wife and lover, "Ms. Fitzgerald and I were out for a walk and got caught in the storm. We came here to wait it out and ran into Mr. Connolly. I guess he had the same idea."

"You?" Eileen sneered and jerked her head toward Aoife. "Out with her? Do you think I'm thick?"

"Of course I don't think you're thick," Gethsemane said. "I don't even know you. But Ms. Fitzgerald and I *were* out for a walk. I asked her about native plants that might be toxic and she graciously agreed to point some out."

"A nature tour?" Eileen asked. The sneer remained.

"Yes, that's right." Gethsemane sniffed. "That fragrance you're wearing. Is it Vainglory?"

Eileen tossed her hair. "Yes, it is."

"I thought so." Gethsemane hated Vainglory. Her rival at Vassar wore it. It cost two hundred dollars an ounce. "You have refined tastes, Mrs. Connolly."

"Thank you, Dr. Brown." Eileen ran her hands over her skirt and patted her hair, her composure returned. "Not everyone appreciates such an exclusive perfume." She looked at Teague.

Aoife slowly exhaled.

Gethsemane offered Eileen her hand. "Please, call me Gethsemane."

"Storm's over," Teague said. "They're like that around here. Blow in fast and unexpected, rage like the coming apocalypse, then blow over quick as hell can scorch a feather." He took his wife's arm. "You take the car and go on home. I'll follow along on foot."

"Don't be ridiculous, dear." Eileen extricated her arm. "We're going to the same place, we'll ride together." She looked at Gethsemane and Aoife. "I'm sure the ladies can make their way back."

Teague frowned. "I don't know, Eileen. I think I ought to—"

Eileen's lips pursed.

"That's kind of you, Mr. Connolly," Gethsemane said, "but Ms. Fitzgerald and I will be fine. The cottage isn't too far and she can call a cab from there."

Eileen relaxed. "You see, no need to be gallant. You come home with me."

"Well—" Teague hesitated.

"It's all right, *Mr. Connolly*," Aoife said. "Dr. Brown and I will finish our nature walk. I want to show her two of my favorite poisonous wild flowers—Housewife's Tongue and Widower's Joy."

Eileen lunged. Teague grabbed her again, throwing her off balance, then half-steered, half-dragged her from the room. Gethsemane and Aoife listened as the new volley of venom faded away down the stairs.

Aoife threw her arms around Gethsemane and hugged her. "Thank you."

"Aw, shucks," Gethsemane said in her best mock cowboy voice. "'T weren't nothing."

"It took guts, stepping between Eileen Connolly and the target of her wrath. She's the most stylish woman in town with the dirtiest mouth and the foulest temper. She's sometimes violent."

"Lucky I didn't know that."

"Don't sell yourself short." Aoife clapped Gethsemane on the back. "I'll bet you'd keep calm faced with a fire-breathing dragon."

Aoife and Gethsemane walked together as far as Carraigfaire Cottage. The just-rained scent of wildflowers and wet earth clung to the air. The women didn't speak much as they picked their way around puddles, trying to avoid the deepest mud. Aoife did point out the names of a few wildflowers along the way and explained their traditional uses.

"For veracity's sake," Aoife said with a laugh.

The cottage came into view around a curve. Lights shone in the windows and peaty smoke rose from the chimney.

"Charming place," Aoife said. "Do you like it?"

"I do." Gethsemane nodded. "Now. It took some getting used to."

"Seems strange to see the cottage all lit up and inviting again. It sat dark for so long after Eamon and Orla died."

"Did you know the McCarthys well?"

"Well enough to say hello and chat a bit. Mostly Orla. She came by the pharmacy quite often. Dad sold stationery supplies then. Orla swore he stocked the best pens in the county. Said her poems flowed as smooth as their ink when she wrote with them."

"What do *you* think happened to Eamon and Orla?"

"Eamon pushed Orla over the cliff and then poisoned himself."

"You really think that?"

Aoife remained silent for a long while. "Not really, no. I think they met with foul play." She looked at her feet. "Not that I'm one to go about saying such things."

"What if I told you that I found evidence—irrefutable evidence—proving Eamon couldn't have murdered Orla?"

"You're serious?"

"As tax season. And what if I told you I'd given the evidence to the police?"

"I'd tell you to be careful, Dr. Brown."

"Gethsemane."

"Be careful, Gethsemane. The cliffs aren't the only treacherous things in Dunmullach. There's some who would go to great lengths to keep their secrets secret."

*   *   *

Gethsemane invited Aoife in to use the phone.

She declined. "I've got my mobile and my car's parked farther down the road. Thanks again for running interference with Eileen."

"Don't mention it."

Aoife took a step, then stopped. "May I—" She hesitated. "May I tell you something?"

"Sure."

"Remember at the pharmacy you were looking at photos and you asked me what happened to Oisin Ardmore?"

"You told me he died." Had Aoife mailed her the article from the *Guardian*? "You seemed reluctant to talk about it."

Aoife nodded.

"It still hurts, even after all this time. Not just because of my feelings for Oisin, but because of the effect his death had on Dad. Oisin truly was like a son to him. Dad shut down. Couldn't function. We were afraid he'd lose the pharmacy."

"He recovered?"

"Eventually. But that's not what I wanted to tell you." Aoife paused, tears in her blue-green eyes. Gethsemane waited. The pharmacist continued, "The guards said he died of a heart attack."

Eamon had told her as much.

"Oisin started doing drugs when he went to university. The pressures of class, the wrong crowd of friends, you know the story."

"You think Oisin died of an overdose?"

"I think drugs killed Oisin."

"I don't understand."

"Oisin wasn't a kind person when he was using. Cruel, even. He hurt people, badly. More than one grew to hate him. Hate him enough to feed him drugs he didn't intend to take. Hurt breeds vengeance."

"You think someone poisoned Oisin to get revenge? Someone he'd hurt. Did he hurt you, Aoife?"

Aoife gasped. "Oh, God, no. Not me and not Dad, I swear.

Oisin left the drugs alone when he was with us. When he was with others...I'm talking crazy, aren't I? What're the odds of another unsolved murder written off as something else? Too much coincidence."

"Something must have aroused your suspicions. Me asking questions about Eamon and Orla?"

"No, not you. How well do you know Siobhan Moloney?"

"Not well," Gethsemane said. "Enough to suspect I wouldn't want to tick her off."

"Siobhan stopped in the pharmacy asking about Dad's old inventory records. She wouldn't say why and I was afraid to ask. You didn't push Siobhan Moloney. She may have looked like a carnival fortuneteller in those get-ups of hers, but beneath the caftan beat a cold, mercenary heart."

"You wouldn't have records from that long ago. Would you?"

"I have records from the day the pharmacy opened. We Fitzgeralds are packrats. That's not what I told Siobhan, though. When she left, I started looking through the old logbooks. I noticed discrepancies in inventory around the time Oisin died. Discrepancies in the amount of drugs ordered from suppliers and the amounts actually on the shelves in the stockroom."

"What kind of discrepancies?"

"Dad didn't record specifically which customers bought which drugs but he, or one of his assistants, did note in the inventory logs when a drug was sold or was returned to the supplier. He and his assistants also did a bi-weekly count of the stockroom supply. According to the books, around the time of Oisin's death some drugs were unaccounted for. They weren't sold or returned and they weren't on the shelves. I think the drugs were stolen and used to murder Oisin."

"Did your Dad notify the authorities?"

Aoife shook her head. "I told you, Dad was in no shape to do much of anything after Oisin died. He turned running the pharmacy over to others for a long time. I doubt he knew about the theft."

"Wouldn't whoever was running things for your dad have known?"

"Maybe the fox was guarding the hen house."

"You know who did it, who stole drugs and poisoned Oisin."

"I don't know. Not for certain. And I don't want to go around pointing fingers. Word gets around town...I meant it when I said some people would go to great lengths to keep secrets."

"I'll make you a deal. Bring me your evidence and I'll take it to the police. To Inspector O'Reilly. No one except him will know it came from you."

"I'll think about it." She checked the time on her mobile phone. "I'd better go. Thanks again for Eileen and thanks for listening."

"Before you go, did you mail me something? A letter?"

"No. Someone mailed you a letter? Here?"

"Never mind. Drive safely."

"About the lighthouse—"

Gethsemane winked. "What lighthouse?"

Gethsemane waited until Aoife disappeared around the curve, then peeled off her mud-caked shoes and opened the cottage door. The leather-soap smell hit her full in the face.

"Where the devil have you been?" Eamon's voice boomed through the hallway.

"Out walking." Gethsemane tossed her shoes in a corner. "Like I said."

Eamon mimicked her. "Out walking."

"Your American accent sucks." Gethsemane headed for the study.

Eamon's voice followed her down the hallway. "Out walking in a bloody gale force storm. You might've been killed. The winds on the cliffs can throw a grown man over the edge. Think what they'd do to a wee thing such as yourself."

Gethsemane poured herself a bourbon.

"Thanks for giving me credit for enough sense to come in out of the rain. I rode out the storm in the lighthouse." She flopped on the sofa.

Eamon materialized next to her.

"Oh. Of course, the lighthouse. Sorry. And my American accent's better than your brogue."

"Not." Gethsemane sipped. The bourbon's slow burn down her throat warmed her. "Guess who I found in the lighthouse?"

"Kieran?"

"Your brother-in-law."

"Teague? What was he doing up there?"

"More like *who* was he doing. Aoife Fitzgerald."

"Aoife? Teague and Aoife? You're jokin'."

"And just when it looked like I'd spoiled all the fun, guess who arrived to liven up the party?"

"Tell me."

"Your brother-in-law's wife."

"Eileen? The she-devil of County Cork? Whoo hoo!" Eamon slapped a hand through the arm of the sofa. "I bet poor ol' Teague would've preferred to take his chances with the wind. Being dashed to pieces on the rocks wouldn't have been half as painful as listening to that harpy shriek at him."

"Not that I condone adultery, but in Teague's case I'll make allowances. What'd he ever see in Eileen?"

"It's a long, complicated story that's no more fun hearing than telling. Eileen Rafferty Connolly's been a dirty piece of work since the age of twelve." Eamon leaned away from Gethsemane and looked her over. "You seem to have escaped unscathed. Didn't even muss your hair. When Eileen attacks, she doesn't give a damn about collateral damage. How'd you manage to stay out of the kill zone?"

"I told a fairy story about Aoife and I being on a nature walk and running into Teague accidentally."

"She bought that?"

Gethsemane emptied her glass. "No, but she bought it when I

complemented her on her refined tastes and her exquisite perfume. Stroking her ego defused her long enough for Teague to drag her out."

Eamon laughed.

"Guess what else?"

"I'm no good at guessing."

"Aoife believes you were murdered. She believes Oisin Ardmore was murdered too. Poisoned with drugs stolen from her pharmacy."

"A mad poisoner on the loose in Dunmullach? Except Oisin died in Cork."

"Cork's not that far away."

"Does she know who did it?"

"She has a strong suspicion, but she wouldn't name names. She's nervous—afraid. She also won't go to the police herself. I told her I'd go."

"Hmmm." Eamon looked worried.

"'Hmmm' means it occurred to you Aoife's reluctance to speak up for fear of reprisal means the killer is still alive and well enough to kill again."

"Oh, so you can read my thoughts now?"

"Am I wrong?"

Eamon rolled his eyes. "Well, no. Not wrong so much as partially right. Aoife might be afraid of a grey-haired murderer or she might be afraid of a murderer's offspring. Secrets and grudges get passed down through the generations like the family silver in these parts. It wouldn't be beyond the pale for a son—"

Gethsemane held up a finger. "Or a daughter."

"A woman?" Eamon raised an eyebrow.

"Eileen's a woman. She'd stab you in your sleep."

"Aye, point taken. Or daughter to commit murder to save the family's reputation."

"First and second generation murderers notwithstanding," Gethsemane stood, "once Aoife tells me what she knows, I'm going to O'Reilly and I'm camping out in front of his office until he agrees to open an investigation."

"Don't suppose it would do any good to tell you to be careful?"

"When am I not careful?"

Eamon glowed orange-yellow. "No, not one damn bit of good."

Ten

Gethsemane spotted them on her way to the pub after school on Wednesday. In an alley between the pizza parlor and the Laundromat, partially obscured by a dumpster, Eileen Connolly and a man who was not Teague leaned against a wall. The man buried his hands to the wrists in the back pockets of Eileen's skinny jeans. Gethsemane couldn't see Eileen's hands, but from the closed-eyed, opened-mouthed expression on the man's face she guessed what Eileen's hands were doing. She hurried past.

Inside the pub, Gethsemane found Inspector O'Reilly in a booth at the back. File folders covered the tabletop. A full pint glass sat neglected near his elbow. As Gethsemane wound her way toward him, dodging tray-laden waitresses, it dawned on her he sat in the same booth Siobhan had used to conduct her business. A chill halted her for a moment. She ignored the looks—from Nuala, Pegeen, and Deirdre at a table near the window, from Jimmy Lynch at the bar with the pub regulars—aimed in her direction. She nodded hello to Francis as she slid into the booth opposite Inspector O'Reilly. He kept reading.

"Afternoon, Inspector."

O'Reilly didn't look up. "Afternoon, Dr. Brown."

They sat in silence. O'Reilly flipped pages. Gethsemane pulled his pint glass toward her.

"Are you going to drink this?"

"Help yourself," he said.

Gethsemane sipped the dark bitter liquid and made a face. She couldn't pretend she liked lager. She pushed the glass back. "Aren't you going to ask me what I want?"

"You'll tell me, whether or not I ask."

"You're right, I will. I may have evidence pointing to a murderer."

O'Reilly raised his head.

"Got your attention?"

"For a moment," he said. He motioned to a waitress.

"Thanks, but I'm good."

"The drink's for me. I suspect I'll need something stronger than a pint."

"Since you're having one anyway, you can buy me a Bushmills Twenty-one. Neat," Gethsemane said as the waitress approached.

"Make that two," O'Reilly said to the waitress. He turned back to Gethsemane. "What evidence?"

"I don't actually have it yet."

O'Reilly leaned back against the bench, closed his eyes, and pinched the bridge of his nose.

"Don't start," Gethsemane said. "I'll have evidence soon. Well, as soon as Aoife Fitzgerald finds it."

"Aoife Fitzgerald?" O'Reilly sat up. "What's she got to do with it?"

Gethsemane unfolded the newspaper clipping she'd received in the mail and slid it toward O'Reilly. "Someone sent me this piece about Oisin Ardmore. He was a student at University College in Cork. He died suddenly and his death was blamed on a drug overdose."

O'Reilly skimmed the article. "I know the case."

"You know the—? How?"

"One of my mates, fella named Kildare, heads the cold case unit with the Cork Garda. He's working this."

"As a homicide?"

"Yes." O'Reilly set the article on the table but didn't slide it back to Gethsemane. "What's it got to do with you? Aren't the McCarthys enough to keep you busy?"

"I told you, someone mailed that article to me. I didn't go looking for it."

"Who sent it? Aoife?"

Gethsemane shrugged. "No idea. Aoife said not her. I asked her about Oisin—did you know they grew up together?—and she told me she thought he'd been deliberately poisoned. And she had an idea of who'd done it."

"Did she say who?"

"No." The waitress set the whiskey on the table. Gethsemane ignored her. "But she said her father's inventory records could prove the drugs used to murder Oisin were stolen from her pharmacy."

"Where are the records?"

"At the pharmacy. Aoife's afraid to bring them to the police herself, so I volunteered to bring them for her."

"Of course you did."

"What's that supposed to mean?"

"It means you've a habit of getting mixed up in things you've no business being involved in." Gethsemane opened her mouth to reply, but O'Reilly's raised hand stopped her. "I don't want to argue, Dr. Brown. I need you to get those—No, never mind. I'll see Dr. Fitzgerald and get the records myself. I do want you to come to the station and give a statement, though. Kildare's coming to town. I'll introduce you. He'll get a kick out of you. He's attracted to hard-headed women."

"I am not hard-headed. I just don't give up when I know I'm right about something. And I'm right about the McCarthy deaths." She drained her glass and stood up. "Wait." She sat back down. "How do the Cork police know Oisin's death wasn't accidental? There was nothing in the article."

"The Garda don't reveal everything to the press. Have to keep some details back in case we get a confession. To answer your question, the drug used to poison Ardmore wasn't a party drug and it wasn't prescribed for him. No reason for him to be taking it on his own."

"What was it?"

"Cardiac drug. Digitalis."

Eleven

"I'm sorry, Headmaster, Mr. Dunleavy." Gethsemane glanced at the clock for the third time. "We'll proceed without him. Ruairi, you'll take the solo. Feargus, you're first chair."

"I warned you. Unreliable." Dunleavy harrumphed and tugged his lapels.

"I'm sure there's a reasonable explanation, sir." Riordan pulled a handkerchief from his pocket and dabbed his forehead.

"Of course, Richard. Typical Nolan."

Feargus signaled the oboe for an A. The boys tuned, brass, woodwinds. Another A and the strings tuned. Ordered, efficient. Gethsemane climbed the podium and raised her baton.

The door banged open on the downbeat. "Sorry I'm late." Colm's voice drowned out the opening notes of *St. Brennan's Ascendant*.

Gethsemane kept her back to him. "Colm Nolan, report to Headmaster Riordan's office."

"Headmaster's right here."

"My office, Mr. Nolan."

Feet scuffled, the door slammed. Gethsemane raised her baton again. She pretended she didn't hear Dunleavy's comment as Eamon's melody filled the room.

"Such a disappointment."

*   *   *

"I've got it." Francis burst into the faculty lounge and locked the door behind him.

Gethsemane and the math teacher had the room to themselves. Gethsemane grabbed a steaming pot of coffee. "Got what?"

"The tox report." He unfolded a sheet of paper from an envelope.

Gethsemane relaxed and poured herself a cup of the coffee. She poured tea for Francis and joined him at the table.

"Read this." He slid the sheet toward her.

"Digitoxin, Digoxin, Digoxigenen, Dihydrodigoxin...What is this?"

"I asked the chem teacher. It's a list of active metabolites of digitalis found in the bourbon. The bourbon was laced with digitalis. Toxic levels."

"How toxic?"

"In high enough doses digitalis causes lethal cardiac arrhythmias. If McCarthy drank from this bottle..."

"This is the second time this week I've heard of someone dying from digitalis poisoning. First, a guy in Cork named Oisin Ardmore, forty-something years ago, now Eamon, twenty-five years ago. The papers wrote Oisin's death off as an accidental drug overdose, but O'Reilly says it was murder."

"When'd you see O'Reilly?"

"The other day at the Rabbit."

Francis toyed with his teacup. "What were you doing in a pub with a Guard?"

"Telling him about the newspaper clipping about Oisin Ardmore someone mailed me." She omitted the detail about Aoife's evidence. The fewer people who knew, the better.

"Why the pub? Why not the station?"

"What difference does it make?"

"You meet folks at the pub to socialize."

"Since when do you care who I socialize with?"

"I don't care." Francis blushed. His cup clinked loudly against his saucer. "What's this about a newspaper clipping?"

"Someone, I don't know who, mailed me the article about Oisin's death. No note or anything identifying the sender came with it."

"What's it got to do with McCarthy?"

"*Two* digitalis poisonings? You don't think they're related?"

"Seeing as how there's over a decade between them, no. Digitalis isn't hard to come by. Easy enough to grab some from the medicine cabinet and dispatch some unfortunate soul. Unless you think McCarthy murdered Ardmore and offed himself the same way when the guilt finally caught up with him."

"Ridiculous. Eamon McCarthy no more killed Oisin Ardmore than I did. Eamon didn't kill Oisin, himself, or anyone else. He's not a killer."

"You sound as if you know him personally."

"I, uh—" Did Grennan believe in ghosts? "I know of him. He didn't seem the type to murder anyone."

They both jumped at pounding on the door. "Who's in there?" an angry voice cried. "Who locked this door?"

"Ah, bloody—" Francis let the visitor, a stubby balding man with a bad tie, into the lounge.

"What's going on in here?" The man blustered. "Who locked that door? This lounge is for the use of the entire faculty."

Francis whispered to Gethsemane, "Teaches Latin and Classical Greek. It's gone to his head."

"If the two of you—" He pointed his stubby finger back and forth between Gethsemane and Francis "—want to fraternize during school hours—"

"Fraternize? Were we fraternizing, Grennan?"

"I'd call it cavorting."

"Cavorting? Canoodling."

"Consorting."

"Keeping company."

The Latin teacher harrumphed and stomped over to the teapot. Gethsemane refolded the toxicology report. "Thanks for this, Grennan. I'll take it to O'Reilly. At the station."

Eamon materialized on the bike rack in the faculty parking lot.

Gethsemane jumped. "I swear, Irish—" She glanced around. She didn't want anyone to see her talking to what would appear to be herself.

"Digitalis, huh? That was the bitter and slightly spicy substance slipped into my bourbon?"

"How did you—"

"I was in the lounge. I read the report over your shoulder."

Gethsemane rolled her eyes.

"Hurry and take it to your Guard. See what he makes of it."

"O'Reilly is not *my* Guard."

"Is Grennan your maths teacher?"

"No."

"You were the one who said 'canoodling.'"

Eamon winked.

She made it to the station in time to catch O'Reilly pulling out of the parking lot. He rolled down his window. "Have you spoken to Miss Fitzgerald since she told you about the drugs theft?"

"No. I thought you were going to go see her."

"Haven't been able to catch up with her. I left messages. If you do see her, ask her to call me, please."

"Sure."

"Thanks. Sorry, but I have to go." He rolled up his car window then rolled it down again. "You'd best stand back. We don't want to bump into each other this time. The car will hurt."

Gethsemane, toxicology report still in her pocket, watched him drive away. Had he spooked the pharmacist by trying to contact her? She'd promised Aoife she'd take the evidence to the police herself, not that she'd send the police to fetch it. She'd better go see Aoife and make things right.

Gethsemane knocked a half-dozen times before giving up. Aoife wasn't home. She wasn't at the pharmacy either. Gethsemane checked there first. The assistant on duty would only tell her the pharmacist was out and wasn't expected back soon. Had Aoife been frightened into hiding?

She heard the stilettos on the driveway before she saw Eileen striding to the porch, as bejeweled as the night of the lighthouse confrontation. Skin-tight leopard print pants took the place of the miniskirt. A cloud of Vainglory surrounded her. Gethsemane steeled herself.

"Where is she? Where's the slag?" The only difference between Eileen and a dragon was a lack of smoke billowing from her nostrils.

"Where's who, Mrs. Connolly?"

"Don't play innocent with me. You're standing on her bloody porch, ain't ya?"

"I've no more idea where Aoife Fitzgerald is than you."

"Oh, I've a feckin' brilliant idea where she is and who she's with. It's no coincidence my Teague's out of town at the same time that slut's nowhere to be found. Away on business, he says. I'll give *him* the business." She shoved a vermillion-tipped finger under Gethsemane's nose. "And if you're a part of this—this conspiracy—to keep a man away from his wife..."

Time to end this. The best defense..."Mrs. Connolly, you've got me all wrong. I would never dream of interfering with the sacred bonds of marriage. Especially yours. You and Teague inspire me. I can only hope someday to have a marriage half as vital as yours. Maybe we could get together and you could share your secrets for keeping your marriage vibrant. You could invite your friend. Is he single? Dating anyone seriously?"

Eileen's eyes narrowed and she stepped back. "What friend?"

"The guy I saw you with near the pizza parlor the other day. It looked like you were helping him get his zipper unstuck. So sweet of you. But hey, if you can't count on a friend to help you with a stuck zipper who can you count on? Am I right?"

"So help me, if you tell anyone—"

"I do need to speak with Aoife, but about more important things than your social connections. But since Aoife's not home, we should probably leave. You should leave. Come back some other time."

"I'll do that. And I'll see you some other time too."

"I'll look forward to it. You, me, Teague, dinner. Invite your buddy, make it a foursome."

Eileen walked away without a word. Her scent lingered. Gethsemane sneezed. God, she hated Vainglory.

Twelve

"The boy's chronically late." Gethsemane played Saint-Saens' "Danse Macabre in G Minor." The day had not gone well. Riordan had reminded her that her continued employment depended on his, meaning Dunleavy's, continued faith in her ability to lead St. Brennan's to victory. He'd hinted replacing Colm as soloist would be a sign warranting that continued faith.

"Maybe his watch is slow." Eamon joined her at the piano, his hands melding with hers as their fingers flew over the keys.

Static shocks coursed up Gethsemane's arms. "He wears a Rolex. Rolexes don't run slow."

"Maybe he has bladder control problems."

"At sixteen? Maybe he's just arrogant and inconsiderate and thinks the universe owes him." Maybe Dunleavy was right. Damn.

"No worse than any other teen lad. Trust me, I used to be one."

Their fingers reached for a chord. "Did you ever let being a teenager interfere with music?"

"Of course. I was fourteen, thought I knew more than my parents, my instructors, everyone. I went about my lessons arseways, generally acted the maggot. You know how it feels, wanting to live normal like the other kids. You resent music for taking over your life, for separating you from the crowd, making you stand out, alone. It's why you played softball, a *team* sport."

"Yeah, but I quit music to play ball. I knew it was one or the other. I didn't try to do a half-assed job of both."

"Boys aren't as logical as girls. I think the testosterone surge damages brain cells."

"What brought you back to your senses?"

"Orla threatened to never speak to me again unless I got straight. Peg threatened to toss me off Carrick Point Lighthouse."

Gethsemane dropped her hands to her lap. "I have to demote Colm. Give the solo to Ruairi and make Feargus concertmaster."

"You're afraid Peter Nolan won't be happy about his nephew not headlining the show?"

"I am not." Her elbow shot through Eamon's ribs. "This is my orchestra. I decide who plays. Not the judges."

"But?"

"If I do what's best for the orchestra, Dunleavy and Riordan will think I caved to them. I don't cave."

"I noticed."

Gethsemane played Mogwai's "Kill Jester," channeling her misgivings to the keyboard.

"What's Dunleavy got against Colm? The boy aggravates me, but I'd drag him from a burning building if it came to it. I suspect Dunleavy'd let him burn."

"Perceptive of you. Has nothing to do with the lad, per se. Dunleavy's have hated Nolan's for three, four hundred years. Family disputes over money and property. Part and parcel of being the two wealthiest families in the village."

"It's personal with Dunleavy. More immediate than a four-century-old grudge."

"Colm's ma broke her engagement to Dunleavy to elope with Colm's da. Didn't help the whole village thought she got the better deal in Nolan. Young, handsome, and rich instead of old, dry, and rich."

"Now I get it. Brutal enough being thrown over halfway to the altar. Having to deal with the offspring of a union you desperately never wanted to happen, downright diabolical. Dunleavy denies

Colm the solo, he gets some measure of revenge on the woman who he believes wronged him."

"Your dilemma: keep Colm as soloist and pacify Peter Nolan or dump Colm as soloist and pacify Dunleavy and Riordan."

"My solution: drop Colm to first violins because he doesn't possess the maturity to handle the responsibility of soloist and don't worry about Dunleavy, Riordan, or Peter Nolan."

"Spoken like a true maestra."

"Thank you."

"Be careful. You're claiming ownership of the St. Brennan's orchestra. You risk finding it hard to give up once you win your job back in the States."

Colm sauntered into the music room ten minutes late for his appointment. Gethsemane let him wait until she finished grading a student quiz, one of several stacked on her desk. "Have a seat."

Colm nodded at the pile. "Too bad you don't have an assistant. The senior instructors get a boy to help mark papers."

"I'll manage. You're late." As usual.

"Sorry." Colm crossed his legs and leaned back in his chair.

"Do you mind telling me where you were when you were supposed to be here?"

Colm shrugged. "Mr. Jameson wanted to see me after practice today. He's going to start me in the game against St. Michael's."

"And all the other times you showed up late?"

"Mr. Jameson."

"Soccer."

"Football," Colm emphasized the word, "is important, Dr. Brown."

"So's orchestra, except, apparently, to you." Gethsemane pushed aside memories of her own year of high school sports. She'd given up music, made a choice. She hadn't tried to juggle both. "You can't be a football star and a violin virtuoso at the same time. Which is why I'm giving the solo to Ruairi."

"Ruairi? You're coddin'?"

"No, I'm not."

Colm knocked over his chair. "You can't do that. I *deserve* the solo. I'm better than Ruairi."

"Colm, you have the gift of transforming beautiful music into transcendent music. You lack discipline and dedication. Your attitude, frankly, stinks."

"But Ruairi? He sits like a mouse staring at his shoes, not saying a word unless you speak to him."

"He's shy. I can work with shy. He plays almost as well as you. I can work with almost as good. I can't work with indifferent brat."

"If I can't be soloist, I quit the orchestra."

"I hope you don't mean that, Colm, but it's your decision."

"You won't win without me."

"We'll try."

"Dunleavy's put you up to this."

"This is my decision. I'm the maestra."

"So that's it, then?"

Gethsemane slid an exam from the top of the stack. "Pick up your chair."

Colm righted the chair and stomped to the door, jostling several other chairs on the way. He paused at the threshold. "We'll see what happens."

Gethsemane braked her bicycle at the junction of the road to town and the road to Carrick Point. She looked out over the village as she ran through the meager contents of her pantry. Guinness stew at the pub sounded better than peanut butter and jelly on stale crackers at home. Gethsemane turned her bicycle toward town. She hummed "I'll Tell My Ma" as she pedaled to the Mad Rabbit, admiring the red and gold fall foliage she passed. She had just reached Bunratty's Off License when a tremendous boom tore through the air. Gethsemane nearly fell off her bicycle. At the far end of the street flames and black smoke shot into the air. The pharmacy. Gethsemane raced to the scene. Dozens of townspeople gathered on the sidewalk, talking excitedly, gesturing, and shouting for help. A few people tried to get near the burning building, but the flames drove them back. Soon the shriek of sirens drowned out the voices of the onlookers. Firefighters and police officers took over the sidewalk, pushing spectators farther down the street. Something caught Gethsemane's eye as she moved back—Teague's car parked in the pharmacy parking lot. Shards of glass glittered on the car's roof. A chunk of smoldering masonry protruded through the smashed windshield.

Thirteen

"It's a damned shame about Teague." Eamon shoved his hands into his pockets and leaned against a bookcase. Gethsemane read the titles through his chest. "He was a good man. Orla adored him." His aura glowed a sad yellow.

"I'm sorry," Gethsemane said. "I liked Teague and Aoife."

"Eileen's havin' a hooley, I bet. Shed of a husband without the bother of annulment or scandal of divorce. She'll play the sympathy card and wear widow's weeds for a week or three then bring that boyfriend of hers out in the open."

"You knew about that?"

"Everyone except Teague knew about that."

Gethsemane picked up the newspaper from a console table under the window. The explosion at Fitzgerald's Apothecary dominated the *Dunmullach Dispatch*'s front page: *Explosion Kills Two, Gas Leak Suspected.* "At least Teague and Aoife were the only ones in the pharmacy when it blew up," she said. "Things could've been worse. What if it had been one of the gas lines at St. Brennan's instead?"

"Hmm," Eamon said.

"What's hmm mean?"

"It's Irish for 'I wonder.'"

"About...?"

"You noted it yourself. There've been an awful lot of violent deaths in Dunmullach this past few weeks."

"This is different. Someone murdered Hurley and Siobhan. The explosion was an accident."

"So says the *Dispatch*."

"You disagree?" Gethsemane folded the newspaper. "Bashing a guy's head in and shooting a woman with an arrow take plenty of chutzpah but minimal skill. Blowing up a building—at least without blowing up yourself and half the neighborhood—requires some technical know-how."

"Eileen knows how. Her father owned a demolition company and her eldest brother disposes ordinance in the army."

Gethsemane smelled the faint aroma of leather and soap. "You think Eileen murdered two people?"

"The two people being her husband and his lover." Hints of blue surrounded Eamon. "You've met Eileen. She's capable of murder."

"Capable of spontaneous violence, maybe. But of a well-planned murder? One that required patience and precision timing?"

The fragrance and the blue glow dissipated. "You're right, it's not really Eileen's style. She'd prefer ripping your eyeballs out to long-distance killing." Eamon moved closer to her. Her cheek buzzed as his fingers brushed it. "I've been thinking. You've been working nonstop between getting ready for the All-County and trying to light a fire under O'Reilly."

"Hmm."

"What's hmm?"

"It's American for 'he's getting ready to sugar me off.'"

"No sugar coating. Forget about murder. Focus on the All-County."

"Forget about proving you didn't kill your wife? Forget the one thing that's kept you from resting in peace for a quarter of a century?"

"But you *did* prove I didn't murder Orla. You put O'Reilly on to that videotape."

"I haven't proved she didn't commit suicide. Or fall

accidentally. And I haven't proved that you didn't poison yourself."

"Let it wait. At least until after the All-County."

"I expect to be on my way back to the States after the All-County. Peter Nolan? The Boston Philharmonic? Remember?"

Eamon stared at his shoes.

"I remember."

Gethsemane passed a hand through Eamon's shoulder. "Why the change of heart?"

"When we started the body count held at two—Orla and me. Truthfully, I thought our murderer had escaped human justice and was dead and rotting in hell. But now—" Eamon paced. "God, I hate admitting I'm wrong."

"But now you think one person killed Teague, Aoife, Hurley, and Siobhan, the same person who killed Orla and you."

"Aye."

"When I suggested a connection between—"

"I said I was wrong, didn't I?"

"As much as I enjoy hearing those words from your mouth, let me play Devil's Advocate. No one knew Aoife's plans except me. Aoife wouldn't have told anyone. Well, maybe Teague but he died with her. Why kill Aoife if you didn't know she could prove you were a murderer?"

"Who did you tell?"

"No one. Well, you. O'Reilly. But that's it. And I don't peg O'Reilly as the murderer."

"Where did you tell O'Reilly? At the garda station?"

"At the Rabbit."

Eamon groaned.

"What? I didn't stand on top of the bar and make a general announcement. We sat in a booth near the back. No one came near us other than the waitress and she only stayed long enough to take our order and bring our drinks."

"The barmaids at the Mad Rabbit have ears like parabolic microphones. They're the grease that keeps the Dunmullach gossip wheel turning."

"Wait." Gethsemane gasped. "Are you saying the waitress overheard me then told the killer?"

"Told the killer, the killer's uncle, the postman, the butcher..." Eamon sat next to Gethsemane on the piano bench. She shivered as his hand passed through hers. "I'm not blaming you, mind. You weren't to know."

She pulled her hand away and hugged her shoulders. "I could've guessed. I grew up in a small town. I've lived away so long I forgot how gossip spreads."

"It's not your fault." A blue halo framed Eamon's head and sparks popped. "Damned busybodies ought to have their tongues cut out and their lips sewn shut."

Neither Gethsemane nor ghost spoke for several moments. Eamon broke the silence. "Quit."

"I can't. I told you."

"Sure you can. Quitting's easy. Don't ask any more questions, don't dig up any more clues. Stick to orchestra business. Quit snooping. Better disgraced than dead."

"You sound like O'Reilly."

"O'Reilly's got sense under that stupid hat."

"I don't get why you want me to stop. I'm helping you."

"Do you really not know I don't want to see you harmed? A bloody maniac's on the loose with six murders to his credit. A seventh murder would be easier than slipping on ice. I'd rather you not be number seven."

"When did you start to care?"

"I don't know. I didn't mark the date on the calendar. But I do care, a great deal. Which is why I'm telling you—begging you—stop."

"Quitting's not who I am. It's not in my DNA. My father's father was a brilliant cellist who couldn't land a gig with a professional orchestra because he was black and it was the nineteen-twenties. He didn't quit the cello and go back to tailoring, he started his own orchestra. My mother's parents were sharecroppers. When she was born the plantation owner's wife congratulated Grandma on the birth of 'another little cotton picker.' Everyone told Mother poor, black, country girls don't get to be doctors, so she became a doctor. My father battled mental illness, hiding it so he could attend lectures in college instead of group therapy in an institution. Everyone thought he'd do well just to stay out of a padded cell, so he became dean of the mathematics department. Succeeding despite everything being against you, beating the odds, is a family tradition." She moved to the window and stared out at the threatening clouds hanging low over the cliffs. "I don't look good with my tail between my legs."

"Your tail's going to wind up six feet under if you're not careful."

"I'm careful. Anyway," she said, trying to convince herself as much as Eamon, "I don't think I'm in real danger."

"Are you daft or are you just trying to provoke me?"

"Six victims. What did you all have in common?"

"We never saw it coming."

"Exclude Orla. She died first so let's say she was the real target. The murderer feared the rest of you could expose him. He killed you as damage control."

"Which puts you squarely in the crosshairs."

"Or not. 'Cause, let's face it, I have no idea who our killer is."

"I doubt such a fine point will trouble him as he's dispatching you from this life to the next."

"If he took me seriously as a threat, wouldn't he have come after me already?"

"Just because no one's come after you yet doesn't mean they won't."

"Thank you for worrying about me—"

"But you've no intention of acting like you've got some sense and dropping this before you get hurt."

"That's not exactly how I'd have put it."

"Well, it *is* exactly how I put it." Leather and soap filled the room as Eamon glowed bright orange-yellow. "And damned if I'm going to stick around to watch you get your fool-self killed. Damned stubborn." Eamon vanished. As the leather and soap aroma faded, his faint, disembodied voice cautioned, "Be dog wide. Please."

Gethsemane's usual ability to rationalize a situation away failed her by lunchtime, forcing her to admit Eamon was right. A serial killer—six victims certainly qualified one as a serial killer—would sooner add her to the hit list than risk exposure. Her best hope of avoiding the victims' fate, short of high-tailing it out of Ireland, was to get conclusive evidence of Orla's murder to O'Reilly before the killer got to her. Which meant she had to find some conclusive evidence. Fast.

She needed a clue. From one of the villagers? Nuala Sullivan? Too unstable. Deirdre Lynch? Too much risk of a run-in with her sociopathic brother. Father Keating didn't gossip and Kieran didn't talk at all. Mrs. Toibin had gone out of town for the rest of the week. Pegeen Sullivan didn't like to talk about the past. Who could blame her? She had a hunch. Thinking of the Stinney case, she rode to the library to take a stab at back issues of the paper.

An hour spent scrolling through microfilmed copies of the *Dunmullach Dispatch* reminded Gethsemane why facts beat hunches. Four decades' worth of reading turned up nothing more interesting than a photo of Headmaster Riordan and a man she didn't recognize holding archery trophies won at the annual Michaelmas Festival and Field Day Games. She fast-forwarded the microfilm, tuning out the blurred images zipping past on the screen and the whir of the spindles as film unwound from one reel onto another. She pulled out pen and paper and wrote down what she knew—someone murdered Orla and Eamon twenty-five years ago and the same person recently murdered four more people to keep from being exposed for the original murders. She wrote one word about what she could prove to O'Reilly's satisfaction—nothing.

The *thwap, thwap* of the end of the film pulled Gethsemane back to the room. As she pulled the reel from the spindle she noticed the label on the film box—*Please rewind*. She swore loudly, drawing a dirty look from the man in the next carrel. She apologized then swore again, under her breath, as she reloaded the film and flipped the machine's lever to reverse. An image scrolling across the screen caught her eye. She pressed pause. How had she missed it? Eamon's wedding photo, claiming half of the March twenty-fifth issue's front page. Orla and Eamon beamed in each other's arms. A wreath of flowers crowned Orla's flowing hair. A matching boutonniere graced Eamon's lapel. The accompanying article—an adulatory ode to the ripped-from-the-fairytales romance between world-renowned composer and acclaimed poet—took up the rest of the front page and most of the second. She judged from the percentage of the *Dispatch*'s front section given over to the wedding coverage and the number of people in the photos, the McCarthy nuptials rated as Dunmullach's event of the year. Everyone in town seemed to appear in at least one photo, many alongside international celebrities. Gethsemane leaned closer to the screen. *Almost* everyone in town. Pegeen Sullivan wasn't in any of them. She and Orla and Eamon were the oldest of friends. Odd to miss an old friend's wedding, especially when the barman and the postmistress managed to make it.

The closing chime interrupted further speculation about Pegeen's absence. Gethsemane returned the microfilm and went upstairs. She reached the first landing as Inspector O'Reilly descended. He zig-zagged to avoid a collision and dropped the overstuffed file folder he carried.

"Sorry, Dr. Brown." He tucked his hat under his arm as he bent to collect the fallen papers.

Gethsemane stooped to help. She glanced at the papers as she handed them back. "None of these seem to be about the McCarthy case."

"Because," O'Reilly stuffed papers back into the file, "there is no McCarthy case. As I've explained. Repeatedly."

"You still say that? After all that's happened? You've admitted Eamon McCarthy couldn't have pushed his wife off a cliff. Why can't you admit someone else did?"

"After all that's happened, I still have no evidence Orla McCarthy didn't jump or accidentally fall."

"You have proof Eamon and Oisin were poisoned with the same drug."

"But none that McCarthy didn't spike his own whiskey."

"What about Aoife's evidence of drug theft?"

"Evidence that no longer exists." O'Reilly, hat in one hand, files in the other, tried to move past her.

Gethsemane stepped in front of him. "So Eamon's death remains a suicide and the case remains closed."

"A succinct summary of the situation, Dr. Brown." He spoke in the tone St. Brennan's schoolmasters reserved for boys in the lower school who tried their patience. "While I appreciate your interest in Dunmullach's crimes, please understand the cold case unit consists of one man—me—and these," he held up the expandable file, "are the cases my superiors want me to close. Expeditiously." He stepped past her on the opposite side. "Again, please excuse me."

Gethsemane blocked him a second time. She ignored the muscle twitching in his jaw. "What about the recent murders?"

"What about them?"

"You *will* concede those were murders? At least Hurley and Siobhan. You can't accidentally bash your head in with a cricket bat or commit suicide by shooting yourself in the chest with an arrow."

"Not only will I admit Hurley and Miss Moloney were murdered, I'll concede Connolly and Miss Fitzgerald were murdered too. However, none of those murders are cold cases. Therefore, they're not my concern. They're active investigations being conducted by the homicide unit. *Once* again, excuse me."

Gethsemane shifted a foot.

"If you step in front of me, I'll arrest you for hindering an officer."

Gethsemane let him pass. When he reached the bottom of the stairs she called after him. "You know they're all connected."

O'Reilly paused, but didn't turn around.

"The murders," Gethsemane said. "One person committed all

of them. Whoever killed Eamon and Orla McCarthy twenty-five years ago killed Hurley, Siobhan, Teague, and Aoife this month. Solve one murder, you've solved them all."

O'Reilly looked up at Gethsemane and tipped his hat. "I'll pass that along to my colleagues in homicide."

"Don't patronize me, Inspector. A serial killer is running loose in Dunmullach and *one* of us is worried about it."

Gethsemane grabbed her bike, her renewed determination fueled by frustration, annoyance, and anger. Damned if she'd let O'Reilly put her off, damned if she'd let a murderer keep killing, and double damned if she'd let Eamon down. She pedaled for the Rabbit with a new plan—turn the tables and use Dunmullach's gossip wheel against the murderer.

The Rabbit held a thinner crowd than usual. Francis sat at the far end of the bar, drink in hand, empty glass at his elbow. The Sullivan sisters sat at a table near the door. Deirdre Lynch sat alone in a booth, surrounded by books, head bent, pen flying across paper. No Jimmy Lynch.

"Evening, Grennan." She took the barstool next to Francis and signaled Murphy.

"Same to you," Francis said.

"Bushmills Twenty-one?" Murphy asked.

Gethsemane nodded. She cleared her throat, raised her voice, and said to Francis, "I need to ask you something."

"Ask." Francis motioned for a refill.

Certain she had at least one barmaid's attention, Gethsemane asked, "Who murdered Orla McCarthy?"

All pub chatter ceased at once, as if someone had flipped a switch.

Francis, caught mid-sip, choked. He looked around the room and then back at Gethsemane. "I love the way Americans get right to the point."

"I *know* she was murdered. I can't prove it—" she glanced

around the bar "—yet, but I know it. I don't know *why* she was murdered. Motive points to suspect. But everywhere I dig for a motive, I hit a dead end."

Francis signaled for refills. "Name the most common motives for murder."

Gethsemane counted on her fingers. "Love, money, revenge, honor."

Francis sipped his drink. "Consider love. People have killed in its name as often as they've killed in the name of religion. The gardaí, and everyone else in town, assumed Eamon murdered his wife after a lovers' quarrel then killed himself in a fit of remorse. You've debunked that theory.

"Money."

"The McCarthys had plenty, Eamon from fame and Orla from family."

"Revenge."

Francis leaned against the bar. "My auntie was at school with Orla. To hear her talk, Orla was sweetness and light incarnate, adored by all. Doubt anyone had a vendetta against her. Eamon, on the other hand...I recall something about a brouhaha between him and a rival composer. Name-calling, lawsuits, that sort of thing. I think Eamon's the one who came out on top. Would being on the losing end drive a man to murder? You'd know more about the evil that lurks in the hearts of musicians than I."

"Not in this case. The rival died three years ago, car accident in Berlin. And we're looking for a motive for killing Orla, not Eamon."

"What better way to avenge a wrong than by destroying what your target loves? And the McCarthys died twenty-five years ago which is longer ago than three. Trust me, I'm a maths teacher."

"But four more people have been murdered within the past few weeks."

"A single killer?" Francis arched an eyebrow.

"You prefer a multitude of homicidal maniacs roaming Dunmullach?"

"Single killer it is." Francis drained his glass. "So far, we've ruled out love, money, and revenge. What does that leave us?"

"Honor," Gethsemane said. "Kind of old-fashioned. Anyway, there were no angry male relatives or cuckolded husbands in Eamon's past. He was that rarest of rarities, a man one hundred percent devoted to the wife he loved more than his own life. He never cheated. So cross honor off the list and we're back where we started. Nowhere."

"But haven't we slighted perhaps the most important motive of all?"

"What?"

"Jealousy, of course. Jealousy encompasses crimes professional, romantic, and pecuniary. So who was jealous of Eamon and Orla? Willing to kill the Joneses rather than try to keep up with them? Any scorned lovers lurking in the wings?"

"Enough!" Pegeen Sullivan slammed her glass on the bar. Amber liquid sloshed onto Gethsemane's arm and lap. "This isn't a game, some academic exercise for your amusement." Pegeen swung her arm, missing Gethsemane by an inch and knocking Gethsemane's glass to the floor. She shouted, "We've had nothing but grief since you came to town. Four dead in fewer weeks. 'Tis your doing."

Gethsemane leaned away from the shrieking woman. "I didn't kill anyone."

"You've brought a curse to this village, poking your nose where it don't belong. Digging up the dead instead of letting 'em rest. Stirring up ghosts."

"Do you mean ghosts in the metaphorical sense, Peg," Francis asked, "or is another Sullivan sister seeing things?"

"Shut yer hole, Frankie," Pegeen said. "These murders are her fault sure as if she'd swung the bat or shot the arrow."

"That's a bit harsh now, isn't it Peg?" Murphy said.

Pegeen put her nose an inch from Gethsemane's. "Eamon's dead and beyond caring what anyone thinks of him. Leave it alone."

"I'm sorry, I can't do that."

Pegeen slammed a fist on the bar and pointed at Gethsemane,

Francis, and Murphy. "To the devil with all of you." She shook a finger at Gethsemane. "You especially. Go to hell or go back to the States, just leave Dunmullach and leave well enough alone." She stormed out of the pub. The door slammed behind her.

"Wow," Gethsemane said. "Zero to intense in five seconds."

"Peg took Eamon's death pretty hard," Murphy said, mopping up the mess from the bar.

Gethsemane waved away another drink. She borrowed a towel and dabbed at the wet spots on her blouse and skirt.

"Not as hard as she took his marriage," Francis said.

Murphy exchanged Francis' empty glass for a full one. "Don't you go tellin' tales out of school, Frankie."

"'S not a tale if it's true."

"What am I missing?" Gethsemane asked

"Pegeen was particularly fond of Eamon," Murphy said.

"You don't get sent to St. D's for being *fond* of someone," Francis said.

Gethsemane swiveled on her barstool back and forth between the two men.

"What's St. D's?"

"St. Dymphna's. The old insane asyl—" Murphy corrected himself. "Beg pardon, the old 'mental health facility' just outside of town." He jerked his head southward. "Closed down five, six years ago."

"Pegeen was committed to a psychiatric hospital?"

"Don't get too excited. Half this village has been resident at St. D's at one point or another, including Eamon McCarthy. Mental illness is as common in Dunmullach as Irish eyes a smilin'. I think it's something in the water." Francis signaled for another drink. "Which is why I only drink this." He raised his glass.

"Other folks have to drink water, Frankie," Murphy said, "because you don't leave 'em anything else."

Gethsemane cut in. "Did you say Eamon was committed to a psych hospital?"

"Not committed. Checked himself in. Back before he and Orla

married. Nothing much to it. Eamon went through a rough patch and needed a rest is all."

"Exactly where outside of town is St. Dymphna's?"

"About half a kilometer south of here," Murphy said. "Up on Golgotha."

"Golgotha? The place of the skull? Bizarre name for a place meant to help people recover their mental health."

Francis snorted. "The only thing ever recovered at St. Dymphna's was fees from the health authorities."

Murphy explained. "We call it Golgotha. Carnock's the place's real name. A miserable pile o' rocks up Mulligan Road. Forlorn place to stick an asylum. More likely to turn a man into a header than cure him."

"About how long would it take to get out there?" Gethsemane asked.

"Why the interest?" Francis asked.

Gethsemane shrugged. "No special reason. Curiosity."

"Translation, she's headed up there to poke about."

"Nothing much up there to poke at," Murphy said.

"Except patient records."

Murphy shot Francis a look.

"Don't you go encouraging her."

"Dr. Brown needs no encouragement from me," Francis said. "She's a woman who knows her own mind."

"She's a woman who didn't suddenly turn invisible. She can hear you," Gethsemane said. "Go back to the part about the patient records."

"When they closed St. Dymphna's they didn't relocate the patients' charts. They left 'em behind, down in the basement."

Gethsemane had seen abandoned hospitals on *Ghost Hunting Adventures* where everything—charts, equipment, supplies—had been left behind where it lay, as if staff and patients had been taken up in the Rapture or abducted by aliens, dry land versions of the *Mary Celeste*. She'd only half-believed such places existed. "They left charts out in the open, where anyone could get to them?"

"Who'd be fool enough to go up there after 'em?" Murphy asked.

"They locked the doors," Francis said.

"Locked the doors. Right." Gethsemane climbed down from her barstool. "Please excuse me, gentlemen. Thank you for the whiskey." She nodded at Murphy and placed money on the bar. "And for the information." She nodded at Francis. "I'll see you at school, Grennan." She eyed the three-fourths empty glass in his hand. "I'll try to keep the orchestra rehearsal volume *pianissimo*."

Gethsemane left the pub. She stood on the sidewalk for a moment, eyes closed, and breathed in the smell of coming rain. Eamon neglected to mention his stay at St. Dymphna's. What else had he neglected to tell her? Was his stay somehow connected to Pegeen's? Or to the murders? Gethsemane shrugged on her mac and pulled up the hood against the beginning drizzle. She wouldn't confront Eamon about the psych hospital just yet. She'd go to St. Dymphna's first and see what the records held. She climbed on her bike and pedaled toward Carraigfaire Cottage. Preoccupied with plans for her escapade, she didn't notice Kieran watching her from a nearby alley.

Fourteen

The next morning, Gethsemane headed straight to her bicycle, pausing only long enough to consult a map she'd found at the cottage. She felt a twinge of guilt as she passed congregants in their Sunday best gathered in front of Our Lady but she kept on south to Carnock. She stopped at the base of a rocky outcrop and stared up at the towering derelict hulk of a building perched atop it. As she pedaled up the tortuous strip of cracked asphalt leading to the summit, images of Poe's House of Usher stuck in her head. The desolate patch of land deserved the nickname "Golgotha."

She leaned her bicycle against a gnarled tree bordering the overgrown semi-circular drive in front of the former psychiatric hospital and examined the massive brick building, half its windows boarded up, the other half with broken panes of glass looking like so many black eyes. A wind sprang up, carrying with it a hint of leather-and-soap. A faint voice suggested—or did she imagine it?—she forget about spooky basements and moth-eaten records and do something sensible like ride back to the Mad Rabbit for a drink. She ignored it and approached the abandoned asylum.

Chains and a padlock barred the front doors. Gethsemane picked her way through waist-high weeds and peered into one of the un-boarded-up windows. Mold grew on a mug in the windowsill, cobwebs hung from light fixtures, dust covered the nurses' station. She walked around the building, trying to find a

way inside. On her second circuit, she discovered a maintenance
door falling off its hinges. Several minutes of vigorous pushing,
kicking, and swearing yielded an opening large enough for her to
slip through. Her eyes adjusted to the building's dim interior as she
fumbled along a grim corridor to an even grimmer stairwell. She
felt her way down to, she hoped, the basement. Cobweb-laced
windows set high in the walls let in just enough light to see she
stood in another hallway, this one with doors at the far end. She
crept to the first and turned the knob. Locked. She tried another. A
storage room. A third. The morgue. She shuddered and slammed
the door. As she turned to go back to the stairwell she noticed a
second hallway branching off to the left.

Faded signs pointed the way to the records department.
Gethsemane followed a maze of corridors to a door with *Records*
stenciled on it in worn, flaking gilt. Hinges creaked as she stepped
into a room half a large as a football field. Gray metal shelves
crammed full with dust-covered brown folders of varying
thicknesses filled most of the space. Signs suspended overhead
labeled with letters of the alphabet indicated which charts occupied
a particular row. Gethsemane started toward the *M*'s, then
hesitated. Annoyance and suspiciousness about Eamon's
withholding his psychiatric history battled guilt over prying. She
changed direction toward the *S*'s. The Sullivans had enough
baggage to fill a travel supply catalog. She'd start by uncovering
their secrets.

Gethsemane walked down the row, pulling charts from the
shelves at random until she found a Sullivan. The typewritten label
affixed to the cardstock cover read *Nuala Sullivan*—Pegeen's sister.
Gethsemane blew dust from the chart, sneezing as the thick cloud
tickled her nose. She opened the chart to the first page.

She closed it after reading a decades' long history of mental
illness. Nuala had been labeled a pyromaniac at age eight. Age
twenty-one brought a diagnosis of schizophrenia. Nuala had
shuttled between the asylum and jail more than two dozen times
before her thirty-fifth birthday. Gethsemane remembered their

previous meetings. Was Nuala haunted by ghosts or by hallucinations? And did pyromaniacs blow things up?

Gethsemane traded Nuala's chart for one a quarter of the size—*Pegeen Sullivan*. Unlike her sister, Pegeen only had one admission to St. Dymphna's. She'd attempted suicide on March twenty-fifth, thirty-seven years ago, Eamon's wedding day.

"No wonder she missed the wedding," Gethsemane said aloud.

She read on. Pegeen stayed at St. Dymphna's for three weeks, after which her psychiatrist deemed her no longer a threat to herself or others and released her. Pegeen cooperated with all aspects of her treatment program during her stay except one—she refused to divulge why she drank a tisane brewed from foxglove.

Gethsemane re-shelved Pegeen's chart. She took a deep breath. Time to find out what put Eamon in St. Dymphna's.

McCarthys filled most of the *M* section's shelves. She hoped that only meant McCarthy was a common name in Dunmullach. Eventually, she pulled down Eamon's record, a folder about the same size as Pegeen's. Another deep breath, then she flipped open the cover.

She relaxed by the third page. Murphy spoke true. Eamon checked himself into St. Dymphna's for a "rest"—from a grueling tour schedule, a copyright battle with Ulbrecht, wedding preparations—and checked himself out two weeks later. He spent the interim entertaining elderly ladies on the dementia ward with show tunes.

Gethsemane put the folder back and dusted her hands. Guilt edged out irritation. Eamon probably hadn't thought his "stay-cation" worth mentioning. She wouldn't mention it either. She turned to go, then jumped at a thud behind her. A chart, three times as thick as Eamon's, lay on the floor beneath a newly empty space on a shelf just above her head in the L section. On the label— *Maureen Lynch*. She stood on tiptoe and slid the chart back into its slot. It fell again as soon as she put her feet down, landing open, almost on her toes.

"Eamon? Is that you?" She sniffed. Nothing on the air except the odors of dust and mildew. But maybe? The faintest hint of white roses and vetiver?

She stared down at the chart. Maureen Lynch's first admission to St. Dymphna's occurred on her eleventh birthday. Gethsemane picked it up. Continued reading brought back memories of paging through her mother's *Diagnostic and Statistical Manual* as a teenager. Maureen Lynch qualified as a "textbook case" of chronic mental illness. Her abbreviated life consisted of a series of increasingly long psychiatric admissions punctuated by increasingly short stays outside. Her diagnoses progressed over the years from quaint melancholia and hysteria to coldly modern major depression with psychosis and schizophrenia.

Gethsemane gasped. About two-thirds of the way through, Maureen Lynch became Maureen Sullivan. She kept the surname through a half-dozen more admissions, each coinciding with a desertion by her husband, Joe Sullivan. By the seventh, final, admission she was Maureen Lynch again. She'd been committed after the church granted her now-former husband an annulment. Maureen stabbed Joe's new girlfriend, a barmaid from the Mad Rabbit, then ran naked through town brandishing the bloody knife while screaming about what part of Joe's anatomy she intended to cut off. According to a police report neatly stapled into the chart, she'd been subdued by Oisin Ardmore and her youngest daughter—Pegeen—and taken into custody. Six weeks later she'd committed suicide by hanging herself in St. Dymphna's laundry room.

Gethsemane closed the file and reached up to replace it on the shelf. She held her breath. It stayed put. She crossed her arms against a sudden chill. Pegeen's sister started fires and her mother went after people with knives. Pegeen's suicide attempt seemed mundane in comparison.

Gethsemane looked at the shelves again. Her hunch paid off. She pulled down a chart labeled *Deirdre Lynch*. The record's family history section exposed Deirdre as Maureen's niece. Her problem list included homosexuality—considered a mental illness at the time of Deirdre's admission—and DeClerambault's Syndrome—

erotomania. Hadn't Eamon said Deirdre Lynch had an unhealthy attachment to Orla? Hadn't she witnessed the depth of Deirdre's devot—

Too late, Tchaikovsky warned her. Gethsemane's collar jerked up and back then something—someone—shoved her forward. Hard. A sharp pain lanced her eyebrow. Deirdre's chart slipped from her hand...

She awoke lying on the floor. Her forehead throbbed. Dark liquid mingled with dust in a pool around her face. She touched her cheek. Sticky. She held her hand in front of her eyes. Her fingers looked blurry...and red. She tried to count them. One, two, four...Her fingers moved away from her. The room dimmed...

Gethsemane coughed herself awake. She sniffed. Smoke! She sat up, sending pain shooting through her head and graying her peripheral vision. She lay down again and let her eyes scan the room. The shelf above her held nothing other than a red stain on its edge. The nearby shelves stood empty as well. She pushed herself up onto an elbow. Flames flickered from a small mountain of charts piled in front of the door. She rolled over and tried to crawl but the room's spinning thwarted her. She lay down once more and tried to force herself to think. She felt drowsy. Noises. Pounding. Wood cracking. Footsteps. *Oh, please, let them be coming closer*.

She yelled. "I'm in here!" Or did she imagine that too? She tried again. "I'm here!"

Everything went black.

Gethsemane blinked. And blinked. And blinked. The room faded into focus. Not the records room. Not a room at St. Dymphna's. A room with bright overhead fluorescent lights, one of which flickered and buzzed. A hospital room. Gethsemane closed her eyes.

"Dr. Brown? Dr. Brown, can you hear me?"

Gethsemane opened her eyes again. Three faces blocked her view of the lights—O'Reilly, Francis, and a man who looked familiar. And angry. She couldn't tell which one had spoken.

"Yes," she said to all three. "I hear you."

"How do you feel?" O'Reilly asked.

Gethsemane answered after a quick self-assessment. "Nothing from the chin up."

"Don't worry, miss." A fourth face, framed by a stethoscope, displaced the other three. "The feeling will return once the anesthetic wears off."

"Anesthetic?" Gethsemane asked.

The stethoscope nodded. "I gave it to you before I stitched up your forehead."

Gethsemane raised her hand to her head. A bandage covered her eyebrow. She remembered the sticky substance on her face and the red stain on the shelf. She shut her eyes. She wanted to ask questions but had difficulty putting words together in the correct order.

Inspector O'Reilly saved her the trouble. "You're lucky Kieran Ross saw you riding out to Carnock and followed you. What the hell were you doing up there?"

"I think Americans call it snooping," Francis said.

"Investigating." Gethsemane opened one eye.

"In Ireland we call it trespassing," the angry stranger said. Gethsemane recalled where she'd seen him—the homicide unit at the garda station. She didn't know his name. He continued. "And breaking and entering. Have you gone mad?"

A commotion spared her an answer. O'Reilly pulled back the curtain enclosing her stretcher. Two uniformed police officers dragged Nuala Sullivan, handcuffed and struggling, down the hall. Pegeen followed. The sight reminded Gethsemane of—something.

"Let me sister go, ya scabby gobshites!" Pegeen pulled at one of the officer's jackets. "She's done nothin'!"

"Nothing?" The officer dodged a foot. "You call smashing the grocery store windows and setting the fruit bins on fire nothing?"

"She's crazy," the other officer said, ducking an elbow. "All kinds of crazy, just like your ma. Belongs back in the looney bin, she does."

Crazy. Mother. Crazy mother. Gethsemane pressed her temples. Whose mother was crazy? She could taste the memory hovering at the edge of consciousness. She willed her synapses to start firing.

"You shut it." Pegeen grabbed the officer's arm. "My mother wasn't crazy. Neither is my sister."

"Both bat shite crazy. Whole damn Lynch clan's crazy and has been since your family tree was still an acorn."

Pegeen punched the constable. He staggered backwards and lost his grip on Nuala. Nuala bit the other officer and she and Pegeen bolted down the hall and out the door. The officer ran after them. The angry detective ran after the officer and O'Reilly ran to assist the fallen constable, then he and O'Reilly ran after the others.

"Once or twice a century Dunmullach wakes up," Francis said. "Glad I was here to see it."

Gethsemane propped herself up on her elbows. "Maureen Lynch."

Francis repeated the name. "So?"

"Pegeen and Nuala's mother."

"What about her?"

"She stabbed someone. And threatened to emasculate her ex-husband."

"Not surprising," Francis said. "The family does have a history of violence on the Lynch side. And a history of improvidence on the Sullivan side."

"What kind of violence?"

"Besides resident sociopath, Jimmy, and his father and his father before him? Deirdre's thrown a few punches in her day. She'd fixate on some bird, fancy they were best mates, then ramp up to ninety if her feelings weren't reciprocated. Her ma was the same. She once put a woman's eye out. You can trace most of the town's property damage to Nuala. And Peg flies off the handle if anyone reminds her the Lynches aren't the full shilling."

Another commotion arose. The four police officers dragged the two Sullivan sisters kicking and screaming back into the hospital.

Several hospital staff descended on the group. They managed to carry Pegeen and Nuala down the hall and out of view through a set of swinging double doors.

"Wow," Gethsemane said.

"You Americans put things so succinctly," Francis said.

"It's a gift." Gethsemane sat up and swung her legs over the side of the stretcher. She clamped a hand over her now-throbbing forehead and looked around. "Where're my clothes?"

Stethoscope tried to push her back down onto the stretcher. "Hold on."

Gethsemane shook him off. "I'm fine, Doctor." A stabbing pain behind her eye contradicted her. "At least I will be after a good night's sleep."

"You've suffered a head injury *and* smoke inhalation. You need to stay in hospital, at least overnight," the doctor said.

"No thanks."

"If it's the food you're worried about," Francis said, "it's better than the stuff they serve at St. Brennan's."

"I'm not worried about food. I'm worried about cops and their questions." She hopped down from the stretcher. "I'm not in the mood to be interrogated or charged with a felony."

An argument ensued with the doctor while Gethsemane gathered her blood-and-soot-stained clothes. She won after she promised to stay home from work the next day and to have someone check on her frequently throughout the night. She wondered if he would have acquiesced if he knew the someone was a ghost.

"You're wearing that out?" Francis asked.

Gethsemane looked down at her voluminous hospital gown and at the ruined outfit bundled in her arms. Then she looked at Francis's jacket.

He sighed and handed it to her. "I'd best take care. I'm liable to turn into a gentleman, hanging around you."

Gethsemane thanked him. "Ride home?"

"Don't want much, do you?"

"C'mon, Grennan," Gethsemane said as she pulled on the jacket. Voices spoke in the hall. "Before Inspectors O'Reilly and O'Grumpy get back."

Francis ushered her to the clerk's desk. Gethsemane ignored the displeased look from the homicide detective and the amused look from O'Reilly as she signed out of the emergency room.

Fifteen

A good night's sleep, a hot shower, and the breakfast Eamon had insisted she eat somewhat restored Gethsemane the day after her attack. Her head still ached but she rode to the garda station anyway and gave her statement to the same angry police officer who'd harangued her in the emergency room.

Afterwards, she wound through the station's gray-green halls to O'Reilly's office. She found him seated across from a blond man of similar age but brawnier build, dressed in a plain suit and tie with worn-at-the-heels brogans. O'Reilly wore leather oxblood slip-ons. The men stood when she entered.

"Should you be up?" O'Reilly offered her a chair. "Are you feeling all right? You snuck out of the hospital."

"I'm fine. I hate hospitals."

"A head injury's serious. So's smoke inhalation—"

"Mother her to death, why don't you, Iollan?" the blond interjected.

O'Reilly blushed. "Dr. Brown, meet DI Kildare, from Cork. Donny, Dr. Brown, St. Brennan's music director."

"A pleasure. I've heard a lot about you."

"I'm not nearly as bad as he says." Gethsemane nodded toward O'Reilly.

Kildare touched his forehead. "What happened?"

Gethsemane fingered the bandage over her brow. "A little run-in with a homicidal maniac."

"Dr. Brown's added amateur detective to her long list of accomplishments," O'Reilly said. "Her investigation prompted me to take another look at the McCarthy case."

"Did you just—"

"Don't gloat."

"Iollan tells me you know something about a case I'm working. Oisin Ardmore."

Kildare. O'Reilly mentioned him at the pub the day she showed him the clipping from the *Cork Guardian.* She glanced at O'Reilly's desk. The familiar news story lay on top of a pile of papers. Gethsemane reached for it. "Someone mailed a copy of this to me around the time Siobhan Moloney was murdered."

"Dr. Brown tipped me off about Aoife Fitzgerald's pharmacy logs." O'Reilly's face fell. "I'm sorry I didn't get to her in time."

A moment of silence passed in Aoife and Teague's remembrance. Gethsemane recalled why she'd come to see O'Reilly. She pulled Francis's toxicology report from her pocket. "Speaking of tips, Inspector, I meant to give this to you."

"What is it?" O'Reilly unfolded the sheet.

"I, uh, found the bottle of Waddell and Dobb used to poison Eamon."

"You *found* the bottle. Care to tell me where?"

"Not especially."

Kildare raised a hand to cover a grin.

O'Reilly raised an eyebrow. "Go on."

"Long story short, Eamon and Oisin were both poisoned with digitalis."

O'Reilly set the toxicology report on his desk. "This is when I mention 'chain of custody.' How many hands did this bottle pass through before you 'found' it?"

"Um..."

"That many. Which means—"

Gethsemane raised a hand. "I know, I know. You can't use the evidence because the bottle could have been tampered with. It wasn't but it *could* have been."

"You're learning."

Kildare picked up the report. "Hmm. Let's assume the lady's right—"

Gethsemane smiled and bobbed her head. "Yes, let's."

Kildare continued. "The same poison killed both Ardmore and McCarthy."

"Years apart," O'Reilly said.

"True. But what if your—our—murderer figured he'd gotten away with one digitalis murder so why not stick with the tried and true? Any connection between the murdered men?"

"Yeah," O'Reilly said. "Half the village. Ardmore hailed from Dunmullach."

"Oisin was murdered in his dorm room wasn't he?" Gethsemane asked. "Whoever killed him had to have access to his dorm."

"My nephew's finishing his first year at uni," Kildare said. "I visited him once. His lodging was like a bloody train depot. Always people in and out. Not always people he knew."

"Maybe our poisoner's not a 'he,' Donny."

"What're you thinking?"

"Not to get too detailed in mixed company," O'Reilly nodded at Gethsemane, "but let's be honest, Donny. When you and I were at university we had our fair share of people in and out of our lodgings."

"And?"

"And more than a few of them were of the fairer sex."

Eamon materialized in the entryway as soon as Gethsemane opened the door.

"Where the hell have you been?"

"Hello to you too. You know I went to the police station."

"For this long? I thought the killer had finished what he started up on Golgotha."

"I stopped to see O'Reilly. He introduced me to his buddy,

Inspector Kildare. He's with the Cork An Garda Síochána cold case unit."

"Don't talk to me about O'Reilly." Eamon glowed blue. "Feckin' eejit wouldn't suss a murder if it happened on his front porch."

"He believes."

"What?"

"O'Reilly believes. He believes you and Orla were murdered. He's reopened your case."

"Holy Mary, Mother of—Whoo hoo!" A bright red aura replaced the blue and the full spectrum of his cologne—leather, oakmoss, fern, pepper, hay—permeated the room. "I've waited twenty-five years for that. Thank you, darlin', thank you. How'd you change his mind?"

"By being knocked unconscious and nearly immolated."

Eamon, a somber yellow, hugged Gethsemane and kissed her forehead. Her skin buzzed where his melded into hers. "I am sorry for that, darlin'. I'd rather roam the earth until three days after doomsday than see you come to harm."

"Hey—" Gethsemane's voice cracked. She cleared her throat and tried again. "Takes more than a desperate serial killer to stop Gethsemane Brown." She tapped her bandage. "There's more. Kildare thinks whoever poisoned Oisin Ardmore also poisoned you. I agree with him. Question is, who hated both of you enough to kill you?"

"No one," Eamon said. "Not that I can think of. Oisin and I weren't close."

"You must have had a common enemy. Someone who you both knew. Think, Irish."

"I *am* thinking. There's no—" Eamon vanished then reappeared by the window. Gethsemane could see through his chest out the window to the distant cliffs. "There's no one I can think of. No one in common."

"Did you know your aura turns gray when you lie?"

"I'm not lying. I can't think of anyone who'd want to kill us."

"Hurt you, then. Make you sick. Or make Oisin sick and kill you. Or make you sick and kill Oisin. I doubt digitalis poisoning is an exact science. Who disliked one or both of you enough to be willing to risk killing you to punish you?"

"No. One. No one, I tell you."

"Who are you protecting, Eamon? The man or woman who killed your wife? The person who followed Orla up to the cliffs, put their hands on her back, and pushed—"

"Stop it! Just—stop." Eamon pointed at a bookcase. A slim volume of Orla's poetry floated down and fell open to a photograph tucked between the pages. "Orla loved this snap. The four of us home from university, Orla and me from Trinity and Peg and Oisin from Cork. Peg convinced us to sign up for the Michaelmas Festival field games. We were happy, Peg, Orla, and I. Even Oisin seemed— well, he'd left the drugs alone. We had a grand time. Orla wrote one of her earliest published poems about that day."

Gethsemane examined the photo. A young Orla and Pegeen stood arm-in-arm, flanked by equally youthful Eamon and Oisin. Bows and arrow-filled quivers lay at the boys' feet. Trophies stood at Pegeen and Orla's. Trophies like the one Headmaster Riordan held in the newspaper photo in the library's *Dispatch* archives. "Archery trophies."

"Aye. Peg and Orla took first and second in the women's division." Eamon laughed and glowed brighter. "Orla's win was a fluke. She hit home with her poetry, but when it came to sports her aim was as accurate as a clock without hands. Peg came by her win honest, though. She was captain of the women's archery team at University College."

Gethsemane placed the photo back in the book and closed it. She traced the title—*Poems of Love and Friendship*—with her finger before she spoke. "Eamon, you said Pegeen and Oisin dated for a while. Why'd they break up?"

"Dunno. No particular reason. Just one of those college romances that burns bright like an ember and flames out just as fast."

"Just one of those things." She recalled Shakespearean levels of drama during her Vassar days when college romances ended. "Who dumped whom?"

"Didn't pay much attention. Oisin, I think."

"Your best friend gets her heart broken and you don't pay attention?"

"I thought she was worlds better off without Oisin. I told you I didn't much care for him. I'm pretty sure I told Peg so. She'd have confided in Orla."

"Why are men so clueless?"

"It wasn't a big deal. Peg grieved for a week or so then never brought it up again."

"She didn't try to kill herself?"

"No, of course not. Why would she?"

"For the same reason she tried to kill herself when you married Orla. That *is* why she missed your wedding, isn't it? I saw the newspaper coverage of the day. All those photos and Pegeen's not in a single one. I'm not crazy about weddings, but I wouldn't miss my two best friends' big day without a good reason. Like being on suicide watch in a mental health facility."

"How do you know Peg tried to kill herself?"

"St. Dymphna's. I read some charts before I got clobbered. Pegeen's. Nuala's. Their mother's. Yours."

"You neglected to tell me."

"We're even. You neglected to tell me you'd been committed to St. Dymphna's."

"Voluntarily admitted. I was exhausted. I needed a rest. No big deal. Nothing sinister."

"Pegeen's admission was anything but voluntary. She didn't check herself in for a 'rest.' I'm a psychiatrist's daughter. I know what prompts involuntary commitment. A doctor or a judge determines a patient is a danger to self or others."

"That was ages ago. Ancient history. What's it matter now?"

"It matters your best friend attempted suicide on your wedding day. We're not talking got drunk and threw up on the bride. We're talking almost ended her own life. Something triggered her. Something drastic."

"I don't know."

"Don't know or won't say?"

"Don't know. She never told me why she tried to kill herself. I didn't even find out until after I returned from my honeymoon. Nuala had gotten into some trouble in Limerick. I thought Peg had gone to fetch her."

"Guess, then."

"I can't guess. I can't fathom why she'd want to end her own life."

"I'll guess. I guess you and Pegeen had an affair. I guess you broke it off to marry Orla. I guess Pegeen doesn't handle rejection well, that she takes after her mother in that respect. She—"

"Shut up! Don't you say such things." Eamon vanished, replaced by a blue-white orb which glowed like the Holy Spirit on the apostles at Pentecost. The orb hovered an inch from Gethsemane's nose, sizzling and popping. The smell of burnt leather blasted her full in the face. She fell back on the sofa and shielded herself with her arm.

"Okay, I'm sorry, I take it back. You never had an affair with Pegeen. Calm down."

Eamon re-materialized but remained blue. "I *never* had an affair with anyone. You know I'd have died before I'd cheated on Orla. Pegeen and I were *only* friends and never more than that. Could *never* be anything more than friends."

"Did Pegeen know that?"

Eamon looked at the bar. "God, I wish I could have a drink."

"What happened on your wedding day, Eamon?"

"Nothing."

"Eamon, what happened?"

"Not on my wedding day." Eamon's shoulders slumped. "On the eve of my wedding. I spent the day up at the lighthouse, hiding from Orla's wedding-happy female relations. When I came home that evening I found Peg waiting for me. In my bed. Starkers."

"Naked in your bed meant she wanted out of the friend zone. Then what happened?"

"Then I made her put her clothes on and I took her home. Nothing more. I swear by all that's holy, I took her home and left her there."

"And the next morning she poisons herself."

"I didn't know what she was going to do, did I? If I'd had any idea—"

"Damn." Gethsemane ran to the bookcase. "Stupid, stupid girl." She scanned the shelves.

"What're you doing?" Eamon asked.

"Looking for—" Gethsemane pulled a heavy volume down and flipped through pages.

Eamon appeared next to her. "A dictionary?"

Gethsemane kept flipping pages. "Pegeen drank foxglove tea." She ran her finger along a page. "Here it is. *Foxglove. A plant belonging to the genus digitalis, principally Digitalis purpurea. Chemical constituents include digitoxin, digitonin, digitalin...*It's digitalis in plant form." Gethsemane closed the book. "Pegeen attempted suicide by overdosing on digitalis, the same drug used to poison both you and Oisin Ardmore. Nuala tried to tell me with her tea party stunt. The foxglove in the sandwiches tasted the same as the digitalis in your bourbon—bitter and slightly spicy—because they were the same thing."

Eamon went back to the window. "I don't like where this is going."

"Pegeen was a champion archer," Gethsemane said. "Siobhan was killed with an arrow."

"Could be a coincidence. Bashing in a skull with a cricket bat requires no special skill. Neither does pushing a woman off a cliff."

"Which means Pegeen could have done both." Gethsemane spoke more to herself than Eamon, "But what about the pharmacy?"

Eamon kept his face to the window. Gethsemane strained to hear his whisper.

"Peg worked at Fitzgerald's over summers to earn money for school. That's where she met Oisin."

Gethsemane smacked her forehead. "Nuala, again. She didn't care what Agatha Christie did in the war. She ratted on her sister. She wanted me to know Pegeen worked as a pharmacy assistant. That's how she learned about poisons. It's also how she got easy access to drugs. I bet Aoife's logbooks would have shown Pegeen was the assistant on duty when the drugs went missing from inventory."

"I wish you'd stop saying those things. Pegeen was my friend. Orla's too."

"Your friend was in love with you and humiliated herself trying to make you love her. You rejected her."

Eamon protested.

Gethsemane held up a hand. "I don't mean you deliberately tried to hurt her. You did her a favor. But in her mind you rejected her. Oisin rejected her. Her father rejected her. Her mother responded to rejection with homicidal violence. Pegeen took a page from mom's playbook."

Eamon said nothing.

Gethsemane paced and chewed her thumbnail. "But how'd she manage the explosion?"

"Her father," Eamon said.

"Her father?"

"Joe Sullivan used pyrotechnics in his magic shows. Eileen's father supplied them. Whenever Joe performed in town, Pegeen and Nuala would help him set up his shows. It was the only way they could spend time with him."

"Meaning Pegeen knew how to shut Aoife up and at the same time keep anyone from ever seeing the evidence against her. Poor Teague was just collateral damage."

"Peg hated Teague. He said some ugly things about Nuala once. Peg never forgave him."

"Or a bonus." Gethsemane slammed her fist into her palm. "Damn. I bet a first class ticket to Boston Pegeen used her own records as kindling for that fire she started at St. Dymphna's. She destroyed all hard evidence linking her to digitalis, in pill *and* plant form. Everything else is just circumstantial."

"Don't you sound the right legal eagle?"

"My eldest sister married a judge." Gethsemane resumed pacing. "Pegeen Sullivan has gotten away with murder for forty years. There's *got* to be something to use against her, some way to stop her."

"There is. Let O'Reilly do his job."

"I don't even know if O'Reilly considers Pegeen a suspect. We didn't until just now. Of course, I'll *tell* O'Reilly Pegeen's the killer..."

Eamon's aura turned blue-yellow. "Stop it. Stop talking."

"But I need something to *show* him. He definitely falls into the seeing is believing category."

Eamon materialized in front of Gethsemane so close she walked through him. Her skin sizzled. Her head spun.

"Please stop," Eamon said. "Please. Just. Stop. Talking. I've known Pegeen Sullivan her whole life, I counted her among my closest friends. Now to find out—to think she—just...Stop." Eamon vanished.

"Eamon?"

No answer. Silence. No cologne, no orbs. Gethsemane picked up the photograph of Eamon, Orla, Oisin, and their killer. They stood close, beaming at the camera, carefree, with no idea that three of them would die at the hands of the fourth.

"Why'd she wait ten years?"

Gethsemane yelped and dropped the photo.

Eamon appeared in front of her. "Orla and I were married for ten years. If my rejection of her and marriage to Orla drove Pegeen to kill me and my wife, why'd she wait ten years to do it?"

"She was hospitalized after her suicide attempt."

"For weeks, not years."

Gethsemane snapped her fingers. "Maybe the hospital she went to for medical stabilization before being transferred to St.

Dymphna's would still have the records. The lab reports would show a high digitalis level in her blood. How long do they keep records at non-psychiatric hospitals in Ireland?"

"Don't change the subject."

"I'm not changing the subject. I don't know why she waited. I'm not privy to the inner workings of the jealous serial murdering mind."

"Explain the gap. If Pegeen killed out of jealousy, why'd she wait so long?"

"Revenge is a dish best served cold?"

Eamon shook his head.

"Tell you what. I'll ask her."

"The feck you will." Blue surrounded Eamon's head. "Not two minutes ago you tell me my oldest friend is a deranged killer who murdered me, my wife, and a string of others. Then you say you'll *ask* her if she did it as calmly as asking to borrow the sugar? Have her over for a cuppa and ask if there's anything she wants to get off her chest? Are you not the full bloody shilling?"

"I'm all twelve pence, thanks."

"Stay away from Pegeen."

"I'll stay away from Pegeen if I can figure out how to get her to confess without going near her."

"Bloody hell, woman." Eamon threw up his hands.

"Face it, Irish, we have to get Pegeen to confess. She's destroyed the evidence against her. A confession is the only way to stop her."

"Oh, no." Eamon waved a finger. "Don't you go 'we'-ing. I'll have no part of this."

"*You're* skeptical of Pegeen's guilt and you're one of the people she murdered. As hard as it is to convince you, how much harder will it be to convince a jury? A half competent lawyer might have her dancing a jig down Main Street in less time than it took to bring the case to trial."

"So let the garda get a confession."

"Sure. *After* I convince O'Reilly to suspect her and *after* he gathers enough evidence—oh yeah, there isn't any left—to get an arrest warrant and *after* he arrests her and she lawyers up and blah, blah, blah. She could have killed a dozen people by then. Confession first, then O'Reilly."

"She doesn't need to kill a dozen people, she only needs to kill you. If you're right about her—and I'll *reluctantly* admit you probably—"

"Definitely."

"She won't hesitate to finish what she started." Eamon jabbed his finger through Gethsemane's bandage into her skull.

She shuddered as her head buzzed. "Then it's a race. I get her to confess before she kills me. And don't go poking your finger into people's brains. It's rude."

"Listening to reason's obviously not on your agenda, so what're you going to do?"

"Come up with a plan. Maybe you could—"

"No. I've told you I want no part of this confession nonsense. I won't help you get yourself killed. I've done dead. It's not much fun. Don't be in such a rush to join me."

"I can't just sit back and wait."

"Don't wait. Write O'Reilly a note outlining your theory, catch the next train out of town, swallow your pride and borrow plane fare from one of your siblings, and mail the note from the airport as you're boarding a plane back to the States where Pegeen can't get at you."

"You mean run."

"Yes. Just as fast and as far as you possibly can."

"I won't run."

"Darlin', Gethsemane," Eamon leaned down to look Gethsemane in the eye, "I've seen this movie. It doesn't end well. Be sensible."

"You're not going to talk me out of this. I know what I have to do."

She headed for the hall.

Eamon called after her, "Where're you going?"

"To bring a murderer to justice. And since you won't help me, I'll find someone who will."

"O'Reilly, like I told you?"

"Francis Grennan. I'll let you know what we come up with." Gethsemane marched to the door.

Francis lived in the bachelor schoolmasters' quarters, Erasmus Hall, on the eastern edge of St. Brennan's campus. Gethsemane found him bending over a rose bush in a garden in the rear of the Georgian building.

"Hoy, Grennan."

Francis waved. "Looking for new lodgings? The west wing's nearly deserted. You'd have your pick of suites."

"I'm looking for you." Gethsemane noticed he held a spade. "What are you doing?"

"Planting roses, while the soil's still warm. 'James Galway' and 'Galway Bay.'"

"Math teacher, amateur botanist, archer, rosarian. I hope your many talents include getting women to say things they don't want to say."

"According to my ex-wife."

"Ex-wi—Never mind. I need your help. Again." Gethsemane explained about Pegeen having committed all the murders and her dilemma over lacking evidence. "So, how do I trick Pegeen into confessing?"

"Trick her into confessing to—" Francis counted on his fingers "—six, seven murders?"

"Yes."

"You don't. Pegeen Sullivan may be insane, but she's not stupid. She's not going to admit anything."

"Pegeen Sullivan is a cold-blooded killer who's gotten away with murder for decades. If someone doesn't stop her she'll go on killing."

"Allow me to ask the obvious. Why you?"

"Who else *but* me? My digging into the McCarthy murders woke a sleeping dragon. It's up to me to slay it. With your help."

"Remind me why you come to me whenever you need help with something dangerous."

"Frankie, I think this is the beginning of a beautiful friendship."

"*Casablanca* explains every situation." Francis set the spade down. "I don't know what it is about you but I can't seem to tell you no."

"Have you got any ideas? Short of water-boarding?"

"Give me a day to think on it. I'll meet you tomorrow after school at the Rabbit."

"Not the pub. Word would be all over town before you finished your first drink."

"I drink fast. Maybe before I finished my third. But I see your point."

"How about Carnock? It's isolated, no one will see or overhear us."

"Golgotha? Are you fecking serious? You won't get me near that place, I don't care how many *Casablanca* quotes you throw at me. Let's meet at The Athaneum. Come to think of it, that's probably the best place to set up Pegeen. She's a history there with her father. Having to face those demons might throw her off-kilter, give us the advantage."

"I knew you were my only man. Excellent idea. How do we lure Pegeen to the theater?"

"I don't know yet, do I? I said give me a day, not half a minute."

Gethsemane hugged Francis and kissed him on the cheek. "You're a sound fella, Grennan."

Francis blushed and backed into a rose bush.

"Take some advice. Go to O'Reilly and tell him what you know."

"You too? I'm not running."

"Don't run. But don't wait for proof you might not get. If this plan goes arseways, which it probably will, at least the guards will have some idea of where to start looking for your murderer."

She *had* to stop Pegeen. What could she use against her? Gethsemane walked back to her bike. Two of Pegeen's first three victims were men who'd rejected her, like her father. Maybe she—

Something caught her eye as she mounted the bicycle seat—a cigarette butt and a shiny object, a button or a pin, near a copse of hedges. One of the boys sneaking a smoke, probably. No big deal.

The smell hit her a few yards past the garda station. Not leather and soap. White roses and vetiver. She stopped. "Orla? Orla McCarthy, are you there?" The fragrance wrapped itself around her and drew her attention to the Athaneum up ahead. Why not go there now, look around, try to come up with a plan herself to lure Pegeen?

She tried front, side, and back doors of the theater. All locked. Halfway through her litany of curses about her luck, the back door latch clicked and the door swung open. She peered inside. "Orla?"

"No." A blast of leather and soap accompanied Eamon's voice. "It's me." He materialized next to her. "I'm here to talk you out of this suicide mission."

Gethsemane followed him inside. Eamon walked instead of vanishing and reappearing as he usually did, letting his aura's saffron glow illuminate their path backstage. They stopped in front of Sullivan the Magnificent's poster.

"This is your fault, Joe." Eamon glared at the magician's likeness. "If you hadn't been such a shite father—"

"How can we use that against Pegeen?"

"I'm not helping you do this. I'm here to talk sense to you."

"We've had this conversation. I've plenty of sense, enough to know that without a confession, Pegeen gets away with murder. Murders, multiple."

"Damn it, woman, I've lost my oldest friend. I don't want to lose my newest too."

"Eamon, I am your friend, which is why I can't let Pegeen get away with what she did to you."

"I can't watch this." Eamon vanished, leaving Gethsemane to find her way out in the dark. She missed a flash of straw-colored hair slipping outside just before her.

Sixteen

Back at her teaching duties the next morning, Gethsemane pretended not to watch the clock. She jumped as soon as the lunch bell rang. She couldn't wait until after school to speak to Francis.

She waded through a tide of hungry boys to be met at the door by the headmaster's secretary. The woman handed her a telephone message slip. "You received a call from the garda station. Said it was urgent you meet Inspector O'Reilly at Our Lady."

Gethsemane thanked her. The inspector had been out when she'd gone to see him after meeting Francis. In Cork, she'd been told. Maybe he'd found something concrete to tie Pegeen to Oisin's death. She stopped by Francis's classroom on the way out but he'd already gone to lunch. She'd fill him in later. She'd have to hurry if she wanted to meet O'Reilly and make it back to school in time for her first class after lunch.

Eamon sat at the piano concentrating on the final movement of a new concerto. Crumpled paper littered the floor. A pen floated across a sheet of music paper, leaving a complex design of musical notation in its wake. He didn't hear Pegeen come in.

"You could stampede a herd of elephants through a room and you wouldn't hear it while you were composing," she said. "Some things never change."

Eamon spun. The pen hovered in the air for a second then clattered onto the piano keyboard.

"Yes," Pegeen said. "I can see you."

Eamon spoke.

Pegeen waited until his lips stopped moving. "Can't hear you, though." She chuckled. "Funny, isn't it? All those years we knew each other you could hear me but couldn't see me. Not really. Orla blinded you to the truth. I could see her, too, for a while. 'Til I borrowed one of Father Keating's spell books and banished her."

Eamon's mouth moved again.

"Did you never wonder why you couldn't find her? Why she never found you? The sight of the two of you together during life sickened me. Couldn't bear the idea of the two of you together in the afterlife."

Eamon glowed blue then froze. Why couldn't he form an orb?

Pegeen recited something in Latin.

Eamon traced the pattern in the carpet through his outstretched hands as he dematerialized. He faded—solid, semi-solid, transparent, nothing. The last thing he heard was Pegeen's, "Don't worry. Wherever you're going Orla won't be there. I made sure of that."

Gethsemane pulled up in front of Our Lady of Perpetual Sorrows. The yard was deserted. She leaned her bicycle against the fence and walked into the church, calling out as she went through the narthex into the nave. "Inspector? Inspector O'Reilly? I'm here. You wanted to see me?"

She passed rows of empty pews on her way to the chapel. No one there. She continued to the chancel and climbed the three steps.

"Inspector? Where are you?"

She stepped behind the rood screen. No one in the choir stall. The message said to meet O'Reilly *at* church. Maybe he hadn't meant *in* church.

A noise. Or not. Hard to be sure with "Pathétique" blaring in her head drowning out all other sound. She stepped back into the nave. Still nothing but empty pews.

"Inspector? 'S that you?"

No answer other than Tchaikovsky.

"Father Keating?"

No response. Gethsemane shivered. Empty churches were as eerie as darkened theaters. And she'd ignored her inner warning system to her peril these past several days. Better wait outside. As soon as she checked one final place. She walked to the sanctuary and knocked on the sacristy door.

"Father Keating? Are you in there? Is anybody here?"

"I'm here."

Gethsemane spun. Pegeen Sullivan sat in the choir stall.

"Will I do?" she asked.

"Actually," Gethsemane said, "I'm expecting Inspector O'Reilly. He's probably waiting for me."

"In the poison garden, maybe?"

"Please excuse me."

Pegeen blocked her path. "About that message..."

Gethsemane froze, less to do with Pegeen's words than with the object she held in her hand—a gun. "Inspector O'Reilly's not coming, is he?"

"Not in your lifetime." Pegeen motioned to the choir stall. "Have a seat."

Gethsemane sat on one of the benches.

Pegeen sneered. "So you thought you could trick me into confessing to murder, did you?"

"Not murder," Gethsemane said. "Murders, plural."

Pegeen spat.

"I'm pretty sure spitting in church is sacrilegious."

Pegeen cocked her revolver. "Well, when you meet God you can ask Him what He intends to do about it."

"Something involving fire and brimstone, most likely."

Pegeen raised the revolver and pointed it at Gethsemane's

chest. "You've quite the mouth for someone on the wrong end of a weapon."

"Sorry, habit. I get smart when I'm nervous. Right now I'm fecking brilliant."

"Soon enough you'll be fecking dead."

Gethsemane tensed. Was the choir stall's wood thick enough to stop a bullet?

"Please be so good as to sign that note, Dr. Brown." Pegeen motioned to the bench next to Gethsemane.

Gethsemane looked down at several items laid out near her: a typed note, a pen, an open bottle of Waddell and Dobb Double-Oaked, and a lead crystal whiskey glass filled with bourbon and ice. "Ice, how thoughtful."

"Sign the note," Pegeen said.

"I never sign anything without reading it first."

"I'll summarize for you. It's your suicide note. You describe how stupid you felt when you discovered that Eamon McCarthy *had*, somehow, managed to kill his wife and then himself, after all. You couldn't face the humiliation and ridicule of being wrong after all the trouble you'd caused so you decided to end it."

"An honor suicide? By drinking poisoned whiskey? Just like Eamon?"

"I like the symmetry of it."

"And you really think you can get away with this?"

Pegeen smirked. "I got away with all the others."

"It doesn't faze you, does it? All this killing."

"I never killed any who didn't deserve it."

"That's how you justify serial murder? You convinced yourself that seven people—"

"Eight," Pegeen said, "including you."

"Or nine? Grennan knows about you. Won't you have to kill him?"

"Let Frankie's death be on your head. You shouldn't have dragged him into this."

"How about ten? O'Reilly? Eleven? The cold case inspector

from Cork? They know Oisin was murdered. They know the McCarthys were murdered. They know Oisin and Eamon were both poisoned with digitalis. How long before they discover you tried to kill yourself with the same drug? How long before they connect the deaths to you?"

"Stop it." Pegeen tightened her grip on the gun.

"When does it end?" Gethsemane kept her eyes on Pegeen's hand.

"When it's over...When I decide it's over! That's when it ends! Sign the damned note!"

Gethsemane took a deep breath. She forced the fear from her voice. "No, I won't sign it. I'm not signing a bogus suicide note," Gethsemane said. "I'm not making this easy for you."

Pegeen balled her free hand into a fist and clenched her jaw so tight Gethsemane thought she might break teeth.

"Did the others make it easy for you?" Gethsemane asked. "Oisin?"

The unpleasant smile reappeared. "Quite easy. I just slipped some digitalis tablets in with the pills he usually popped. Washed 'em right down with his cider, never noticed."

"What about Orla? Throwing someone off a cliff's not as easy as mixing pills with their alcohol but she was a tiny thing. Couldn't have put up much fight. Or was she tougher than she looked?"

"Not tough at all."

"Why'd she go out so late?"

"Thought Eamon had come home early from Dublin to surprise her."

"Wonder where she got that idea?"

"Someone slipped a note under her door. Eamon's handwriting's pure easy to copy. Been doing it since we were at school. Used to write his English papers for him."

"How thoughtful."

Pegeen frowned. "Didn't he show his appreciation? Orla'd never have done any such thing for him. I did more for Eamon than Orla ever did and he thanked me by marrying that silly cow. The silly cow who hurried up to the lighthouse to meet him. Running up Carrick Point Road all alone so late at night. Easy to slip, twist an ankle, go tumbling off a cliff. She never saw it coming."

"Another sneak attack. They seem to be your specialty. Ambush with a bat on a drunk. An arrow to the heart from—how far away?"

"Across the green. Clock tower."

"No big deal for a champion archer. But why do it? Why kill Hurley? He and Lynch helped you, covered for you by shifting blame for Orla's death to Eamon. Was it your car Jimmy saw?"

"I've no idea whose car he saw, if he saw one. Probably another of his lies. I didn't drive, I took the footpaths over the cliffs. Hurley and Lynch weren't helping none but themselves. Pathological opportunists, both of them. They saw a chance to be rid of a thorn from their sides and grabbed it. Lucky me."

"So you killed Hurley because...?"

"Because your snooping got him to thinking maybe blackmail would be a way to supplement his pension. Back in the day, before the booze took hold, he was a decent investigator. Some vestige of the garda he once was remained under that alcohol-sodden exterior. He got hold of that damned evidence box—"

Gethsemane interrupted. "And did what he failed to do twenty-five years ago. Examined it. And connected what, the bourbon bottle, to you? So you killed him and stole the evidence box. But you missed the bottle stashed among Hurley's impressive collection."

"Aren't you the clever one? I'd have had more time to search for it if you hadn't been Janey-on-the-spot raising the alarm."

"I'm not apologizing. What about Siobhan?"

"Blackmail is a common pastime in Dunmullach," Pegeen said. "Siobhan saw me buy a bottle of the Waddell and Dobb. She found out I'd stolen tablets from the pharmacy too. Aoife shot off her mouth, no doubt. I stopped Siobhan from bleeding me and Aoife from telling anyone else."

"Siobhan mailed a newspaper clipping to me, didn't she?"

Gethsemane asked. "A hint there might be more to Oisin's death than an accidental overdose. That his death might be connected to Eamon's."

"You kept asking questions, poking your nose into others' business. When she saw you weren't letting it go she thought you might be willing to pay for information."

"Or that you'd be willing to pay more for her silence."

"Siobhan underestimated me."

"A mistake."

"Her last." Pegeen nodded at the bourbon. "Enough talk. Drink up."

"I'm not thirsty," Gethsemane said. "I'm not in a hurry either. Satisfy my curiosity. Why'd you wait so long after Eamon and Orla were married to kill them?"

"I'm a patient woman. I gave Eamon time to come to his senses, to see Orla for what she really was."

"An intelligent, beautiful, kind woman, beloved by all?"

"No!" Pegeen took two steps toward Gethsemane. She took a deep breath and stepped back. "No. Manky slapper. She didn't deserve Eamon."

"But you did."

"Yes, I did! I *did* deserve Eamon. I'm the one who was there for him. I'm the one who was there for all of them. After everything I did for them, I deserved to be loved." Pegeen wiped away a tear. The gun wavered in her hand.

"So, what, you figured ten years, long enough to see the light? Time to force the issue?"

"I had to act, didn't I? Stupid cow went and got herself pregnant. I ran into Orla in Limerick, coming from a specialist's office. Didn't want to see the local GP, sodding useless gobshite he was. She and Eamon had tried so long to start a family. She couldn't wait to tell me. Went on and on about how happy they'd be. Bitch."

"Gee, I can't imagine why she'd want to share her good news with her lifelong friend."

"Not a thought for my feelings. Did she care where I'd fit in?"

"So you fixed her."

Pegeen nodded. "I had to act fast, before she could tell Eamon. He was in Dublin that day so I took my chance. I fixed her good same as I'm going to fix you. Drink up. Your ice is melting."

"I take my bourbon neat," Gethsemane said.

"You'll take it now." Pegeen re-aimed the gun. "Stop stalling." She laughed, a sound as ugly as her smile. "Or are you hoping Eamon will come along and save you?"

"What do you mean, 'save me'?"

"I know Eamon's ghost haunted Carraigfaire. I've known since the day of his funeral."

"You knew Eamon's ghost was stuck here, thanks to you, and you never let on, not even when Siobhan was doing her psychic hotline routine?"

"Did you really think you were the only one in Dunmullach who could see him?" Pegeen spat. "You're nothing special. Nuala and I both have the gift."

Gethsemane wiped spit from her cheek. "Funny, Eamon never mentioned your being able to see him. You certainly couldn't converse with him. He would've told me. Sad, really. Even in death he took no notice of you. Pathetic. Or maybe he noticed you but just didn't want to talk to you."

"Shut. Up." Pegeen cocked the revolver again. "And drink up."

"Are you thick *and* a header or just a header? I'm not drinking anything. I *won't* make this easy for you."

"Drink or I'll—"

"Shoot? Won't that pooch your suicide scenario?"

"People have been known to shoot themselves."

"Not from a distance of three feet."

Pegeen stepped closer. Gethsemane rose slightly from the bench. Pegeen stopped. She shook her head and stepped back. Gethsemane sat back down.

"Makes no difference if it's suicide or homicide," Pegeen said. "You'll be dead, either way."

"And you'll be in need of a really good lawyer. They'll know it was you."

"Not after I get rid of Frankie."

Gethsemane snapped her fingers. "When I mentioned Inspector O'Reilly, did I forget to mention I left him a note at the garda station? Given your penchant for torching evidence and killing witnesses, I took Grennan's—and Eamon's—advice and told O'Reilly all about you. In writing. And I signed *that* note. I'm sure it will stand up as evidence."

Pegeen clenched her jaw again. She pressed the heel of her free hand against her brow.

"Shut up and drink the bourbon."

"You really *are* crazy if you think I'm going to help you kill me."

"Don't say that."

"What, that you're crazy? Isn't that what they called you while you were locked up at St. Dymphna's?"

"Shut up about that."

"Crazy just like your mother. Well, maybe not *just* like her. Your mother at least had the balls to go after your father out in the open. No sneaking around for her, faking suicide notes and drug overdoses. When she got kicked to the curb she—"

"Shut up! Shut up! Shut up!"

"Keep it together, Peggy. I know it's difficult, you being from a long line of crazy. Your mother, your sister, your cousins. What was it that cop at the hospital said about your family tree?"

"Stop it!" Pegeen pointed the gun directly at Gethsemane's forehead.

"You're losing it, Peggy. That's what they'll say, you know, that you're daft. But, hey, that should help you in court. They *do* have the insanity defense in Ireland, don't they?"

"Shut up!"

"Off your nut. Touched. Not the full shilling."

"If you say one more word, I swear I'll—"

Gethsemane chanted a sing-song, "Crazy Peggy, looney Peggy.

Peggy heads the ball. Crazy Peggy can't keep a man so crazy Peggy kills them all."

For an instant, Gethsemane was back in high school in the bottom of the ninth in the final game of the state championship. She picked up a grounder then dove as she hurled the ball to the catcher to tag the runner out at home. Then she was back in the choir stall, the lead crystal whiskey glass flying from her hand toward Pegeen as she dove under the bench. Ice and bourbon splashed her as she hit the floor.

Instead of the sound of a bullet crashing through wood into her flesh, the opening chords of "St. Brennan's Ascendant" blared from the pipe organ in the loft above the chancel. Pegeen's shot went wild as the whiskey glass hit her in the arm. Her gun skittered to a stop just out of reach of both women. Gethsemane scrambled under the bench as Pegeen leapt forward, both grabbing the gun. Gethsemane bit Pegeen. Pegeen slammed Gethsemane's head against the choir stall. Gethsemane kicked, sending the gun clattering down the chancel steps onto the marble floor of the nave. Pegeen punched Gethsemane then grabbed the bottle of Waddell and Dobb Double-oaked. Bourbon poured down her arm as she raised the bottle above her head.

A shot echoed as the rood screen exploded inward. Pegeen flinched and dropped the heavy bottle. Gethsemane tumbled her to the floor as the shrill of police sirens rose in the distance. Ruairi stood in the aisle, still holding the revolver.

Gethsemane yelled. "Ruairi, run!"

Pegeen broke free. She kicked Gethsemane and ran down the chancel steps toward Ruairi, who dove between pews. Saoirse, Feargus, Aengus, and Colm popped up from between other pews and hurled prayer books at Pegeen.

Gethsemane jumped onto Pegeen's back as the church's doors flew open. O'Reilly and a squad of uniformed officers burst into the nave. Pegeen wriggled out from under a startled Gethsemane and ran out the south transept exit, guards in close pursuit.

The children helped Gethsemane to her feet.

"What are you all doing here? How did you—"

Colm threw his arms around her. "I'm sorry, Miss, I'm sorry."

"Sorry for what, Colm?"

"I heard you and Mr. Grennan talking about luring Miss Sullivan to the theater. I was sneaking a fag in the bushes and I heard what you said. Part of what you said. I thought you were planning to prank her. I was so mad, I wasn't thinking."

"Tell her what you did, Colm," Saoirse said.

Colm stared at his feet and fingered the torn spot on his lapel where his Head Boy pin used to be. "I told her. I was furious about Ruairi getting the solo so I told Miss Sullivan you were planning to trick her. I didn't know she'd killed anyone." His voice cracked and tears flowed. A frightened teen replaced the arrogant bully.

"Kieran was at the theater," Saoirse put an arm around her older brother. "He heard what you said about the murders. He told me and I told Colm. I wanted Colm to tell our parents. They listen to him."

"Then I realized what I'd done," Colm said, "and I couldn't tell them."

Ruairi stepped forward. "So he told us. We called the guards and came here as fast as we could. We just ran out of school."

"You should have seen the teachers' faces," Aengus said.

"They thought we'd all gone mad," Feargus added.

Colm sniffled. "It was all Ruairi's idea, coming here. He's the hero."

Gethsemane put one arm around Colm's shoulders and the other around Ruairi's. She smiled at all the boys. "As far as I'm concerned, you're all heroes. And you all get an A."

Away from the church Pegeen kept running—from the gardaí, from Gethsemane, from her past, from her ghosts.

The gardaí would follow but they'd waste time getting in their cars. She knew short cuts up the cliffs. She'd make it to the lighthouse. She'd have time.

Seventeen

The green chiffon with the train? The beaded navy? Gethsemane went through Orla's evening gowns. Custom dictated a plain black suit for the podium but she wanted to make an impression at the All-County, not blend in with the boys. The backless silk brocade. Guaranteed to keep all eyes on her.

"If they've got my back for the whole performance, might as well give 'em something to look at, right, Irish?"

No comment. No aroma. No ghost. She'd forgotten. Eamon was gone. She hadn't seen, heard, or smelled him in weeks. She returned home from her showdown with Pegeen to an unfinished concerto and a sense of oppressive gloom. She'd recounted the details—except the news about Orla's pregnancy, no need to push the knife deeper—about Pegeen's confession, eighth murder attempt, and suicide, repeatedly, without effect. No orbs, no cologne. She was talking to furniture.

What happened to him? Where had he gone? She wanted to believe Eamon had crossed over once the murders were solved and was enjoying a celestial bourbon with Orla in paradise. But she couldn't shake the feeling something sinister underpinned his disappearance.

Gethsemane held the silk brocade in front of the mirror and examined her reflection. "I wish you were here, Irish. I'd trade the trophy and a case of Waddell and Dobb for a bit of your snark."

* * *

The auditorium lights dimmed in concert with the stage lights rising. The boys quieted in their seats as Feargus took his place near the conductor's podium. At his signal the boys tuned their instruments. Polite applause greeted Gethsemane as she stepped on stage, followed by a confident Ruairi. Gethsemane raised her baton. All fell silent. She held the gaze of each boy for a moment, telegraphing trust. Nods for Ruairi, Colm, and the Toibin twins conveyed encouragement and thanks. Then the downbeat. Strings and flutes sounded, joined by the rest of the orchestra and then Ruairi, tempo increasing as Gethsemane led them in a dance of hope and struggle, frustration and defeat. The melody crescendoed into Ruairi's solo. He bowed the cadenza, filling the Athaneum with the anguish of generations of St. Brennan's. Tears dampened many cheeks.

Gethsemane raised her baton again. The boys played the coda, flowing without pause into the andante second movement. Gethsemane guided them through the nuances of the theme and variations, the notes surrogates for the sacrifice and determination to re-form, phoenix-like, and surge onward to restore St. Brennan's pride.

The final movement. Allegretto. Gethsemane coaxed the boys into pouring all of their dreams, desires, wishes, and ambitions into the rondo, evoking the passion of St. Brennan's triumphal ascent from the nadir of shame to the summit of victory.

The last notes faded. Gethsemane held her breath. Silence. Two seconds, five, ten. Applause thundered, accompanied by calls of *"bravo!"* and "maestra!" Gethsemane turned to accept the standing ovation from audience and judges. Eamon should have been there to share it.

A distant rumble. Thunder? Did it rain in—wherever this was? Eamon pivoted slowly. Nothing but gray fog all around. He seemed to be standing on gray linoleum. More gray above him. Where the hell had Pegeen sent him? Homicidal bitch. And how long had he been here? Not a clock or calendar in sight—in wherever here was.

The noise increased. Not thunder. Applause. The All-County? Either that or a rugby match. Dunmullach hadn't won a rugby match since before the last time it won the All-County. Who'd earned the applause? St. Brennan's? True he'd composed his most brilliant concerto. But Gethsemane'd only had a few weeks to pull the boys into competitive shape. Assuming she'd survived Pegeen. She must have. He'd have run into her if she hadn't. Wouldn't he? Would she have been sent here? Eamon looked around for something to put his fist through. Or throw. Or kick. Or—anything. Was this Hell, a vast nothingness? Couldn't be Heaven. Damn Pegeen. Eamon hoped this wasn't Hell. He hoped fires raged in Hell and that Pegeen Sullivan burned in one of them.

"Congratulations, Dr. Brown."

Gethsemane excused herself from the group of congratulatory parents. Peter Nolan stood behind her.

"Thank you," she said.

The tall, slim man smiled at her, his teeth as perfect as his blonde hair. "Grand prize. I confess, I didn't think you could do it. When I heard a new teacher planned to prepare an orchestra and premier a new composition in only six weeks I thought, impossible."

Gethsemane shook the executive director's hand. "I confess I'm happy I proved you wrong."

"Bit of luck, finding an Eamon McCarthy concerto under the floorboards."

"You never know what you'll find when you open yourself to all possibilities."

Richard Riordan and Hieronymus Dunleavy stood with a man and woman Gethsemane didn't recognize. Riordan cradled a golden trophy as tall as a junior school boy. He clapped Gethsemane's shoulder with his free hand. "The heroine of St. Brennan's." He introduced the two people as members of the school board.

"My pleasure and privilege to meet you, Dr. Brown," the man said. "Congratulations on your victory."

"Thank you," Gethsemane said, "but it's St. Brennan's victory, not mine."

"You're too modest, Dr. Brown," the woman said. "Hieronymus and Richard told us how hard you worked. St. Brennan's owes you a great deal."

Dunleavy shook her hand. "I hope I can count on you for input into the design of St. Brennan's new auditorium and music room, lend your technical expertise on matters of acoustics and space."

Headmaster Riordan shifted the trophy. "Please come see me in my office Monday morning. I want to discuss something with you."

Gethsemane agreed to the meeting then headed to the lobby for canapés and wine. Ruairi, Colm, and the Toibin twins intercepted her.

"You guys were fantastic," Gethsemane said.

"We couldn't have done it without you, Miss," Ruairi said.

Gethsemane laughed. "I was about to say the same thing."

"Ruairi's violin solo put us over the top," Colm said.

Ruairi blushed. "You'd have been better."

"I wouldn't have. I mean it. Even Uncle Peter said so."

"Well, I think you're *all* amazing musicians," Gethsemane said. "And not half bad as a rescue squad."

"So we can have Monday off?" Feargus asked.

"No," Gethsemane said, "you may not."

Peter Nolan interrupted. "Do you have a moment?"

"Of course, sir."

"Call me Peter." They moved to a quieter area. "My nephew, Colm, speaks highly of you. He says you're an excellent teacher. Do you enjoy teaching?"

"Yes, I—"

He cut her off. "Would you enjoy life in Boston more? I'm sure you've heard I'm looking for a new music director for the Philharmonia."

"Someone mentioned it."

"Watching you conduct, it occurred to me a maestra was who I'm looking for." He inclined his head toward the parking lot. "May I drive you home?"

Gethsemane's heart skipped a beat. Boston. The States. Musical directorship of the Philharmonia. Hers for the asking. She'd dreamed of this. So why did the feeling in the pit of her stomach feel like dread instead of joy?

"Gethsemane?"

"What? Oh." She snapped back to the present. "Actually, I have my bike."

"In that dress? You're joking. I have my Mercedes." He offered her his arm. "We'll send someone back for the bike."

Eamon paced. He longed for a piano. Or pen and paper. Or a book. Laundry. Garbage to take out. Anything, as long as it was something to do. He didn't mind the quiet. The nothingness drove him crazy. Burning in Hell sounded like the better deal. Not that eternal torment was a hooley, but it beat being bored to death. If he could've found a wall he'd have punched it.

Eighteen

Moe Franklin, four thirty-six. George Washington, four twenty-six. Neal Arlett, Four twenty-five. James Milner, four oh-six.

Gethsemane paced until she ran out of baseball stats. Then she roamed the cottage, straightening things that didn't need to be straightened. Boston was within her reach. Why wasn't she happier?

She took a deep breath. Nothing but peat and rain. No soap, no cologne. No Eamon. She needed him. He'd sort her out. He'd make her laugh. She missed him.

Music. She picked up her violin. Running through Paganini's Violin Caprices would calm her. A knock on the door interrupted her halfway through the thirteenth. Tchaikovsky in her head replaced Paganini on the strings.

Two men stood on the porch, bundled against the cold—Billy McCarthy and Hank Wayne.

"Afternoon, Dr. Brown," Billy said.

"Mr. McCarthy. When'd you get in?"

"Drove in from Dublin this mornin'. Took care of some business in the village, thought I'd come up to see how you were gettin' on. And call me Billy."

Gethsemane couldn't take her eyes off of Hank Wayne. Patent leather wingtips, bold pin-striped pant legs peeking beneath a gray overcoat—cashmere, probably—matching scarf, silver pompadour as perfect as the white teeth displayed in his crocodile smile. Expensive and flashy, like his horrid pink hotels.

"Is this a bad time?" Billy asked.

"What? No. Sorry." Gethsemane moved aside to let the men in. "I just—you caught me by surprise. And call me Gethsemane." She took their coats.

Billy nodded at the other man. "Allow me to introduce—"

"Hank Wayne." Gethsemane shook the hotel magnate's hand, wincing as his bulky diamond ring dug into her fingers. "I recognize you from your picture in the papers. I've stayed at a few of your hotels."

"Glad to hear it." Hank spoke with a generic American "news anchor" accent. Coached, Gethsemane suspected. He clapped her on the shoulder. She staggered.

"Gethsemane is a classical violinist, Mr. Wayne, world class. And a conductor." Billy turned to Gethsemane. "Congratulations on Boston, by the way. Whole village is talking about it."

Dunmullach's gossip mill strikes again. "Thank you. But I haven't accepted the offer yet."

"Not into music." Hank puffed out his chest. "Too busy for frivolities. Leave that stuff to the wife and kids." He brushed past Gethsemane and Billy down the hall, poking his head into rooms. He lingered at the music room. "Say, McCarthy, get rid of this piano and this'd make a fine lobby." He slapped a hand against the door frame. "Have to knock out a wall."

Lobby? Wall? Gethsemane turned to Billy. He wouldn't meet her eye.

She eased past Hank. "Eamon McCarthy and his wife adored this cottage. They restored it from a ruin themselves. They built their lives together here. Eamon composed some of his best work on that piano." She pointed at the Steinway.

Hank snorted. "They're twenty-five years past caring."

Of all the arrogant—Gethsemane frowned. She'd give her right hand to be able to hurl one of Eamon's blue orbs. Right between Hank's cold blue eyes. Where *was* Eamon?

Billy, his cheeks an embarrassed red, chimed in. "Mr. Wayne knows Aunt and Uncle's legacies form an important part of Carraigfaire's charm, its allure."

"'Specially since that nut job serial killer threw herself off a cliff. True crime's a money maker. The publicity should draw tourist dollars for the next three to five years," Hank said.

Tourists. Eamon would hate tourists. "So you're going ahead with plans for the museum?"

Hank snorted again.

"Perhaps not an entire museum. A memorial room. A tie-in to that American woman's book. Sales have rocketed since the, uh, situation here." Billy smiled like a school boy explaining how the dog ate his homework. "Thanks to you, Gethsemane. Clearing Uncle's name, restoring his reputation. Perhaps you'd contribute to the memorial. I'm sure your story of how you stopped a deranged killer would fascinate guests—people."

"Sure." Gethsemane didn't try to keep the sarcasm from her voice. "I could lecture on my adventures as an amateur detective. Or hold séances. Summon Eamon's ghost to do parlor tricks and sign autographs, pose for a few photos."

Gethsemane and Billy jumped at a crash. The shattered remains of a vase surrounded Hank's feet, his face blanched as white as his hair.

"Don't worry." Billy hurried to scoop up the pieces. "Only a wedding gift from Amiri Baraka. I'm sure it can be repaired."

Hank ignored him and pointed at Gethsemane. "You've held séances?"

Hank's reaction reminded her of something. She didn't answer the developer.

Hank glared at Billy. "You know how I feel about the supernatural, McCarthy."

Gethsemane snapped her mental fingers.

The Wayne Terror. Hank's childhood run-in with the dark side of paranormal. Not a hoax, judging by his expression. She tried not to gloat.

"This is Ireland, Mr. Wayne. You can't spit without hitting a supernatural creature in the eye."

"She's exaggerating," Billy said.

"If you," the words nearly choked her, "buy a home here and you're worried, you could paint the doors and window sills blue to keep the spirits out. Works in New Orleans." She couldn't resist a pointed look at Billy. "It wouldn't be hospitable, though."

"Door's already blue," Hank said.

"Gethsemane has quite the sense of humor." Billy's eyes begged her to stop. "You Americans."

"I don't find humor in the supernatural."

"Dunmullach's ghosts are hysterical," Gethsemane said. Wayne would get a real kick out of Eamon. Right back to Michigan.

"Ghosts, pshh." Billy's voice trembled despite his dismissive wave. "Misinterpretations of natural phenomena, isn't that how you explained it, Gethsemane?"

"I was wrong. But don't worry, Mr. Wayne. If you experience any paranormal trouble while you're here, go see Father Keating. He has an extensive collection of occult material he inherited from his brother, a trained exorcist. I'm sure Father'd find something in his books to help you."

"Exorcist! That means demons."

"No, no demons in Ireland," Billy said.

"Not technically demons. Evil spirits." Gethsemane counted on her fingers. "The Dearg-due, the dullahan, Balor, the Sluagh...Place is lousy with 'em."

"She's kidding again, Mr. Wayne."

"Aren't you happy to learn the place is haunted?" Gethsemane asked, her tone a model of innocence. "Paranormal tourism is the rage. Draws in lots of tourist dollars."

Bravado vanished, Hank stormed to the hall and grabbed his coat. He shoved his arms in his sleeves. "McCarthy, we need to talk." He tore open the door and stomped out to the car.

Billy grabbed his coat and ran after him.

Gethsemane sank to the hall bench and watched Billy's car pull away, Wayne gesticulating in the passenger seat. That jerk was after this cottage. She had to save Carraigfaire. *Eamon* had to save Carraigfaire. She had to find him. Fast.

ALEXIA GORDON

A writer since childhood, Alexia Gordon won her first writing prize in the 6th grade. She continued writing through college but put literary endeavors on hold to finish medical school and Family Medicine residency training. She established her medical career then returned to writing fiction.

Raised in the southeast, schooled in the northeast, she relocated to the west where she completed Southern Methodist University's Writer's Path program. She admits Texas brisket is as good as Carolina pulled pork. She practices medicine in El Paso. She enjoys the symphony, art collecting, embroidery, and ghost stories.

The Gethsemane Brown Mystery Series
by Alexia Gordon

MURDER IN G MAJOR (#1)

Henery Press Mystery Books

And finally, before you go...
Here are a few other mysteries
you might enjoy:

LOWCOUNTRY BOIL

Susan M. Boyer

A Liz Talbot Mystery (#1)

Private Investigator Liz Talbot is a modern Southern belle: she blesses hearts and takes names. She carries her Sig 9 in her Kate Spade handbag, and her golden retriever, Rhett, rides shotgun in her hybrid Escape. When her grandmother is murdered, Liz high-tails it back to her South Carolina island home to find the killer.

She's fit to be tied when her police-chief brother shuts her out of the investigation, so she opens her own. Then her long-dead best friend pops in and things really get complicated. When more folks start turning up dead in this small seaside town, Liz must use more than just her wits and charm to keep her family safe, chase down clues from the hereafter, and catch a psychopath before he catches her.

Available at booksellers nationwide and online

Visit www.henerypress.com for details

ARTIFACT

Gigi Pandian

A Jaya Jones Treasure Hunt Mystery (#1)

Historian Jaya Jones discovers the secrets of a lost Indian treasure may be hidden in a Scottish legend from the days of the British Raj. But she's not the only one on the trail...

From San Francisco to London to the Highlands of Scotland, Jaya must evade a shadowy stalker as she follows hints from the hastily scrawled note of her dead lover to a remote archaeological dig. Helping her decipher the cryptic clues are her magician best friend, a devastatingly handsome art historian with something to hide, and a charming archaeologist running for his life.

Available at booksellers nationwide and online

Visit www.henerypress.com for details

PRACTICAL SINS
FOR COLD CLIMATES

Shelley Costa

A Val Cameron Mystery (#1)

When Val Cameron, a Senior Editor with a New York publishing company, is sent to the Canadian Northwoods to sign a reclusive bestselling author to a contract, she soon discovers she is definitely out of her element. Val is convinced she can persuade the author of that blockbuster, The Nebula Covenant, to sign with her, but first she has to find him.

Aided by a float plane pilot whose wife was murdered two years ago in a case gone cold, Val's hunt for the recluse takes on new meaning: can she clear him of suspicion in that murder before she links her own professional fortunes to the publication of his new book?

When she finds herself thrown into a wilderness lake community where livelihoods collide, Val wonders whether the prospect of running into a bear might be the least of her problems.

Available at booksellers nationwide and online

Visit www.henerypress.com for details

CPSIA information can be obtained
at www.ICGtesting.com
Printed in the USA
LVOW10s2345050417
529721LV00009BA/713/P